# THE WANTED ONE

## A FALCON FALLS SECURITY NOVEL

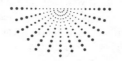

## BRITTNEY SAHIN

EMKO MEDIA, LLC

*The Wanted One*

By: Brittney Sahin

Published by: EmKo Media, LLC

Copyright © 2023 EmKo Media, LLC

This book is an original publication of Brittney Sahin.

Chief Editor: Michelle Fewer

Editor: Ashley Bauman

Proofreader: Judy Zweifel, Judy's Proofreading

Cover Design: LJ, Mayhem Cover Creations

Photographer (front photo): Wander Aguair

Model: Travis S.

Back image: istock license

Ebook ISBN: 9781947717367

Paperback ISBN: 9798853496859

*For my girl Marni Mann*

*For motivating and encouraging me.*
*For not letting me give up on writing this book while I was*
*having a rough few months.*
*And now I can release a book I'm truly proud of ...*

*I'm so blessed to have a friend like you in my corner.*
*Thank you.*

*-Britt*

# CHAPTER ONE

### JACK

WASHINGTON, D.C.

I BARELY MADE IT TWO STEPS IN THE DOOR BEFORE A PETITE woman in a tight navy-blue dress abruptly blocked my path and slapped a sticker to my chest. "You're number nine tonight."

My focus fell to her hand as she traced a manicured nail along the number written in red Sharpie beneath the little words: "My name is."

"Not 'my number is'?" I teased, then peered at her face framed by thick, black hair.

Her green eyes glinted as she stepped back and did a quick inventory of my appearance. I'd decided on dark denim jeans and a black button-down with the sleeves cuffed at the elbows. For whatever reason, my friend and colleague—the same person who insisted on this little dating adventure tonight—all but demanded my forearms be on display. Hell if I knew why.

Clearing my throat, I waited for her eyes to return to my face, curious if she'd ever respond to my joke. The woman did have my ego inflating a tad as her gaze continued to linger on my chest. At forty-two, I was divorced and had been single for what felt like forever. So, I'd take the boost when I could get it.

Of course, the woman had to be fifteen years younger than me (or God help me, more). *Probably more.* And because I was feeling on the awkward-nervous side I went ahead and added, "So, I'm not a ten, huh?"

She stared at me for a beat. *Damn.* Not even a smile from her, let alone a laugh.

"No names tonight." Long fingers tucked her dark hair behind her ear as she gave me another once-over before finally setting her sights on my face. "You'll have to make it to night two before you earn names," was all she gave me.

Shit, I really was out of my element. I would have felt more comfortable in the midst of a fight with an M4 or a Glock to keep me company. Missions. Operations. Hunting HVTs (high-value targets). *My* thing. Fuck, that was a list. So, *things,* plural.

I shook my head and smirked as my mother's voice popped into my head with a quick lecture about my poor grammar, internal monologue or not.

"Are you okay, sir?" The woman tipped her head in question as her bright green eyes flew down my body again.

*Third time checking me out, huh?* And damn, not even her intense gaze or the "sir" stirred a below-the-belt reaction. *Am I broken? I mean . . . fuck, maybe?*

"I'm fine." *That's a lie.* I was about to speed date, so no, I wasn't remotely fine. "Uh, where do I go? What do I do?" I finally took a minute to look around the dimly lit dining room that'd clearly been reserved for the night. The fact I was just taking notice of my surroundings was more proof I wasn't acting like myself. *Maybe I should leave.*

"To table nine, of course." She stabbed a finger in the general direction of *over there*. "You'll hear a buzzer, and the women will rotate to you every fifteen minutes. We'll be starting soon."

"Wait, what?" My hand went back to my chest, covering the number. "Since when do the women have to move around? Call me old fashioned, but shouldn't the guys have to get their asses up and do the walking?"

A light unexpected chuckle tumbled from her lips. "Do you open doors for the opposite sex, too? Walk on the streetside of a sidewalk alongside a woman to keep her safe?"

"Of course. Why wouldn't I?" It took me a second to realize she'd been sarcastic. Just great.

With her fourth perusal of my body—this time to my crotch—I backed up a few steps.

"How old are you, Nine?"

Did I detect a hint of seduction in her question? And why the hell did I feel like this woman was about to call me "daddy" and mean it in a *very* different way than I was used to? *Time to hit the brakes.* "Old enough. But not that old." *That's all you're getting from me.*

"Mmmhmm." The peek of her tongue between her lips had me turning to search for my seat among the rows of small tables. Why on earth had I let Mya convince me to try speed dating?

Mya Vanzetti worked with my security company, Falcon Falls, part-time. She also freelanced with a group of Marines, but I had a feeling that'd be ending soon. One of those Marines had feelings for her she didn't reciprocate, and it was getting awkward for them to work together. At least that's what Mya had spilled and told me in a slew of drunk texts last weekend.

Finding my spot, I politely nodded at the guy at my nine

o'clock who was patting his brow with the bottom of his tie as I settled in my chair.

Anxious, I peered around the room again, clocking every guy in there, assessing for possible threats. Not in the competition-for-a-date department, but more in the "could anyone be an enemy of the state" kind of thing. Force of habit.

The week prior, my team had been in Scotland handling a high-value target, and things went sideways. Really, really fucking sideways. The kind of shit show that had me hanging from the side of a building while my life flashed before my eyes. Thankfully, my teammate, who was now safely back home in Alabama with his wife, hauled me back to the rooftop and saved my ass before I became a permanent fixture on the road fifty feet below.

That moment, though—those precious seconds I kept myself from falling before the rescue—had me sweating less than I was now.

The wild thing? I *did* want to date. I *did* want to meet someone and start a family. I was certain my nerves tonight had more to do with me slowly surrendering to the idea I'd never meet my "the one" the way my best friend and many of my teammates already had. Well, for a second last month I thought I'd met her, but then she slipped away before the sun came up, and . . .

My fingers curled inward at the memory of the woman I needed to shake free from my mind if I had any hope of surviving the evening.

But damn, I still wanted her. How in the hell did I let a woman I'd spent less than six hours with get inside my head so much?

The sound of a dramatic buzzer from somewhere behind

me snapped my attention back to the moment, and I looked over to see women filtering into the room from a back door.

A brunette wordlessly slid into the seat across from me before I had a chance to stand and pull out her chair. "Hi," she whispered.

"Hey, how's it going? I'm, um . . ." *No names, right.* "Number nine." I smiled, doing my best to give her one of my better ones.

*"Give them your sexy lopsided smile. You know, crook the side of your lip and flash just a hint of teeth. It'll drive them crazy,"* Gwen Montgomery had suggested. She was my best friend's twenty-four-year-old niece.

Like Mya, Gwen had also been pushing me to "get out there." She even set up a few dating profiles for me (not that I had asked her to). In fact, I'd begged the opposite. To leave my dating life, or lack thereof, alone.

But she was as stubborn as Mya, and she'd had me matching up with people online before I could protest. I'd been too overwhelmed by all the swiping left, right, fucking horizontal, to ever actually meet anyone in person, though.

Hell, I'd almost given in and asked Gwen to put her hacking and coding skills to better use by helping me find my mystery woman instead.

"I'm number eleven." The woman gave me a little nod, pulling my thoughts back to the present.

"Ah, nine-one-one." *Another corny joke, really? Exit stage left.* I inwardly groaned.

She gave me a shy smile, her red lips parting a touch, and I couldn't help but smile as well.

*Okay, maybe you like corny?* "So." I drummed my fingers on the table, thankful there wasn't any grease or dirt under my nails from cleaning my rifle earlier.

"The no-name thing is . . . probably to protect first impressions." Her hesitant tone had me curious to ask why.

"So, if my name—"

"Began with a J, for instance, it might be problematic," she cut me off, and she dropped her forearms onto the table and locked her hands together as if wringing out some tension.

I arched a brow. "J, huh?"

"Yeah, every guy I know with a J name is a heartbreaker." She proceeded to list off every J name in the book— ironically pretty much every J name but mine.

"I feel slightly offended on behalf of those Js." I chuckled. "Also, what if they're not all heartbreakers. Maybe they're more of the hold-your-heart kind of guys?" *Hold? Shit.* Now my palms were as sweaty as dude eight's forehead.

"Why does holding my heart feel a little . . . cringe? Like something a stalker or serial killer might say. *Silence of the Lambs*, you know?" It was her turn to shrug. This was going great. "Oh, oh, or Dahmer." She abruptly lifted her hand and snapped her fingers. "J name, too. *Jeffrey* Dahmer. See." She smirked, proving her point.

"Right, right." I nodded, going along with it, because damn, what else was I going to say now? So, I sat in silence waiting for her to go on, and she did. For a solid fourteen minutes. I kept track on my Apple watch. Her shyness had melted away as she began talking about her recent bad dates. None of which had a J name.

The relief that hit me when the buzzer went off was overwhelming. Three more not-so-great "dates" later, and I was finally sitting across from someone who gave off decent vibes.

"So, I'm here to make my mom happy. Why are you

here?" she greeted in a direct, no-nonsense tone. Her number was six, and I opted not to make any sixty-nine jokes.

"Truth?" *Why the hell not at this point?* "I've been lonely. My teammates are all falling in love, and I'm getting a bit depressed at the fact I have no one. And I'm supposed to be the comedian on my team, so the blues just don't work for me, you know?" I spat out. "Then I started to develop what I thought were feelings for a teammate, and that went sideways." *Nearly as sideways as that almost-plunging-to-my-death incident last week.* "Mya friend-zoned me hard and fast. But she was right. And it took me meeting, and then losing, the woman of my dreams last month to realize Mya was never the right one for me."

*Woman of my dreams? Way to word vomit that out.* Sure, the American I'd met at a bar in Cape Town had officially been occupying my thoughts for twenty-seven days now, but who was counting? She was probably even why I'd nearly gone man-over-building in Edinburgh. She'd been on my mind that day. That laugh of hers . . . God help me that laugh kept playing on repeat in my thoughts.

And how could she not be in my head after the most incredible night of my life? Apparently, it hadn't been as memorable for her since she ditched me before sunrise.

"Are you okay?"

I blinked, remembering I was on a date with number— what was it again?—then looked up at the blonde who reminded me a little bit of the therapist from the show *Lucifer* Gwen had made me binge-watch with her this year. "Did I just say all that out loud?"

"You did, but my job is to get people to open up to me, so I—"

"Holy shit, you're a shrink?" I hadn't meant to interrupt. My mom had taught me better than to cut off a woman.

7

"No, prosecutor. I'm notorious for bringing the heat in the courtroom during my cross-examinations, and I always make people crack. Spill their deepest, darkest secrets."

I swallowed and shifted back in my seat. I had way too many secrets and didn't need to spill any more with a stranger.

"I honestly didn't expect you to share the truth with me like that, though." She stole a look at her thin silver watch. "This has to be a record for me."

"Well, neither did I." Before I could summon an apology for my odd behavior, a flurry of movement pulled my attention to the main door. I swiped a hand down my face before looking up at the ceiling while sighing. "Speak of the devil—*wait, devils.*" I tilted my head toward the entrance. "Mya and Gwen are here, great."

Mya and Gwen breezed past the woman who'd assigned my number, ignoring her protests, and rushed my way. *This can't be good.*

"What are you two doing here?" I pushed back in my seat and stood.

My date, number six—*right, that's it*—whispered, "Mya's the one who friend-zoned you, right?"

Mya's lips parted, and she gave me a funny look before snapping out, "We need you. Now. Wheels up."

"Sorry," I quickly tossed out to the prosecutor, complete with a shrug and what I hoped was a roguish smile. "Time to go save the world." Another bad joke. But hell, it was probably the truth. Well, save *someone's* world. Someone's life.

"What's going on?" I asked them once we'd escaped the restaurant and were outside by the street in front of a black Suburban.

"Get in," Gwen commanded instead of answering as she

hopped into the passenger seat, leaving me to slide into the back with Mya.

My teammate, Oliver Lucas, was behind the wheel. He looked back at me and grinned. "Number nine, huh? Really? You're a solid ten in my book, man."

I shook my head at his echo of my bad joke from earlier. "Thanks, brother." I rolled my eyes and peeled off the sticker. "So, what's the emergency?"

"They won't even tell me. These two are being cryptic. Just assembling us like we're the freaking Avengers or something," Oliver replied while pulling onto the road, joining the traffic.

"Yeah, that's worrisome." I frowned and peeked at Mya as she busied herself with texting someone, fast fingers flying over her screen. "Who are you talking to?"

"Mason," Mya answered without looking my way. "He's joining us."

Oliver braked hard at the mention of the Marine, and Mya jerked forward. On instinct, I shot my arm out to stop her from going forward since she was unbuckled.

"Fuck. Sorry. There was a squirrel," Oliver piped up before driving again.

"Yeah, a squirrel in the middle of the streets of D.C. that you spotted but I didn't see," Gwen said with a light laugh, her British accent rolling through her words. "Absolutely."

"I happen to have great eyesight. And what? There are squirrels in D.C."

*Yeah, sure.* Oliver wasn't a fan of Mason Matthews, and everyone knew why. Mason had once been Mya's friend with benefits that she was now struggling to work with, soooo, why in the hell was he joining our op?

"We need single guys. He's single," Mya said as if that'd clear everything up. Nope. Not even a little bit. "And the rest of his team was pulled away on a last-minute mission, and he doesn't want me going on this op without him since he was helping me run leads on it, and—"

"Slow down there, buttercup," Oliver commented. "What-in-the-what are you talking about? This was supposed to be a mission with your Marine crew and we're your backup plan?"

The man sounded offended. Maybe I was, too.

"It's their area of expertise. Well, originally, I thought it was connected to trafficking, but I'm pretty sure I was wrong. But yeah, we were working on this thing together. Plans changed, though," Mya explained, frustration edging her tone.

"Dealing with human traffickers is their specialty, right," I said grimly, my skin crawling at the mere idea our op would be connected to that subject. Human trafficking was something I so desperately wanted to will away from existence in the world. I'd Jedi mindfuck it gone in a heartbeat if I could. Use my first genie wish on it. Second wish? Bring my parents back to life. Third (but like really not that low on the list)—have my mystery girl never have ditched me that morning.

I worked my top two buttons free, wondering if that'd help me breathe a bit better.

"Like I said, now we don't think it's a trafficking op, but we'll explain everything when we're with the others." Mya shoved her phone into her purse wedged between her jeaned legs. "We won't be bringing everyone with us undercover because our mission is . . . well, it's a unique one. Single people needed, and a lot of Falcon is now hitched, so . . ."

*Unique?* "And that means?" I probed, hoping to get more out of the two women before we got to the airport.

Gwen shifted in her seat and peered back at me. "We're going to Brazil. To um . . ."

"Brazil?" Oliver murmured. "Okay, but why do we need to be single?"

"Well, um . . ." Mya and her damn ums now, too.

*Not good.* "What do you not want to tell us?" My voice was almost hoarse that time.

"A friend of a friend needs our help, and to help we need to partake in this dating competition thing. Go undercover as contestants," Gwen said, biting the bullet, dropping the shit news on us. "Mya's been helping me, and things all kind of came together for the op at the last minute. Like as in today we secured the official invites."

"Are you for real?" *Of course you are, or I wouldn't be here. But damn.* "And by 'secured,'" I said with air quotes, "you mean you hacked the list and got us on it?"

Gwen nodded. "It wasn't easy. I'll explain more at the hangar, but for the show . . . well, think *Survivor* meets *Love Island.* Maybe a little *Naked and Afraid,* too," Gwen casually tossed out. "Not like *The Bachelor,* though."

"Because that's supposed to make me feel better?" *Shit.* Speed dating was bad enough. But to go undercover in a dating competition? I hung my head, cursed, then did it again for good measure. "Fuck my life."

# CHAPTER TWO

## JACK

THERE WAS NEVER REALLY A TIME I QUESTIONED MY JOB. Okay, maybe when I tried my hand at real estate after the Army because my then-wife had forced me to leave the military . . . yeah, I regretted that.

But never in all my years as Army Special Forces did I stop and wonder what I was doing. Hell, not even as part of Ground Branch for the CIA did I second-guess my choices. And before this moment, I never doubted my decision to join Falcon Falls Security.

Standing inside the private hangar watching Gwen argue with her father, Wyatt Pierson, did have me taking a second or two to rethink my life choices, though. Because the idea of going undercover in a dating competition was sure as hell not what I signed up for when I joined the company.

"I don't see why in the bloody hell you need to go, too," Wyatt said, his British accent deepening as he yelled at Gwen and slid his arms across his chest.

The defiant lift of Gwen's chin was followed by her stabbing the air at her old man. Not that Wyatt was old. We were close in age. "This is my op. I'm pulling everyone in

12

for help. Of course I'm going. My friend's friend is in danger."

"*Your* op?" Wyatt stepped back, the vein bulging at the side of his neck. He looked toward Gray Chandler and Carter Dominick, my two team leaders standing alongside the private jet, as if hoping for an assist, especially from his brother-in-law, Gray.

But Gray wouldn't be joining this mission since he was married. As were three of our other teammates: Sydney Hawkins, Jesse McAdams, and Griffin Andrews. So, I assumed they'd be working from behind the scenes. And actually, Griffin's wife was in her third trimester, so he wasn't spinning up regardless.

Although Wyatt didn't work with us—he was a Navy SEAL and part of an off-the-books team under the President's command—our paths often crossed, especially on any op involving his daughter.

"Dad." Gwen's tone softened that time. Ah, she was about to try the honey-instead-of-vinegar approach with her father, who I had to admit was a bit overprotective when it came to her at times. Then again, he hadn't even known he was her father until just before her twenty-first birthday, so I was pretty sure he felt like he had a three-year-old under his protection instead.

"You're agreeing to this? Just like that?" Wyatt focused on Carter again. After all, it was Carter's money that funded our ops. It was his jet they were standing in front of, and it was Carter's worldwide web of mysterious connections that helped us out on almost every op.

Carter casually slid his hands into his pockets and arched a dark brow. "Your daughter says she needs our help. Do you really want her going alone? Because you know she will. Well, with Mya."

The man had a point. I was happy to keep my mouth shut on this decision. Not my fight. Well, not completely.

But there was a part of me that needed to get away. I always went a little stir crazy in between ops. Not that I wanted my next mission to involve dating. God no. But, Brazil . . .

"Who is this friend in danger? What's the story behind our impromptu mission?" I spoke up, needing more intel.

Gwen peered around the hangar before returning her attention back to her father. At least Gwen gave Wyatt a heads-up she planned to work with us this time, unlike the op in Turkey last fall that brought Gray and the woman of *his* dreams together.

"This friend an ex? A hacker?" Wyatt relaxed his arms to his sides only to bunch his hands into fists. "He's a bloody criminal, isn't he?"

"*Former* hacker. And Harley's one of my best friends. But it's not him in danger, it's an ex-girlfriend of his." Gwen focused on Mya as if unsure what to say, and Mya did a little one-shoulder shrug as if tongue-tied, too.

Mya's focus seemed a bit off. Maybe she was nervous about bringing her former friend with benefits along for the op? Oliver and Mason didn't exactly play well together.

"Harley reached out to me last month when he found out his ex fell off the grid. He asked me to help try and track her down. His, um, coding skills are rusty since he put them aside for a different life," Gwen quickly explained. "My trail took me to a dating competition his ex was part of. It's a streaming-type show but aired over the internet and not with any major network. But the show has sponsors that fund it. Anyway, his ex was a runner-up during their last season when it was hosted in New Zealand."

"So, she disappeared there?" I asked.

"No, ten days later. And when I did some more digging, I discovered other women who were part of past seasons have mysteriously disappeared, too. Always a female competitor who placed in the top three couples to win the money. But never a woman part of the winning couple, though. So, no one is getting robbed and taken for the money." Gwen played with her charm bracelet, smoothing her thumb over the SEAL trident charm Wyatt had given her. "I don't think it's a case of trafficking, or a money crime, but I'm not sure what in the hell is going on, so—"

"Kidnapping," I cut her off. "Someone is kidnapping these women."

Abandoning her bracelet, Gwen fiddled with the silver rings on her left hand. I wasn't used to seeing her so fidgety.

"So," Mya picked up when Gwen went quiet, "if we have any hope of figuring out what happened to these women, and stopping anyone else from disappearing, we need to join their seventh competition. We put eight of our names, well, aliases we cooked up, on the waiting list." She peered at Carter. "But we only managed to get six to drop out."

"First of all, didn't that look suspicious to whoever is running this thing?" Gray asked, stepping away from the jet, eyes on Mya. "And secondly, how'd you convince six to drop out?"

Gray echoed my exact thoughts—we were usually on the same page—but when I cut my attention to my other team leader at Gray's side, I put two and two together. "Ah, Batman's money," I joked. "You figured if these people signed up to win the contest for the money, you could offer them an easier payout to drop out instead."

"Yeah, but we had to do it in a way that wouldn't draw attention." Mya let go of a heavy breath. "We put together a fake competition, acting like they were poaching the guest list from them, offering them a better deal. Stuff like that happens all the time in the online entertainment world."

Gray shifted to face Carter. "So, you were part of this and didn't tell us?"

"We went to Carter yesterday when Mason's company had to spin up unexpectedly on another mission. We asked Carter if he could help instead," Mya said. "And Mason chose to hang back and work with us on this. He knows Brazil well. Especially the area we're going to because it has a history of, um, trafficking in that region."

Yeah, I could narrow down the list of locations quickly based on that factoid.

"And you're really expecting us to go undercover and participate in this thing, and what, make it to the end to see if someone comes after one of us?" I asked, uncomfortable with the plan.

"This has all been kind of on the fly, so I think we have to make it up as we go," Gwen said with a small, nervous smile.

*Like sending me to a speed dating event just to pull me away.* I stared at her blankly, waiting for her to continue. This was going to be a shit show.

"I'll understand if you don't want to do this, because there are more questions than answers . . ."

"Yeah, but that's always how it is with us." Not wanting Gwen to feel bad or guilty for the fact I hated this op, I teased, "Our missions are real page-turners. It's what we do."

"Thanks, Jack." Gwen's uneasy smile became a genuine one, which made me feel a little better.

"As soon as Mason gets here, we should roll out. The meet and greet cocktail hour is tomorrow night. We'll make it just in time," Mya announced. "We'll have to act like we don't know each other, though. I used our first names with fake last names."

"And our aliases had to be unique based on the other contestants and who they previously chose for past events," Gwen tacked on.

Wyatt offered a nice little reality check and pointed out the important elephant in the hangar by saying, "You all realize a show means you guys will be on camera." He turned to face Carter, the man who'd gone rogue from the CIA and was wanted by people all over the world. "How's that going to work, for you especially?"

"The show is filmed weeks before it's broadcast online. Nothing is live streamed," Gwen countered. "That's kind of suspect since almost all these things these days are live, which makes me wonder what they're editing out. What don't they want the public to see?"

"The women that have gone missing, does it happen before or after the show airs? That's an important detail," I pointed out. "Otherwise, it could be any wacko with Wi-Fi watching the event online going after these women."

"They've all gone missing before their show aired, which is why I think someone connected to the show is behind the disappearances. Plus, in each case, there's been an excuse as to why the women mysteriously went missing," Gwen explained.

"Meaning someone is making it look as though they chose to go 'off the grid,' but your friend Harley isn't buying it?" I asked.

"Exactly. The show has only been around for two years. Four events last year, and this is their third one this year. So, having women go missing in such a tight timeframe, all with ties to the event, should draw attention either way," Mya shared. "But these women aren't all disappearing from

Delaware, you know? They're from all over the world. No way to connect the dots unless you know what you're looking for."

"Well, lucky for your friend Harley, you think outside the box," Wyatt said to Gwen, his expression softening into one more of pride than frustration. "Let me guess though, these missing women, they don't have strong family ties, do they? No one *reputable* to come looking for them when they vanished?" And he was back to passively aggressively poking at her for her choice in friends.

*Man, you're such a dad.*

"Yeah, I guess you could say that," Gwen said without letting that dig from him rock her resolve.

"And all six seasons, a woman went missing? Just one?" I asked, and Mya nodded. "Same exact pattern?" Based on my knowledge on the matter from reading fiction only, serial-type assholes usually had weird quirks, kinks, and shit like that. "Was the first time different?"

"The women were all taken ten days after the end of the game, *excep*t for season one—she's our anomaly," Mya answered. "She vanished after the show publicly aired."

"So, the first time was probably unplanned. After that, they decided to do it again but made adjustments not to draw attention back to the show." I was disgusted that someone could do something like this once, never mind have the forethought to cover their tracks so they could continue to do it again and again. "And uh, do these women have anything else in common?"

"The women are all smart from what I can tell, boasting different skills on their applications. But everyone who's part of the show is required to have unique skills." Gwen paused and glanced at Mya. "Every woman on the show is in their twenties or thirties, so we can't really use that to narrow it down, but all the missing women are blonde."

"That's why you dyed your hair back to blonde?" Oliver asked, eyes on Mya. Her nod only seemed to make him more frustrated. "Of course, you're painting yourself as a damn target."

"Just bloody great," Wyatt hissed, eyes on his blonde daughter.

"Anyway," Gwen began, "we're obviously working to get the names for the production crew, judges, and sponsors involved to narrow down our suspect list."

Before we could continue bouncing ideas around, Carter shot Gwen a hard look, a warning embedded there. "Just so we're clear, my face *never* ends up online."

"Like I told you last night," Gwen quickly replied, "I'll never let the show see the light of day. Trust me, I'll hack the hell out of it before that happens. But with any luck, if these people running it are bad guys, it won't matter. They'll be behind bars before then."

"I love your confidence, really." I sensed a "but" coming from Gray. "But like you said, Gwen, lots of question marks. Those of us not going undercover can do some more intel gathering from the outside. Sydney will remain Stateside, so she can be our point of contact here for anything we need. But once Jesse gets here, the two of us will fly down there. We'll need to pull together a secondary crew. You may need an extraction or backup at some point."

"My team is wheels up tomorrow for the Middle East. I can try and get out of it, but—"

"No, Dad," Gwen interrupted Wyatt. "I'm sure Falcon has plenty of other trained operatives on standby who can have our six when or if needed. You need to relax."

Wyatt snorted. "I swear if anything happens to you . . ."

Gwen lifted her wrist and shook her charm bracelet. "The tracker trident charm you cleverly planted is right here. And come on, they've got my back. Worst case, Carter can just fork a guy to death if we get in trouble." Her lips teased into a slight smile.

And, yep, that happened—Carter really had killed a guy with a fork on the last op Gwen had taken part of—but Carter grumbled, clearly not amused by her comment.

"And Jack's like an uncle by extension of Gray. He won't let anything happen to me," Gwen went on, still feeling the need to bulldoze her way through her obstacle of a father.

"I'm just curious why you sent me to a speed dating event tonight. It's like y'all knew I'd need the practice for this undercover work." At the very least, they could have given me the heads-up my night was going to grind to a halt right when I was hitting my stride.

"Wait, speed dating?" Gray grinned.

"That really is just a weird coincidence," Mya said before Gwen could respond (or lie). I was having my doubts about these two right now. "And you're awfully grumpy tonight." Mya tossed a thumb Gray and Carter's way. "They're supposed to be the grumpy and broody ones." Her gaze cut to Oliver. "He's the frustrating one." Oliver kissed the air to annoy her, and she rolled her eyes. "But, Jack, you're the—"

"Unwanted one." *Damnit. What was with the verbal vomit tonight?* I shook my head and slammed my hands to my hips.

"Not true." Mya pouted, but then Gray motioned for me to follow him away from the others, and I hesitantly joined him on the other side of the jet.

Gray was the only one who knew about the woman I met post-op in South Africa last month. We'd wrapped up a quick job working with one of Carter's old friends, Camila Hart. And since we weren't leaving until the morning, Camila invited us to drinks at the hotel bar. She never made it to the bar because Carter beckoned her for something important— not that she ever spilled and told us what—which meant I wound up alone with Gray.

Not even ten minutes into the night, Gray's wife had called, and I ordered him to go back to his room and talk to her like I knew he wanted to. And that was when I met her. *The* her. The woman I couldn't seem to forget. The woman I so desperately *still* wanted.

*"She didn't give you a last name? Tell you where she was from?"* Gray had asked when he'd caught me sulking on our ride back to the U.S. the day she'd ditched me.

*"Not even a first full name. Just that everyone calls her Charley."*

Worried something had happened to her, I'd hacked the hotel's surveillance camera using the bare-minimum skills I had in that department. Thankfully, no one had abducted her, but I'd also had to watch her willingly leave the hotel lobby on her own . . . like the night before meant nothing to her.

I'd taken screenshots of her image from the camera, tempted to run it through our facial recognition software to get a name and address, but even that felt a little too psychopath-stalkery for me.

So instead, I kept trying to convince myself that I only wanted her because I couldn't have her. That it wasn't because our time together had been great, hell, amazing even. That it was simply because she'd left me wanting more with no way of getting it. Like some weird mindfuck thing. *Maybe I was reading too far into the situation. It was only one night . . .*

"Dating might be a good idea," Gray said, snapping me from my thoughts. "Maybe not speed dating, though. You need to get back on the horse. Or whatever that saying is." He slapped a hand over my shoulder. "I'm worried about you, man. You can't keep fantasizing about that woman. It just wasn't meant to be."

"And, what, you think I'll meet the woman I'm meant to be with while undercover for a dating game?" I almost laughed at the absurdity of how that sounded.

"Hell, when it comes to us . . . you just never fucking know."

# CHAPTER THREE

## JACK

### IN THE AIR

"DO YOU WANT TO TALK ABOUT WHAT HAPPENED TONIGHT?" Mya asked softly as she sat next to me.

Sighing, I closed the worn-out Dean Koontz book I'd been reading—my go-to comfort read when I was nervous. Yeah, reading a serial killer thriller as a "comfort read" sounded a bit off even in my head.

"Well, a lot has happened tonight, buttercup," I teased, stealing Oliver's nickname for her, earning myself a playful elbow in the side before she started to fasten her seat belt. "What exactly happened that *we* need to talk about?"

"What that date of yours said tonight at dinner about—"

"Friend-zoning me?" I said under my breath, somehow not feeling the stain of embarrassment crawl into my cheeks. I'd already pretty much admitted to Mya one late night six or so weeks ago I'd mistakenly started to confuse our friendship for more.

"Yeah, why'd you tell her that?" Mya lifted a dark brow, which didn't match her new blonde hair color.

23

I leaned my head back and closed my eyes, stifling my groan the best I could. *Why did I tell her that? No clue.*

My mom's advice from forever and a day ago came to mind: *"Don't be friends with women you're attracted to—nine out of ten times it doesn't end well."*

*"And what, I can't be the exception?"* I'd replied. *"Pretty sure Dad was the exception for you,"* I'd reminded her, peering at my father reading the newspaper across the table.

Mom had been worried I'd eventually fall for Gray's sister, Natasha. But she'd fallen for one of our close friends instead, and that hadn't ended well. And now Gray's sister was married to Gwen's father, Wyatt. So, it all worked out in the end.

"We *are* friends, right?" Mya reached for my arm and gave it a squeeze. Well, she tried. I'd been spending more time at the gym to alleviate my "tension," and my biceps were a bit "more" lately. I was pretty sure that was the word Gwen had used to describe them the other day.

After a quick look around the cabin to ensure we didn't have eyes or ears, I told Mya, "Yeah, we are friends. That was just some verbal vomiting earlier. Not used to speed dating I guess."

Part of me wanted to tell Mya the truth, to tell her why I was more messed up in the head than usual. To tell her about the blonde with blue-green eyes that I couldn't shake from my thoughts. The one dimple that had killed me every time it'd appeared when I'd had her laughing. Or how her fingers would drum the column of her throat every so often, a habit I was pretty sure she was unaware she kept doing, but . . .

"Who are you thinking about?" Mya's question rumbled through my head. Great, caught daydreaming again.

"No one." I frowned and flipped open the book, but she set her hand over mine and closed it.

"Don't lie to me. There's someone on your mind, I can feel it. Come on, out with it. If we're friends, talk to me. I tell you things all the time."

I grumbled, "Not everything."

"No, just the important things." She smiled.

I looked over where Oliver was talking to Gwen and Carter. Our "third wheel"—aka the Marine—was sitting alone near the cockpit.

"How are we doing this?" I deflected. "Four of us guys. Two of y'all. You said we have to couple up or something at this event? We're short two women." *And who will you pick? Oliver or Mason?*

"We'll figure it out," she said, waving a dismissive hand as if it were no big deal.

Another thing Mom said when I was fumbling my way through my dating years, before I married Jill, *"The man the woman acts like she can't stand is more than likely the one she wants."*

*"Mom, I think you read too much."*

*"There's no such thing as 'reading too much,'"* was all she shot back. *"And your dad benefits from my reading."*

"TMI, Mom. TMI." My return volley had been delivered with an inner cringe and an outer wince. I'd still been in high school during that conversation, but hell, if Mom was alive today, I'd say the same to her.

Was it so wrong that I wanted the kind of love my parents had shared? Dad died shortly after her. Like he hadn't been able to go on breathing air without her there.

My parents had me at an older age, so it wasn't like they'd died young. Late seventies. But that didn't change the pain of their loss.

A chill crept down my neck at the memories of losing

them, and I focused on the man Mya "couldn't stand"
—Oliver.

Before I had a chance to continue the conversation that I
didn't want to have with Mya, Carter flicked his wrist,
motioning for us to join them. Mason was on his feet, too.
The turbulence seemed to obey Carter as well, and the plane
went still. Of course that man could control the skies. Made
perfect sense.

I set aside the book, unbuckled, and trailed behind Mya to
get to the others.

"We have a little more information about what to expect,"
Carter announced once we were together near the bedroom
door in the back of his plane—that room saw more action
than I did.

Oliver snatched Gwen's arm to keep her from falling
when a bit more turbulence snuck up on us, and Gwen gave
him a small smile of thanks.

For a minute, some of us had thought Gwen and Oliver
might wind up dating. At one of our teammates' weddings in
the spring, even when Oliver had been glaring at Gwen's
date, it hadn't been because of jealousy, but because he knew
her date, and not a shocker, the guy was a dick.

But lucky for Oliver's life (as in Wyatt not needing to kill
him), it was clear who Oliver wanted—the woman *he*
"couldn't stand."

"So, what do we know?" I folded my arms, uneasy for so
many reasons.

"There are twenty-four contestants and on day one they
split people into three groups of eight," Mya began. "For the
first week, the teams will compete against each other in
different events. By the end of the week, one team is
eliminated. By Friday, we'll be down to sixteen people, and
it'll be couples against couples from that point on."

"That's assuming we're still there by Friday," Carter said. "I'd prefer we wrap up this op before then."

Mya shot Carter an uneasy look. "I get that, I do. But this undercover assignment is different from our norm. Eyes *and* ears on us a lot. We'll need to be extra—"

"Stealthy," Gwen finished for her, giving Carter a pointed look.

Carter grunted out, "I'm stealthy."

"Sure, but you won't blend in. Not there. Maybe when you're kitted up in your military gear you can, um . . . but in a suit you stand out a bit more. In jeans, too." A blush I didn't want to see on Gwen made its way to her cheeks. She freed her blonde hair from its ponytail, allowing the waves to partially hide the red appearing on her neck.

Carter took a step back, bumping into Mason. I wasn't used to seeing that man uneasy, but Gray's niece seemed to trigger his defenses.

*Yeah, please, keep the wall up between you two. Don't make me fight ya.*

"Are we wearing microphones?" Ah, Mason for the win with the all-important question. He also saved Gwen from potentially turning as red as a Crayola crayon.

*Shit.* How in the hell would we talk in private about the op if someone was always listening?

Gwen shook her head. "No, it's not a traditional show like the ones on a professional streaming network. But I did hack the lodge's camera system. Looks like they did things mostly old school—wired cameras instead of wireless ones to record us when they don't have a camera person directly on us. The Wi-Fi is spotty in the jungle, so I went ahead and created a code for Gray to use to hack those camera feeds from the outside so they can keep an eye on us."

"But if the signal is shit at the lodge, doesn't that mean

Gray might lose us on camera?" I hated to point that out, but I assumed Gwen, a cyber genius, would have an answer to that.

"Yeah, they'll have to link up to a satellite to maintain the signal. Once they've got a SAT-feed, they'll be good to go," Gwen reassured us with easy confidence as she reached for her laptop from the couch and popped it open. "I've gone ahead and marked all the safe spots free of cameras and Wi-Fi where we can talk in private if need be."

"If they're using mostly wired cams, we should be able to spot those areas fairly easily, too," I noted. "Do they take our phones when we arrive, too?" How would we communicate with Gray if we were going in dark?

"No tech allowed. Not even phones, but we'll sneak one in so we can touch base with Gray." Gwen's eyes went to Carter's crotch as if suggesting he hide his phone where we'd hopefully not be searched. Carter glared at her, then pivoted his focus back to her screen, waiting for her to continue. "Um, so, with the Wi-Fi being shit, that also means—"

"The bad guy is probably on-site watching the show in real time to pick his next victim," Mason interrupted her.

"Exactly." Gwen nodded. "I have a feeling the person responsible for the missing women won't ever show their face on screen for Gray and his team to see and run a background check, even though I'm sure they'll be on-site."

*Which is why we're undercover and not going to be in the jungle with Gray tomorrow watching from afar.* "Unless there are two assholes. One working for the show relaying information and footage to someone at a safe distance away." In my experience, there was often more than one target.

"True," Gwen responded. "I'll also do my best to tiptoe around and see what I can hear or find out, too." She'd left that detail out back at the hangar, presumably so her father didn't tie her down and stop her from boarding the jet.

"Why you? Why not one of us?" Oliver asked, his thoughts circling around the same concerns as mine: *what if you get caught?*

A sly smile crossed Gwen's lips. "This wouldn't be my first time snooping around a place, even with cameras on me. I've got this, just trust me."

"And I'd like to return you home safely to your father." Carter's sharp tone seemed to catch Gwen off guard, but she schooled her expression quickly as he continued his mini lecture. "Let's not have you wind up becoming one of the missing girls."

"I appreciate the concern, but I have a bag full of toys that'll help us." A nervous laugh fell from Gwen's lips. "That sounded kinky." She waved a dismissive hand, brushing off her comment. "Anyway, what I mean is, I have some gadgets I'll plant around the property to be *our* eyes and ears on those trying to stay behind the scenes."

"And Gray can pick up on the signals?" This was sounding more like a doable plan, except for the Gwen-creeping-around-the-property part.

But there was one lingering question on my mind. How in the hell did we prevent ourselves from getting axed in week one? "If we're going to have to stay longer than Friday, who picks who stays and who goes? How are the winners chosen?"

"There are judges who award points based on the competitions. The team with the least points gets cut," Gwen said. "I've never seen the judges on camera in previous seasons, but my guess is there are people behind the scenes making these decisions. And what if—"

"One of the mystery judges is our bad guy," Oliver finished for her.

*Yup, shit just got even creepier.* Human trafficking? Fuck

that. And serial stalker-murdery types? Fucking fuck them, too.

I didn't want to be the one to say it, but what if Harley's ex was already dead? The book *Kiss the Girls* had given me damn nightmares back in the day about a similar subject. And spoiler: they were serial-collector-type guys who should've had their dicks cut off and used to choke them to death. I remembered watching the movie adaptation with Morgan Freeman, and I was certain it was around then I'd made the decision to do everything in my power to serve and protect the innocent.

I shook free my memories and focused on Gwen as she shared, "I hacked their system and did a little rearranging to ensure we're all on the same team this week. I picked two other women I thought were—"

"What?" I blurted, and Gwen's smile said it all. "My type?" *Please tell me you're not still trying to match me up.*

"I honestly don't know your type at this point because you . . ." Gwen cleared her throat.

*Thank you for not finishing that sentence.* No one there needed to know there was zero consistency when I'd attempted to do all the swiping on that dating app. Not that I'd gone on any dates.

"Five contestants received special invites to the event—two males, a brunette female, and two sisters—so I didn't attempt to bribe them to quit," Gwen explained. "One of those sisters is blonde, unsure about the other, so *that's* why I chose them to be placed in our group. I didn't want to split them up."

"Were you able to see if the six missing women from the other seasons had applied or were an invitee?" Oliver asked her.

"Harley confirmed his ex was invited," Gwen said. "But

only two of the six missing women were invited. Almost all the invitees have a social media presence, though. So, it's possible most of the invitees are extended the invitations because of their follower count. You know, to help boost the show's views when it airs. One of the invitees I placed in our group has a big following on TikTok, so that's probably why she was invited."

"Wait." *That doesn't add up.* "I thought the missing women didn't have strong ties to the world to decrease the chances anyone notices when they disappear? Why in the hell would our suspect pick someone with a high following count on her Insta or whatever? That doesn't make sense."

"Yeah, but the two women who went missing with an online presence didn't have any family and moved around a lot. The person, or people, who took them clearly did their homework," Mya explained. "And sounds like our suspect is rigging the game to ensure their favorites wind up in the top three, which may narrow our list to one of the show's judges."

"And what's the background for the two women you placed in our group?" Mason asked. "You said one is a TikToker?"

"Yeah, Lucy and Charlotte Braxton. Lucy is the TikToker. I couldn't find anything on her sister," Mya said. "I also couldn't find any address for them. No known information at all, other than what Lucy shares on TikTok."

"You run their faces and names through our program to learn more?" Since it was all last minute, I wasn't sure if they'd had time to do that yet, but knowing Gwen and Mya, it'd be on their to-do list.

"I forwarded what we had about every contestant to Sydney before we boarded. No photo for Charlotte. And her TikToker sister, Lucy, must use face altering filters for her posts, because our software couldn't get a read. And that might push her up higher on the targeted list, especially since she's blonde."

"Guess it's good you placed them in our group, then," I said with a nod. "We can keep a closer eye on 'em."

"Yeah, and I'm sure we'll learn more about the sisters when we meet them," Gwen added with a touch of hesitancy. "Since we'll be, um, snuggled pretty close together."

"Say what?" Oliver frowned.

"The details aren't listed on the main server I hacked, but I think we'll wind up sharing a suite together. Possibly beds, too," Gwen said. And now I knew why she hadn't shared these details back at the hangar in the presence of her father. "Looks like they have three suites prepped. Three beds in each suite."

"Yeah, those numbers aren't numbering," I spoke my thoughts out loud. "Nine beds for twenty-four of us?"

"My guess is that each team gets a suite. Each couple gets a bed. And one unlucky, or maybe so-called lucky, couple winds up getting their own room from each team," Gwen noted.

Carter focused on Gwen, and there was no mistaking the grit to his tone when he snapped out, "I'm sure as hell not sharing a bed with you."

Gwen peered at him, a comical look crossing her face. "I'm struggling to believe a man like you is afraid of my dad."

"I could be your dad," Carter bit back.

"Aw . . ." Gwen ran her nail down the buttons of Carter's dress shirt. "*Daddy*."

"You walked right into that one, man." Oliver slapped Carter's back, and Carter tossed him an if-looks-could-kill glare that even had a shiver flying up my spine.

"Anyway," Mya said, rolling her eyes at Oliver, "all that matters is we find out what happened to the missing women."

"I should also mention we're going light on this op." Carter's shoulders dropped a touch.

"Light as in not a lot of artillery?" I asked. "Or like no-luggage light? Because all I have is what I'm wearing."

Carter probably had a closet of well-tailored suits waiting for him in every city around the globe. I'd bet money on it. Me? I'd have to do some last-minute shopping. And what was I supposed to wear to this kind of thing? Shit, I still couldn't believe I was on a plane to Brazil for this undercover mission.

We were flying into Tabatinga, in the northwestern part of the state of Amazonas. From what we'd learned, the resort for the event was also on the border of both Peru and Colombia as well. That tri-border area was well-known for trafficking, which didn't sit well with any of us, especially Wyatt.

"I'm having trouble finding someone at the airport to look the other way so we can offload weapons," Carter let us know. "By the time Gray and our extract team arrives, I'll hopefully have someone to help them out, though."

"Of all places you can't get help?" Oliver smirked.

"I have connections in the bigger cities," Carter grumbled. He had family on his father's side in Brazil, and the man was fluent in Portuguese among other languages, so this had to be more than a little frustrating for him. "But believe me, I'll find a person. We'll just be going undercover unarmed."

"Pretty sure we can't bring a rifle in with us anyway," I stated the obvious.

"Plus," Oliver said with a shit-eating grin, "there's always utensils."

"Seriously? Do you want him to throw you from the

plane?" Mya jerked a thumb Carter's way. "Or, maybe if I'm a good girl, Carter will let me throw you out."

"Buttercup, you wouldn't know how to be a good girl if your life depended on it," Oliver murmured as if the rest of us weren't even there, causing Mya's cheeks to heat as he stared at her.

"Well," Mason said, clearing his throat, "this trip is going to be the opposite of fun. And if we're not careful, someone just might get killed."

# CHAPTER FOUR

## CHARLOTTE

### PALMA, SPAIN

My body was sore today. Even more than normal. I'd taken a group of tourists to the other side of Mallorca for a cave-diving adventure, and I'd been up since four in the morning. And in three hours, I had to report to job number two of three—tending bar. Summer was always my busiest season for work, but since I mostly survived off tips, I couldn't complain. Busy was good. Just . . . exhausting.

Sitting in my tub, I grabbed my phone and opened the TikTok account I'd created to keep tabs on my sister. I only followed her and one other girl who made delicious meals. I promised myself one day I'd find time to make them. Just not today. *Maybe tomorrow.* Hell, it was always tomorrow. The thing was, the tomorrows kept happening, and all the promises to myself of things I'd do never did.

I smiled at the sight of my sister's face in her post from an hour ago. Well, Lucy on TikTok was hardly Lucy in real life. I made her use filters to disguise her identity. I'd done as much begging to keep her offline as I possibly could, but my sister was even more stubborn than me, and I'd lost the battle. So, a fake name and filters that would conceal her identity had been the compromise. Plus, a virtual private network to hide her location. I never imagined she'd wind up with over a million followers, though. Then again, my sister had the kind of personality men and women gravitated toward, so I shouldn't have been shocked.

I clicked play on her post, which she'd titled, Lucy's Dating Advice Series, Part 7. *This should be interesting.* My sister was great at doling out words of wisdom, but not so great at following them herself.

"Hey, everyone, get ready with me while I talk about what not to do when it comes to dating," my sister began while applying mascara. "Do not put the person you met five minutes ago on a pedestal, people. If you have, take them off and stand on it yourself. Use it to reach your own goals and dreams. No one should ever stand above you . . . you need to know your own worth."

Less than a second later, the door flung open to my bathroom, startling me, and I almost dropped my phone into the tub.

"Was that my voice I just heard?" my sister asked, barreling into the room and heading straight to my closet.

"Yeah. I was listening to you steal the words *I* just gave you last week. You know, about a certain guy in your life and how you keep putting assholes who don't deserve your time on a pedestal."

When Lucy returned from my closet carrying one of my suitcases, I swapped my phone for a nearby towel.

"Where are you going, and why with my suitcase?"

"You mean, where are *we* going?" Lucy set the bag down, then squatted in front of the vanity and snatched my makeup bag from beneath the counter. "And also, you give great advice that the world should hear. Just because I don't take it doesn't mean someone else won't." She tossed me a saucy look over her shoulder and winked.

With her back to me again, I stood and wrapped the towel around my achy body. "I'm not going anywhere, and neither are you."

Lucy pushed upright and spun around to face me, a determined look etched between her brows. "You've been bossing me around since I was fourteen. Running me all over the globe. It's my turn to tell you where we're going, and no questions asked this time."

"I boss you around to keep you alive," I reminded her while stepping out of the tub. "And like hell am I going somewhere no questions asked."

My sister's eyes softened as she wrinkled her nose, and I knew . . . I just knew what was going on.

She was running.

But from this week's latest jerk face or a new problem?

My sister fell hard and fast for "bad boys." Did she have anxious attachment issues? Probably. And with how our lives had been for the last eleven-plus years, I didn't blame her.

I tightened the towel around my breasts, preparing myself for a delicate lecture. "Lucy, you know I'm all about 'catching flights not feelings,' but before we discuss the impromptu vacation, I need some honesty here. Tell me the truth. What's wrong?"

Lucy positioned her back to the counter and folded her arms over her plain white tee partially tucked into her denim shorts.

When she didn't open her mouth, I focused on her phone wedged in her front pocket. "When your mood starts depending on whether a guy texts you or not—"

"Why do I do it?" She slowly worked her eyes up to my

face. "Let some guy's texting habits impact my mood? So what if he leaves me on 'delivered'?" She lifted her hand and tossed it in the air. "Or worse, on 'seen'? I'm too good for ninety-nine percent of these men, and yet, my stomach hurts whenever it happens."

I closed the space between us and wrapped her in my arms. "You know why. But that doesn't mean you have to keep letting your past dictate the present. Your future."

"How come you're not like me?" she asked once I freed her from the hug. "You couldn't give two fucks if a guy doesn't message you back. Hell, you ghost, not the other way around."

"I don't ghost." I frowned. "Not on purpose, at least. We just move a lot. So, why get emotionally invested in some guy?"

"Oh I don't know, because you're over thirty now, and maybe you want a family of your own one day?"

"You're my family," I protested.

"But I'm not your daughter. You took on that role eleven years ago, but I'm twenty-five. I'm all grown up if you haven't noticed." Another pout from her, and she knew what those did to me. "Even if I don't always act like an adult, because yeah, maybe I do put these undeserving men on pedestals when they don't even pull out the chair for me." She sidestepped me and abruptly snatched the suitcase and held it between us. "I need to get away, and I want you to come with me. Plus, this is kind of for work. In fact, they extended the invite to me because of my social media following and my adventure series. I guess you need certain skills for this show, so . . ." She paused for a moment. "With them being so eager to get me to join, I used that to my advantage to bargain. I told them I'd only go if they offered you an invite as well. I explained you have survival skills like me, too."

"An invite? Survival skills?" *What?* "We just moved to Spain. I can't up and leave, especially not for some online thing." *Maybe in six months, sure.* "I work three freaking jobs to make ends meet."

"Exactly why we should do this. And it'll be great material for my TikTok and YouTube channels. It's, um, well, a dating game hosted in Brazil this season. In the Amazon rainforest, actually. It's their seventh event, I think. And the location is always somewhere new with different challenges. Plus, if one of us wins—a million bucks split between the winning couple. Can you imagine?" Her cheeks went pink.

I was seconds away from snatching her arm and demanding she look me in the eyes. Because what if this was a trap? The event simply bait to catch us?

But her excitement and the way her eyes lit up about the trip had me resisting the urge to speak my thoughts.

"With that kind of money, maybe we could settle down in one spot for more than a year?"

That was a kill shot I hadn't seen coming from her. My shoulders dropped. "Since when do you want to be in one spot for long?"

"I don't know, maybe the only way I can get over my issues is to stop doing what I always do . . . what *we* always do. Let's stop running."

"I'm sorry that's been our life for eleven years." I sighed. "But what choice do we have?"

"Your paranoia is why we run, Charley. No one is going to find us. It's been forever. We don't look anything like we did eleven years ago."

"But with advanced technology, what if someone did discover it's you on that TikTok account? And since they can't get our location, they're drawing us out?" *There. I said it.* And no, I wasn't being paranoid, I was being careful.

Her dramatic eyeroll she'd perfected over the years left me shaking my head. "It's not. No freaking way. Come on." She shook her head right back at me. "You know, I'd just been getting used to Cape Town, and poof," she said while snapping her fingers, "you made us move."

I was pretty sure that situationship of hers from Cape Town was the real reason she'd been pissed when I demanded we "get out of Dodge" so fast and come to Spain. Screw that asshole and how he love-bombed her only to pull away and make her miss him.

*"Why is it harder to get over someone you were never even in a relationship with?"* Lucy had asked me last week as if I'd know the answer to that. I had no advice to give in that department, because I was still hung up on a guy I had no business wanting.

And speaking of that guy . . .

"Someone found us in Cape Town, so we had no choice but to move again." I snatched my suitcase from her and let it plop unceremoniously to the ground. It wasn't exactly Louis. "I can't go on vacation for some dating game thing. And there won't be filters available for you, which means you're not going either. I can't have your face online. Not your real one."

She waved her hands in the air, trying to shoo away my rejection. "The show won't air until three weeks after we've already left, so it's fine. And like I said, we look nothing like we did when we lived in California. I highly doubt those after us will be watching some dating game show." She rolled her tongue along her lips, and I knew that look. She was artfully plucking the right words from her head to use against me. Well, to try and get her way. "A half a million dollars means you won't need to bust your ass teaching yoga, taking tour groups all across the island, or dealing with assholes trying to touch your tits at the bars you work at."

Okay, maybe not artfully chosen words. More blunt than anything. But no less accurate.

*But come on, could we actually win some dating game thing?* I didn't even know the exact location in Brazil or the details, and yet, why'd I feel like I was slowly giving in to her? And what if my fears that someone had recognized her on TikTok were spot on?

"Important side note," she went on when I didn't voice my thoughts, "I still don't think anyone found us in Cape Town."

My turn to roll my eyes. "Ohhh, please."

"Just because some handsome stranger chats you up in the bar and does the impossible of winning and wooing you over, does not mean he was a threat."

"Except it was all a trap. And I fell for it. Hook, line, and sinker." *Mom never would've been so careless.* "I got sloppy. Stupid. And for a moment, I let myself forget . . ." Forget the reason why we ran and always maintained a level of anonymity, because that stranger had given me the best night of my life. Hell, just the memory of the way his lips had slanted over mine gave me butterflies, and I hated myself for having a visceral reaction to a memory. But I wouldn't back down from my belief our night together wasn't some happy accident.

"You're neither sloppy nor stupid. I just don't believe he—"

"He had a gun. And his passport didn't match the name he gave me. That's why he's an asshole. An asshole regardless of whether he was there for us, by the way. And I should have known the second he'd said his name that it was an alias. Jack London. Sure, sure, he had the same name as the author of *Call of the Wild*. And I didn't question that the second he said it?" I really had been off that night, hadn't I?

"You shouldn't have been snooping while he was asleep."

"I had to get to work and didn't want to wake him, so I was searching his jacket for a pen. Shockingly, the room didn't have one. I didn't expect to find a gun instead."

"You really think someone who targeted you passed out after baiting you to his room, only to allow you to escape his grasp?" She snorted. "Come on."

"I dodged a bullet. Quite literally," I said instead of answering her question. I didn't want to admit she had a point. And I was getting good at dodging things I didn't want to think about. "The idea of me falling for some guy I just met . . . maybe he slipped something into my drink to make me all googly-eyed, talkative, and—"

"Happy?"

"The point is—we're not going to this game. I can't believe you ever signed us up for this." I had to get back on track. Focus on the objective at hand and talk my sister out of this wild idea of hers.

"A half a million dollars, Charley. Between the two of us —two chances at winning. Let me take care of you for once. You've been busting your ass playing mom for eleven years now."

"It's not a hardship looking after you." I hated knowing she thought that. She was my sister. My family. I'd give my life for her, and I almost did when I was twenty. Not that she knew every detail about what happened after Mom's accident. Some truths were better off buried beneath pretty plants to disguise the ugliness beneath. Not that our constantly-on-the-run lifestyle could be described as a "pretty plant," but I did my best to run to pretty locations, at least.

"I think it's time we stop. What if we're safe now?"

"The guy who seduced me to his hotel room last month is evidence of the fact we're not safe," I reminded her.

"Well, there could be other reasons that guy had a gun and different passport on him. Doesn't mean he was sent after us." She began packing my makeup bag as if we were going to Brazil.

I covered her hand as she gripped my tube of mascara. "My job is to keep you safe. A half million dollars to put you in harm's way is not worth it to me."

"But it's not your job. It never should have been. You have to let go." She dropped the mascara and faced me. "I'm doing this with or without you."

I hung my head. "Please, Luce."

"Don't Mom me. Don't 'Luce' me." Mom's name for her. *Shit.* I knew she hated it when I called her that because it . . . hurt her. It hurt me, too. I missed her so damn much. "I need to do this. I'm sorry. You're either coming with me, or you're going to have to finally let me go."

My stomach ached, and my chest became tight. I went over to the window and peeked through the blinds, catching sight of the beautiful skyline of Mallorca. The Cathedral of Santa Maria, or as locals called it, La Seu, sat regally on the Bay of Palma. Mom would've loved it there. She'd always wanted to travel. To see the world. And now we were doing that for her, just not in the way Mom would've wanted for us.

I let go of the blinds and peered at the words inked inside my wrist, **Never Let Go.** "I'll never let go."

*"Where you go, I go,"* Lucy had said to me at fourteen when I'd tried to force her to live with Mom's trusted contact in London instead of going on the run with me. I wanted her to have a shot at a normal life. But the paranoia that someone would find her and I wouldn't be there to protect her had

been too much, so I'd given in to her begging to come with me.

When Lucy remained quiet, I released a heavy breath. Hoping like hell this game wasn't a trap, I murmured, "Where you go, I go."

# CHAPTER FIVE

## JACK

### TABATINGA, BRAZIL

INSIDE THE SHARED LIVING ROOM OF OUR TEMPORARY lodging, I gently pushed Mya's hands away from my wrist as she tried to roll my sleeve to my elbow as if I didn't know how to do it myself. "I know, I know. Show my forearms."

Mya lifted her hands and fake pouted while stepping back, and I busied myself with the job of cuffing my white linen shirt sleeves, eyes on the window instead of focusing on the task at hand.

We had to leave for the event soon, and we'd be traveling down the river by motorboat to get there. No roads in or out. Not exactly comforting. And with the canopy of trees, a helo extract would be tricky unless done over water.

The last time I'd been in Brazil had been with the CIA, protecting Gray's sister, Natasha, on an intelligence-gathering operation in Sao Luis on the coast. It'd been a totally different mission, but ironically, a similar cover story: single businessman seeking adventure. Only this time, my cover story had some partial truths, such as being a Green Beret. It helped fill the event requirement that contestants have certain backgrounds and skills to help with the "survival" aspects of the game. I still couldn't figure out if the contestants were supposed to be there for love, money, or adventure? I supposed all three.

On this trip I was going as Jack Hughes. It was always easier to keep our first names on missions so we didn't screw up and slip when overtired and overworked and call someone by the wrong name. Or refuse to respond to someone when they called us by the "wrong" name.

Done with my sleeves, I faced the room again and found myself asking, "What's the deal with the arm thing anyway?"

Mya exchanged a look with Gwen, and Gwen stood from the couch, swiping her hair clinging to her cheeks away from her face.

It was humid as fuck in there. Sweat dripped down my back even though it was only in the low eighties outside and there was a little A/C unit working double time. It was huffing and puffing like the train in *The Little Engine that Could* book I'd just read to my goddaughter, Emory, last week. Natasha and Wyatt's daughter—Gwen's half sister—was ridiculously adorable, and she made me wish . . . *want* to have a kid of my own one day.

*Why am I thinking about having kids right now?* I blinked and tore my focus away from the on-the-verge-of-death A/C unit to focus back on Mya and Gwen, still waiting for them to answer me.

Gwen slid a few silver bangle bracelets onto her wrist. "You have great arms, Jack," she said, catching me by surprise. "Arm porn. It's a thing, and you should rock it."

I grunted. "Yeah, I didn't need that answer. The last word I want to hear from you of all people is 'porn.'" Just because we weren't related, and she wasn't my niece, didn't mean she didn't feel every bit like an extension of the only family I had left—as in the Chandlers, my best friend's family.

"But she's right. And, just so you know, you have plenty of other sexy qualities aside from your personality," Mya added.

Were they trying to give me an ego boost knowing how nervous I was since this wasn't just any op? Of course, with my luck, I'd be the only one not paired up and get kicked out before the night even began.

Mya began mussing up my hair I'd just worked hard to tame with gel. "You have incredible hair. Thick brown locks with natural golden and coppery highlights."

"You mean gray," I joked. "That's gray." But I did have great hair. I was with her on that. Tapered at the sides. A bit longer and unruly on the top and parted to the left.

"Oh, and you have ink. Ink is hot." Gwen winked. "And I know everyone likes to tease you that you're like Ryan Reynolds, but personally, I'd say you remind me of that guy from *Vampire Diaries*. Ugh, what's his real name?" She snapped her fingers. "Paul Wesley. Mmm. Yeah, definitely him."

I looked back and forth between the two of them, anxious for the other guys to come back so they would stop showering me with compliments like it was their job. "I have no idea who or what she's talking about."

Mya closed one eye. "Yeah, you know, I can see it. Ryan's humor but looks-wise . . . well, damn, now I can't unsee it. I used to have such a crush on that actor, too."

"I hate you two," I grumbled. "You prepared this little speech to give me, didn't you?"

Walking past them, I started for the balcony overlooking the river. I pushed open the door and went outside, pulling the door closed behind me. Hopefully they took the hint and stayed inside with the A/C.

It may have been hot and humid there but being in the place boasting the "Lungs of the Planet" meant the air was fresh. I sucked in a deep breath, detecting a hint of smoke to it. Deforestation and fires had been problematic lately. Hell, there was even a timber-smuggling trade route now. Fuck, could no one just leave a good thing alone? Just let the forest be.

I gripped the railing, finding the bolts a bit loose, and took a small step back. We were on the third level, and I wasn't looking to cliff dive into the river below. "Careful," I warned Mya at the realization I wasn't alone. Nope, she definitely didn't take the hint. "Some screws are loose." I chuckled at the double meaning there since I was feeling a bit off myself.

Mya nudged me in the side with her elbow. "I promise you'll find someone to make you happy one day." Well, that was quite the pivot I hadn't anticipated.

I tossed a look behind me to see if we were alone. Gwen was busy typing on her phone in the living room. "Don't worry, I won't mistake your silly compliments—if that's what they were—for flirting. I'm on the friend train now, I promise."

*"It takes meeting the right one to realize you were interested in the wrong one."* That was yet another saying from my mom finding its way into my head. I swear the woman was still with me even though she'd died years ago.

Some days I missed my parents more than I cared to admit to anyone. I drank the pain away, too. Kept the pain to myself. Bottled it up. Then used the bottle to try and convince myself I didn't need a love like theirs to be happy.

It crushed me that my parents never saw me wind up with

my "the one." They'd died while I'd still been unhappily married to Jill.

"I'm jet-lagged, but I swear I saw her at the airport today. Even chased after her. Did the embarrassing shoulder-turn-around thing. It wasn't her, of course. And I felt like a fool." *And I just spoke my thoughts out loud, didn't I?*

I was truly starting to think I hallucinated that night with Charley in South Africa. If I didn't have evidence on my laptop she really existed, I'd go ahead and sign myself up for therapy.

"Saw who? Chased after who?" Mya grabbed my arm-porn arm, yeah, I'd never forget that, and urged me to face her. "Tell me. Please."

"Don't give me the puppy dog eyes." I frowned.

"But like . . . these eyes work six out of seven times." She smirked, and it was a smile that would've killed me before meeting Charley. The kind of kill-me that happened to Mason. To Oliver. To any single man with a pulse. I doubted even Carter was immune to Mya.

But there I was, obsessed with a ghost. A woman who left me alone. It was Charley's smile that haunted me and might have possibly forever fucked my chances of falling for someone again. I felt it right down to my bones. She was my "when you know, you know" as my teammate Jesse said about the love of his life, Ella.

*What if I did upload her face to our facial recognition program to get a hit? Find out her name. Where she lived. Chase after her like some psycho from a Dean Koontz novel? What was the worst that could happen? Get rejected again?*

"Earth to Jack." Mya gently tugged my arm. "We have to leave soon. Spill. Who has you in a daze? And if she hurt you, so help me I'll—"

"You'll what?" I gave her a hesitant smile.

"Just stop stalling and tell me."

I dropped my eyes to her hand over my forearm. "I met someone on my op in Cape Town last month. You weren't with us for that job. You were with the Marines." I swallowed. "Well, I mean, I met her the night before we flew Stateside. She was at the hotel bar. We wound up talking, and well, we didn't stop talking until the morning."

Mya's lips parted in surprise. "You had a one-night stand?" She was straight up beaming. Color rising in her cheeks. Eyes bright. "Why am I so shocked by that?"

"I didn't, actually." And I kind of hated Mya knew I wasn't some fuck boy. No, it was my wife who cheated. I was ridiculously loyal. "We went to my room, but we only talked." *Kissed, too.* But I didn't need to tell her that. "Then I passed out at some point, and when I woke up, she was gone."

"Oh." Her brows pinched tight, and she shot me those puppy dog eyes again, but they were full of sympathy that time.

"Yeah, exactly. I had the best night of my life, and Charley and I didn't even fuc—" I cleared my throat, recalibrated, then tried again. "Just talked. About nothing, and yet everything, at the same time."

I knew the little half-heart-shaped scar on her chin was from falling off her bike while speed racing the boy next door at twelve.

And she loved standing in the rain and catching drops on her tongue during storms. Even if bolts of lightning cracked through the sky, she'd just stand there with arms open wide living in the moment.

I also knew she'd lost both her parents at different points in her life. That she'd swear she could hear her mother guiding her in her head. Directing her in life as to where to go and what to do. Just like me.

But I didn't know other details. Her last name. Age. Any living siblings or family. Not even what she did for work. She'd dodged that question, and she never asked me how I earned a paycheck.

"I can't get her out of my head. God help me, I want to." *Well, I don't really want to. I need to, though.*

"Wow, Jack. I don't know what to say. I'm just a bit . . . well, your extra weirdness these last few weeks makes more sense now that I know you're feeling this way."

I was nervous to even peer at Mya with her knowing the truth.

"Gray know?"

I shrugged. "Of course." My best friend was the only one I was truly comfortable talking with about the *anythings* and *everythings* in my life.

"You try to find her? Pull her photo from the hotel surveillance? I mean," Mya began while tipping her head toward the suite, "we can help you track her down."

"I can't do that. I want to. But I can't search for her." I faced the view again and gripped the railing while hanging my head. "I've got a feeling she doesn't want to be found."

# CHAPTER SIX

## CHARLOTTE

THE AMAZON WAS NOTHING LIKE I'D EVER EXPERIENCED before. Brazil had always been on my bucket list of places to live, but I'd held out, worried I'd never want to leave. And that was my life—leaving beautiful places behind. But this place . . . well, maybe we could stay a while.

Shivers managed to rack my spine at the thought despite the warm air washing over us in the courtyard of the "players' lodge" as our tour guide had called it. The lodge was in the thick of the jungle, and we were surrounded by not only beautiful greenery but crawly things everywhere I looked. Thank goodness for the bug repellant I'd doused myself in.

We'd yet to receive our room assignments, but I'd felt the welcoming rush of the A/C unit hit me from one suite while walking by a building with a thatched roof. From what I'd noticed, each little house-like building had a veranda, including a cute bucket swing and hammock.

While Lucy had distracted our American-accented tour guide with her concerns about caimans, jaguars, and anacondas in the jungle, I'd taken the chance to try and determine where the cameras may have been strategically placed. Thankfully, I was pretty sure Wi-Fi sucked, and I'd tracked some of the wires to the cameras they'd done their best to blend in with the environment. I sure as hell didn't need anyone listening to any private conversations I had with my sister, so I wanted all my bases covered.

While the rest of the women had gathered in the courtyard, I'd located what I believed to be a dead zone for recordings and planted myself there, waiting for the start of the game.

*I can't believe I'm here.* That I'd quit my jobs yesterday to take part in a dating competition to try and win money. But I saw how much Lucy wanted this—well, needed this—and she was stubborn enough to come with or without me. I couldn't let that happen, so, here we were.

"It's views like these that more than make up for the fact we haven't been in the States in over a decade," my sister said in a soft voice, coming up alongside me while offering a drink. More like a peace offering.

"I guess." I accepted the glass, took a sip, discovering it was a club soda and tequila, better known as "Ranch Water." I clinked my glass with her red frozen daiquiri before taking another sip.

"Do you remember that day you caught me with the bottle of vodka in my bedroom? Pretty sure after that lecture I didn't touch alcohol until my twenty-first birthday. And now here we are . . ." Lucy's unexpected comment commanded my attention, but while my eyes focused on her face, my mind tried to drift in a completely different direction.

I simply stared at her instead of responding, finding myself lost in a daze.

My sister's nose was a touch smaller than mine. Her eyes more green than blue. And her blonde hair borderline brown when she wasn't highlighting it. She was far more Dad than me in looks, and I was a spitting image of Mom. And just like her in every other way, too.

And not a day went by I didn't wonder what things would have been like for me—for Lucy—if Mom hadn't raised me to be just like her. What if Dad hadn't left Mom in so much debt when he died? Would Lucy and I still be in the States? Would Lucy be married now with a house and picket fence to keep a dog in the backyard?

And would I be . . .? I honestly didn't even know what I'd wanted in my life before the decision was snatched from me. I couldn't even remember if I'd had dreams and life goals.

"I guess you don't remember that day like I do," Lucy said, a slight catch of emotion in her tone.

"No, I do," I murmured, still distracted by my thoughts. "I yelled at you for drinking alcohol straight from the bottle. You were only thirteen. And I'm glad you trusted my opinion enough to abstain from touching anything again until you were legal."

"Technically, I was legal at eighteen in every other country we lived in. But you made me wait until twenty-one," she reminded me with a little laugh. "You were momming me before you actually had to 'mom' me." She took a small sip of her daiquiri.

"Mom did her best," I said, feeling the need to defend her as usual. I knew where this conversation was going, and it never painted Mom in the best light.

"Mmhm. You're far more paranoid than she ever was. Maybe if she had been as careful as you are, we wouldn't even need to be here."

I closed my eyes, doing my best to push the picture of Mom's car accident, broadcast on the news that horrible day, from my mind. It was all there in my head like it was happening in real time, though.

I'd shut off the TV when Lucy had walked in the room that night, hoping she wouldn't recognize the Ford Mustang on the screen. But I'd been too late. Lucy's soda had fallen to the floor, splashing all over the beige carpet.

"Mom was paranoid. She taught me to be like this," I admitted, opening my eyes.

"Maybe you don't need to be quite so paranoid, though." Lucy flicked at her straw, a frown marking her lips. "You made us fly into Peru, worried they'd intercept us at the airport in Brazil. We used old aliases in case someone was tracking our new names for this event. And—"

"You wanted to come here, and we did. It just had to be by my rules." I sipped my drink, hoping she'd let go of the uncomfortable conversation.

"Yeah, okay." The resigned sigh that left my sister's lips lacked the dramatic emphasis I'd anticipated from her. That was progress.

I peeked over at the other female contestants. Most of them were huddled by the kidney-shaped pool. Little lanterns with fake candles surrounded the water, and I assumed that meant we wouldn't be taking a dip tonight.

"Should we go talk to the others?" Lucy asked, following my gaze.

Eight women were chatting up a storm near the untouched table of food while two women were off to the side of the group. Not together. Just not with the others. Kind of like they were as unsure about being there as I was.

"I don't know. Is this going to be a *Hunger Games* thing, and they're our enemies, so we don't want them to hear our game plan?"

"I hope not. Pretty sure people died in that game," my sister reminded me.

"Right. Been a minute since I've read that series." Or any book for that matter. I worked a hundred hours a day.

"Women will see you as competition regardless, though," she said. "You're smoking hot."

I did feel kind of "hot" but not exactly like myself. My hair was down instead of in a messy bun or side braid like normal. Little diamond studs adorned my ears, making me feel princess-y for some reason. Probably because I normally wore simple silver hoops. It all felt like I was trying to be someone else. Well, more "someone else" than I usually tried to be.

But it was mostly the dress my sister bought me that had me uneasy. All silk. So thin it showed every part of my body as it clung to me like a second skin.

Sleeveless and backless. A sweetheart neckline with built-in bra cups that didn't do such a great job at hiding my breasts.

*"You have a great body. Shoulders women would kill for, perfect back muscles . . . and don't get me started on your breasts."* The memory of her last exaggerated comment on my appearance as she'd helped me zip my dress at our hotel before we'd headed to the event had me nearly chuckling even now. *"And with how your breasts look in this dress, well, they could make it to the Seven Wonders of the World list."*

They weren't that big, just big enough to cause me back pain here and there.

"Ohh, the men are finally coming out," she said a bit too eagerly for my liking a beat later, interrupting my thoughts. "And also, damn. They're all pretty good looking so far." My sister loosely wrapped an arm around my back as if worried I might take off in the opposite direction from the twelve men heading our way.

And yeah, I'd rather take my chances with the jaguars in the jungle than small talk with a bunch of guys.

From what I could tell as they walked toward us, most were already armed with drinks. That could be an advantage for us. After tending bar for so many years, I was often able to read a person based on their go-to drink.

A muscle-y guy with arms about to tear the sleeves of his polo walked several paces ahead of the pack. He had a beer in hand, his eyes laser-focused on the women like they were targets and he'd do anything to land a bullseye.

*Not my type. Not even close.* Then again, did I have a type? *Sure, sure.* Guys who gave me fake names, made me laugh, and carried a handgun. Gah, I had to stop thinking about—

*No. Flipping. Way.*

He stopped dead in his tracks at the same time my thoughts fell straight through the cracks to Hell—a place I had apparently been transported to as well. Because HE was there.

As if in slow motion, his glass tumbler fell to the pavers by his loafers and the liquid sloshed onto some other guy's jeans next to him. He kept his eyes laser-focused on me, and I'd swear he'd had the same reaction Lucy had the day she'd seen Mom's car accident on the news. Frozen in shock.

"It's him," I whispered. "Jack London."

"Wait, what?" she shrieked in a low voice.

"The one who dropped his glass."

"The guy staring at you like he's seeing a ghost?" She tugged me closer, hooking her arm around my waist so I didn't take off.

"How'd he find us?" And why was he still standing there like a statue of fucking gorgeousness while the others maneuvered around him to get to the cluster of women?

"He looks stunned to see you," Lucy stated the obvious, but maybe it was an act? The man fooled me before. What was his game plan now?

"It can't be a coincidence. No way." I stepped back, and my sister went with me, unwilling to release her death grip on my forearm.

"He's still not moving," she pointed out.

Oh, I was aware, since I was staring right back at him. Jack, or whatever his real name was, looked like a movie star —(with an action hero vibe)—standing there in his khaki linen pants and white linen shirt. Sleeves rolled to the elbows. Top few buttons undone. Hair artfully styled in a messy way. His golden-tan throat bobbed from a swallow I managed to clock from twenty feet away. Okay, I probably made that up, but in my head, there was definitely a gulp.

And if he was that hard-swallow shocked . . . what'd that mean? Was my sister right? A wild accident we were both there?

*No, no. Nothing is ever* that *accidental. He's undercover. Just like in Cape Town.* But how in the world would he have found us?

"What are we doing?" Lucy finally let go of me.

Jack STILL wasn't moving. His arm was finally down at his side, though.

The woman from the lodge who'd provided our tour came to his side and started to crouch for the glass that somehow hadn't broken when it'd connected with the hard ground. And it was only then that Jack finally budged.

He bent forward and snatched the glass before she could, and I read the apology to her on his lips. Another skill I had. Lipreading. It came in handy, especially reading men from across the bar before they made an ass of themselves toward one of my female patrons.

When he was upright again, he focused on one of the other guys who happened to be looking his way. The man's brows were pinched tight. He was the only guy there in black slacks, a black dress shirt, and tie. His attire matched his dark hair, eyes, and his energy.

I caught a subtle nod from Jack his way. They knew each other, didn't they?

"There are two of them. They've got to be here for us. No clue how, but this is a trap." I went over to a nearby bar-top table and discarded my drink, ready to grab my sister and make a run for it. But there were no roads in and out of the place. Boat ride or helicopter exit only, and I didn't have a captain or pilot on standby. *Shit.* Before I could come up with a game plan, the host walked out to greet everyone.

"Good evening." The man's voice boomed as he clapped his hands together. "Now that we're all here together, let's get started." Based on the research I'd done, he was American. Born and raised in Kentucky, but I didn't detect an accent. He wore jeans and a crisp white button-down shirt. His blond hair and green eyes completed his pretty-boy look. Mid-forties maybe. "As many of you already know, I'm your host, Stephen."

"We can't run now. How would we even leave?" Lucy whispered even though we were in a safe-from-a-microphone zone. "If they're really here for us, they won't make a scene and just snatch us, either," she continued in a low voice while the host went on about the lodge and its amenities. I was doing my best to focus on Jack, along with his dark-haired friend, instead of paying attention to Stephen's commentary.

"They could have an exit planned, though. Unlike us," I hissed, angry at myself for ever agreeing to this trip in the first place.

When the host began motioning us all over to join him by the pool, it took my sister pinching me to remind me to move.

Was I really doing this? Were we not running? My entire body was taut. Every nerve ending fired up as I finally did as instructed.

Stephen had the men line up in front of the women. Lucy was at my side, but it was my luck I wound up directly across from Jack. Barely five feet between us now.

Jack had the same sexy trimmed beard he'd had in Cape Town. His blue-green eyes were just as I remembered, a similar color to mine, and they were firmly fixed on me. That sculpted jaw was tight, like he was clenching his back teeth. Less shock now, a touch more "pissed off." He studied me with a cold glare, as if remembering I'd left him alone without so much as a word. He'd missed out on his mark. Let me slip through his fingers. The only person he should be angry at was himself.

*What's your real name?* He hardly looked like a Kevin, as listed on his passport.

Stephen began introductions. Sharing names. He ran down the line of men, ending with Jack *Hughes*. Jack's brows dipped in what might have been an apology the second his last name was revealed.

*Jack London my ass.*

When it was time for the women's names, Jack's lips parted as Stephen said, "Charlotte Braxton." Braxton had been the last name my sister used for her TikTok account, so I'd been stuck with it for this charade.

"Charlotte," Jack mouthed as if testing out the name on his lips to see if it worked for me. And I'd swear he was acting as though he wasn't aware that was my real first name.

He deserved an Oscar for how he'd fooled me in South Africa, but like hell would I let him do it again, even if the man did things to my body with just the way he was looking at me.

There shouldn't have been a flash of heat in my stomach that traveled between my thighs when he angled his head and held my eyes like he owned me. And why in the hell did the idea of a man "owning" me turn me on? That was about as "me" as the dress I had on.

I shifted uncomfortably in my nude heels, and his eyes dropped to my legs. It was almost torturous how his attention walked ever so slowly up my body.

*I hate you. And yet, at the same time, I want you. Hot and heavy headboard-banging-the-wall kind of sex. Or hell, no bed at all. Annnd perfect. Just perfect. That's where my head is at.* If the Wi-Fi wasn't shit, I'd find a way to watch my sister's TikToks to remind myself of the advice she'd borrowed from me.

Stephen continued about the rules. Something about being divided into teams, and our teams would compete against the other groups the first week. Then an elimination round based on points. But it was all a blur, because I was stuck in my thoughts, remembering my night with Jack last month.

I was supposed to be meeting a friend for drinks at the hotel where she was staying. She was one of the only women I'd remained friends with after moving. Normally, I forced myself to lose touch with people. It was better that way. Safer for my sister. For me.

But Mila was different. I'd met her seven years ago while we were in Santiago. Mila didn't know my real identity, and I had a feeling she kept some stuff from me too, and yet . . . I still trusted her enough that when it was my cue to take off for a new city, I promised her I'd stay in touch. Gave her an email address. And we'd met up three times since then. I'd been disappointed when she'd texted at the last minute to say she couldn't meet me at the bar. I'd stood to leave, and Jack had bumped into me, his drink spilling onto my shirt.

*"Fuck, I'm so sorry,"* he'd said, then winced as if also sorry for swearing in the presence of a woman. I loved that he hadn't tried patting down my breasts to "dry me off" with a napkin, taking a chance to get a feel. Instead, he'd ordered club soda and snatched a few napkins and offered them to me. Then he bought me a drink. Things just . . . progressed from there.

We'd talked until closing. And neither of us seemed to want to leave one another, so he'd invited me to his room.

*"I'm not trying to be an asshole, I promise, but if you want to keep talking, my room has a balcony. We could sit out beneath the stars and chat?"* he'd suggested, a handsome smile forming on his full lips.

To be honest, it was kind of shocking we hadn't had sex that night. After nearly four hours of epic conversation, he kissed me, and it was a hell of a kiss, but he hadn't even tried to take it any further. Since when did bad guys have a moral compass? *And how had I read him so wrong all night?* Well, he wasn't that great of a bad guy, he did fall asleep while on the job.

Realizing I was currently staring at his crotch, which was not my intention, I stole my focus toward the host just as he shared the fact I'd be teamed up with Jack.

We'd just been assigned to the same group of eight. *Oh crap.*

My heart stopped. We'd be sharing a room. Competing *together.* I had to assume there were cameras in the rooms. Microphones, too.

"I'll explain more of the rules as we go to keep things a mystery," Stephen went on. "Tonight's objective is for you all to become familiar with your teammates. Figure out your strengths and weaknesses. Learn to trust each other . . . if you can, of course."

"And how do we get to know each other?" the guy with the big biceps I'd noticed earlier asked.

"We'll be doing a series of icebreaker rounds within your teams this evening. You'll be awarded points by the judges. And no, you can't see the judges, but they can see you." Stephen opened his arms, then pointed to one camera that was visible in the corner of the vine-wrapped pergola behind us. "You'll be coupled up by the end of the night. And one couple from each team will sleep together in one of the jungle treehouses where there will be no cameras." He gestured toward the thick bank of trees, but he didn't share how that "lucky" couple would wind up there.

*So, to sleep off camera, I have to be alone with one of the guys in the woods? This just keeps getting better.*

"The other three couples will share a suite. Three beds in the suite. Each couple will sleep together in their designated bed. And there is a camera in the suite."

An uncomfortable band of pressure pushed into my chest, and I released the word, "No," into the warm air.

My sister nudged my back with her fingernail, a warning not to speak my thoughts out loud again.

"If you have a problem with the rules, there's no one forcing you to stay, Charlotte," Stephen said to me.

I stepped away, on the verge of taking his offer to leave, but my sister's palm went flat on my back before she hooked her arm around my hip, a request not to run.

I wasn't about to leave without a plan in place. I just needed air. Well, different air. Air that wasn't being shared with the man who'd been in my head the last four weeks. The man I'd guiltily thought about while using my vibrator to get off the few times I'd had the energy to do so since Cape Town.

"I need a second. Excuse me," I said, and my sister unhanded me. But of course, remained at my side, walking with me away from the others.

Stephen's continued explanation of the icebreaker rounds for the evening fell to the wayside as I made my way to one of the microphone dead zones I'd mapped out upon arrival.

"We need to figure out a way to leave," I whispered just in case I'd missed a hidden microphone somewhere.

"You still don't know if he's here for us," she mouthed back.

I turned to the side to put eyes on Jack. He looked as though he wanted to walk over to where we now stood, but he was holding back. He must not have wanted to give up the fact that we knew one another. Something just didn't add up. "How could he not be, though?"

"If he's really a bad guy, and we even managed to find a way to safely leave, he'd follow us, right? We won't be safe," she pointed out. "Our best chance is to do the whole 'keep your enemies close' thing, and see how this plays out. I really don't think he'll make a move on camera. That can't be his plan."

I hated being there in the first place, but now my bad gut feeling was supercharged in Jack's presence.

"Also, I don't want to leave. I still think there's another reason your mystery guy is here. And yeah, maybe it is for you. But maybe it doesn't have anything to do with . . . you know. What if he's—"

"Obsessed with me?" My eyes widened, and I faced her. "That'd be bad, too."

"I'd give anything for a hot and funny guy to be obsessed with me. Just FYI." She reached for my arm and gave it a little pinch. "If you're not running, we should head over before people start asking questions."

"Fine. But if I think we're in danger at any point, we slip out in the middle of the night, and we take our chances in the jungle. I memorized the way we came by boat. We can follow the path along the river to get back to the other hotel if necessary."

"Okay."

I didn't believe her "okay" or her nod. But she didn't give me much choice, or another chance to plead my case, because she left my side and rejoined the others.

"Hugs or handshakes. And then we'll do the first round," Stephen was saying as I made my way back over. He gave me a questioning look, which wasn't the best sign. I knew there was a chance I could wind up cut and not Lucy. And that hadn't been a huge deal before, since I could have waited for her at the other hotel located ten kilometers away. But now? Now I had to either last as long as my stubborn sister did, or force her to leave if I was eliminated first.

"I'm a hugger," my sister said and opened her arms to some guy on our team named Mason.

Mason had dark hair and gray eyes, and those eyes flew up and down Lucy's body so fast I nearly missed it before he accepted her invitation for a hug.

The two women in my group busied themselves with introductions to the other guys as Jack stepped around them to get to his target. Me.

"Hi." He extended his arm, offering me the handshake option instead. "I'm Jack."

I wet my lips while deciding what to do. I hated that he didn't smell like bug repellant. And I hated that whatever cologne he had on didn't repel me, either.

I stepped forward and ignored his outstretched arm,

opting for a hug with one purpose in mind. I slung my arms over his shoulders, and he went completely still, as if shocked I'd gone with that choice. When his hands slid to my bare back to complete the whole "hug thing" I hated him again. Hated that his big hands felt good there. Felt freaking perfect. One even slid up my spine beneath my wavy hair, and he held the nape of my neck.

*Own me.*

*Take me.*

*Fuck me.*

NOT the thoughts that should've popped into my head. But they'd joined the chaos of my mind, nevertheless.

I pushed away the ridiculous inner monologue and brought my mouth to his ear and whispered, "I don't know what you're doing here, but this can't be a coincidence."

He kept hold of me, and chills danced across my skin as he returned the favor with his mouth to my ear. "Same, Charley. Same."

There was so much meaning in those three words. In that deep voice. I was so distracted it took me a second to realize someone else was talking to us.

"You, uh, going to let go of each other?"

I forced the lump down my throat, ignored the fact I knew my body was covered in goose bumps, and I pulled away from Jack London-Hughes.

"I'm Oliver."

I looked toward the new guy. He had a friendly smile with warm, kind eyes. "You can call me Charley." I smiled back at him and, since I had to keep up with the hugs now, offered him a quick one-arm one.

I moved on next to the other two guys—Mason and the intimidating-looking man in all black who I believed was in league with Jack, Carter something-or-other.

"Charley, huh?" my teammate, Mya, asked, her tone a bit . . . questioning.

"Mmhm. Mom wanted to call her Lottie. Dad preferred her full name," Lucy spoke up. "My rebellious sister went with her own choice, Charley."

I glared at her. *TMI, Lucy.*

"My mom's name is—" Gwen, I think that was her name, let go of whatever she'd planned to say and shook her head. "I like Charley," she tossed out as if that completed her dangling sentence.

I shot her a hesitant nod, unsure what to make of any of my new teammates.

"Now that we have the introductions done," Stephen said with another loud clap, stealing my focus back his way, "it's time for the first kiss."

"Kiss?" I blurted, unable to stop myself, and I shifted to the side, slamming into a hard wall of . . . well, Jack. My focus fell down the length of his body. *You that hard everywhere else?*

When our eyes met, there was a twitch to his lips as if he'd read my thoughts. Like he was holding back a, *Why yes, do you want to find out just how hard?* response.

"So, um, kiss?" I must've missed the kissing part when I'd made my dramatic exit from the group earlier.

"The best way to get to know if you have chemistry with a person right off the bat is to kiss. Let's see how many men on your team are frogs. And how many are princes." Stephen grinned. It was less creepy and more like he was trying to sell me on something I sure as hell didn't want to buy.

"Kiss them? All four of them?" I focused back on Jack. He slid his hands into his khaki linen pockets, but his eyes weren't on me this time. They were on the sky, as if this idea was as troubling to him as it was to me.

And this wouldn't be our first anything. In fact, I was pretty sure our kiss in Cape Town had broken records. It'd been a make-out session. One where this so-called bad guy had never even slid his hand beneath my shirt or my skirt. He'd shown me something that sadly I wasn't used to from most guys: respect. And people wondered why I was still single.

"Of course." Stephen's response barely registered, because now all I could think was that I may have had Jack's motives for being in Brazil all wrong.

I didn't think Lucy was on the right track, though, either.

But I'd for damn sure find out who the hell he really was and what in God's name he was doing there.

And so help him, if he was a threat to my sister in any way . . . well, screw whatever weird feelings and desires he inspired within me, I'd lay him out to keep her safe.

Because like I'd done at twenty, I'd do whatever the hell I had to, to protect Lucy.

Even if that meant killing someone.

Again.

# CHAPTER SEVEN

## JACK

*HOW IS THIS POSSIBLE?* IT MADE NO FUCKING SENSE.

Charley had looked as stunned as I'd felt when I'd walked out there. Probably even more shocked, which was saying a lot.

I hadn't taken her for the type to join a dating game competition for money. But what were the odds she'd not only be there, but she was one of the women Gwen had prearranged to be in my group?

And now I had a new mission: protect the woman of my dreams. The same woman who'd spent the last ten minutes looking at me like she wanted to kill me.

*She thinks I'm a liar*, I had to remind myself. I gave her a different name—my real name, ironically—in Cape Town, so of course she'd be wondering why I was using a different one. But hell, that still didn't explain her bailing on me last month.

Carter turned his back to the host and looked toward the sky as he whispered, "There something you want to tell us?"

"I know one of them. Charlotte," I said from the corner of my mouth like a bad ventriloquist. Before I could add the obvious problem with that, our host reminded us about the impending and expected kiss with each of the women on our team.

*Kiss Mya? Gwen?* That'd be awkward enough. But set my mouth to Charley's after I'd felt her body shudder in my arms during our hug? I'd swear she'd been on the verge of threatening me had Oliver not unglued us from one another.

Regardless of her reasons to be pissed at me, aside from the last-name thing, there was one thing undeniable. We had chemistry. Whether she wanted to accept it or not, it was there. Fucking electric. And I knew I wasn't hallucinating shit that time. I'd never felt anything like it in my life. The same charge of energy we had between us at the hotel was present now.

"Kiss them? All four of them?" Charley asked, her blue-green eyes glinting.

I slipped my hands into my pockets, curling them into tight fists at the idea of watching my teammates kiss Charley. My hands were going to be spending quite a bit of time in those pockets, hopefully preventing me from breaking the arms of those same teammates. Yep, that sounded crazy, because she wasn't mine.

*But you feel like mine. Why the fuck do you feel like mine?*

Aside from Carter now knowing I knew Charley, I was certain Mya had connected the what-the-fuck dots, but she was a better actor than me. She didn't even chance a confused look at me to determine if by some wild turn of events she was "my" Charley.

Stephen continued, "If you think this is awkward now, well, then you may want to bow out before things get a bit more extreme."

I should've done more homework on what to expect for

this dating game thing. Watched previous shows or something.

"Got it," Charley responded with grit in her tone I couldn't help but admire.

A moment later, the women were directed to line up in a row. All twelve women stood in front of the pool, grouped by fours based on their team.

"Each guy will take a turn going down the line of women on their team. Kiss must be on the lips," Stephen casually explained, opening his hands to the sky.

"And if we don't want to kiss someone on our team?" Mya asked, her gaze bouncing from Oliver to the host.

"You're going to wind up losing this competition pretty fast if you can't handle a kiss," Stephen commented.

Mya shot me a hesitant look, and clearly, I wasn't the only one uncomfortable with the situation. It couldn't be easy for her to kiss Mason when the man needed to be getting over her. But to kiss Oliver in front of Mason? She was a good person, and I knew it'd pain her to do that to Mason even more.

And while the thought of kissing Mya or Gwen was uncomfortable, the bigger issue was I really didn't want to kiss anyone other than . . . well, the woman who was currently staring at me like I was an enemy of the state. Ironic, given I hunted those people down for a living.

"Okay, then. Let's get started. One at a time," Stephen announced. "Once you've kissed all four women, swap places with your next teammate."

Mason stepped up first while I drifted to the end of the line. Distraction did me wrong. I was stupid. Should have taken that first spot. Instead, I'd be sitting there in my discomfort, hoping I didn't have to go all caveman and claim Charley from one of my teammates.

I watched Mason's back muscles noticeably pinch together beneath his black tee as he started toward Mya, who happened to be first in the line.

From the corner of my eye, I spied Oliver lowering his head, eyes on the pavers instead of watching what turned out to be a quick kiss. "It's done," I said under my breath, letting him know he was safe to look. He'd never admit it'd been hard on him to watch the woman he "hated" kiss someone else.

Mason kissed Gwen next. Quick and fast.

Charley's sister was third in line. Mason leaned in for the kiss, and I was a bit surprised when that one lasted longer. Even more shocked when her hand went to his hip, drawing him even closer.

Mason stumbled back a moment later as if shocked by whatever the hell had just happened. A quick, audible throat clear from him, then a, thank God, faster-than-fast kiss with Charley, and he was done.

I'd swear the column of the man's throat was red. Not necessarily embarrassed at having us watch him kiss four women, but the fact I was pretty sure he'd enjoyed kissing Lucy.

I stole a look at Lucy, wondering if I'd see the same reaction from her. She seemed impacted, too. She began murmuring something to her sister at her side, but Charley's eyes were on me as she whispered back to her.

"You're up next," Mason prompted Carter, who'd yet to budge.

Carter finally stepped forward, adjusted the knot of his tie, then sped through the line so fast I nearly missed it.

When it was Oliver's turn, he appeared even more hesitant to step forward than Carter had been.

I stole a look at Mason to check on him, but he wasn't

looking at Mya. His focus was on Lucy. *Must've been some kiss.*

"Any day now. Just get it over with," Mya blurted at Oliver, who was still standing before her like a statue of indecision.

Oliver's back was to me, so I couldn't see their actual kiss. But I was pretty sure it lasted longer than any of us, especially him and Mya, expected. When he backed up from her, he hurried down the line at the same rate Carter had, not taking his time with anyone else the way he had with Mya.

And then it was my turn. *Just get it over with.* I unglued my hands from my pockets and went over to Mya.

She gave me a nervous little smile. I couldn't believe we were all in this situation. Never in my wildest dreams did I think I'd be doing something like this. I leaned in and set my mouth to hers. Quick and fast. Friendly.

With Gwen, I had to forget she was Wyatt's daughter for a second during our kiss.

Lucy was next. How in the hell was I kissing Charley's sister, and in front of her? I kissed the side of her mouth, barely catching her lips, hoping our host didn't spot that. Best I could do in the situation.

My heart was going to pound right out of my chest once I was before Charley, though. I was sweating. Skin on fire.

Charley's blonde hair was styled differently from Cape Town. She had long bangs now, swept off to the side that blended in with her wavy hair. She was as gorgeous as I remembered.

Her breasts lifted and fell as she breathed through her nose. And when her eyes met mine, I tensed at the memory of the last time our mouths had touched.

"Just do it," she whispered the directive since I was stuck in the echo of last month's encounter.

I forced myself to dip my head and slant my mouth just over hers, our lips barely a breath apart, then closed my eyes and waited to see if she'd meet me the rest of the way.

The moment her soft lips met mine I nearly groaned. At the feel of her tongue skimming the seam of my mouth, I almost cursed.

Instead, I took it as an invitation to meet her tongue with mine. The "polite" term French kissing could kiss my ass. This was more like fucking with our tongues. It was hot. Borderline dirty. And being in the presence of others, including those watching on camera, only seemed to ramp up the energy between us.

I couldn't stop myself if I tried.

She'd have to break the connection, give me some signal when she was ready to back off.

Her hand landed on my chest, lingering for a moment before climbing up to my shoulder, and she held on to me as we made out, and the rest of the world faded away.

*My mission? What fucking mission? She's my new mission. The bad guy, aka the Wizard of Oz man-behind-the-curtain, never fucking heard of him.*

"Ahem." It took Stephen loudly clearing his throat to finally break the spell. "Like I said, a kiss can reveal chemistry."

When I eased my mouth back from Charley's, she blinked a few times as if wrapping her head around the moment we'd shared—and fuck, it was a moment, no denying that—then she slowly withdrew her hand from my shoulder.

She must've forgotten the pool was right behind her, and when she stepped back, she knocked into a lantern, pitching her toward the water. I quickly shot my hand behind her back and hauled her into my arms. Her hands landed on my chest for support, and she stared up at me with a swirl of confusion in those beautiful eyes.

"Fast reflexes," I overheard Stephen comment as Charley righted herself. "Nice catch."

Once I knew she was safe from going into the water, I let go of her. I gave her one last look, then forced myself to rejoin the guys.

Carter's brows lifted as I headed back his way, a question in his eyes.

*Yeah, join the club. I have a lot of questions, too.* I huffed out a deep breath, willed my hard-on to go down, then turned toward the host. I couldn't remember what was next during the icebreaker round, too lightheaded from that kiss to think straight.

"Next up, you'll each take turns answering a series of questions," Stephen shared as a few staff members from the lodge began carrying out a table and . . .

*Shit.*

"A polygraph?" Oliver piped up at the sight of the recognizable equipment. He tossed a quick look Gwen's way, probably wondering why she hadn't given us a heads-up that'd be part of the game.

Was this new? Did someone running the show suspect something was off given the sudden change in contestants at the last minute?

We still had no idea if we were dealing with just one serial-collecting psychopath somewhere or a team of criminals. The entire show could be a cover for some shady shit. Or have absolutely no connection to the disappearances whatsoever. Jury was still out. Too early to tell anything.

Hell, it could even be a hide-in-plain-sight kind of bad guy, like our host.

One target we could handle. An armed team, though? I

didn't like those odds without worrying innocents would get caught in the crossfire.

"And what if we answer with a lie?" Lucy asked.

Stephen smiled. "You lose two points. And lose an article of clothing. But two back-to-back lies and, well, you strip down to nothing but, well . . . you'll see."

I supposed losing clothes was better than our covers being blown. Beating a lie detector test wouldn't be a problem for me. Nor for Carter. The CIA trained us to handle that shit. But I wasn't so sure about Mason and the others. I shared a worried look with Carter, on the same page of concern with me. Some of us might be out the door before the game even really began.

"Let's do this, shall we? This time, we'll have the men start on each team." Stephen gestured toward the table beneath the pergola by the pool.

"This is going to end with some of us butt-ass naked," Oliver said under his breath as Mya neared us.

"Do your best to be honest," Mya whispered. "I don't want to see your ass, thank you very much."

"Sure you don't, Butter—" Oliver cut himself off, as if remembering he shouldn't already have a nickname for his teammate. He cleared his throat as Carter was called over first.

*Good.* Carter would be fine. I wasn't worried about him. No one could crack that man, I was sure of it.

I set my back to one of the columns of the pergola and buried my hands in my pockets, nearly forgetting we were on camera. Gray and Jesse weren't arriving until tomorrow, though, so we'd have to do our best not to get ourselves in trouble, at the very least, before then.

A woman in a light blue wrap dress sat on the other side of Carter with a laptop in front of her to check his honesty.

"I'm Shannon," she introduced herself. "And are you ready?"

Carter looked my way for a moment, gave me a subtle nod, then faced her.

"Is your name really Carter?" she asked him, her accent noticeably American.

"Yes," he replied.

"Have you ever killed a man?"

Well, that was a quick pivot of what-the-fuck. I pushed away from the column, unsure what he'd say. He could lie, sure. But I was trying to remember the cover story Gwen had cooked up for him.

"Yes."

"When? Why?" Shannon probed.

"Traveling in Europe, and I was jumped. The guy had really bad table manners. And it was a him-or-me thing," Carter casually shared, and I spied Oliver trying to hide his smirk at Carter's semi-truthful and slightly comical answer from when he'd forked a guy to death last year in Zurich.

Polygraph tests were usually yes or no questions, or short answers. But I had a feeling a lot of what was going on here was theatrics for higher ratings. *Not that we'll let this footage ever air.*

"Interesting," Shannon said after a moment. "And who was the best kiss of the four?"

I about stumbled at the rapid change yet again.

Carter peered at our group. I knew he didn't want to answer. He didn't even want to fake an answer. "No comment," he went with.

Shannon pushed her glasses to the bridge of her nose. "Not a choice."

"Charlotte," Carter relented with the lie even I could detect.

Did a CIA-trained operative just let a question about a kiss be what broke him? But yeah, the machine buzzed.

Carter wordlessly loosened the knot of his tie, slid it free from his neck, then flung it to the pavement.

Shannon drummed her fingers at the column of her throat. Was she sweating? I supposed sitting across from the broody dude could make anyone's pulse uptick. "And, um, ahem, if you could screw anyone on your team, who would it be?"

Carter grumbled, "No one."

The damn polygraph was either overly sensitive and misreading Carter, or my team leader was off his game. Would the man seriously rather get naked than divulge a name? Who in the hell on our team did he want to sleep with?

"Your time is up. If you can't be honest, how will your team depend on you during the game?" Stephen asked him. "Clothes off." He twirled a finger, motioning for Carter to stand.

Carter's jaw and fists clenched. Hell, his ass cheeks probably did, too. Not a visual I wanted in my head.

But obeying someone else's orders would be more difficult for Carter than stripping in front of twenty-plus people.

Shannon stood and offered him a large, bright green leaf that seemingly came from nowhere. "You can have this, though, to, um, cover yourself." Her gaze dipped straight to Carter's crotch, and her cheeks flamed to match her red nail polish.

Carter angled his head and replied in a flat voice, "I'm going to need a much bigger leaf."

# CHAPTER EIGHT

## CHARLOTTE

"Well then. I didn't expect ink beneath that shirt, but wow," Lucy said into my ear as Carter tossed his black dress shirt. His back was to us, and he had a tattoo of black feathery wings inked on each side of his shoulder blades, and when his back muscles pinched, the wings came together like he could fly.

*Are you the fallen one? A fallen angel?*

He pivoted to the side, giving his back to the other two women on our team, Mya and Gwen, and began unbuckling his belt. For whatever reason, he'd rather Lucy and I see him strip. That was interesting.

I turned, offering him privacy, then snatched my sister's arm, urging her to look away as well. But she appeared stuck in some stupefied trance by a guy who had to be almost twenty years older than her.

*No daddy issues allowed. Please, God. We have enough issues in your dating life.*

I heard his belt connecting with the pavers, and my mind wandered. Was it just his belt? Had he removed it from his pants before dropping it? Was he dragging out the efforts to hide his embarrassment? He didn't strike me as that type of guy. Would Jack be that kind of guy? Shit, what was wrong with me?

"Lucy," I hissed when she'd yet to follow my command.

"Oh, yeah. Right." Lucy faced me, flushed.

"Guess you weren't lying about needing a bigger leaf," I overheard an unfamiliar voice say. Maybe a woman from another team. And I guess that answered the question about the belt.

I sure as hell had no plans to strip, but I also couldn't afford to tell certain truths if asked. Heels, panties, and a dress was all I had on.

"You can put your briefs back on," Stephen directed after a chuckle. "We were kidding about the leaf. And the nude thing."

Carter grumbled something. It was more like a growl. He wasn't happy. And I got the feeling you did *not* want to piss that man off. But at least complete nudity wasn't on the table tonight.

"Next up, Mason," the host announced a few seconds later, forcing us to return our attention to the polygrapher.

But when I spun around, it was Jack I noticed first. He was scrubbing the back of his hand along his jawline while staring at the polygraph machine. Was he worried about lying, too? Hell, was our entire team a bunch of liars?

I had to remind myself Lucy and I were there for the money, which meant we couldn't afford to lose any points if we truly had a shot at winning. But there was still the hurdle of Jack being there to get over before I could consider making it as far as the finals.

"Ever shot a gun?" was Mason's first question.

"Yes," he quickly answered.

"Why?" the interrogator, Shannon, asked.

Mason shrugged. "Marines."

While he was peppered with a few more questions, I stole a look at my sister. Lucy was focused on . . . damnit, on our nearly naked teammate, Carter.

Carter, in only his tight black briefs that didn't leave much to the imagination, leaned his muscular body up against one of the pergola columns. His arms were folded across his chest, but he didn't seem all that shy about his current state.

Lucy seemed to be focused on the veins that cut down his sculpted body and disappeared into his briefs, though.

"Last question, who on your team would you like to spend the night with in the treehouse if you were given the chance?" Shannon pressed, fingering her red nails through her blonde hair, which hung in loose waves around her face.

Mason looked straight at Mya, then his attention dipped to Lucy.

*Well, the plot thickens. Why do I sound like some silly contestant in a game show? Oh, right. Because I am one.* I nearly face-palmed myself for the annoying thoughts. *Chalk it up to this weird situation and the fact "Jack London-Hughes" is there.*

"Mya," Mason finally revealed, and no lie detected. But why'd his answer have Oliver mumble a curse under his breath?

"Something off to you?" Lucy whispered as Mason traded places with Oliver in the hot seat.

"You're just asking me that?" I almost laughed, but I kept the outburst to myself that time.

Oliver seemed to get off much easier than both Mason and Carter in the question department. He handled each question with ease, like he was plucking answers from the sky without a worry in the world.

Then Shannon hit him with what felt like the unavoidable

million-dollar question. The one that broke each man in some way, shape, or form: "Who do you want to have sex with?"

Oliver dragged a palm down his face and said, "Gwen."

Buzz.

He peeled his shirt over his head, revealing ink on his shoulder that went down his bicep.

"Try again. Remember, you lose everything aside from your underwear, and more importantly double the points, if you lie again," she reminded him.

Oliver closed his eyes and murmured a name too low to hear.

"What was that?" Shannon asked.

Another mumble from him.

"I can't hear you," she was quick to snap out.

Oliver's eyes flashed open as he rasped, "Mya. I'd fuck Mya."

No buzzing. But Mya's face went pale at his words.

Damn, this all felt really personal. And I even got goose bumps at the exchange.

Oliver stood abruptly, knocking the chair over. Without so much as a word, he walked over to the pool area, and his muscles flexed with every step.

"Now this is starting to feel like a dating show," Stephen piped up. "Last male contestant on this team is Jack."

*Oh geez.*

Jack grabbed the chair from the ground and took a seat. His palms landed on the table before him, and he kept his focus on the woman across from him.

"Have you ever met anyone here before tonight?" was a question I sure as hell hadn't expected, and Jack's gaze flew my way.

But the second he said, "No, I don't know anyone here. Tonight is my first time meeting everyone," and the thing didn't buzz at his lie . . . I knew I was in even more trouble than I thought.

I barely heard his answers to any of the other questions. Almost missed the fact he'd said he'd been a Green Beret. But what if that was a lie, too? How could I possibly know what to believe?

*Who are you, Jack London-Hughes?*

"Who was your best kiss?" That question rocked me back to reality.

Jack looked my way. "Charlotte."

No buzz.

"Who do you *not* want to have sex with?"

"Gwen," he quickly remarked, and when I peeked at Gwen, she didn't look remotely offended.

"If you could be anything, anyone you wanted, right now," the woman continued, her tone soft and almost wispy that time, "who would it be?"

I focused back on him. Jack's jaw clenched, and his chest lifted and fell with a heavy breath. His eyes focused on the table as he revealed, "A husband and father."

Why did his answer feel so . . . painfully honest? Why did it hurt my chest so much to hear? Why did it make me want to believe that of all his answers, that was the most genuine?

"Last question," she began, never referring to a list of questions on paper so she either memorized them or made them up as she went, "based on first impressions, if you have to pick someone on your team to marry and be the mother of your children, who would you pick?"

That was a twist on her sex question, and yet, it felt even more intimate.

Jack shook his head, then began working his fingers over the buttons of his shirt. "No comment. Don't ask again," he ground out, then pushed back in his seat while opening his shirt and slid it back off his shoulders, allowing it to fall to the pavers as he stood.

I gulped at the sight of the hard planes of his chest. The sexy ink on his shoulder and at his side. The way his ab muscles flexed as he took a few deep breaths and let them go. There was just so much to take in. I wanted another question. I wanted him to lie. I wanted his hand to go to his belt buckle, and for him to be in the same situation as Carter.

And mostly, I needed to get a grip, remembering he'd already lied. And to me.

"Okay, then." Shannon looked at Stephen, deferring to him for what was next.

"Time for the women," Stephen instructed, and I blinked and tore my focus from Jack's muscular frame. The idea of sitting in that chair and doing the very thing I always avoided, talking about myself, was nauseating.

Lucy was ordered first up, and she was hit with different questions. They were more skills-based, as if the show wanted to ensure we hadn't fudged our "list of extracurriculars" to earn ourselves a spot in the game.

But it was the next series of questions for Lucy that made me physically ill.

"Any living family aside from your sister?" Shannon asked, and Lucy shot me a worried look before shaking her head no. "Where do you currently live?"

*Guess we're not going back to Spain.*

"Mallorca," Lucy tossed out, knowing I was crawling out of my skin.

Shannon asked her a few more questions, thankfully ones I could stomach, before Lucy finally swapped places, putting Gwen up next.

Gwen had been hit with similar questions to Lucy, and

Carter seemed a bit thrown at how easily Gwen had confessed she'd choose him to sleep with.

I'd swear my entire team knew each other, not just Jack and Carter. Not that I'd yet to confirm that theory. Just a hunch. But the way they all looked so uneasy, how they peered at each other during the lie detector tests, told a much different story from the one they were showing the host.

Mya went third. She lied about her best kiss when she shared it'd been with Jack. Then she lied about who she'd sleep with, in which she'd given Carter's name. And that meant she'd have to strip. But only to her underwear? Or did she get to keep her bra? Or damn, was she like me and not wearing one?

"Panties *and* bra can stay on if you'd like," Stephen told her.

"Gee, thanks." Mya removed her dress, her gaze bouncing back and forth between Oliver and Mason as the material pooled around her wedge sandals. Her matching frilly pink panty set seemed to snag the attention from the guys on the next team over.

*There's awkward, and then there's this.*

"Charlotte, you're up," Shannon called me over.

I sat in the hot seat and did my best not to look at the man I wasn't supposed to already know.

She tossed me a few softball questions to warm me up. Nothing I couldn't handle.

"Do you have any secrets?" was her fourth one.

"Don't we all?" was my way of dodging the answer, and she tipped her head as if to say, *True.*

"What are you really good at doing? What do you do best?"

What was I supposed to say to that for an answer: *I'm great at avoiding answering personal questions?* Or the other truth, the one I didn't want to admit, either? "Surfing," I said, making up my mind to go with the not-quite-a-lie answer; although, it was certainly not what I was best at. *No buzz. Nice.*

"Are you attracted to anyone on your team?" she asked next.

I opened my palm, waving my hand toward the four men. "Um, have you seen my team?" They were all good-looking men with rock-hard bodies. Muscles for days. I was also dodging again. I didn't want to confess which one of the four men made my pulse race.

"And if your life depended on it, which of the four men would you want to save you?"

"I don't know them well enough to answer that." *Well, hell, that was pretty much the truth. Why'd I get buzzed?* I looked toward Jack, his arms crossed, studying me. I supposed my subconscious mind had a different answer. Jack, I'd choose him, even if it didn't make sense.

"Looks like there is someone," she said, reading my thoughts. "But maybe we'll wait to see how everything plays out to get that answer. You don't have to remove any clothes for that one."

I almost grumbled a sarcastic *thank you* but kept my mouth shut. But was she suggesting I'd need my life saved by someone on my team later?

"Charlotte, have you ever killed someone to save another life?" Well, that was oddly specific compared to Carter's question.

If I answered no, she'd know I was lying. If I told the truth, she'd ask why. And I couldn't answer that. So, I sighed at what I'd have to do, and went with, "No comment."

Hearing the buzz, Stephen started heading back our way from observing the team next to us.

"So, do shoes count as removing something?" Even as I tried to laugh it off, there was no way to hide the struggle in my voice.

"No." Stephen matched my nervous laugh with what might have been kindness. But maybe it was just impatience.

I stood and reached beneath my dress to find the hem of my panties, doing my best to expose as little as possible. I slid my panties down my thighs, then allowed the dress to fall back in place as I shimmed free of the nude satin underwear. I stepped out of them, then snatched them from the ground.

I settled back in the seat, and my heart nearly broke free from my chest at the way Jack pinned me with a dark, broody stare.

Goose bumps I couldn't conceal came back and I shivered under his gaze.

"Last question," she began, and I knew what was coming. And I also knew if I didn't answer honestly, I'd be losing my dress. "Who would you like to share a bed with tonight?"

My shoulders relaxed. "Easy." Thank God for her wording on that one. "My sister."

# CHAPTER NINE

## CHARLOTTE

WITH THE CANOPY OVERHEAD, WE WERE SHIELDED FROM ANY last bits of evening light as all twenty-four contestants walked the trail in the jungle. We had to complete our third icebreaker round before we learned where we'd be sleeping tonight, and being told to march into the woods without knowing why wasn't exactly thrilling.

There were two cameramen walking with us, as well as two guys who worked for the show holding obnoxiously bright lights. Based on how and where they aimed them, I assumed they were more for the purposes of helping film whatever we were about to do and less about helping us see so we didn't trip.

With no time to recalibrate after the polygraph fiasco, Stephen had ordered us to the jungle path. We weren't allowed to change, nor had we been allowed to put back on the clothes some of us had lost. So, I was bare beneath my dress. *But* they'd given us all black rubber boots to wear. I guessed that was better than the alternative of going barefoot or doing the impossible and walking through the jungle in heels.

"Can we talk?" I paused hesitantly at Jack's voice just behind me, then carried forward after pretending to fix one of my boots.

"Not a good idea," I whispered back.

"Is your name really Charlotte?"

I stopped walking, knowing we'd fall behind the others, but with the cameramen ahead of us, I opted to take my chances and get this out of the way now. I whirled around and faced him, ready to put a stop to his questions and hopefully avoid drawing attention to either of us. He must not have expected my abrupt change in direction, because he was too close, and we collided.

My hands landed on his muscular chest, and instead of biting my tongue, I snapped back, "Is your name really Jack?"

He snatched my arms as if worried I'd float away. Drift into Never Never Land. Pretty sure we were already there. "Yes," he shot back.

"Mmmhmm," I dragged out on purpose. "Sure. Jack London? Jack Hughes? Or?"

"Or what?" he asked, a touch of humor in his tone.

Frustrated, especially at how I hated the way his body felt so damn good beneath my palms, I wiggled free from his touch and started to face forward. But my normally steady legs betrayed me for the second time tonight, and my knees buckled.

When I lost my footing and went backward, Jack snatched hold of me. But rather than just righting me and sending me on my way, he lifted me from the ground, scooping me into his arms. For a second, I wondered if he'd toss me over his shoulder and carry me like I was some petulant kid who needed a time-out in my room. Or a spanking.

*No, no, no. Don't go there . . .*

But my brain did.

In fact, it went there in 4D.

On a bed. Jack flipping my dress up, exposing my bare ass. His big hand connecting with my skin with a loud thwack. Me bucking forward just before he palmed my ass cheeks to soothe the mark.

*Oh God, help me. I'm into red flag carriers. Just like my sister.*

"You just want to fall tonight, don't you?" he asked, and I hated I couldn't see his face clearly enough to read the expression that went along with his jab.

"You should've let me fall. Both times," my stubborn self responded. I wasn't used to men rescuing me. Or doing anything remotely heroic. And I could never allow myself to get used to having someone to rely on.

"Oh yeah?" he asked, his tone casual.

I grunted. Not very ladylike. And I didn't care. "Why are you still holding me?"

"Because there are ants crawling all over the place. And if I set you down, you might wind up pissing them off even more than you already did when you tripped."

*Oh, okay, well, in that case, my pride could shove it.* "How can you even see them?" I craned my neck to search out the trail, keying in on a tiny beam of evening light that spliced through the canopy. It was just enough to illuminate the buzz of movement on the ground.

Yeah, being covered in ants wasn't on my to-do list. Not that I had lists. Lists were for normal people with normal lives. People who didn't panic move, as Lucy called it, at every sign of a possible problem because they *didn't* have anyone to save them from falling. Or, well, from dying.

"Maybe you should walk a bit faster, then? Before it's just

us and the ants alone out here," I suggested, returning my attention to his face. He shifted just right so the little trickle of light allowed me to make out his strong jawline.

"I will if you tell me what you're really doing here."

*So, you're stubborn, too? Figures.* I unhooked my arm from behind his neck and palmed his chest, contemplating my options. Push away and deal with ants? Or deal with the man whose heartbeat was so steady beneath my touch, I almost felt reassurance and safety with every beat. "Same reason as you. For the money. Clearly. Not for love."

An unexpected laugh rumbled through his chest, and the warmth of his breath fanned across my cheek. The light cutting through the branches and leaves nearly a hundred feet overhead moved, placing him fully back into the darkness again, erasing his features from view. "Try again, sweetheart."

"Do I look like a 'sweetheart' to you?"

"No, at the moment, you look like a pain in my ass. But your ass happens to be pretty much in my hands right now," he fired back, a hint of humor still clinging to his tone.

And that naughty-spanking thought popped back into my head with the same level of intensity as the imaginary swat on my rear end had.

"You two coming or what?" someone called out, interrupting the weird moment we were having.

It sounded like Stephen, but it could've been anyone, the sound of his voice muted and lackluster as it drifted back to us.

The jungle, however, was very much alive and vibrant— every little sound echoing around us. Buzzing. Humming. Chirping. And yet, I was pretty sure I could still make out the sounds of both our heartbeats. They seemed to be competing for attention. Beat for beat.

"Coming. Saved her from an army of ants," Jack hollered as he began walking, still carrying my "pain in the ass" self.

"Let me down," I demanded a minute later, squirming in his arms.

He finally relented and lowered me to the ground. When I faced forward, prepared to flee what I'd worried would be inquisition part two of the evening, Jack snatched my wrist, stopping me from bolting.

"Just tell me one thing," he said a bit more roughly this time. "The question you didn't want to answer back there . . . did someone hurt you or someone you care about? And are they dead?"

How in the world had he read that situation like that? Jumped to *that* conclusion?

I blinked in shock, thankful he couldn't see the rapid fluttering of my eyelashes. "I'm not answering that." I tugged my wrist free of his hold.

"I need to know." Zero humor. Only grit.

I faced him. "Why?"

Jack leaned in and brushed my hair away from my face, tucking it behind one ear. "I need to know if there's anyone still alive who shouldn't be."

Chills coasted over my bare arm. "What are you saying?" Because it sure as hell sounded like he was—

"Does anyone need to die, Charley?"

The intensity of his words nearly knocked me down, but I needed to keep my shit together. No more falling. "I don't trust you, Jack *Hughes*. So, you won't be getting *jack* shit from me." I spun away from him and hurried forward without giving him a chance to grab me again. Although, with his lightning-fast reflexes, I had a feeling if he really wanted to stop me, he could've, ten times over.

Instead, he growled out a curse from behind. He was

keeping up with me like my shadow protector, one I didn't need. Well, definitely didn't want.

After a few more minutes of walking alone with my chaotic thoughts, we finally rejoined the cast of the show. I wasn't sure what I was expecting, but it wasn't finding them gathered at the edge of a cliff.

"Nice of you to join us," Stephen said, turning his attention away from the other contestants and toward me. "Most couples wait to hit the suite before . . . well, anyway, we've been waiting for you all to start."

The cameramen off at his sides snickered, and the "illuminators," as I'd dubbed them in my head, steadied the beams of light toward something just off the edge of the cliff. Lovely. A rope suspension bridge that looked more like a death trap than a walkway.

"Don't tell me you think we're going to cross that piece-of-shit bridge," Oliver spoke the words that had to be on everyone's mind. "It's, uh, missing about seventy-five percent of its steps. And that's gotta be a forty-foot drop into the water down below. Just a small FYI, we're not all lightweights here."

I maneuvered around a few contestants from another team to get to the edge, and a horrible gut-sinking feeling hit me when I got a better look at said death trap. Fifty feet in length maybe. Two thick ropes ran parallel across a ravine with a few wooden planks as "steps."

*Oh, hell no.* I wasn't letting my baby sister go near that.

"Exactly how is this an icebreaker thing?" Mya asked, coming up alongside me.

"More of a trust-building exercise," Stephen shared. "Everyone on the team must make it across the river and back. You'll need to work together if you want to ensure you all complete the task."

"And if we fall?" Jack flanked my other side, taking in the view lit up by what felt like lights bright enough to land a plane in the jungle.

Stephen shrugged. "Then you take a swim. It's deep enough to pillow your fall. Slight current. It's a narrow river. An offshoot from the Amazon, though."

"And there are piranhas, snakes, caimans, and a lot of other dangerous-to-our-health things in the Amazon," Oliver shared.

I'd spent the last eleven years doing everything in my power to protect my sister, how could I place her in harm's way like this? And if this was only night one of the competition, what was in store for us next? Money wasn't worth it.

"We're not doing it." I focused on my sister to let her know my mind was made up.

"I've done plenty of ropes courses before," Lucy responded, talking to me like it was just the two of us, the world fading into the background. "We've got this."

"No. This is different." I crossed my arms, a slight chill sweeping over my skin. Part nerves. Part nighttime in the jungle. The weather was changing without the sun. And my imagination was conjuring up the potential of a jaguar creeping up on us. I chose to ignore that paranoia part of my brain for now.

"What happens if we don't, at least, try to cross?" Lucy asked Stephen.

"You can pack your bags and leave," he answered in a flat tone. "Now, make up your minds. Team one is going first."

"And who is team one?" *When did we get a number?*

"You're team one," Stephen said with a dismissive chuckle, then he went over to the cameramen and began pointing, issuing directives about the lights.

"And if there's nothing left of this piece-of-shit bridge after team one is done?" someone from another team called out.

"Then your teams luck out, and you don't have to complete the challenge," Stephen replied. "It was just the luck of the draw that team one was chosen first."

*Luck of the draw my ass.* I planted my hands on my hips and peered around at the others. This was my chance to leave. To bail and get a safe ride out of there and away from this entire mess. We had to take it.

"No," Lucy said, reading my mind. "I'm doing this. I'm done running, Charley. I need to do this, for me." My sister's trembling voice and strong words about did me in. "If the women cross first, since we weigh less, that should put less stress on the bridge, right?" she went on, letting me know the conversation I'd never actually started was over.

I caught sight of Jack peering at my sister as if he'd picked up on the double meaning of her "done running" comment. Yeah, she was talking about way more than just running from the jungle. *Damnit.*

"But even if we all make it across, we still have to make it back, so it won't matter about our weight," Mason pointed out. "I'd rather test out the boards and see which are the most reliable. Find the best path first before you all cross."

"Chivalry hasn't died, huh?" Lucy asked him, and with the lights on us, I caught an innocent smile flicker across Mason's lips that came and went fast.

Shit, if we wound up staying through this thing, my sister was going to actually fall for someone. As long as it wasn't for someone twice her age, like Carter, I supposed worse things could happen.

"You know, this look works for you," Gwen interrupted

my thoughts, and I followed her eyes to the man standing next to her in his black briefs and rubber boots.

Carter stepped into the shadows, his tone almost fatherly, as he snapped back, "We need to focus on getting across the bridge right now."

"Yes, sir," Gwen replied with a smile.

Why'd it feel like she just poked a grizzly? Well, in our case here, a jaguar. Much more fitting for the man, too. Sleek. Terrifying. Deadly, even. And he'd so much as admitted to killing someone during his inquisition. *We have that in common, huh?*

"We should go across barefoot," Carter continued, ignoring Gwen's "sir," as he stepped back into the light and began removing his boots. Without waiting for anyone to agree, he went over to the two ropes on one side anchored to nearby thick trees, and he gave the top rope a tug. The bridge did a little wave, swaying to the side, and one board in the middle immediately detached without much effort and fell to the river below.

"That's a bad sign," Lucy said as he tested the bottom rope, then moved on to the other side for a check.

"I think the ropes are durable. We need to avoid the actual steps," Carter said, turning back to face our team.

"It's narrow enough that if we straddle the bridge and place one foot on each rope, then hold the top one we can, in a sense, tightrope our way across without using the shitty boards," Oliver suggested.

"That's what I'm thinking." Carter's gaze went to Gwen as he said, "Your dress is fine." He looked at me and Lucy next. "But you two need to lose a few inches. The material will get in your way when you spread your legs."

"That sounded so fucking wrong." Oliver chuckled, but Carter seemed to ignore him and brush off his comment.

"I've got you two covered," Mason said, producing a pocketknife. He shrugged as he peeled open the blade. "Snuck it in. Thought it might come in handy during the game."

"Marines," Oliver said under his breath.

"Can you help me cut my dress?" my sister asked him, and Mason gave her a hesitant nod, then knelt before her.

Her dress was like mine, and I winced at how much he cut away and where he put his hands on her to do it.

*Shit.* I didn't have any panties on; so, when Mason started my way, I shot my palm up to stop him. "I can do that myself, thanks."

He gave me the knife, and I wound up making a mess of the bottom of my dress but didn't remove anything, just poked a bunch of ragged holes in the fabric.

"Can I please help you?" Jack asked, his tone surprisingly soft.

I checked the location of the rest of our team, relieved to find them talking near the entrance of the bridge, testing the strength of the ropes again.

"No panties," I reminded him. "Do your best not to accidentally touch me *there*."

He dropped to one knee before me, knife now in hand, then looked up. "Did I try and touch you *there* last time?" he murmured.

I planted my hands on his bare shoulders when he began to rip the fabric. I didn't need to fall and accidentally get stabbed. "No, you didn't," I relented.

"So, why would I do it here?" When I kept quiet, he added, "You should just trust me." He paused for a second before tossing out, "Right, forgot. Trust is off the table."

"Your sarcasm is noted. And not appreciated," I grumbled as he finished the job of shortening my dress with efficient movements. When he was back on his feet, he closed the knife, and I couldn't help ask, "Learn to do that in the Army?"

"Sarcasm. Noted," he echoed back, then dipped his head, bringing his mouth to my ear. "And yes, I was in the Army, *sweetheart*."

"Is the Southern accent even real?" The Texas drawl was unmistakable, but could have been part of his act and I'd never know. I'd watched a lot of *Walker, Texas Ranger,* Dad's favorite show when I was little. For whatever reason, it was always the seemingly insignificant things I remembered about him more than anything else.

With Jack's mouth still lingering near my ear, he responded in a deep voice, "Everything about me is real." Then he pulled away and turned his back, choosing to be done with me for now. His turn to walk away.

"Ready?" Lucy waved me over, and I did my best to pull myself together and join everyone by the bridge.

The other two teams came back over, and I had to assume they'd all already discussed their own strategies to cross the bridge. Of course, maybe it'd be their luck they never had to try.

I hung back. Listening. Observing. A few nods of agreement. And then Mason opted to go first with Lucy behind him.

My heart leapt into my throat the second my sister planted her feet onto the ropes on each side of her. Carter was behind her, helping her hook her arms over the tops of the ropes to ensure she didn't fall before she even began. Mason was an arm's reach away from her, and he tossed a look over his shoulder as if ensuring she was all set and safe.

Carter and Mason maintained a slow and steady pace,

neither of them rushing her and keeping themselves like a protective cocoon, which made me feel a little better.

I released a sigh of relief once the three of them successfully made it across the wobbly-ass bridge. I removed my boots, surprised to see Carter coming back across on his own. He stealthily moved without any hint of fear. He and Jack boxed Gwen in next, becoming her own personal shields.

I gasped when one of Gwen's feet slipped, but Carter was just behind her, and he freed his hand from one rope to reach for her hip. With his hand securely around her, she was able to find her footing again.

Stephen came up to the edge, standing near me. He was nodding as if impressed by our strategy, and I had to assume the others would abandon whatever plans they'd made and do the same now that they'd had it modeled for them. I had to admit, this really was a team-building exercise. And the fact the guys were willing to go back and forth to keep us safe, well . . .

I just wasn't used to that kind of self-sacrificing behavior. And it was hard for me to believe this was all an act from both Jack and Carter. My instincts were usually spot on about people. But that didn't answer my suspicions about why in the world he had a gun and fake passport back in Cape Town. Or why he was here now.

I supposed there was only one way to find out, and that was to ask him. But I wasn't sure if I was ready for that conversation. One thing at a time. Like crossing the bridge.

I was the last in line to go, and Jack and Oliver were going to be my "escorts."

"You ready?" Jack extended his hand, and it felt like a peace offering. I hesitantly accepted it and joined him and Oliver at the bridge.

Oliver positioned himself on the ropes, facing me instead of the direction we were supposed to go.

I set one foot on the left rope as Jack held my waist from behind, keeping me steady. With my second foot in place, he helped me loop my arms over the top ropes. My legs trembled at my unsteadiness, and I adjusted my feet, so the ropes were at the center of my soles. I let go of a sigh as my balance improved slightly.

"You've got this," Jack said once Oliver began moving, remaining close in front of me.

"Sure, sure," I mumbled under my breath, trying not to look down. I knew I'd lose my balance and get dizzy if I did.

We were halfway across when the rain began seemingly out of nowhere. Heavy enough to cut through the canopy.

"Welcome to the rainforest," Jack said calmly. "Slow and steady. You're almost there."

And that's when I did the dumbest thing ever. I looked down. Followed the path of the rain pelting over my body to my left foot no longer on the rope. And my arms slipped, too.

"Fuck," Jack hissed from behind.

I felt his hand go to my side to try and grab me, but I lost my hold of the top ropes and dropped like dead weight, far too fast for even the best of the best to catch me.

I managed to grab hold of the bottom rope and loop my arm around it, clinging to it for dear life, but there wasn't a chance in hell I'd last longer than thirty seconds there.

Jack shifted off the ropes and laid himself flat across the three boards there, hooking his arms around mine. "I can pull you up. Grab hold of me."

I stared up at his wet face, water rivulets falling onto me. From the corner of my eye, I spied Oliver using only the ropes to maneuver around Jack.

"I can't. I'll slip, and we'll both go down," I whispered. "Just let me go so you don't fall, too."

Jack adamantly shook his head.

My body was shaking, and Lucy was crying out something to me. But I was in a weird foggy state of disbelief as I clung to the rope and Jack clung to me.

One board beneath him cracked and joined the rain falling into the river. If he didn't let go of me, he'd be next. There was no sense in the two of us plummeting into the river.

"I'm letting go," I told him.

"Don't you dare," he hissed, his eyes widening despite the rain battering his face and lashes. "We'll pull you up. Oliver's got my legs pinned. I'm good. I'm going to hoist you up."

"Then all three of us fall," I cried, the rain masking the quiver in my lip.

Jack's jaw strained as he worked against gravity, trying to hoist me up without putting too much pressure on the shitty boards barely holding his weight.

"You can't pull me up how you're positioned, and I can't hang on much longer." I looked over my shoulder, catching sight of the water visible because of the show lights. Lights that were now trained directly on us.

"I've got you. Trust me," Jack said, his tone somehow as steady as his heartbeat had been earlier.

But my heart? Right now, it was going to thump straight from my chest.

"I can't . . . hold. I'm sorry."

"Oliver," Jack gritted out. "Let go of me," he warned.

"Why?" Oliver snapped out.

Jack looked into my eyes and said, "Because she's about to fall, and I'm going in after her."

# CHAPTER TEN

## JACK

THE SECOND CHARLEY LET GO, I DOVE IN HEADFIRST. THE water didn't exactly cushion the fall. No, it still hurt like a motherfucker upon impact, but it was deep enough to prevent dying, so there was that.

I swam to the top and broke the surface and quickly scanned every direction, searching for Charley. There was a slight current, but thankfully, these weren't river rapids.

The second I saw her head pop up above the water, a swell of relief hit me. The water was too murky to see through, and the rain made it even worse. Had she not resurfaced, I'd have been forced to feel my way around in the dark. And I didn't even want to think about what else could be lurking down there.

"You good?" I swam over to her.

She turned toward my voice as I caught up with her and hooked my arm around her waist. I didn't want her out of my reach in case something tried to bite us.

The rain was still pounding down over us, intensifying the current and we bobbed in the water for a moment as I used my free arm to keep us from going downriver or back under again. She shifted so her body was practically against me, and I may have tugged her a little tighter to me, just for safety's sake.

"Feel like I've been spanked all over," she said with a laugh, lifting her chin to catch fresh rain on her lips as the crew above shined the spotlight down over us.

And fuck if it didn't make me smile, remembering she'd told me her love for standing in the rain back in Cape Town.

"Are you okay?" I heard Oliver yell.

"We're fine," I called back, finding Charley's eyes again. Thankfully there was enough light to see her features, including the ghost of the smile still there. "Let's get you out of here before we have company."

"Right." When the hem of her dress floated to the surface around her, she quickly pushed it down with her free hand.

Yeah, and that was a good reminder that this woman had no panties on. Yep, we needed to get out of there. Stat.

"Stephen said we had to make it across the river and back," she said.

Did she really give a damn about points? Or was it because her *sister* did? And did I even care?

Of course I did. I'd have done whatever she wanted, or *needed,* to do. And there was also the fact I had to stay in the competition not only to find the bastard taking women but prevent Charley or anyone else from being his next victim.

The fact that motherfucker *(yeah, I know, Mom, could be plural . . . those motherfuckers),* could be watching us now, in this position, boiled my blood.

I focused back on the immediate task at hand. Getting her to safety.

We were only about ten feet away from the other side of

the river now, and I wasn't comfortable with staying in the water any longer than necessary. It wasn't just a matter of getting out, there was also a rock wall we'd need to scale if we wanted to get to the bridge to cross back over. Although, the wall looked safe enough with numerous ledges on it.

"Let's get you out of the water and figure out next steps," I told her, urging her to get a move on.

I breathed a sigh of relief when we reached the edge unscathed, but then her startled scream had me hoisting her up out of the water as fast as possible. I had no clue what made her yelp, and I had no intention of taking the time to find out.

I quickly joined her. "We need more light," I hollered up to the crew on the other side of the river. "Think something bit her."

"A gator-caiman thing . . . or piranha . . . or a tree branch, I don't know . . ." She set her back to the rock wall, breathing hard and fast.

There was a slight overhang from the rock wall that shielded us from the rain. So, she stretched out her legs, and I knelt before her, thankful for the light so I could get a decent look. There were two fresh cuts on her right calf muscle. It looked like nails had dragged across her skin.

"You need antibiotics when we get back." Bacteria in the water plus an open wound, bad combination.

"So, what's the plan?" Her tone remained surprisingly calm considering we were on the side of a river in the rain and an unknown *something* had left two marks on her leg. This woman was just . . . well, something else.

"One second." I stood and looked around, spotting a lone branch a few feet away. I maneuvered along the narrow ledge and snatched a handful of leaves from the branch, then used them to pat at her open wound and clean the blood the best I could. I didn't need her slipping on her own blood while mounting the rock wall.

"How are your climbing skills?" Using her hand as a visor to shield her eyes from the bright lights still on us, she studied the cliff back to the bridge. But before I could answer her, my focus fell to her legs.

The dress was nearly at her waist, and . . .

"Uh, my skills are good." I forced my attention up before I caught sight of more than she'd want me to. But that wasn't a great idea either. Her breasts were fighting to break free from the tight top of her wet dress. And it took me a lot longer than it should have to look away. But I wound up staring at her legs, and damnit.

"Oh my God." She cursed and clamped her knees together at the realization she was nearly exposing herself, then her other hand made a beeline for the top of her dress to fix the material there.

"I didn't see anything." Doing my best to help her forget I *almost* caught a glimpse of her, I turned to clock our surroundings again.

Stephen was up top looking down at us, a cameraman tight to his side training his equipment and light our way, the rest of the contestants packed around them.

"Are we really required to try and finish this challenge when she's been hurt?" I shouted up at him.

"It's not that bad," Charley protested, much to my frustration.

"It's a survival dating game show," Stephen hollered back, his words echoing off the rock walls surrounding each side of the waterway. "The rest of your team has already crossed back to us. If you don't want to be cut, then find a way back over."

"Since when was that a rule?" I hissed, but it was doubtful he heard me.

Charley secured a hand at the nape of my neck, urging me to look at her, and I gave her my attention. "I'm not leaving without Lucy, so let's climb this wall and get back across. Let's finish this, okay?"

The determined grit in her tone had me on edge. And I was starting to worry she had more secrets than I did.

"Yeah, okay." At my agreement, she let go of my neck, and I stood and offered her my hand. "It'll be wet when we fuc—" I dropped my curse as I hauled her off the ground. "Wet" and "fucking" did go together, but in a much different way than our current "fucking climb" situation I was about to go with. My dumbass mind went straight to the gutter, imagining this woman wet and ready for me instead. *What the hell is wrong with me?* "You, uh, should go first."

"So, you can catch me when I fall?"

"How about you just not fall for a fourth time tonight?" I caught myself smiling, then dismissed it to focus. "Let's just get this over with." I sidestepped her and searched out a better route up. The overhang would be too hard to climb unless she was a skilled boulderer, so we'd have to go about ten feet over.

"The rain's slowing as quickly as it started," she said, reading my thoughts.

"Still wet." I jerked a thumb toward the wall, motioning for her to go first. There were enough ledges and resting places that would make it easy for me to scale, even in the rain. And with her being nearly half my size, she'd be fine, too.

With her back to me, she reached out for the wall, searching for a hold. The first ten feet appeared to be the most challenging, but it'd be relatively safe from that point on. No potential of free-falling to our deaths.

The woman of my dreams, who was very much real and standing in front of me, wet and nearly naked—*fuck me*—mounted her foot to the wall, then eased herself up, going flat with the surface. She tested a vine dangling down at her side for support, tugged it two more times for good measure, then used it to help propel her up another step. *Nicely done.*

But at her next step, she slipped and slid down right into my arms.

Her dress hiked up, and her naked ass pressed against me.

I went still. My linen pants didn't do much to hide my body's natural reaction to having her there. And fuck me, that also meant her bare pussy was . . . so close.

For a split second, my dirty thoughts played out a scene where she asked me to finger fuck her right there against the wall. Not that I'd make love to this woman with an audience, and sure as hell not on camera. But in my head? Yeah. In my head it was safe to imagine her begging me to touch her. To have her moan my name.

"Jack?" she murmured. "Your body is blocking my ass from the cameras, right?" Her hands left the rock wall and skated down her silhouette as she tugged her dress back in place. Well, what was left of the dress.

"Yeah, I'm not moving, don't worry."

"Okay, good. Otherwise, I'll need to destroy the footage somehow." She tossed a look over her shoulder only I could see since we were still under the spotlight. A perfect TV moment. "Know any hackers just in case?"

I laughed. *Because yes, I do, in fact. One is on our team. But she's on the good side. No dark web shit.* "Don't worry. This show won't ever see the light of day."

*Why in God's name did I just spill that top-secret bit of*

*news with a woman who didn't even trust me, and who had her own mysteries I still needed to unravel? Like for one, why'd you leave me that morning?*

Instead of pressing me for more information, she returned her attention back to the task at hand. She scaled the most challenging ten feet without falling, and the rest was quick and easy from that point on.

Once we were both topside, we made our way to the bridge. It was missing three more boards than before. Mya was at the other side of the bridge, looking at us. "You two okay?"

"We'll be fine. Her leg needs attention, though." I faced Charley. "You ready?"

"The rain's stopped, so I think we can do this," she said with the confidence I needed to hear.

Carter made his way across this time to help. "You gave Mya a heart attack," was his greeting, and I'd swear there was a touch of worry in his tone he was working to mask. "Glad you're okay."

*So, you do have feelings. Who'd have guessed, you're human after all.*

"Uh, thanks." Charley shot him an awkward little smile, the lights from the other side panning across our faces.

Done with this show's shit, and ready to be on solid ground, it took two minutes to get across that time, and I was damn relieved it was over. Lucy ran over to us and pulled her sister into her arms for a hug.

"I'm not hanging back to watch the other teams," I told Stephen during their embrace. "I want her to get this wound looked at. With her open cut and bacteria in the water, she needs antibiotics."

Stephen crouched before Charley to check her leg, making me uneasy given the short length of her dress and lack of panties. "Your team really learned to trust each other out there, even in the thick of danger," he said while righting himself. "And you going in after her, knowing you'd lose points for falling, says a lot." He gave me a tight nod of approval that I didn't give a shit about. "You two will be coupled up."

Charley spun toward me at his announcement, and I couldn't get a read on her look. Was she happy or pissed about that? Whatever she was, she was masking it from me.

"But since she fell," Stephen continued, "and you both lost an article of clothing earlier, you don't have enough points to win the treehouse sleepover."

"And who does have the most points?" Lucy asked as I grabbed my boots, sliding them on in preparation for the journey back to the lodge.

"You and Mason. You'll be staying in the treehouse." Stephen peered at the rest of my teammates. "The judges have matched Carter and Gwen. And Oliver and Mya. Those not in the treehouse will be sleeping in building one. Your beds, where you'll sleep as couples, are being prepped now." He looked back at me. "We'll have a medic waiting for you when you return. If you think you all can find your way back in the dark, you can go ahead. If not, stay until the other teams are done."

"I'll take my chances in the dark." I was anxious to get the hell out of the jungle.

"Am I really sleeping in a treehouse with Mason?" I overheard Lucy whisper to her sister once we were all "booted up" and on the move.

I turned my attention to Carter when he came up alongside me, and Lucy and Charley's conversation became too muddled for me to overhear.

"You good?" Carter asked me.

"Not really." I looked back at Mya and the others trailing behind us.

"Is she going to blow our cover?" he asked me, keeping his voice down.

I focused back on the "she" he was referring to since Carter was aware I knew Charley. "Something tells me she has more to hide than we do." My chest tightened at that fact. "So no, I think we're safe." *For now.*

# CHAPTER ELEVEN

## JACK

CHARLEY'S LECTURE TO MASON ON THE *DOS* AND *DON'TS* during his treehouse sleepover lasted nearly five minutes. It was impressive. She could go head-to-head with Wyatt in the parenting department without missing a beat.

And then it dawned on me, Charley probably had to step in as a mother-figure for Lucy at some point since they'd lost both their parents.

". . . And if you so much as touch my sister—"

"Unless I want him to, you mean?" Lucy finished her sister's threat, then gave Charley a pointed look. A plea to back down?

Mason lifted his hands in the air and peeked at Lucy's suitcase on the ground by her booted feet. He snatched it from Lucy's reaching hand before appeasing Charley with a contrite, "Consider me her chauffeur and protector only, ma'am."

"She's overprotective. Sorry." Lucy elbowed Charley in the side, which Charley ignored, continuing her death stare at Mason like he was enemy number one.

*Better him than me for now.* "We need to get your leg looked at," I reminded her, anxious to get her inside our new quarters and have the wound treated before we had more problems.

But then a creeping sensation shot up my spine, and it wasn't from my lack of shirt. Someone was watching us. Not on camera, either.

I had no clue when I'd let Charley in on the fact we were potentially being watched by a psychopath as they picked their next victim—I needed to run it by my team first—but I could keep her from being a sitting duck out there in the open.

I scanned our surroundings, wishing that someone watching us from the jungle was Gray, but he wouldn't be in until tomorrow. And with any luck, Carter's quick call to rally reinforcements would mean Gray had an entire team at his disposal upon his arrival.

"Watch your back out there," I blurted to Mason, forgetting myself for a second. But damn that bad gut feeling.

"Because of snakes? Jaguars?" A nervous little smile crossed Lucy's lips.

I frowned. "Yeah, of course."

Charley gave Mason one last if-looks-could-kill glance, then she hugged her sister and waved her hand at Mason, dismissing him.

Once Mason and Lucy were out of sight, Charley turned her attention on me. I had a feeling I was next on her radar for a list of *dos* and *don'ts.* Probably about sharing not only a room with her, but a bed.

At least the uncomfortable feeling of being watched had gone away, but my relief would be short-lived given we were expected to sleep together with cameras on us.

"She has bad taste in men," Charley said in a tight, semi-defensive voice, like she felt the need to explain her lecture. "She basically collects red flags like souvenirs."

I did my best not to smile at what was probably more of a sad reality than a joke. But then that cute little dimple I had loved seeing in Cape Town popped into view, and my heart thwacked against my chest. The grin I tried so hard to suppress broke through. Yup, I was a goner.

"Not funny, I know." She brushed her fingers across her lips as if guilty for the almost-smile she'd given me. All it did was make me want to replace her fingertips with my mouth. "Anyway, falling for assholes is like an art form for her, so I have to watch out for her."

"I get it. I'd do anything for the people I care about, too." I cleared my throat and motioned for her to head inside. "You're soaked, and you were hurt. We should get you undressed and washed up."

"Undressed, hmm?"

"You know what I mean," I teasingly grumbled, then waited for her to walk ahead of me. I turned to check the jungle area once more, hoping it was just an animal that'd been lurking on us.

I shook my head, hating our situation, but never more thankful that Gwen and Mya had assembled our team at the last minute. Otherwise, Charley and her sister would be there alone, without protection or insider information of what to look out for.

Once inside, I hung back by the doorway to look around the place. "So much for pretending we're on a tropical vacation."

Our room was one large space with three full-sized beds as the only furniture. The beds were all lined up in a row along one wall, and there wasn't much walking room between or around them. If all we'd be doing was getting rack time in there, I supposed it wasn't that bad. I'd seen worse. Our bags were already waiting for us on our designated beds, and Mya and Oliver wasted no time arguing about the sleeping arrangements.

"Pillows between us or you sleep on the floor," Mya snapped. She'd been a great actress earlier, but Oliver tended to get under her skin, and she was losing the plot now. Forgetting she wasn't supposed to know Oliver enough to already dislike him.

"Damn. I've heard of insta-love, but your insta-hate game is pretty strong," I tossed out, trying to remind them they were on camera.

"He has one of those faces you just want to punch, I guess," Mya said, then chucked a pillow at him.

Before it hit him, Oliver snatched it with one hand and cocked his head as if challenging, *That the best you got, buttercup?*

"Where's Carter and Gwen?" I asked as Charley went to our bed and quietly busied herself with unzipping her gray suitcase. "And I thought the medic would be waiting for us."

"Medic's still a no-show. And Carter and Gwen are showering," Oliver said while placing the pillow in the middle of the bed creating a do-not-cross zone. "Not together," he quickly added.

Before I had a chance to inquire about the bathroom and shower situation, the medic finally appeared. "Who needs help?" His Jersey-esq accent pinned him as another American.

"Something bit or scratched her in the water when we took an unexpected plunge. Not sure what," I explained to the medic, gesturing to Charley.

She grabbed a shirt from her bag and took a seat, then draped it over her lap, probably to prevent the medic from getting an eyeful beneath her torn dress.

*Good girl.*

"You should both take a dose of oral antibiotics since you were in that river," he said once he finished cleaning her wound. He handed us each a water bottle and a pill to take. "And I'd recommend a shower."

I nearly choked at his shower comment as I chased the pill down and drained the rest of the bottle.

"She good?" I turned at the sound of Carter's voice to find him entering the bedroom from what I assumed was our bathroom. Thankfully, he was fully clothed in black runner shorts and a white tee. Probably what I'd wear after my shower, too.

Although, Mya and Gwen had done my shopping before we'd come to the lodge, so I had no clue what was in my bag.

"I'm fine, thank you." Charley nodded at Carter, then went to her suitcase and grabbed her pajamas. A tank top and little shorts that were going to be the death of me while sleeping next to her.

"How's the shower?" Mya asked Carter after the medic left us alone.

Not that we were truly alone with a camera in the room spying on us, a major inconvenience if we were to try and talk "shop." Of course, Charley was still an outsider, so we couldn't exactly speak freely right now regardless.

Carter frowned. "The shower was fine. Why wouldn't it be?"

*And why the tense tone? Shit. Gwen.*

She came into the room a moment later wearing a tee that went to her thighs. The black shirt said, *I Paused My Game For This,* in neon green letters with a little controller beneath it. I was certain Gwen didn't play video games, and it was probably an ex's shirt she repurposed for nightwear.

"Just my luck I end up sleeping next to Mr. Grump, huh?" Gwen commented, smirking. She set her eyes on Charley, trying to sell the whole "we don't know each other" thing. "I heard you ask about the shower." She peered at Mya next. "If you like them burn-your-flesh hot like I do, then you'll hate it."

"Is there any other way to take a shower?" Charley focused on me, her eyes narrowing a touch, likely remembering sharing that little tidbit in Cape Town. Perhaps also remembering how I'd told her I usually took cold showers.

*"I heard they help you live longer. Good for your heart,"* I'd said, explaining my rationalization for freezing in the water. *"But if I had a reason to take a long one, I'd be willing to turn up the heat."*

*"I bet you would,"* she'd answered, those long fingers of hers flying down the column of her slender neck as she'd spoken.

Charley tipped her head toward the open bathroom door. "We should probably get this over with." I wasn't sure if her nose was wrinkling at the prospect of a cold shower, or because she was worried I'd opt for a warm shower tonight to prolong our time together in the bathroom.

"There's a privacy wall in there for you to change. A door on the toilet. Curtains for each of the showers." Gwen gave me a lopsided smile, like the kind she'd told me to use myself for dates. "Don't worry. She won't see your junk."

"Thank you for that." I rolled my eyes. Sometimes I felt three decades older than her, not just sixteen years.

Charley didn't wait for me and rushed into the bathroom

while I searched my suitcase for something to wear. I settled on gray loose-fit running shorts and a black tee. I normally only slept in boxers, but . . .

Once in the bathroom, I dropped my change of clothes on the counter, then scanned the room, searching for any surveillance equipment. Nothing I could see, so I peeled my focus to the two showers that were both running. The curtain was drawn closed on the one Charley was showering in, but the partition between the two stalls was lower than the curtain rod. And with my height, if I wasn't careful, I might catch sight of more than she wanted me to see.

"I went ahead and turned the second one on for you so it could warm up a little. I figured after our swim in the river, you might not want an ice cold one," she let me know.

I removed what I was still wearing: my rubber boots, wet linen pants, boxers . . . and *frown*. Because I was trading that look in for a smile. Was that a peace offering from her? When were we at war, though? *And for that matter, why'd you leave me that morning?* I kept all that shit to myself and hopped into the shower that was lukewarm at best and tugged the curtain across. "Thank you."

She didn't waste time, approaching the dark green divider between us, and asked, "We're alone, right?"

"Alone. No cameras in here." I swiped the beads of water from my face and stepped away from the direct spray.

"And how much of me can you see right now?"

*Too much.* I swallowed. Grew tense. *And* hard. "I can see your face. Shoulders, too."

"Just my shoulders? Nothing more, right?" She closed her eyes and shifted back, ducking beneath the spray, then she tangled her fingers through her wet locks, shoving her sweeping bangs away from her forehead.

I couldn't help but smile at the sight. "Well, you have a nice body, and . . ." *Nice body? Come on, man.* "Great, in fact." Nope, not what I should've said, either.

Charley opened her gorgeous blue-green eyes—they appeared a touch bluer tonight with her long, wet lashes framing her irises.

"I didn't mean—"

"I'm sorry I was a bitch earlier," she said, saving me from more than likely butchering my next comment again. "You have to understand it was weird you showing up here. I'm not the most trusting person, and I don't get why you're here," she rushed out in a low voice.

"I didn't follow you here. I'm not some psychopath that tracked you down," I told her, keeping my tone only above a whisper. "I'm not here for you." *Fuck, did I already say too much?*

"Who are you here for, then?" Her brows shot up.

*Shit, shit, shit . . . way to go, Jack. Of course she wouldn't skip over that detail. And fuuuck, she was cute when anxious.* Was it completely inappropriate of me to want to will away the metal partition between us right now? Leaving nothing but our wet, naked bodies on display . . . Damnit, I needed to focus before this shower really did need to be a cold one. "I know I'm still pretty much a stranger. So, asking you to trust me is—"

"Not going to happen. Not yet, at least. I still have questions. And I get the feeling you don't have answers." Back beneath the water spray, she began soaping up her hair. "So, let's see how this plays out."

"The game or us?"

"Both, I guess," she answered hesitantly.

"Okay, but one thing." I grabbed the bar of soap and began lathering up. "My name really is Jack London. My mom was a library director. Books were her thing. She named me Jack on purpose, and trust me when I say I got shit for it in school when we had to read, *The Call of the Wild*." I'd laid the truth out for her, and hoped I could trust her, given I was there with an alias.

At my admission, she quietly tipped her chin toward the spray of the water. Her deep inhalation lifted her chest, bringing her nipples dangerously close to my line of sight.

I forced myself to look away. If the day ever came I got to see this woman naked, it'd be because she wanted me to. I was old school, what could I say? Mom taught me right. But that didn't mean this moment was easy for me. No, it was hard. Really, really fucking hard in fact. So hard, I set down the soap and turned the water on colder.

I palmed the wall and bowed my head, trying to wrangle in the desire burning through me. Stroking my cock in the shower stall next to the woman of my dreams, an unlocked door away from my teammates, wouldn't be a good look for me. An anaconda wouldn't take me out on the trip. No, it'd be blue balls that'd kill me.

"I want to believe you," she finally said, and I kept my hands to the wall while chancing a look at her.

When our eyes met, my stomach muscles immediately banded tight. We had a connection. Something I couldn't explain. Or deny. But I'd been burned so many times in my life, I wasn't so sure I could take it. Especially after she'd already ditched me in Cape Town.

Something brought us together again, though. And I wanted to cling to that "something" and not ask questions.

She tore her focus away from me and turned off the water, breaking the spell. "Will you give me a second to towel off and get dressed before you get out?"

"Of course," I returned, hating the disappointment in my tone.

When she was gone, I hung my head again. I had to get a grip. I was still there on a mission, and I couldn't lose sight of that. No matter what.

After another minute, maybe two, I turned off the water, and toweled dry.

Mya and Oliver came in just as I was pulling my shirt over my head. She closed the door, looked around the room, doing a quick camera check, then asked, "You okay? That's her, right?"

"What do you mean, 'her'?" Oliver faced Mya, but she kept her focus sharp on me.

"Yeah, that's her. From Cape Town," I admitted reluctantly. "This is a weird coincidence."

"She and her sister were invited to the event. An event you're undercover for," Mya whispered. "This can't be a coincidence, but I don't understand it."

"Neither do I. But she's not ready to open up and trust me. The name I gave her there is different from the one I'm using here," I quickly shared.

Oliver lifted his hand in the air. "Is someone going to catch me up?"

I nodded at Mya, giving her permission to enlighten him, because I didn't have it in me to share with him my sob story.

"A chance meeting at a hotel bar in Cape Town on Falcon's op there last month led to the two of them sharing a night together, only for her to slip out in the morning without a goodbye." Mya's summary of events was better than I could've done, but it still hurt to hear.

"And now she's here," Oliver said. "So, it wasn't really a chance encounter in South Africa. She was there for a reason.

You were her target that night, Jack. Clearly, you're still her mark."

I went tense at his suggestion. At him implying Charley was after me. "No," I spit out my retort, arms locking at my sides.

"I hate to say it, but in this case, guilty until proven innocent." Mya gave my forearm a squeeze, then encouraged me farther away from the door. "Sydney couldn't find out anything about her and her sister, remember? Maybe that's because their names are aliases, and Lucy used filters on TikTok to hide her identity."

"Charley had no idea I'd be here. They were invited before our *aliases* made it to the contestant list at the last minute," I reminded her, placing a big hole in her theory.

"Yeah, I guess. But don't you think something is still off about all of this?" she asked, and Oliver nodded as if—shocker—they actually agreed on something.

"Obviously," I grunted in frustration. "But fine, I'll keep my mouth shut about why we're here for now." Charley would need to learn to trust me first, and I had a feeling we were on the right path to that, but one wrong move, and I'd lose that trust in a heartbeat. "I better go out there before I have to lie and say we're having a threesome." I started for the door, swiped my dirty laundry from the counter, and then left them alone.

Back in the bedroom, the light was already off, and I assumed Carter and Gwen were in their bed. Charley must've chosen a side of our bed since I didn't see any movement in the room. At least no one had come knocking wondering why we were all in the bathroom together.

The fact I was about to sleep—well, share a bed—with the woman who'd been running a marathon in my head since last month was just so damn wild. And yet, as Mya and

Oliver had frustratingly pointed out, somehow, I had a feeling our encounter in Cape Town wasn't an accident. And that also meant us being stuck together in the jungle couldn't be either. I'd thought it was fate, that I was there so I could protect her, but Mya's doubt was infiltrating my head and throwing me off.

I tossed my clothes by the bed and peeled back the covers. The second I was next to her, my weight made the shitty mattress dip down, and the headboard-less bed groaned.

"How's your leg feeling?" I whispered. With my eyes beginning to adjust to the darkness, I could not only feel her shifting to face me, I could make out her silhouette as she moved.

"It's fine."

Even with the lights out, I was pretty sure our faces were only inches apart. Our lips damn close. Maybe our bed was even smaller than Mya and Oliver's, because I doubted we could place a pillow between us.

"You smell good," she shocked me by saying.

"I smell like you." Damn that comment. "Sorry, that sounds weird. But, you know, we used the same type of earthy-smelling soap."

"Mmhm. But it smells better on you."

"Oh, does it now?" Was she giving me an inch here? Checking to see if I'd try for a mile? Fuck if this woman didn't already have me so wrapped, I'd give her an entire zip code.

And that also concerned me. What if I was too invested in Charley to see the truth? To see Charley as the *threat*, not the threatened one?

"I wish I . . ." She let her thought linger, and I hung on to it tighter than that damn rope bridge.

My hand shot beneath my pillow, and I plumped the sad piece of cotton up as much as I could, waiting for her to continue. Hoping she would, at least. When she didn't, I shared, "I wish you never left that morning without saying goodbye." I kept my voice low enough that the cameras wouldn't pick up my words. *I wish you'd tell me the truth so I could stamp out any lingering doubts. Kick Mya's warning to the curb.*

"I had to go," she said after one of the longest minutes of my life.

The woman was starting to give me anxiety with all her pauses.

*What if you're just a great actress? What if that little scar on your chin wasn't from a bike race? What if your parents are really alive, and you knew about mine, and you used that information to try and draw me in? Relate to me to get me to open up. Was it a trap? Did you drug me, so I'd pass out that night? What were you after? Who are you really?*

I hated the seed of doubt Mya had planted. Hated myself even more for not acting like a man with twenty years of operational experience dealing with some of the worst terrorists all over the world. In my line of work, the only people I could trust were on my team. And I didn't mean my jungle-love-show team, which made Charley one huge question mark.

"Why'd you *have* to go?" Despite the montage of warnings and reminders pushing through my head, I had to ask. *Talk about collecting red flags like souvenirs.*

No response.

"Well, when you feel like you can trust me, will you tell me?" I eased the question out in a steady tone.

Another painful pause. Slightly shorter than before. "Even

if I can ever trust you, there are some things just better left unsaid. Safer for you not to know."

*Safer?* That had my pulse picking up. More alarms sounding.

"Don't ask," she murmured before I could do exactly that. "Goodnight . . . Jack."

# CHAPTER TWELVE

## JACK

It took me a second to figure out if I was in some weird dream when I woke up, or if the last twelve hours had been real. Was the woman who'd been in my head since last month really in bed next to me?

I usually slept on my stomach, but I'd woken on my side this morning, and Charley was facing me while asleep. Her hands were tucked beneath her face, but did I play capture the flag with her leg in my dreams? Why, yes. Yes, I did. And that leg was wedged firmly between mine, the weight of my top leg not disturbing her in the slightest.

Not wanting to relinquish that small personal victory, I reluctantly tried to ease her leg free without waking her. Our covers were bunched at the bottom of the bed, making the task a bit easier. The A/C hadn't done wonders to keep us cool while we'd slept, and one of us, or maybe both of us, must've gotten rid of the blanket during our sleep.

Once I'd managed to successfully move her leg, she decided to kill me by scooching her body closer to mine, as if she hated the space there as much as I did. But having her pelvis flat against me, and her hand now sliding to my arm, was going to seriously fuck with my already existing morning wood. Not to mention her tank top was twisted, showing a hell of a lot of side boob—and the woman had great breasts, so yeah, my cock was on high alert.

I dragged my eyes back to her face. To the beautiful woman before me. *You're real. Last month was . . . real. Not some fever dream concocted by my lonely, attention-starved brain.*

Her hair was a sexy mess. She'd let it air dry in her sleep, and her long bangs covered one eye. Her lips parted a touch, and I wanted to lean in and capture the soft moan that escaped.

She tortured me by smashing those perfect tits to my chest; she was playing with fire. Arching into me. Rotating her hips in small circles as if chasing an orgasm I'd happily give her if she were awake and asking for it.

I squeezed my eyes closed, doing my best to prevent my body from responding. I refused to reposition myself so she could have better access to what she was searching for in her dream, which I assumed—fuck that, *hoped*—was my cock. I didn't want to think about who else she could be dreaming about, or I'd wind up jealous of a fantasy. And that'd be ridiculous.

When her hand went to my bicep and wandered along the ridges of muscle, I figured she was awake. But she'd told me back in South Africa she was a deep sleeper, and from the looks of it, she appeared to also be an active participant in her dreams. Because her body was joining whatever was happening in that beautiful mind of hers.

I tipped my head, catching sight of her ass peeking out from her short shorts. Then I dipped my chin to see the swell of her flesh. With her shimmying, the thin fabric of her shirt had moved to reveal one of her nipples.

I stifled a groan and bit down on my back teeth, remembering we had eyes on us. *The cameras.* I didn't need some sicko getting a view of her body like this. Not that I should have a view, either.

Doing my best to move without waking her, or crashing to the floor, I eased back toward the edge of the bed. Her hand fell to the mattress between us, and I reached for the cover, prepared to drape it over her, but went still when she whispered, "Ohhh," and her hand dove beneath her shorts.

*O* would officially be my favorite letter from now on.

Her tongue slid along the seam of her lips as her free hand went beneath her top and she squeezed her breast.

"Touch me," she murmured suggestively, *still* asleep.

I gulped at the erotic moment happening before me with the woman I'd been fantasizing about for almost a month. I had to get it through my thick skull that she wasn't asking me to finger her or bury my face between her legs and go down on her. No, she was asking the guy in her dreams. Lucky bastard.

I backed away from her a bit more, then finally got my head on straight and covered her so no one could witness her getting herself off.

Part of me wanted to wake her up, because we weren't alone in the room, either. I didn't need Carter or Oliver hearing my . . . *My what?*

A quick glance toward the bed next to me revealed Gwen and Carter weren't there. I twisted to the side to clock Mya and Oliver's bed. They were both asleep, bedding still covering them, so I had no clue if they'd wound up in the same precarious state as Charley and I were now.

Where in the hell had Carter and Gwen gone? Maybe Gray reached out on the phone we'd snuck in?

I focused back on Charley, her mouth was relaxed, and

she didn't appear to be moving beneath the covers anymore. Did she finish in her dream? Climax?

She appeared deeply asleep again, so I quietly slid my legs to the side of the bed and stood, ensuring the cover remained on top of her in the process. Grabbing running shoes and a ball cap from my suitcase, I snuck my way out to the veranda. I sat on the bucket swing out there, sucking in a breath of fresh air as I laced up, doing my best to calm down my dick and heart.

After a few minutes of jogging the trail, hoping to conceal the real reason I was out there so early—to find my teammates and make sure they weren't in trouble—I made my way to the main lodge area.

I was already sweating even though the temperature couldn't have been that bad yet. But it was sure as hell humid out. Plus, I was still screwed up in the head from watching that beautiful woman fondle her tit and clit.

*Now, I'm rhyming. This is why I don't date.*

Nearing the main lodge building where we'd first been greeted upon arrival last night, I caught a whiff of something I loved almost as much as the feel of my Glock at my back (which I was missing right now) . . . *coffee.*

I slowed my pace before switching to walking. I swiveled my ball cap forward, looking to shield my eyes a bit as I neared the main area, unsure who I'd come across.

Once inside, I recalled the map in my head that Gwen had provided for where there'd be no cameras and took that route.

I peeked into each room down the one hall. All empty so far, and I was also starting to wonder if I'd hallucinated the coffee aroma.

*Where are you two?*

Based on what I remembered from Gwen's map, the next room up was a decent-sized library. Gwen had figured it may have been one of the possible locations for the judges to watch the contestants from a safe distance.

When I stopped by the open doorway, the last thing I'd expected to see was Gwen pinned to a bookshelf clutching Carter's shirt while they . . . *kill me now* . . . made out.

"What in the actual fuck is going on?" I murmured, breaking the silence. If I watched my team leader kissing Gwen any longer, I'd take my chances and try my hand at knocking him out. Maybe all the extra work at the gym would come in handy after all.

Carter quickly backed away from Gwen and dragged his hand over his mouth before facing me, his breathing a touch ragged.

"Shit, you startled us," Gwen whispered, tossing an angry hand my way.

I stepped into the room and locked my arms across my chest, feeling like her father had hijacked my body, a reprimand on the tip of my tongue.

"We heard someone coming." Gwen approached me, waving a hand to ask me not to overreact. "I had to think fast. Two people having a hot moment seemed plausible if someone found us. I grabbed him and made him kiss me."

*Made Carter kiss you? Sure, sure.* No one made Carter do anything. I cocked a brow and shot a hard look at Carter, waiting for his side of the story.

"I needed to call Gray. She wanted to plant some of her gadgets in here," Carter explained, keeping his voice low. "This room has a strong Wi-Fi signal, but no camera."

I freed my arms from my chest, semi-satisfied with his response, then checked the hall, ensuring we were still clear.

"Gwen was right, they watch us from this room." Carter pointed to the only wall in the room free of books. Two flat-screen TVs were mounted there, but they were currently off.

There was a box with antennas on a table by the TVs and a mess of thick cables on the ground. "And no cameras in here because they don't want anyone watching them watching us."

"We'll have eyes and ears on them in the room now, though. Gray can pick up the signal and get names on whoever comes in here." Gwen motioned to a book on the shelf, and I assumed she hid a device there.

That was something. A step in the right direction. I couldn't believe I needed to remind myself I was there on an op and not for other reasons. But Charley being there had thrown my focus. The curveball I'd never have predicted. And who could've?

"Let's talk outside." Carter urged us to walk, and we managed to get out of the building without encountering anyone from the lodge or show.

"You get ahold of Gray?" I asked once we were in the clear from the main building.

"He and Jesse are here in Brazil with the team I managed to pull together. He was able to offload the weapons, too." Carter removed his shades from his pocket and slipped them on.

We were in an open area where the trees were most likely cut down for the sake of constructing the lodge, and the sun was now high enough in the sky to also signal to my stomach it was breakfast time. But today, I was hungry for something other than food. I shoved the messed-up thoughts of kneeling before Charley to taste her from my head and asked, "Who'd you call to come in and help?"

Hopefully it was someone not only Carter vouched for, but a team I could trust with my best friend's life out there. Gray was looking to grow his family, and I'd made a promise to his wife, even his cute dog, Lucky, that I'd ensure he always made it home. No matter what.

Hell, a few months ago, we even shook on it when Gray wasn't in the room. Well, Lucky and I did. He'd been snuggled in the crook of my arm when I took his paw and we'd made a deal that I'd look after his "dad."

"Camila," Carter said, drawing my attention.

"I thought she was on a job in Vancouver," I noted as we turned down another trail that would soon put us in view of the three "treehouses" set up in the jungle. "How'd you pull that off? Her job finish early in Canada?"

"She was . . . already in Brazil. Canceled her job in Vancouver," Carter shared, a bit hesitantly. "It's like she knew we'd be needing her team's help."

"Knowing Camila," Gwen spoke up, "she probably did. Doesn't she get visions?"

Carter grumbled something under his breath. He was still trying to wrap his head around the fact Camila somehow "just knew things" and she'd kept that a secret from him for so long. From what I remembered, unless I was confusing shit in my head, Carter and Camila had known each other most of their lives, and the truth about her visions had only come out during an op together in South America last year.

"Camila said she owes us one after assisting her on that op in—"

"Cape Town," I blurted, cutting off Carter, and I abruptly stopped. Camila had invited me to the bar only to cancel on me. Then I bumped into . . . Charley. *And now Charley's here. Camila's here. What the . . . ?* "Camila knew."

"Camila knew what?" Carter faced me, hands going to his hips.

Gwen spun to the side. "What's wrong?"

"Last month, before we flew home from Cape Town, I was supposed to meet Camila at the bar. She said you called her away, so she couldn't make it. That's when I met Charley."

Since Gwen didn't look shocked at the fact I knew Charley, I had to assume she'd been briefed on that fact. And Carter had more than likely shared that news with Gray on the phone, too.

I shook my head, then focused back on Carter, who was hanging his head as if uncomfortable with the new information.

"I didn't call her away that night," Carter revealed as he stroked his jawline.

Gwen stood between us. "Are you saying you think Camila set you two up because—"

"Because somehow, she knew Charley would need saving here. She knew I'd wind up on this op. Shit never makes sense with her. And she doesn't tell you anything. She just drops you into situations, and you have to figure it out yourself," I rambled, feeling even more fucked in the head than when I first saw Charley by the pool last night. Fate hadn't brought Charley and me together. It was Camila's handiwork. But even worse, that meant Charley was in danger.

"Camila told me when she says too much about her visions, it can often make things worse," Carter pointed out.

*True.*

"Well, Lucy and Charley are blonde and the right age. And based on what Lucy shared during the polygraph, they apparently have no family aside from each other," Gwen stated the facts as my jaw and gut tightened.

*Making them prime targets.*

"Do any of the judges have a say in who gets invited to the show?" Carter asked her.

Gwen frowned. "We don't even know the judges' names

yet, let alone who is making the decisions about contestants." She tipped her head toward the main building, a subtle reminder to the camera she'd planted in the library to hopefully get some IDs.

Before I could manage a comment, my attention swerved to one of the treehouses. Lucy was in the doorway, and Mason was on the other side of her, leaning in and—

"Something tells me that kiss is real," Gwen commented, an amused chuckle following her words.

My attention had been stolen again, though. Charley, Mya, and Oliver were walking our way. Charley abruptly stopped, locking on to the kiss.

And she looked pissed, but not because Mason more than likely had his tongue in her sister's mouth. No, I was pretty sure she was upset with me. Well, with all of us on her team. And damnit, we needed to talk now, or I had a feeling this woman would slip away for good this time. I couldn't let that happen, especially not if she was in trouble.

"Don't." Carter extended his arm, blocking my path. I hadn't realized I'd even taken a step in her direction. He removed his shades and pinned me with a hard look. "You want a word with her? Fine. Then earn enough points to sleep in the treehouse with her tonight. No cameras there. You talk to her then and only then." He arched a brow, waiting for confirmation I'd understood his order.

I let go of a gruff breath and hissed, "Roger that."

# CHAPTER THIRTEEN

## CHARLOTTE

### FIVE MINUTES AGO

"Why is your arm covering my boobs?" I overheard Mya hiss. When I turned to see what they were fussing about, I found my bed empty.

"Shit, sorry," Oliver remarked, sounding genuine.

As he stood from the bed, Mya clutched the bedding to her chest like she was naked.

*Doubtful.* I looked around the room. "Where is everyone else?"

"Maybe on a walk?" Mya suggested. "Coffee run?"

Without responding, I went ahead and grabbed my stuff from the suitcase, needing to go check on my sister. In the bathroom, I quickly washed my face and brushed my teeth before changing into jean shorts and a tee.

When I returned to the bedroom, Oliver and Mya stopped whatever hushed conversation they were having.

"Don't go out alone," Oliver spoke up after I dumped my stuff on the bed and started for the door.

"I'll be fine." I had no plans to stop and wait for a

chaperone. My sister had spent the night with a stranger in a treehouse meant for sex, and I had to ensure she was both physically and emotionally okay.

"Stop," Oliver called out, and I whirled around on the trail to find him and Mya catching up with me.

Oliver hadn't bothered to change—not that he'd needed to. Gym shorts and a tee were perfectly acceptable jungle attire—but Mya was still in what she wore to bed. And no woman I knew slept with a bra on if they could help it. Mya sure as hell hadn't, and I barely choked back a laugh when Oliver turned his attention to her and his gaze went laser-focused to her breasts.

"Mya. Fuck. Seriously," Oliver grunted.

"Then look away." She didn't seem shy about the fact he could see her nipples piercing her T-shirt. So apparently, she didn't care if he saw her, only the cameras.

Oliver cursed again. "Neither of you should be alone. And you need to go change or put on a bra, and I don't want"—he faced me—"you here alone either. So, we need to head back to the room together."

"Why can't we be alone?" I folded my arms, looking back and forth between them. "Three-headed snake going to get me?"

"I mean . . ." Oliver pointed, and I followed his finger to see a snake wrapped around a tree branch not far away, and I cringed and backed up a few steps. "Okay, granted, it only has one head. Think one is enough based on his, uh, thickness and length."

Mya slapped the back of his head. "Thickness and length, huh?" Her gaze snapped another direction a beat later, and I followed her eyes to see my sister there.

"Lucy," I said under my breath at the sight of her outside the treehouse door. Mason had his hands braced at the top of the doorframe, and he was leaning in and kissing her.

It wasn't a long kiss. Hell, maybe no tongue involved. But it was surely meant to be a private moment. Instead, they had an audience, including a tree-hugging snake.

Mason eased back a second later, as if he knew there were eyes on him. His arms fell to his sides as he stared straight at *Mya,* like he'd been caught doing something that'd upset her.

I looked at Mya. Then Oliver. "Who is the ex? And who is your situationship you're using to get over your ex?" I'd watched too many of my sister's TikToks and was now sounding like her.

"I'm sorry, what?" Oliver blinked, eyes on me for only a split second before he went back to studying Mya as if trying to get a read on her reaction to the kiss.

"Don't bother answering," I said in frustration. "It's clear you all know each other. I may be overly perceptive in general, but you two are going to make it obvious to everyone soon." I focused on the trail again, discovering my sister's kiss had even more spectators.

Jack, Gwen, and Carter were just up ahead, but they weren't walking our way, simply standing there in surprise, same as us.

"It's not what you think." Mya reached for my arm as if worried I'd run and tattle to Stephen that the game was rigged. Yeah, not my concern. "Don't talk to him here. It's not safe." Those weren't the words I'd expected from her.

My normal instinct would've been to pull away, but there was something about her, and hell, about all of them, that made me want to do the very thing I never did—*trust.*

"And Stephen is on his way with cameras," Oliver added, but I was too focused on Jack to even notice Stephen.

Why was Carter blocking Jack's path to me?

I looked toward the treehouse to see my sister climbing down the ladder with Mason just behind her.

"Breakfast is ready if you want to eat before the first competition of the day," Stephen called out, his booming radio-host voice jostling my attention his way.

"And what's the first event?" my sister asked, joining me with a sheepish grin as if I hadn't caught her hand in the cookie-kissing-jar.

Stephen removed his Ray-Bans and smiled. "You'll soon see."

When I pivoted to locate Jack again, he was almost right in front of me. He flipped his hat backward as he completed his approach, making me feel stupidly turned on. "How's your leg?" He crouched and reached for my calf without waiting for an answer.

I resisted the urge to set a hand to his shoulder for support when my foot slipped free from my flip-flop as he examined the wound I'd forgotten about. His thumb smoothed over the bandage the medic had placed there, and I sucked in a shaky breath. "Fine, I think."

I peered down at him as he peeled the edge of the bandage aside to check for himself, and I had no choice but to set a hand to his shoulder, in no mood to fall and give him the opportunity to catch me again.

"Okay, looks good." He righted the bandage, helped me put my flip-flop back on, then kept his eyes on me as he stood upright, forcing me to finally let go of him. He tipped his head, continuing to study me. "Sleep well?"

"As good as can be expected." I frowned, unsure what to do next. I felt like I was stuck in quicksand, slowly sinking into the abyss as I stared into this man's gorgeous and mesmerizing eyes. Eyes that turned my brain to mush. No easy feat. Downright impossible. Well, it had been impossible until this tall, sexy man with great biceps, a killer smile, and an even better personality found his way into my life.

Jack leaned forward, catching my forearm in the process, and brought his mouth to my ear. "I'll tell you everything tonight, I promise." His warm breath sent a trail of goose bumps streaming down my arms. "But we need to win a night in the treehouse first."

He freed my arm, then stepped back, searching my eyes for confirmation I was on the same page.

And was I? Did I really want to spend the night alone with him?

Yeah, I supposed I did. I needed answers. And I hated that I also wanted a hell of a lot more than that from him.

* * *

Breakfast beneath the pergola with the morning sun cresting the sky in such a beautiful setting should have been a moment to savor. Instead, I was fumbling with something as basic as a, *thank you,* as Jack wordlessly handed me a coffee just how I liked it. A little milk. Two percent, always. And one sugar.

"You remembered," was what I went with instead of courtesy.

Standing poolside at the buffet table, he tore a pack of sugar for his own cup, then dumped it into his black coffee. "Of course I did," he answered without catching my eyes.

We moved down the food line, side by side, and when we both reached for the last croissant, our pinkies brushed. Just that little touch had my stomach turning. A good turn. Not the run-for-the-hills kind.

As I stood there pondering what the hell that meant, Jack

reached for the croissant and set it on my plate, then grabbed a donut for himself instead.

It was hard to believe less than twelve hours earlier, in that same spot, we'd both answered uncomfortable questions during the polygraph test, and now we were about to break bread together. And I was going to give a man who had a gun and fake passport in Cape Town the benefit of the doubt and wait for his explanation when we were alone at night.

That wasn't like me. Run first, ask questions later. I'd survived ten-plus years on that motto. So, why was I changing now? My chest tightened as I set my eyes on Lucy heading to our team's table.

*For her, that's why.* Because she wanted some stability. A normal life. And the money from this competition could help with that. I just had no clue if I even knew how to do normal when the time came.

Jack and I joined the rest of our team at the picnic table, where he went around to the other side and pretty much forcefully wedged himself between Gwen and Carter. I didn't think anyone missed the eyeroll from Gwen.

Lucy sat across from me on Gwen's other side, and I was between Oliver and Mya.

A few bites of food later, I looked up to see Jack licking the frosting from his donut. Taking his sweet time to swipe his tongue along the top of it. His eyes met mine, and he went still, as if he'd just realized the way he was eating his donut was borderline erotic.

Memories of the way he'd kissed me one day earlier flooded back. Along with the memory of how he'd expertly used that tongue to kiss me in Cape Town. And then there were my fantasies where he'd sink between my thighs and make me come hard with his mouth.

My throat was parched, and I swapped the croissant for

bottled water and chugged down a few healthy swallows, needing to cool off and get my shit together.

"Maybe we should try and get to know each other a bit before the games today," Gwen suggested as I set the bottle down, doing my best not to make eye contact with Jack again.

The woman who'd given the polygraph test last night happened to be walking by, and I assumed Gwen's comment was to keep up with the pretense we were all strangers.

"Sure, what do you want to know?" Oliver asked her.

"Age for starters," Gwen said.

"Almost thirty-five," Oliver commented.

"Same," Mason said. "Thirty-four."

So, Mason was only nine years older than my sister. I could handle that. Not that we were supposed to be there for love.

"I'm forty-two," Jack said.

Wow, I was not expecting that. I'd thought he was still in his thirties. We'd talked about so many things back in Cape Town. But professions, past relationships, and age hadn't come up. I'd done my best to avoid the first two topics. The art of the dodge was my specialty, after all.

"Thirty-one." The number had shot from my mouth a little too fast and Jack's shoulders fell with obvious . . . disappointment. *Too young for you, then?* Clearly, I needed to get a hold of his skin care routine since he thought I was older, and I thought he was younger.

Lucy lightly kicked me beneath the table, snagging my attention. I could read her thoughts: *age-gap romance.* But did eleven years qualify? Mom and Dad had been a decade apart in age, and I'd never thought anything of it.

The rest of the table offered up their ages, and I shoved the croissant in my mouth as if that'd help silence my thoughts as Carter grumbled, "Forty-something," as his answer.

"Any pets at home?" Lucy asked next.

"A dog," Carter was quick to say.

A few others at our table began chatting and sharing more details, but I barely heard anything after that. I wasn't sure how much of this "get to know you" conversing was for show, and were their answers all true?

When I chanced another look at Jack, even though I'd promised myself I wouldn't look his way again during breakfast, he was quietly studying me. We spent a solid minute in that gaze. *Eye-fucking. Is that a thing?* Pretty sure it was a thing, and we were doing it. The man knew how to stare me down well. So well, it felt like he could pin me to the ground and remove my clothes using only his mind. Hell, he could probably get me off without even touching me, and . . .

Ohhh, that dream last night. I remembered it so clearly. God help me, I hoped I didn't act any of it out in my sleep. I had the tendency to have vivid dreams. Well, Mom called them night terrors. I used to sleepwalk after Dad's death when I was thirteen, and it'd lasted a few years. I kept reliving the night I'd found him unconscious on the living room floor from a heart attack.

The dreams had started up again in my twenties after Lucy and I had gone on the run, but they'd thankfully come to an end after years of self-help videos since I couldn't risk therapy and accidentally reveal my secrets.

"Breakfast is over." Stephen's announcement interrupted my thoughts, and he began corralling us back toward our suites. Orders were relayed to change into swimwear and then meet up in five minutes in one of the grassy areas behind the

BRITTNEY SAHIN

pool where a team of people seemed to be preparing what looked like a mud bath.

I changed into my red one-piece swimsuit. Full coverage in the front, not so much in the back, but it was my safest option. Jack had on black swim trunks. Simple. Basic. And he looked hot as hell in them.

When he offered to apply sunscreen to my back, I fumbled the tube. "Lucy can help, but thanks." I wasn't ready to have this man's hands sliding cream over my body. Okay, more like I knew I'd have a physical reaction to that happening, and I didn't need him or anyone in our room to see my body respond to his touch. Especially not anyone watching us on camera.

Once we were outside, everything happened fast. As I'd dreaded and suspected—mud wrestling. But only for the women. Chauvinists. I supposed that beat wrestling in Jell-O. But getting slathered up in mud, forced on my knees to pin down other women while the guys watched . . . yeah, well, if I did make lists, that'd have been on my "Hell No" one.

I won all my rounds, though, so . . .

The obstacle course that followed must've been designed for Olympians. It pushed me to my limits and had me questioning whether I needed to add more cardio into my workout with how breathless it'd made me. *But* my team had won. Determination and grit I'd noticed in each of them packed into their every movement during the activities. They had "the fight" in them, as Mom always called it, and it was easy to recognize since I had it in me, too.

But damn the third event now. An actual fight, where I'd only be an observer because it was "every man for himself" while the women had to watch the men fight. Not mud wrestling like we did, this was a straight up brawl as long as everything was above the waist.

142

All four guys from our team had made it to the final round. They clearly had an advantage. Maybe Jack had been telling the truth and he was military trained. I wasn't sure what to make of that. What'd he do for work now? Was he still tied to anything government-related?

"Wait, hold up. We have to fight each other? Really? We're on the same team," Oliver pointed out after Stephen had made the unsettling announcement.

Mya abruptly stepped forward, hands in the air as if she planned to push the idea away. "I don't like this."

"Relax." Stephen wrapped a hand over her shoulder, and she backed up, forcing his hand to fall.

Oliver glared at Stephen, studying our host as if he might drag Stephen into the ring instead if he tried putting his hand on Mya again.

Stephen cleared his throat and shook off the rejection. "Mason. Oliver. You're up. Winner fights Jack. Final winner fights . . ." He turned toward Carter, the man who'd destroyed the men from the other teams without so much as winding up breathless in the makeshift fighting ring. There was no question about who the boss-level fight would be against.

I had no clue how many points I'd racked up today, but I knew Jack was determined to win the night in the treehouse so we could be alone. But was he willing to hurt his friends in the fighting ring to get it? And I was ninety-nine percent sure they all were friends.

That one percent disappeared when Mason and Oliver faced off. Oliver may have acted like he didn't want to fight his teammates, but the way he stared down Mason in the ring, it looked like he was okay with fighting him. When I looked at Mya, I couldn't help but wonder if this fight for Oliver was more about him fighting Mason for *her* than for team points.

143

I didn't need my sister caught up in that drama. Should've known Lucy would wind up in a red flag situation.

"Who do you think will win?" Lucy squeezed my arm, hauling herself closer to me while we waited for Stephen to wrap up his countdown for the start of the fight.

"I don't know." Both had the same build, and over six-foot height. Muscles for days, just like . . . *Jack.*

My focus landed on where he stood alongside Carter. Jack was shirtless in only gym shorts. Bare feet. No shades or hat to hide the uneasy look in his eyes as he stared right at the fighters.

I swallowed at the sight of him. His entire magnetic presence drew me in from twenty-plus feet away, just as he'd sucked me into his orbit back at that hotel bar in South Africa when Mila had canceled on me that night.

Jack truly was toned and hard everywhere. And the man had great legs. I never knew that was a turn-on for me, because I was an arms girl, but his legs were muscular and . . . perfect. Then there was the stunning ink on his shoulder. And if he really was a Green Beret like he'd said, well, his tattoos seemed to match that: an eagle, pine trees, the American flag, and a few other things, all blended into one artistic symbol that seemed to represent his love for his country. And the finishing touch was the bird wings shielding and protecting the symbols there.

"Well, I guess it'll be interesting either way," Lucy said, but I knew she was rooting for Mason.

I'd barely spoken a word to anyone on my team the entire day, including my sister, aside from what was required during our competitions. We'd been too busy and breathless from our events to chat. "You ever going to tell me what happened in the treehouse?"

She peeked at me from over her shoulder, shielding her

eyes from the evening sun that'd soon be setting. "Nothing happened. He was a gentleman."

I pointed my chin toward the ring where said gentleman had just landed a gut punch to Oliver that looked painful—painful enough Mya had stepped forward, her hand covering her mouth.

Lucy banded an arm across her bare stomach as if she'd taken the blow from Mason instead.

"The kiss you saw was our first one," Lucy finally answered, now fidgeting with her belly button ring. "Well, I mean, our second. But the other didn't count since we had to do it. But um, it just kind of happened as we were about to leave the treehouse, and I'm pretty sure it wouldn't have had we known we had an audience."

"Point for Mason," Stephen called out.

Oliver shook it off and rotated his neck. He looked Jack's way, and . . . oh shit . . . he was going to throw the fight, wasn't he? Oliver didn't want to be the one to fight Jack next, did he?

But when Oliver tackled Mason to the ground and they began grappling, and he forced Mason to tap out, it was clear Oliver wanted to get in a point or two first.

A few more back-and-forth points later, Stephen yelled, "Tied. Next point is the winner."

It'd been hard to watch these two guys go at it, especially when it felt like they really did need to get something out of their systems. I looked for Mya, but she wasn't ringside anymore. Instead, I spotted her up by the pool with her back to the fight.

"Mason chose her last night," Lucy said, and I realized my sister was peering at Mya now as well. "You think—"

"All I know is you need to be careful," I finished for her, then forced myself to watch the last punch thrown to end the match. Mason's left hook snapped Oliver's head to the right, and ouch, that had to hurt.

But Oliver didn't hold his jaw. Maybe it'd been more for show and less painful than it'd appeared. They were good actors, I'd give them that.

"Thank God that's over," Lucy murmured, holding a hand to her heart as she watched Oliver exit the fighting area, his eyes intensely focused on Mya by the pool.

Oliver hung his head as if angry at something—maybe himself—then stood alongside Carter outside the grassy ring, swapping places with Jack. And I felt like I was swapping places with Mya, and it was my turn for my heart to catch in my throat.

As Stephen went over the rules, as if they both hadn't already heard them multiple times, Jack looked my way and frowned. Was he upset about me watching him throw down? Or that he'd be slugging someone he so clearly knew?

His chest had smudges of dirt and grass stains on it from the previous matches, and something told me his heavy breathing had more to do with me than with the adrenaline pumping through him for the fight.

For whatever reason, when Mason threw his first punch, Jack didn't duck. He took it in the chin. Almost as if he wanted some sense to be knocked from him. Or into him.

Jack didn't waste time taking Mason down after that, though. Efficient and quick movements. Hell, he won within two minutes.

"I guess your guy is the tougher one," Lucy commented.

"He's not my anything," I reminded her.

"Sure." She poked me in the side. "But Carter is a whole hell of a lot scarier. So, I think he'll win."

I kept my mouth closed and just gave her a little shrug.

Jack rotated his shoulders, then his neck. They both

loosened up while circling each other, waiting for the go-ahead to fight.

When Stephen abruptly announced, "Fight!" my shoulders jerked, and Carter came at Jack fast. It was a blur of swift movements and Carter had Jack on the ground in seconds, pinning him beneath his body, forcing Jack to tap out.

Carter offered Jack a hand to stand for the next round. I expected him to back off a bit, maybe feign exhaustion after going so hard so fast, but then Carter surprised me by going after Jack without missing a beat yet again.

Carter didn't land his punch, though. He pulled his arm back only to go completely still. His gaze snapped to someone or something off in the distance, and his hand fell to his side as he took a step back.

I turned to see what had thrown him off, but there was nothing there. Mya was back by the ring now, so it hadn't been her who'd stolen his focus.

*Weird.* Oddly, Jack chose not to use that moment to his advantage. He didn't take a shot at Carter while the man had been distracted. And damn that said so much to me about his character.

"You good?" Jack asked him, more than a casual hint of unease in his tone. Carter erased what I'd swear was alarm or concern from his face, then peered at Jack and gave him a tight nod.

Jack scored the next point with an elbow just below Carter's cheekbone that would more than likely leave a mark.

They traded points again. Carter. Then Jack.

"Last point for the winner. And if your team wins the final event tonight, tug-of-war, that means whoever wins this fight winds up in the treehouse. So, make this last point count," Stephen shared.

*Tug-of-war?*

Carter looked over at Gwen, shook his head as if not wanting to spend the night alone with her, then fixed his eyes back on his target, on Jack.

Jack dropped to a knee and swiveled out of the way as Carter rushed him, avoiding the punch aimed at his face. He used his momentum from the turn to pivot back to his feet, and just as Carter faced him, Jack sent a roundhouse kick to Carter's jaw, scoring the final point.

Carter closed one eye and held his jaw, shaking his head as I read his lips when he mouthed to Jack, "Fuck you very much for that."

Well, I was pretty sure it'd been a "fuck you" not a "thank you." Carter seemed more like a "fuck you" guy than a "thank you" one.

I was sure a lot of women found him extremely attractive and would happily take "fuck you" from Carter entirely literally. But not me. No, there was only one man who kept making my heart do a tap dance, and he was currently lifting his hands in apology to Carter.

As if his thoughts were already resting in the same treehouse mine were, Jack turned toward us and set his eyes on me.

With the fight over and won, only one thing stood in our way of a night alone together. And based on the hard look in his eyes as he stared at me, chest rising and falling, he had absolutely no intention of losing.

# CHAPTER FOURTEEN

## CHARLOTTE

I COULDN'T REMEMBER THE LAST TIME I'D PLAYED TUG-OF-war, but I was pretty sure I'd been in eighth grade, and it was when Shane Houser had tried to kiss me after our team won. I'd wound up in the principal's office for socking him in the jaw for it, too. Mom had asked him to take it easy on me by reminding him, *"Her dad just died."*

I probably would have avoided getting in trouble if my smart mouth hadn't shot back to the principal, *"He had it coming."*

The fact Shane hadn't gotten in trouble for trying to plant his lips on mine after I'd said no, still made me angry to this day.

So, I decided to channel my frustrations from all the *"Shanes"* of the world, and I dug my heels in. Funny enough, Jack knew the "Shane" story. I'd shared a lot of random details about myself that night in Cape Town. And I'd never forget Jack's response to that one: *"Let's hope adult Shane never bumps into me."*

I'd chuckled at that, secretly deciding I wouldn't mind

Jack walking into any number of adult assholes I'd dealt with over the years. I mean, I'd handled them just fine, but still . . .

"One more big tug, and they'll fall," Oliver said, trying to encourage us. I was surprised the game had gone on so long given the muscles we had on our team, but the other side . . . well, they may not have been great fighters, but the guys appeared to hit the gym as if staying buff was a job requirement.

This was my team's second round since we'd already defeated the first group. To be declared "winners" we had to win this last one.

"Yup, they're sliding. Losing their footing. We got this!" Gwen shouted loud enough for the other competitors to hear. A little psychological warfare could go a long way.

Not even a minute later, the other team went flying into the mud pit. Their abrupt collapse sent everyone on my side falling on our asses like bowling pins, but Jack cushioned my fall.

"Sorry." I shifted around, only making things worse, because now I was straddling the man. And while everyone worked to get back to their feet, I remained on top of him with my hands planted to his damp chest, not minding the sweat on my palms at all.

"You okay?" He reached for my face and cupped my cheek, acting as though we were alone without both eyes and cameras on us.

"Yeah. You have a wonderful way of catching me when I fall." I smiled, but when he brought his thumb to my right dimple, his touch triggered an uncomfortable memory, wrenching it free from the box I'd locked it in. Screw that unhealed trauma I'd thought I'd already dealt with. I pushed his hand away on instinct and jerked my head back as if he'd slapped me. "Sorry," I quickly apologized as we both got back on our feet, brushing at a piece of grass clinging to my swimsuit so I could avoid his eyes.

"Did I do something wrong?"

When I finally looked up, Jack had his head angled with concerned eyes pointed at me. Based on what he'd done to me at the breakfast table, I knew those eyes could quickly become erotic weapons, able to take my defenses down in seconds.

"Nothing. I'm fine." I was pretty sure I pulled the lie off well, because the lines between his brows disappeared.

"Winners get a dip in the pool. Losers go straight to the shower before you join us at dinner," Stephen piped up from entirely too close by.

"Sure we can't use the pool showers to clean off so we can take a quick dip, too?" one of the guys from the losing team had asked, heading straight for me. "Maybe we could play a game of lifeguard. Give me some mouth-to-mouth." His eyes lingered on my breasts, and I did a quick check to ensure they were still safely hidden beneath my red one-piece swimsuit.

I was about to come up with something clever to say to put him in his place, but Jack stepped to my side. "Eyes up. Eyes on *me*."

"Don't tell me you're already staking your claim here just because you were coupled up on night one," the idiot responded—the same idiot I'd clocked as an immediate no last night at the meet and greet. Far too pretty and polished for me, and apparently, I could add douchebag to the list, too. "It's every man for himself out here. What happens when Baywatch Barbie here wants to trade up at the end of the week for someone a bit less . . . *vintage*."

"Baywatch Barbie?" Oh, I really hated arrogant assholes like this, and I knew exactly how to deal with them. But we also had an audience. Stephen and his cameramen were soaking up every second of the exchange, and I wondered if he'd secretly arranged this made-for-TV moment.

"I took it easy on you in the fighting ring earlier," Jack said, the warning in his tone exceptionally clear. "Don't bother her again. Don't even think about her. Understand?" he added in a tight voice, his anger seething beneath the surface, and that touch of dominance and protectiveness had my thighs tightening, and my heart fluttering.

"Or what?" he asked Jack, snickering.

"You know what vintage means?" Jack tipped his head ever so slightly, never losing eye contact with him. "It means I'm from the generation of 'fuck around and find out.'" Then he flicked his hand in the air, a final *fuck off* warning to him that now would be a good time to walk away.

"Yeah, okay, old man," he said. "But she'll change her mind. I guarantee it. And I just might not be interested by then," the idiot tossed out before starting away with both Stephen and the cameraman trailing behind him.

"Listen," Jack began, a touch of an apology in his tone, clearly opting to ignore the last dig his way, "you seem like someone who can handle herself, so I didn't mean to overstep, but I just—"

"I haven't had anyone around to handle stuff for me in a very long time." And that was the truth. "Thank you." I gave him a little reassuring nod.

He studied me for a few seconds, then returned my nod and asked, "You feel like taking a quiet dip in the pool?"

"Sure, I need to cool off."

He gestured in the direction of the water, like a gentleman offering for me to walk ahead.

When we neared the pool, we discovered the rest of our group already swimming, enjoying a round of fist-bumps and well-intentioned celebratory head-dunks amidst peals of laughter and reassured sighs. Well, except Carter. He had his back to one of the pergola's columns, a disturbed look on his face. He tipped his head, eyes on Jack, a signal for him to join him.

"Give me a second," Jack said before starting Carter's way.

I went ahead into the pool, taking the steps. My sister and the others were gathering in the shallow water, casually talking. Lucy seemed to have everyone wrapped up in one of her stories, talking with her hands. Mason seemed a bit enchanted by her.

I really did love how truly carefree Lucy could be at times, and wished I could let go here and there. But while she couldn't hide it from me, Mom had always done her best to shield Lucy from the dark shit, and I'd done my best to do the same.

Mom had never taught her what she taught me, either. Hell, even the afternoon after I'd slugged Shane, instead of grounding me, Mom taught me the proper way to throw a punch to better protect my knuckles if there was a next time.

I forced away the memories, but instead of joining the others, I swam over to the deep end to try and do a little eavesdropping on Jack and Carter. They were in one of the camera-free zones I'd scouted out as a safe place to talk yesterday.

Jack had his back to me, blocking Carter, which meant I couldn't read their lips. But Jack's back muscles pinched together at something I assumed Carter had said, then he shook his head, turned, and came over to the water, diving in as if he didn't even see me there.

He pushed up to the surface and dragged a hand through his thick, wet hair. He set his eyes on me, and why the hell did he have to be so handsome? Handsome men had never made me lose sight of an objective, and I couldn't allow it to happen this time. I had to remove whatever power his eyes had over me from the equation and remember my current mission: protect my sister and win the money.

Jack swam over to me and offered a quick, "Sorry about that."

"Everything okay?"

"It will be," was all he gave me.

"Today was . . . weird, right?" Small talk and I weren't a thing. Not friends. Neighbors. Not even distant relatives.

"It was most definitely not the norm for me." He smiled, a hint of his perfect teeth showing. "Can't believe you're only thirty-one, though." His unexpected comment threw me off, and even though I didn't verbally say anything, I guessed my face said volumes. "Shit, sorry, I don't mean because you look older . . ." He swam over to the ledge, and I hesitantly followed him.

Setting my arm on the side so I didn't have to keep kicking my legs as hard to stay above water in the deep end, I teased, "You planning on trying to recover from that comment?"

"You're just so wise, you know?" He frowned. "Like, I feel like you're older than me." He shook his head and sighed. "This is going great."

"Perfect, actually. Good to know I look like an antique." And before he could fumble again, I added, "That was a joke." I smirked, but based on his uneasy look, I went ahead and explained what he was trying to say for him, "I've had a life that has mentally aged me. And I've always been a bit of an old soul."

"That's what I meant. And not that thirty-one-year-olds aren't mature, you're just . . . you're different." He grimaced as if still beating himself up for his word choice. "We seemed to click back in Cape Town, and I don't usually click with anyone if they weren't born before 1990. Because fuck, maybe I am *vintage*." He splashed the water at his side as he added, "I just never knew I could relate to someone who didn't grow up drinking from the water hose or using the streetlights coming on as their curfew." He listed a few more things, such as prank calling random people you found in a phonebook. "And don't get me started on not knowing what TGIF used to mean. Parking your butt in front of the TV on a Friday night for *Family Matters, Full House,* and—"

"You don't date much, do you?" I hid a smile, because to be honest, his rambling was cute.

"That obvious?" He killed me with a lopsided smile that was smoking hot when he'd probably meant it as an innocent expression.

"I don't date, either," I admitted. "And while I didn't have all of those experiences, I did watch the reruns for those shows." One shoulder lift later, I asked, "So, does that make me a little bit cooler in your book now?"

He started to reach for my face, then withdrew his hand. "Why do I get the feeling you're not someone who would truly care about being cool, not to someone else, at least?"

*True. But.* "Maybe for the right person . . ." *Where am I going with that?* Hell, I caved. Gave him a genuine smile. Dimple included.

"Ready to clean up for dinner? I'm sure you're anxious to be alone later." Stephen squatted alongside us, killing the mood. Shit, had I really lost myself in the moment and forgotten we were on camera? In a few weeks, people would be eating popcorn while watching us, listening to our private conversation.

*Wait, didn't Jack say the show would never see the light of day, or did I imagine those words by the river?*

"We're ready," Jack said, his eyes catching mine, and I resisted the urge to reach out for this man. To search for his heartbeat to calm me. Guide me through this situation even if that didn't make sense.

Danger and risks I understood. Knew well.

But this?

"You are ready, right?" Jack asked once Stephen had left us alone, and I knew he was asking me something else. Something far different than if I was ready for a shower.

*Am I ready for the truth? To trust him?*

It was a yes-or-no question. But my lips were tight. Breathing had to be done solely through my nose as I stared back at him.

*"Sometimes, you have to let go and simply feel it."* Mom's words popped into my mind. I was sixteen again, sitting behind the wheel of her Mustang. My fifth driving lesson from her that summer.

*"What if I can't trust myself?"* I'd asked her, terror filling my lungs. Sweaty palms gripping the leather wheel.

*"Then you shut your eyes. Only for a second,"* she'd said while wrapping her hand around my wrist, urging me to look at her. *"Sometimes all it takes is a second for you to know which is the right way to go."*

My eyes fell closed. But in that second, Mom's other reminder shot through my head hard and fast. *"But when it comes to men, there is only ever one direction to go. The other way."*

# CHAPTER FIFTEEN

## CHARLOTTE

"WHAT ARE YOU DOING?" I PLANTED MY HANDS ON MY HIPS, watching as Jack maneuvered around the inside of our jungle treehouse, carrying a small cylinder-like metal tube that looked more like it belonged under the hood of a car.

"Ensuring there really aren't cameras in here," Jack whispered.

*This feels very FBI-like.* And just that thought gave me chills, so I shifted the mosquito netting surrounding the bed to the side and sat, allowing it to collapse back together in front of my face.

"Okay, we're good," he declared a minute later.

With his back to me, he bent forward, presumably to hide his device in his bag. And the excellent view of his ass in those jeans was a pleasant distraction from the fact he had spy gadgets on him.

I flicked the netting where it sat on my legs, pushing it away so I could grab my thighs and knead the sore muscles a little. The day's events were catching up with my body. I hadn't realized just how much we'd done until I'd kicked off

157

my wedges to climb the ladder into the treehouse and my calf muscles had screamed in protest.

"So, if we're good, does that mean you're ready to talk?" There was no point in wasting time now. I needed answers, and I'd run out of any patience I had from waiting all day for them.

"Yeah," he said, his back still to me.

I continued working the knots in my thigh muscles, waiting for him to follow up his "yeah" with some information. I peered up at the fan over the bed, which was doing little more than knocking hot air around the room. And there was only so much dead air I was willing to tolerate. "So . . ." I lowered my focus back to find him finally facing me, and my stomach growled, loud enough for him to hear.

"You should've eaten dinner." His eyes went to my hands on my legs as he added, "I grabbed some fruit before we left the dinner table. It's in my bag. Will you eat?"

"Eventually," I promised.

Eyes still lingering on my hands just above the edge of my white sundress, he asked, "Sore?"

"Are you trying to deflect and distract by offering me a massage?"

His brows lifted, eyes shooting to my face. "Do you want my hands on you, Charley?" The seductive edge there had me almost forgetting he needed to tell me something important. "A massage, I mean." An adorable throat clear later, he added, "Would you like one?"

*Yeah, I want your hands on me. All over me, in fact.* "The truth for now would be a good start."

That desire radiating from him only a moment ago slipped away, and in its place was a dark look.

Part of me wanted funny Jack for this moment to help me get through it. The guy who'd made me laugh my ass off back at that bar in Cape Town. Quite literally, too. I'd almost slipped right off the barstool. But he'd swooped one arm out, catching my hip to right me back on the seat before I'd fallen.

This Jack, though, was all hard lines, angles, and intensity. Not that I didn't find broody Jack hot and sexy— hell, broody Jack could eye-fuck me into orgasm—but if he kept looking at me with those worried, haunted eyes much longer, he'd trigger my fight-or-flight mode. And I truly didn't want to run from him, which said volumes considering my typical MO.

One hand left his pocket, but it was only to grip the nape of his neck.

"You're stressing me out," I blurted. "Please. Don't drag this out."

He nodded an okay, or maybe it was an apology, as he lowered his arm to his side. "You're right about us. We all work together." He swallowed, and I did the same. Because damn. "And we're here undercover because women have been going missing after each competition. We're trying to find them and prevent it from happening again."

*My world spun off its axis* was an expression I'd honestly understood a few times in my life. Like now. "I'm sorry, what?" My palms were officially sweatier than when Mom taught me to drive on my sixteenth birthday. And not drive-drive. No, I already knew how to operate a vehicle. Drive as in if I was—

"This is a mission."

His admission wrenched me away from my memory. Mission equated to danger, and . . . *Lucy.* "Lucy was invited here." I stood, maneuvering around the netting. I turned, stepped forward, then backward. Hell, I was unsure which direction I wanted to go. "Is she a target?"

"Potentially. But so are you. He or *she,* I suppose, likes

blondes around your age. Smart and skilled women. And women without families to miss them."

*Of all the people in the world to be selected as targets . . .? Wait, is this some sick joke?*

"Gwen hacked their system and reassigned you and your sister to our group before we even arrived because Lucy fit the description. We didn't know anything about you—your picture was never provided to the show and Gwen couldn't find anything on you based on Lucy's profile—but she didn't want to separate you two since you're sisters," he went on. "We have a team on the outside watching over us, too. Working behind the scenes to narrow down the suspect list."

"These women, do they go missing during the filming of the show? Is my sister in immediate danger?"

"They've always been taken once they returned home, and each time it was made to look like the women chose to fall off the grid, and there's not usually anyone poking around and asking questions. The only reason we learned about this is because someone with a loose connection to Gwen went missing after the last season in New Zealand."

I wanted to feel a little relief at his implication that my sister was currently safe, but how in the hell could anyone feel comfortable knowing women were still out there in danger? Plus, I didn't need a third freaking problem to deal with. Or was it fourth? Because . . . well, was Jack becoming a problem for me, too?

*The team. The gadgets. That all means . . .* "Are you a cop? Fed?" My stomach tipped, turned, and tossed yet again at the new problem I had to tackle.

"I know this is a lot to take in, but you look like you've seen a ghost. You okay?" He took a step my way, and I took three back, the wall stopping me from going any farther.

"Of course I'm not okay. You're here undercover to catch

a serial kidnapper? Killer? Trafficker? I mean . . . those are unspeakable options we're talking about, and my little sister is caught up in this," I sputtered, my body trembling now. I was normally pretty put together. Even whenever paranoia struck and had us packing up our home to move overnight, I didn't panic-walk into walls.

"I won't let anything happen to you or her. You have my word." He placed a hand over his heart, his tone as genuine as the look in his eyes. "And no, I'm not a cop or Fed. I work in private security. And I was on a job in South Africa when we met last month."

*The gun. Passport. Okay, but still.* "So, you don't work for the government at all? And if not now, have you ever?"

"Well, I was in the Army, like I told you. And this isn't all that top secret because I wasn't an officer or agent, but I assisted the CIA with some security stuff," he said with a shrug.

*Shit. Damnit. Hell.*

"And uh, yeah, my team sometimes takes gigs from Uncle Sam, sure. To stop an arms deal, for example." Unknowingly making things worse, he added, "Every so often we have to hunt someone down from a wanted list."

*Oh* geez, *I think I'm going to be sick.* My body moved on autopilot, angling around him as I headed straight for the door. I needed to grab my sister and leave. Abort the money-making-to-live-a-*normal*-life mission.

"Where are you going?" Jack's hand at my waist as I'd brushed past him, stopped me. Not that he'd grabbed me hard. It was barely a touch. I just didn't resist and push forward.

And given everything he'd spilled, I should've kept going. His team could handle the serial kidnapper while I protected my sister from becoming not only a victim that way, but a victim in another way. *So, why am I not moving? Leaving?*

"Charley, talk to me. I know what I said is horrible, and you're scared, but—"

"Did you ever look me up after South Africa? Run my face through any government-type facial recognition thing?"

His hand dropped from my waist, and I slowly turned to face him. The lines in his forehead deepened as he started putting things together in his head. He was adding two plus two and it'd be ridiculous to hope he didn't get four.

"I pulled your photo from hotel surveillance. I just wanted to make sure you left on purpose, and no one abducted you from my room that night. I was confused why you took off, but no, I didn't try to track you down." The tip of his head and tightening of his mouth meant he'd just made it there. To the conclusion I didn't want him to draw.

"What about for the show? Gwen placed us in your group, so you had our names. Did you investigate us then?" I pressed.

"Face recognition for your sister, yes, but there weren't any hits."

*The filters worked, thank God.*

"Who is after you? Who are you worried will find you here?"

*If only it were just one person.* "I have to go." I heard the same urgency in my voice I knew he did, and yet, I still couldn't find it in me to move, which was absurd. Maybe it was because I was tired of running, too. But what choice did we have? Throw in some psychopath looking to take women into the mix . . . I just couldn't wrap my head around the fact we'd really stumbled into a new nightmare.

Was it more plausible someone did ID Lucy even with her filters, and they used the show to draw us out? If we had flown into Brazil instead of Peru, would someone have snatched us at the airport the second we arrived? Did my paranoia save us? And were the cameras at the lodge saving us now because my enemy wouldn't want to be recorded?

My mind continued to race a million different directions, landing on . . . "No cameras in here. Could he come for us now since he's safe from being recorded?" I shook my head, feeling a little frantic. "Lucy. There are cameras in her room, so she's okay for now, right?" *I'm rambling now. This isn't good.*

Jack reached for both my hands and set my palms to his chest, recognizing I was spiraling. Did he know the feel of his heartbeat strangely calmed me down? What in the world was going on with me? With us?

"Are you talking about the man my team is after? The kidnapper? I told you he's never taken anyone from the show." The genuine reassurance in his tone was comforting, but still not enough to fully calm my racing heart and mind.

*No, that's not who I'm thinking about.* I couldn't voice my thoughts; he couldn't know about my dark and messy past. Plus, the truth would place him in an awkward spot, so that was out of the question. "I, um." I forced a nod. "Yeah, the serial kidnapper . . . he won't come to the jungle and attack us?" I hated myself for the lie, but I didn't have a choice.

"Not unless he changes his MO. And if he does that, he'll never be able to use the show to choose women again. He'd shine a light on himself that way."

Yeah, maybe that bastard wouldn't come for us, but there was another asshole that wouldn't care about taking Lucy and me from the show.

And oh, Lucy slept in a cameraless treehouse last night. My palms began to slip from Jack's chest, but he snatched my wrists and held them in place.

*Nothing happened to Lucy last night. He doesn't know we're here. He's not behind this. He would've taken her last night if that was the case.* And the horrible fact women from other seasons were missing suggested that, yeah . . . this wasn't about us. *We're just blonde and match some psycho's wants.*

"You good?" Jack asked, his tone steady but still rippling with concern. And why wouldn't he be worried? I was giving him far too many reasons to question me. "Talk to me. You're nervous, but it's not about my mission. Well, not entirely." He closed his eyes and a few breaths of silence later confessed, "I have a feeling you and I were brought together for a reason. I wanted it to be fate we met, as in . . . well, you know . . . but I'm pretty sure it was because I'm supposed to help you." There was a sadness to his tone that slipped beneath my defenses and momentarily made me lose my edge of paranoia.

*You want me. Feel something for me.* I gulped. *But you'll never be able to have me.* And I had no idea how to admit that to him, especially when I felt the pull between us, too.

"Why do you think that?" I was still trying to decide what to do. Lucy and I were on a team with people connected to the government, caught up in a show being used to kidnap women, and even though the one man I was more terrified of than anyone didn't seem to be behind it, there were still plenty of reasons for us to bail and leave the competition early.

Jack slowly opened his eyes. "This will sound weird, but my friend just kind of knows things. I don't know how to explain it, but we were working with her on a gig in Cape Town, and she was the reason I was at the bar that night. She canceled, then I met you. Now you're here. She's even here. I think she knew you needed help."

Yeah, he was right. That was weird. But maybe it somehow still made more sense than us both accidentally winding up in the same place. "What do you mean she's here? Is that what Carter told you at the pool that made you upset?"

"You really are perceptive. Or maybe I'm just a bad actor." He stroked his jawline for a second. "She was supposed to remain on the outside with my team, but she's smart and fast thinking and is now undercover as a sponsor."

"Wait, what? Isn't that even riskier if she gets caught?"

"My thoughts exactly when he told me."

"Ohhh. That's why Carter lost focus fighting you. He saw her, didn't he?" At least his story kept adding up. Way more than mine would. I couldn't even pretend to lie and say I didn't trust this man, though. I just . . . did.

"Yeah, he noticed her arriving in the distance, and after the fight, he checked the phone we smuggled in. My best friend, who happens to be one of my team leaders, texted from his position in the jungle to let us know the change in plans, that she's on the inside as a sponsor," he quickly explained.

"Gray?" I asked, remembering the stories he'd shared about his best friend back in Cape Town.

"Good memory, and yeah, he's in the jungle right now. And listen, he's not only someone I trust with my life, but he's got the full weight of the United States government at his disposal if need be. So, I promise you, you and your sister are in good hands."

"What do you mean? Who is he?" Because "full weight of the United States government" didn't do wonders to ease my nerves.

"His father is Secretary of Defense. He works for the President."

I whirled away from him, pulling my hands from his grasp, feeling a bit lightheaded. *This just keeps getting better and better.* I peered at the thatched roof, feeling a trickle of sweat slide between my breasts as I tried to find a way to calm down.

Jack circled me, not bothering to try and turn me around.

I had to think quickly, change the subject so he'd forget my reaction to his whole connection-to-the-President thing. "I left you that morning in Cape Town because I was trying to find a pen to leave you my number and stumbled upon a gun instead," I rushed out. "Curiosity had me checking your ID, and I found your passport with the name Kevin. I got scared and took off."

When I found the courage to look him in the eyes, there wasn't anger there for snooping. Just unmistakable relief. "*That's* why you left? Not because you didn't, uh, want to see me again?"

I wet my lips. "I wanted you, Jack. I still . . ." I shook my head, hating myself for this, but I whispered, "But I can't want you. It'd never work. We can never be together." My stomach squeezed at how much I hated those words and the defeated look he gave me next. "We have to assume the reason we met was because of this game and for no other reason. As you said, your friend brought us together."

"What are you saying?" he asked, his tone as tough as gravel.

I tore my hand through my hair, pushing my bangs away from my face as I stole a second to think. "As much as I want to take off now, the idea of a girl going missing because I left, and your team got booted so you couldn't help, isn't something I can stomach." I'd do anything to save Lucy, but I couldn't let someone else's sister or daughter go missing either. "So, let's get through this game, keep my sister from getting taken, find your bad guy, and then we go our separate ways. We can never see each other again after that. And please, please, destroy the photo you have of me. Never run my face, or my sister's, through any recognition program." He opened his mouth to talk, and I shook my head, a plea not to protest. "Also, promise me you'll destroy the footage from this show."

He quietly studied me before his shoulders fell, and he agreed, "You have my word. And the footage will be destroyed." One pause later, he begged, "But damnit, Charley, please tell me what's going on with you. Who are you scared of? Running from? Why won't you trust me to help you?"

"I barely know you. And yet, I do trust you." That one-second feeling Mom told me to listen to had to be why. Everything he said to me washed away any doubts. He was a good man. Safe and honest. "And I, um, do like you," I confessed, "which is why I'm not going to tell you anything. I'm doing it for you. To protect you."

He stepped forward and banded his arm behind my back, drawing my body flush to his. "Fuck my safety." He stared deep into my eyes. "You think I can just walk away from you after this? Forget about the only woman who's made me feel like . . ." He paused, breathing hard, then he demanded, "Tell me you haven't thought about me since Cape Town even after finding the gun and passport."

I couldn't tell him that, so I kept quiet.

In my silence, he angled his head and brought his mouth closer to mine. "And tell me it wasn't me in your dream last night making you come."

*Talk about a subject change.* "Just because I want you doesn't mean I get to have you," I spat out, unable to stop the words or the emotions behind them from flowing. I was in this man's strong arms, feeling safe and secure for one of the first times in my life, and I didn't even know how to make sense of the feeling. It was foreign and new.

"That's bullshit and you know it." The harsh snap of his words didn't cut through the comfort of his embrace, though. "Your sister said she wants to stop running. Let me help you stop running."

"No," I cried, squirming from his embrace now.

"Fine," he snapped out, but he didn't let me go, and for whatever reason, I stopped resisting his hold.

"Fine," I returned, a tremor shooting through my voice.

He was breathing as hard as I was, but we both didn't budge . . . and then he lifted my wrist between us and smoothed his other thumb over my ink there that said, **Never Let Go.** And that's what he appeared he didn't want to do. Let me go. Lose me.

And for some reason, that loosened something inside me. Cracked my defenses, and I found myself pushing up on my toes, setting my lips to his.

He lost hold of my wrist and hiked my one leg to his side, and I drew my body against his. I needed to see if his cock was as hard as I was aroused.

He groaned against my lips in what sounded like both protest and surrender. The moment his mouth softened, and the shock wore off, I could feel the power shift as he backed me up against the wall.

With one hand, he held my wrists together above my head, taking full control. I tensed slightly; this was too close to being cuffed and incapacitated, and my flight mode began to kick in. But when his free hand cradled the back of my head while pressing into me, I groaned and relaxed into him, surrendering to the feelings this man evoked in me. It was at that moment I knew I'd let him do whatever the hell he pleased to me.

Still holding me gently but firmly in place, he broke the kiss and leaned back to find my eyes. "What are you doing to me?" he ground out.

"I don't know." *Because you're doing "it" to me, too.*

I didn't make rash decisions. I didn't go to men's hotel rooms and spend the night talking and making out. I didn't do a lot of things that seemed to be happening with the son of a library director. The son of a mom who raised this man right. I knew it. Felt it. Yearned for everything he could give me, even knowing that after this trip he'd never be able to give me any of those things again.

His eyes fell shut, and he dropped his forehead to mine. "I think I might hate you for this later," he whispered, emotion catching in his voice.

"But for now?" I asked, terrified he might release me and not keep me against him like I so desperately wanted him to do, even if it made no sense.

He lifted his head from mine and opened his eyes, tightening his hold on my wrists. "I guess we're going to *try* and fuck whatever this is out of our systems and hope tomorrow we can move on and focus on the mission. *If* that's what you really want?"

"Move on or sex?" I whispered.

"Both," he grunted, his mouth close to dropping over mine again, an angry but hot kiss a mere breath away.

All I could do was nod. I did want sex, even if that was wild given the heavy conversation we'd just had about a serial kidnapper. But the moving-on part? No, I couldn't say that out loud.

"Aren't you worried sex might make you more attached?"

My pulse quickened as his free hand traveled to the hem of my dress.

Slowly, he began skimming his palm under the dress and up my side where his thumb finally caught the side of my breast. I swallowed a moan, eager and hopeful he'd do more than that.

"I've been attached since Cape Town, sweetheart. You've been in my head every day since. So no, sex won't change the fact I already . . . feel what I fucking feel."

*Ohhh.* Guilt weighed me down. Buried me deep under a pile of emotions I wasn't used to feeling. "Then maybe we shouldn't? I don't want to hurt you," I choked out. "Even though I feel like I might die if you don't take me, I just—"

"Charley?" He palmed my breast and squeezed, giving me what I wanted.

"Yeah?"

"Do you want me tonight?" He enunciated each word, needing a clear and explicit answer from me.

Even with everything he'd told me, including the danger, I couldn't help but murmur, "Yes."

"Then shut up and kiss me."

# CHAPTER SIXTEEN

## JACK

THE MOMENT CHARLEY'S TONGUE MET MINE, I LET GO OF HER wrists, and moved my hands to her hips to keep her steady as she arched into me.

She pushed up on her toes as I bent my knees, bringing her core closer to my cock. She ground against me, moving in circles, searching for relief I had every intention of giving her.

"Please tell me that you have a condom," she said between kisses. "Because I didn't think to bring any on the trip. No plans to have sex."

I stood tall, breaking my mouth from hers. "I wasn't looking to get laid, either." I brought my hands to her face and swiped my thumbs over her cheeks, careful not to touch her dimple that was showing. I didn't want to provoke the same startled reaction from her that happened earlier. "Fortunately, Gwen was a bit more optimistic and forward thinking about our plans tonight and shoved two in my pocket. Against my objections, of course."

Her dimple deepened, and God help me, it was adorable. "Mmmm. I both love and hate her for that."

"Hate, huh?" I arched a brow, curious.

When she stepped back and slipped a hand in my pocket, her fingers skimmed the side of my stiff cock, only a thin bit of fabric separating her from touching me. "I'm not a fan of her hand being this close to you."

I smiled, feeling a bit foolish about the grin on my face given she'd already told me she'd never be with me after this mission ended, but I couldn't help it. "I didn't take you for the jealous type."

"I'm not." Her hand left my pocket, and without ever breaking eye contact, she unbuttoned my jeans and slid down my zipper. "Not normally," she added before working her hand through the hole of my boxers to fist my cock like she owned it.

*And you can have it. Everything. All of me.*

I gritted down on my teeth, doing my best not to turn into a wild animal or go all Tarzan on this woman and toss her onto the bed.

She kept her eyes on me, continuing to stand there as if she wasn't casually stroking my cock inside my boxers. But at the feel of her swiping her thumb over the precum at the crown of my dick, I snapped.

I couldn't stand there any longer and not do something with my hands or mouth. Or both. "Sorry, sweetheart, but it's my turn." I removed her hand from my boxers, then stepped back only to drop to my knees, the tight fit of the jeans, snug on my ass, keeping them from falling with me.

I didn't care if the floors were hard on my forty-year-old knees. I didn't care about anything other than tasting this beautiful woman.

"Lift your dress," I demanded, eyes on hers.

She bunched the lightweight fabric and brought it to her hips, never losing sight of my eyes.

"Tell me you're wet," I demanded, my heart pounding hard and fast. I was in that treehouse to warn her about the dangers and come forward about the truth, not to have sex. But there we were anyway, and it felt right even if it shouldn't have.

"I think you're about to find out just how wet," she murmured, her tone falling over me like a sheet of silk. I dropped my eyes to her nude panties, zeroing in on the wet spot I knew would be there.

She was soaked, and knowing I'd made her that way nearly sent me over the edge.

When I brought the pad of my thumb over the seam of her sex, she bucked forward. But I had every intention of dragging this out. Making her ache with need.

"Open your legs for me," I ordered a bit roughly, and she followed my command like a good girl. I bent in and kissed the inside of her thigh before my hand wandered around to her ass cheek and squeezed.

My lips parted, and I opened my mouth just enough to graze my teeth along her satin-covered sex.

"What do you want, Charley?" I looked up at her, and she pinned the fabric of her dress to her body so she could find my eyes.

"Your mouth on me." The words flowed from her without a hint of shyness, and I loved it. Needed more of it.

"If you want that, then tell me the truth," I murmured. "Was it my mouth between your legs in your dream while you squeezed your tit and fingered yourself in bed this morning?"

Her eyes widened, only for a moment, before her face muscles relaxed a touch, and she nodded. "It's been you since Cape Town. No matter how much I didn't want it to be. Every time I've touched myself, in my mind it's been your hand, your mouth, your cock."

At least we were part of the same fucked-up storyline. I didn't understand it, or how it happened so fast, and I didn't need to. We were there, and that's all I needed.

I hooked my thumbs at the hem of her panties and lowered the satin. My breath hitched at the sight of her beautiful bare cunt; swollen, pink, glistening and ready for me.

Her body shuddered when I dropped her panties to hold her thighs. The anticipation was building for us both. And I could've died a happy man the moment my mouth made contact with her clit, her arousal coating my tongue. But I needed to live long enough to save this woman from whatever she didn't want me involved in, so no dying today.

I also had to shake free the worry or I'd get lost in my head. And the only thing I wanted to get lost in was the moment. With her. Finally, with her.

"Jack . . ." Hearing her cry out my name spurred me on. But her, "Oh my God," as I sucked and flicked my tongue, then stroked what was clearly her most sensitive spot, sent me into overdrive.

Her legs were shaking, and I was worried she might fall, so I ordered, "On the bed."

She wordlessly did as I said and shifted the netting to the side. I slid over on my knees, grabbed hold of her legs and pulled her just to the edge, burying my face beneath her dress, sinking my mouth between her silky thighs.

I worked one hand over her thigh. Gripping. Massaging. Helping ease her muscles in one spot while she tensed beneath my mouth in the other.

"You trying to kill me with a massage while you go down on me?" she whispered before moaning a long O sound.

"Does it feel good?" With my free hand, I dove two fingers into her pussy, penetrating her tight walls.

"Yessssss," she cried the moment my tongue landed back on her clit.

She brought her legs over my shoulders and drew her pussy closer to my face, moving with each stroke of my tongue. Fucking my face. God help me, I loved it. Loved everything about her.

"I'm close. So, so clo-oohhhh," she cried a minute later, climaxing before she even finished her last word.

My heart was officially on the floor. Gone from my chest. And if I'd truly never get to be with this woman again after tonight, well, the jungle could fucking keep it, then. I'd have no use for that particular muscle ever again.

"Jack, I need to feel you inside me," she begged.

I pulled my head from beneath her dress and lowered her legs from over my shoulders before kissing her knee. "You do, do you?" I searched for the condom in my pocket, set it on the bed next to her, then stood and finished the job of removing my shoes, jeans, and boxers.

"I do." She sat up, took off her dress and chucked it while I tossed my shirt. Her bra went next. And she was glorious and completely bare before me.

Standing there, nude in the treehouse, I couldn't help but take a moment to stare at her. God, she was stunning.

Taking my cock in hand, I eyed her luscious tits as they lifted and fell while she worked to catch her breath. "You're so damn beautiful." Emotion swelled in my chest as we locked eyes.

She cupped one breast before rolling her nipple between her finger and thumb like I was desperate to do. "I need you." A shaky breath later. "I *want* you, Jack." She shifted to the center of the bed, making room for me.

I was tethered to the floor by her words. By how she'd said "want" as if somehow knowing that word meant something to me. *I want you, Jack,* played out in my head again. Then one more time. I barely recognized the grit and depth in my own voice as I assured her, "I want you, too."

Getting my feet to work, I moved the netting aside, snatched the condom wrapper, then joined her on the bed.

My head was spinning a little. This wasn't a hallucination. It was real. And all I could do was hope she'd somehow change her mind about us, because there wasn't a chance in hell one time with her would be enough.

I secured the condom on, then swiped my hand from her knee up to her sex. She flinched the second I touched her, still sensitive from her first orgasm, and I was damn determined to give her another one.

I straddled her, placing my forearms on each side of her body to hold the brunt of my weight. Then I used my knee to nudge her legs a bit farther apart.

Her hand went to my chest, and the battle warring in her eyes appeared to be the same one going on in my head. The fear of this being our one and only time.

"You okay?" she mouthed, the words never actually breaking free in volume.

I couldn't answer that with the truth, so I shifted my weight down her body, losing eye contact. I noticed a scar beneath her rib cage, one that looked over a decade old. One she'd yet to tell me about. She'd told me a hell of a lot of other stories that night last month, why not this one? And that made me nervous. *Who hurt you?*

I brought my lips to her skin and kissed the mark, then focused on her nipple, lightly teasing it between my teeth.

She buried one hand in my hair while reaching between our bodies, grabbing hold of my cock. I inhaled a sharp breath of expectation. I'd be buried deep inside this woman soon, and . . .

I sucked her nipple a bit longer, never wanting tonight to end, then finally lined our bodies up again. I slanted my mouth over hers, and she met me halfway. That was exactly how I wanted to take her, with our tongues touching.

Her hand was still on my shaft, and she positioned me at her center.

The second I pushed deep inside her, our connection was complete. I didn't let myself stop to examine the current racing through me. How my entire being, from my head to my toes, felt electrified. Instead, I welcomed the tight walls of her pussy closing around me. Squeezing me.

And I didn't break her kiss and warn her I was beyond screwed in the feelings department when it came to how amazing our bodies felt together. Instead, I thrusted harder, faster, and even deeper, coaxing her to moan and cry and beg for more.

I did the things I knew she needed. Because she deserved it. All of it. And I felt every single reaction from her. Every shift in movement. Every breath. Every touch.

I was doing my best not to come, but being inside her made the wait damn difficult. But I could also tell she wouldn't be getting off from missionary sex. And before the thin rein I had on my control snapped, I asked, "How do you like it? Want it?"

She buried her fingertips into my biceps, holding me tight. "This is perfect, trust me."

I went still and stared down at her. She blew at her bangs, so they were out of her way, allowing me to see her even better. "You can be honest with me. I'm not coming until you do, so I'll happily try every angle until I find a way to get you off, sweetheart. I just might die in the process of holding back while trying."

She chuckled, then let go of my arm to palm my chest. "This really is amazing. But no one has ever asked me, um . . ."

I closed one eye, not wanting to hear about the *anyones* who'd ever tried anything with her.

"I have this idea I'd like to try." She wet her lips. "It kind of popped into my head while we were walking the trail last night. When you picked me up and saved me from death-by-ants."

Lifting my brows, I rasped, "Go on."

"I need to be on all fours." She planted a chaste kiss on my lips, then patted my arm, signaling for me to allow her to switch positions. I wasn't about to object to this woman placing her ass in my face. That was a body part I'd yet to see aside from in her swimsuit.

I slowly eased free from her, checked the condom was still intact, then tried to hide my gasp of pleasure as she went to her hands and knees. I grabbed hold of her hips, taking in the sight of her gorgeous ass and slender waist.

"I kind of want you to do something I've never done . . . but it happened in my head last night." She looked back at me from over her shoulder. "Spank me."

Not what I expected. "I can't hurt you," I shot back the only response I had in me. "Never."

"I think it'll feel good. I mean, no clue, but I kind of want to feel the sting of your hand on my flesh just before you rub your hand over the mark before thrusting into me."

*Well, when you put it that way. Fucking fuck, okay.* "You sure?" I gripped her hips a bit harder, my cock nudging her ass cheeks, ready to go.

"Very," she said with a nod, then faced forward and

lowered her shoulders a touch, fisting the bedding in preparation.

How hard was I supposed to spank her? I was clueless. I wet my lips, drew my hand back, still a bit uneasy, then connected my big hand with her ass cheek.

I instantly felt like a jerk at the sight of the red mark on her flesh, but that emotion disappeared the second she said, "Feel how wet you just made me."

Obeying, I skated my palm to her pussy, and well, damn.

"Now. Please, fill me now," she demanded.

*Yes, ma'am.*

I positioned my cock at her center and pushed deep inside her.

I wrapped a hand around her body and thrummed her clit while we moved together, effortlessly catching the same rhythm.

Leaning in, I kissed her upper back, then buried myself as deep as possible. When she cried my name, the tremor of ecstasy shooting through her, I finally found relief myself. I came hard. Shattered into pieces as I grunted and groaned.

We both collapsed onto our backs a moment later. She turned to the side and set her arm across my chest, hugging me. "That was . . . all of it was . . ."

"Yeah," I murmured in agreement. "Same page." Taking another minute to catch my breath, I faced her, capturing her leg between mine as I'd accidentally done in bed that morning.

She pulled her arm back and planted her hand on my chest, right over my heart. "We're doing that again, right? You have one more condom?" She smirked. "I know you're vintage and all, but tell me you can go for round two soon."

I released a hearty laugh and reached around to grab hold of her ass, then remembered a touch too late she might still be sore from where my hand had left a mark. So, I eased my grip but didn't let go. "I can go again," I promised. "I can go all night with you. But since we only have one more condom, I'll have to be creative in how I make you come."

She chuckled, then closed one eye while tipping her head. "I'm pretty sure we have animals outside listening to us." And then this gorgeous, incredible woman added, "Jack London, teaching those animals the true meaning of the *Call of the Wild*," and I broke into laughter.

*Yeah . . . I'm going to fall in love.*

# CHAPTER SEVENTEEN

## JACK

"Rise and shine, lovebirds."

Not that I ever really fell asleep—too paranoid to do that with Charley in my arms in the jungle, and a possible serial kidnapper on the grounds—but Stephen's boisterous and booming voice just outside the door did have me jolting in the bed a touch.

Charley blinked a few times, slowly coming to. Her blonde hair spilled over her shoulders, covering one breast, leaving the other nipple exposed and taut, teasing me. "What time is it?"

"Sun isn't up yet." I could've figured out something more specific, but my focus was elsewhere. I was doing my best to hold myself back from dipping in to kiss her breast.

Stephen's second knock sliced through my thoughts, cutting off my efforts at fantasizing what it'd be like to wake next to her every morning. I'd have coffee just the way she'd like it on the nightstand as her good morning. Well, after easing her awake with my tongue between her thighs first.

"The next team mission starts now," Stephen announced, killing my second attempt to mentally map out a future with the woman who didn't want one with me. "You have five minutes to get dressed and meet us at the players' lodge. Wear comfortable clothes. You'll be in the jungle all day."

"Did he just say we'll be in the jungle all day, or did I hallucinate?" Charley murmured, but I lost track of everything yet again, because she was naked in my arms and turning to face me. I could feel the wetness between her thighs as she shimmied her pussy against my wide-awake cock.

"Yeah, I'm going to need to fuck you right now," I growled out before flipping her beneath me, unable to stop myself. I laced our fingers together alongside her head and leaned in and kissed her.

"No condoms," she reminded me, a touch of disappointment edging her tone. "And we only have five minutes."

"I can come in under sixty. No problem," I joked. But with her, yeah, no issue there. "Damn the condom problem, though." My shoulders collapsed in defeat, and I let go of her hands as I fell back alongside her.

"Maybe Gwen has more?"

Her question caught me off guard. Because it gave me hope. Was she changing her mind about us?

". . . I forgot," she said, tacking the words to the end of a sentence she never started. Not out loud, anyway.

A heavy, almost painful feeling gathered in my chest and stomach. "Right." I swallowed, then swung my legs to the side of the bed, shoving the mosquito netting away from my face as I sat.

My body tensed at the feel of her hand on the center of my back. "I don't know what to say."

I looked over my shoulder at her. "Do you have anything different to say from last night?"

Her mouth pinched tight, and she shook her head while drawing up the cover, hiding her body.

"Then don't say anything." I stood and moved the netting aside and walked naked over to my suitcase to search for "jungle attire." My dick had yet to go soft despite the pain of her words, so I closed my eyes and took a few seconds to try and will my hard-on away.

"What, um, do you think the challenge will be?"

I opened my eyes at her tentative tone and turned to see her standing behind me. The thin white bedspread wrapped around her like a toga. It was cute that she was hiding as if I didn't already have every inch of her memorized. "I don't know."

Her eyes dropped between my thighs, which didn't help my situation at all. Especially not when I caught her tongue sliding along the seam of her lips as she continued to stare at my cock.

"I'm going to wash up and change in the bathroom," I said, needing a minute alone to steel my thoughts and pull myself together after having another night I'd never forget.

"Yeah, okay. I'll get dressed while you're in there, then."

I nodded, unable to say anything else, then I snatched my things and started for the small en suite.

"Jack, wait."

I froze outside the door, my hand on the knob in preparation to escape.

"Do you hate me now like you said you would?" There was a tenderness there I wasn't sure she'd ever used with me before. Raw and vulnerable. It was enough to make my shoulders collapse before I faced her.

She continued to shield herself with the bedding, and it felt like a secondary wall between us. The first wall—the fact she wouldn't tell me the truth about who she was running from and why—wasn't tangible like the sheet but just as frustrating of a barrier.

"No, I don't hate you." I held my clothes in front of me, feeling a bit strange about being buck naked after she'd sucked the life from me, gagging on my cock mere hours ago.

"But?" She lifted a perfectly shaped brow that disappeared beneath her sweeping bangs.

I expelled a deep breath, wanting to tell her I hated *myself* for taking things further knowing damn well the crushing pain it'd cause me today. But I couldn't get those words out. They would likely make her feel bad or guilty, and I refused to hurt her.

Her eyes fell to the wood floors beneath her feet. "I'm sorry."

"Don't be sorry," I reassured her. "I'm an adult. I made the decision I made." And then I went into the bathroom before she had a chance to look at me and shred me with her eyes.

I closed the door and dropped my clothes in the tight space. Resting the back of my head to the door, I closed my eyes and covered my face with my palm, trying to remind myself I was there for a mission, not to fall in love.

A few frustrated breaths later, I got my shit together, changed and brushed my teeth, then joined Charley in the room.

She'd swapped out the bedsheet for lightweight khaki pants and a white tank top with a black bikini top visible beneath it, the strings tied at the nape of her neck. Her hair was in a messy bun with a few wispy strands around her face. No makeup. Not that she needed any. She was naturally beautiful. And those big eyes of hers pointed my way while she held up her toothbrush. "Almost ready. Let me just brush my teeth, and we can go."

I stepped aside so she could get into the bathroom, doing my best not to circle her waist and draw her to me. To tell her she belonged in my arms. That she'd be safe. That I'd fuck up all the assholes in the world who so much as made her cry if she'd only let me.

I stuffed my shit in my suitcase, put on my running shoes, then waited for her by the door. I needed air. Fresh air. Not air where the smell of sex still lingered. It was going to be the death of me.

I flicked at a piece of lint on my plain white tee that I'd paired with khaki cargo shorts, anxiously awaiting her return. When the bathroom door opened, she gave me a hesitant smile and nod, letting me know she was all set.

After she stored her toothbrush in her bag, I quietly snatched her suitcase and waited for her to successfully make it down the ladder before I navigated the thing, bringing one bag down at a time.

We walked in silence to building one where our team had slept. It was already empty, so I dropped our bags off there and we went in search of everyone at the players' lodge.

"Hey," Carter said the second he spotted me by the pool. "I need a word before we go." He looked at Charley and then back at me.

"She knows," I said, answering the question he was asking without asking.

"I'd still like to talk in private," Carter noted, then tipped his head toward one of the camera-free zones on the backside of the pool area, walking in that direction without waiting for me.

"Yeah, okay." I looked around the patio area of the players' lodge where all the teams were already split up and waiting for instructions. The sun had yet to rise, but there was still enough light out to see everyone. "Be right back," I told

Charley, and waited for her nod of understanding, and for her to join the rest of our team before I joined Carter.

"What's up?" I asked him. "You learn anything new from Gray or Camila?" I was still trying to wrap my head around Camila managing to become even more of an insider than us for this show.

When Carter had summoned me by the pool after our little uncomfortable fight last night, he'd dropped the shocking news on me swiftly and with blunt force, *"I'm going to kill her. If she survives this, I'll . . ."*

I wasn't sure if I'd ever seen Carter react like that about anyone. I supposed it was different since he'd known Camila forever, all the way back to his childhood days in Texas, but the man kept surprising me with these "human-like" sides he rarely revealed.

*"How'd she become a last-minute sponsor?"* I'd asked.

*"Doubt there was anything last minute about it,"* he'd retorted. *"She was just a late arrival, which I'm sure she had a cover story for. And she used my money to put her life at risk, which just pisses me off even more. I mean, yeah, she's on all my accounts and has the OK from me to use the money anytime, but not to risk her neck and—"* He'd cut himself off, his eyes narrowing as if realizing he'd been rambling, an oddity. *"She told Gray to tell me she'll be fine and not to worry, but she thought we'd need someone deeper on the inside and went ahead and made the move."*

"Jack?" Carter prompted, and I'd realized I'd distracted myself with yesterday's memories and forgotten he had something new to tell me now.

"Yeah, sorry. So, what'd you learn?" I folded my arms, but I was unable to stop myself from stealing a quick look at Charley from the corner of my eye.

Lucy had a hand on Charley's arm, and a knowing smile

on her face like she could tell what happened between Charley and me in the treehouse.

"Gray doesn't think our suspect is one of the sponsors. No one from the list has been part of every season, and based on who Camila met when she arrived last night, only a handful of people requested to be on-site," Carter explained, drawing my focus back his way.

"So, you're thinking it's someone who's part of the show's production?" At least we could narrow down our list.

Carter's grimace didn't do wonders for my nerves. "I don't know. Gray tapped into Gwen's library camera and pulled images of the three guys we assume are judges who watched from there yesterday. No red flags. It's possible there are more judges that watched from another room, though."

"So, still in limbo, but why the grim reaper vibes?" I was getting tired of him beating around the bush.

"Camila reached out to Gray and let him know that whatever game was originally planned today was canceled because of a special request made by parties unknown. And that makes me wonder if today's jungle adventure is a trap."

"You think our target suspects something is up, and they're trying to get rid of us?"

"Possibly. So, heads on a swivel."

I started to turn, assuming Carter was done with me, but he shot his arm out, stopping me from joining the team. "Fuck, what else is it?"

Carter lowered his arm, directing a passing glance over our team before his attention stopped on Charley. "I obviously told Gray about your connection to Charlotte yesterday. Camila, no surprise, wouldn't open up about her involvement in any of this."

*But?*

"Gray pulled an image of Charlotte from the cameras here

and ran her photo through our software. Lucy's unfiltered one, too."

My heart fucking stopped. I'd made Charley a promise and clearly remembered the fear in her voice when she'd begged me to destroy her image.

"You two," Stephen piped up, interrupting us, "over here now. Time to go over the rules."

"What is it? Just tell me." I braced myself, knowing Carter was about to lay me out with some bad news. And why wouldn't that be the case? Story of my life.

"Charley's not who you think." Carter kept his voice low and his eyes on her. "She's a criminal, Jack. She was part of a crew involved in a string of heists as their getaway driver. The night of her last heist before fleeing the States, two undercover FBI agents were killed."

I backed up.

Then one step more.

My hand dove through my hair before going to the back of my neck.

*No.*

*No way.*

"She's on the FBI's wanted list." Carter's final words were the nail in the coffin of my heart when he said, "Charlotte *Lennox* is wanted for murdering one of those Feds that night."

# CHAPTER EIGHTEEN

## CHARLOTTE

"It was so incredibly awkward." Lucy sipped her glass of orange juice, her eyes bouncing back and forth between Mason and Mya, quietly chatting about ten feet away from us. "Ever since that one kiss yesterday morning, Mason has barely looked at me. And I'm pretty sure it's because of her."

I chanced a look at the "her" in question, and it dawned on me that Mya's blonde hair didn't match her darker brows. Was she trying to become a target for the bad guy they were hunting? *That's brave.*

Mya met my eyes for a moment, as if sensing she was the subject of discussion, gave me a polite smile, then returned her attention to the man who clearly still had my sister's pulse racing from her overnight adventure in the treehouse. Not that I could be judgy. My pulse was still off the charts because of Jack.

After doing a quick inventory of the camera locations, as well as the three cameramen near Stephen, I admitted to Lucy, "Pretty sure Mason and Mya used to be a thing." The Band-Aid of bad news needed to be ripped off at some point before my sister landed herself in heartbreak territory. "They all know each other. Everyone on our team. Jack told me last night."

Lucy's glass about slipped from her hand, but she saved it from falling and calling more attention to us. "I knew it." She shook her head, eyes wide and pointed their way. "Are they in cahoots together to win the money?" Before I could answer, she continued, "They were all acting weird in the room last night, especially Mya and Oliver. Like as in, they didn't argue. Which would be the first time they've gotten along since we met them." She sipped her juice, eyes volleying between Oliver and Mason. "Oliver and Mason both want her, huh?"

"Okay, that's a lot of questions," I said, my gaze flying over to Carter and Jack. I was growing uneasy at the way Jack's back muscles kept tensing at whatever Carter was quietly sharing with him. "The only answer you need to know is that they're not here for the money," I told her once I found her eyes again. "They work together on a security team. And they're here to catch a serial kidnapper who's been abducting women after each season ends. Six women who'd been contestants on the show are missing."

I quickly snatched the glass from my sister, knowing the truth I'd laid out for her was likely to send it into free fall, and set it aside on a nearby bar-top table.

Lucy's nose wrinkled and eyes narrowed in question as she pinned me with her signature worried look. "Are we in danger?"

"Every woman here is, but I'm also concerned Jack and his friends will figure out who we are." Too paranoid someone would overhear me, I mouthed the words, "They have ties to the government." Thank God I'd taught her to read lips a long time ago.

"I'm so sorry." Her panicky blue eyes met mine. "You were right not to come here."

"It's not your fault." I tried to be as reassuring as possible. Too much panic could show our hand and expose us just as easily as Jack's team's research could. Plus, I couldn't get over the thought we were meant to be here. Even if it didn't make sense.

I looked over at Jack but discovered Carter's eyes on me. A shiver ran up my spine. *If looks could kill. Shit.*

"So, you spent last night learning about this with Jack? Not . . . you know?"

My eyes snapped back to my sister, momentarily forgetting Carter's broody and mildly threatening look my way, and I dipped into my mind to recall every sexy little thing that happened with Jack. Those memories were much easier to latch on to than the heavier topics we'd discussed before making love.

From our kiss, to how he'd buried his face between my legs and used his tongue to deliver one of the best orgasms of my life. To him worshiping every inch of my body with hot kisses. Me tasting him for the first time, even though I embarrassingly choked on his cock. Then riding him hard as I chased another orgasm . . .

*"Fuck me how you want it, not how you think I do,"* he'd rasped, reading me perfectly, knowing I needed to hit a certain spot to bring me to orgasm. I wasn't some romance book heroine who came just because the guy had a magical dick. No, climaxing from sex required work (for me, at least). Different angles and pressure points. And Jack was all in, completely and unabashedly focused on me. It wasn't something I'd ever experienced before. *"I'll love it, too, trust me,"* he'd assured me, as if sensing my slight hesitation to change course.

I'd spun around and rode him reverse cowgirl. I could still feel his hands on my hips, holding me tightly when I'd leaned forward, grinding my clit against him as I rocked to his steady thrusts while holding his strong legs.

*"You're going to kill me. It'll be a nice death, though,"* Jack had said with a hearty, sexy chuckle after we'd both come that time.

Everything was so amazingly different with him than what I'd ever experienced before. I wasn't sure if it was because he was older and more emotionally mature than most guys my age, or if he was just that great of a guy to begin with. But the way he'd guided me, took care of me, and always made sure my needs were met was just . . . well, I didn't have words for it.

"Charley? Your face is pink. Cheeks the color of cherries. You remembering last night?" Lucy asked with a smirk, bulldozing through my thoughts. "So, how many times did he get you off?"

"A lot," I confessed without even trying to fight it, because there weren't many secrets between us. But she didn't need to hear about how the memory of him spanking me was currently turning me on. "We should focus on the reason why they're here, though."

"Right. Missing women." Lucy grimaced. "Do they have anything in common? Like does the bad guy have a fetish of some kind leading him to pick certain women?" She wrinkled her nose at her words, and I could tell our situation hadn't really settled in. The fear that needed to be there was absent from her gaze.

In Lucy's mind, we were discussing a Netflix series, not real life. Then again, we were on a reality show right now, so maybe fiction and true life were becoming one big blur for me as well.

"Blonde. Our age. They're all skilled in some way, but everyone here is, or they wouldn't be on the show, right?"

"Well, that's creepy."

Before I could go on, I spotted Jack and Carter starting our way. Jack's grave look meant sharing more information with Lucy would have to wait.

"Everyone gather around," Stephen hollered, derailing my chance to probe Jack for details about what news Carter had burdened him with. "There's been a change in the schedule, and we've added a new event." He continued to gesture, encouraging us to come closer. "A good old-fashioned treasure hunt has been planned. A little play on the history of the legendary search for the Lost City of Z." Stephen held up a map and pointed to a black X on it. "You won't be tracking down the city, obviously, just a fun little item we've hidden. And this adventure is an overnight experience in the jungle. You have thirty-six hours to retrieve the item and make it back. If you're late, or don't find your 'lost treasure,' you're automatically cut from the competition."

"We're spending the night in the jungle?" asked one of the women with an Australian accent from another team, shooting her hand in the air. "You're for real?"

Stephen lowered the map and began rolling it up. "Yes, and each team will have a different map with a different item to locate. You won't be in each other's way."

"So, this is a survivor thing?" the asshole who'd dared to face off with Jack yesterday asked. "What happens if we get in trouble? Danger? Do you have people on standby to save us from an anaconda? Jaguar?"

"No, you were selected for this competition because you're supposed to already have the necessary skills to complete such tasks," Stephen responded.

I was even more curious about everyone else's skills now

that he brought that part up. I knew mine. Lucy's. Was there a pattern there as well in terms of what the kidnapper looked for in his next victim?

"So," Stephen continued, pointing to three backpacks being carried out by a crewman, "in each bag you'll have basic items, such as canteens, granola bars, a first aid kit, and a few other essentials to help you." He checked his watch. "Everyone on your team must make it back or your entire team is cut," he added while handing out the maps.

Oliver accepted our map, then grabbed the backpack as well.

"Each team will have a cameraman following them around. Don't engage with him. Act like he's not there," Stephen said with a nod. Then he tossed out a quick, "Good luck. Your time starts now," and walked away.

Jack swiveled his black ball cap forward facing as he maneuvered around a few people in his way to get to me. "You want to do this?" he asked, his tone a bit distant. From the looks of it, he'd erected his own wall, copying my moves from the treehouse.

"Not really," I answered flatly as Lucy left us alone to talk. "We don't have a choice, right?"

"There's always a choice." Jack folded his arms, and I lost sight of his eyes as he lowered his focus to the pavers beneath his sneakers. "But I need you to know I'm concerned someone may be on to my people, and they want us to lose this game so we can be cut."

"What makes you say that?"

"Because this wasn't on the original agenda. It's a last-minute add. It's possible we're overreading the situation, though."

"Well, maybe being cut isn't such a bad thing. I don't want Lucy here any longer than she needs to be." It was the truth, but it felt so selfish. Women were missing and another woman at the lodge could be next. "If we lose, then your chances of finding . . ." I let my words trail off when I realized our designated cameraman was now lurking nearby.

"We have someone else on the inside," he whispered the reminder once the cameraman moved on to another part of the patio, and Jack set his eyes back on me.

*And people on the outside.* Was that enough to complete his mission? Was that what he was trying to suggest? Was he giving me a way out? "But?" I felt that word hanging in the air between us even though he'd yet to utter it.

"Carter won't leave without her, and I'm on the same page as him. Camila's like family to him."

"Ca*mila*?" It was the first time he'd shared her name, and my stomach flipped. *Wait. It couldn't be . . .* "Mila."

"Mila?" he echoed back, arms falling to his sides as our eyes met.

"Your friend, is she from Texas, but she's living in South America where her mom's from?" There went my world again. Spinning off its axis as I connected the dots. "Mila was my friend who canceled on me at the bar last month. She was in Cape Town for work. Is she your friend who canceled, too?"

Jack blinked a few times. "You know her," he said under his breath. "Fuck." He cursed again, then backed up a step. "You're not just some random . . ."

I had no clue Mila worked in private security, or that she had "visions." But then again, hadn't she been the one to suggest I move when we'd been neighbors years ago? It was like she knew I needed to get out of there but never directly told me, only planted the seed. And it grew with my paranoia, and Lucy and I took off two days later.

Now the question was, did I still trust her? If she was working with Jack, what if they were both playing me?

No, in my heart I refused to believe that. There'd been plenty of chances over the years for Camila to turn me over if that was the case. And Jack, well, yeah, I trusted that man. I didn't even know how not to at this point.

"We need to go," Carter said, breaking through what was about to become a complex what-if game in my head. "We *are* going, right?" He looked back and forth between us, and I turned my attention to Jack.

I closed my eyes. Just for one second. And I felt it. The decision I had to make.

"Yeah, we're going, and we need to make it back," I said while opening my eyes, making my choice.

"She knows Camila," Jack said to Carter.

The way he shared the news, the grit and decisiveness in his tone, it was as if he was letting him know a hell of a lot more than just that fact.

Carter's brows snapped together before he studied me. His broad chest inflated with a deep inhalation, then he let it go and simply walked away.

"Why do I get the feeling there's something else you're not telling me?" I murmured just before our cameraman approached and pointed toward the jungle, our signal to get started.

Jack frowned and whispered back as we began walking side by side, "Because there is."

# CHAPTER NINETEEN

## CHARLOTTE

"WILL YOU TALK TO ME?" WE'D BEEN HIKING FOR FOUR OR five hours, dodging nature's obstacles, and Jack hadn't uttered a word to me unless it was related to the game. But with our camera guy, a six-foot-four dude who looked better suited for a football field, finally up ahead of us, it was a good time for him to spill whatever Carter told him.

When Jack ignored me, I stopped walking and waited for him to turn. And maybe I was also exhausted. Leave it to me to be the stubborn one who'd refused a snack on our last break. So, a quick rest was needed.

He wordlessly dropped the backpack he'd taken over carrying and removed one of the canteens before facing me. The impending offer of water was appreciated. The continued silent treatment, not so much.

If I mimicked one of my sister's best pouts, would that work on him? Would he open up and share what was bothering him? I swiped back the stray hairs from my messy bun clinging to my damp skin as I waited for him to eat up the distance between us. "What'd Carter tell you earlier?"

More silence was all that greeted me as Jack pushed the canteen my way.

"I'm fine." A straight up lie. I was a bit lightheaded, to be honest.

I folded my arms, but the man didn't back down. He nudged my arm with the bottle and finally made eye contact.

*Bad idea.* I may have sucked at pouting, but I could stare a man down like I was Angelina Jolie in an action flick. The problem was, Jack had that skill as well, and he double downed and hit me hard with his own look. His intensity would have been chilling had it not also ignited my need to win.

"You realize I can do this all day, right?" At least he broke the silence, but the menacing tone from him wasn't doing wonders for my spine. I wilted a touch, and a chill chased up along the curve of my body.

"I don't think we have all day to stare at each other, but I'm game if you are." My words were soft but still carried the appropriate amount of sass I'd wanted.

Only inches of space (and secrets) now stood between us as he dipped his chin, so we were closer in eye level. "Drink the damn water, *Charlotte.*"

"Oh, so it's like that, is it?"

His eyes dropped to my lips for a second like he was contemplating lifting the canteen between us to force me to drink.

"Why are you mad at me? I know it's not about earlier." *About my rejection. And that's for your own benefit, trust me.*

When he met my eyes again, his gaze had softened a touch, and that one look managed to rattle my defenses. My arms uncrossed as more of my self-imposed barrier faltered.

I had to resist the wild impulse to place my hands on his chest and search for the comfort of his heartbeat.

"Pick a reason, sweetheart."

I'd take Charlotte over the bite in his hissed term of endearment, so totally different from how he'd said it to me as we'd made love.

I was exhausted from trekking through the woods, knowing it was possibly a trap, and I still had more questions than answers. My mood was going south, and I was growing crankier on this man more than he probably deserved. But yeah, patience—so clearly not my virtue. Should've had that inked to the inside of my other wrist.

"Please." I had to push the word out. It was uncomfortable and made me uneasy. I didn't beg or plead for anything, not even the truth. And definitely not from a man. Well, not since the one time I'd had to do it at twenty, and I'd vowed never to do it again. "Tell me." I did my best to keep those words sugary instead of full of vinegar, but despite my attempts, and based on the way his bladed jawline tightened and his nostrils flared, I'd been more devil than angel. *I'm a work in progress, what can I say?*

"Drink." The word was a grunt that cut through the air, and his ability to abstain from revealing whatever was in his head was maddening.

I peeked around him, checking the location of our teammates. I was so focused on our stare down, I hadn't even heard anyone grab the backpack, but the bag and our team were about twenty-five feet away and waiting on us. Lucy peeled down the granola bar wrapper as she chatted with the cameraman. *That's it. Distract him for me. Thank you, thank you.*

When my attention returned to my current problem, that problem took one step back and took a sip from the canteen himself. My gaze flitted to his tanned throat as it bobbed with each swallow, and then he completely killed my focus by catching a drop of water on his bottom lip with his tongue.

*Shit.* Wrong time to be thinking about how Jack had gone down on me as if he'd been given a roadmap of my damn vagina to study ahead of time.

"You like to piss me off, don't you?" That was fair, but not what I was expecting as Jack lowered the canteen to rest at his side. "Stubborn and frustrating one second, and then looking at me with hearts in your eyes the next."

"I'm not a hearts-in-the-eyes kind of girl," I scoffed, defending myself. *I'm just stupidly turned on by your tongue. Your eyes. How well you rock a backwards hat.* "But whiplash, I know," I relented since he was technically right.

"You two okay?"

Jack looked back over his shoulder to answer Mason. "We'll be with y'all in a second," he told him loud enough for everyone else to hear before facing me again. He pushed the canteen at me, and I was ready for round two of being a stubborn brat in denying my thirst while waiting for answers.

"I'll drink if you tell me what Carter said to you." I was about to lock my arms across my chest like a kid again, but he cupped my chin with his free hand, catching me off guard.

It was a light touch, but commanding nonetheless, and coupled with the severity of his stare, he had my attention, and I felt obliged to obey.

"You're going to drink, Charlotte. Because you're dehydrated and might faint. And I'm not carrying your ass through the jungle while you take a nap in my arms. Got it?" he borderline growled out the order before letting go of my chin only to snatch my wrist, bringing my hand between us so I'd accept the water.

And I did.

I took it.

My body thanked me about ten times over after I finished drinking.

"Thank you." His gratitude caught me off guard. That should have been my line.

"For being a good girl?" *Where did that come from?* I shoved the canteen his way, and he glared at me while accepting it. The heat in his expression was tangible. Why was I poking the bear?

"You're so far from good right now, what you really need is a—"

"Spanking," I whispered, shocked that word popped from my mouth at a time like this.

His brows slanted as he rasped, "You have no idea how badly I want to swat that ass of yours right now." Oh, he was pissed, and it wasn't from my attitude.

But why? What in the world would he . . . My thoughts died the second I connected the dots. "You know." I stepped back, and Jack's eyes went wide, but this time he wasn't looking at me.

"Get behind me," he whispered, then snatched my waist, not giving me much of a choice but to move into the position he suddenly deemed necessary. "We're not alone."

I tipped my head, trying to look around him, unsure what had his attention. Animal? Person? Three-headed snake?

"I don't see anything," I said, my words nearly dying in his shoulder where I was smooshed against him.

"They don't see us yet," Jack warned. "Don't. Fucking. Move." The words were low, yet their gravity could puncture a hole right through a person.

Jack knew I was wanted for murder, but he was still willing to use his body as a shield from whatever was out there watching us.

He lowered the canteen to the ground, then stood tall,

reaching back to find my waist again. He stepped forward, urging me to walk with him, and then he spun me around, so I was up against a tree twice my width. He pinned himself flat against me, and I felt every ridge of his body press into mine as he held me in that position. "I think we stumbled upon a narcotrafficking route." That was not the answer I expected or wanted to hear. "Carter," Jack called out, the name more like a crackle in the air, nearly blending with the sounds of nature.

"I see them, and they see us. I'm approaching," Carter responded, taking the chance to answer regardless of our shit situation, which meant he must've realized we'd already been made.

I twisted my head to the side to get a better look at him and the others. Carter raised one hand in the air as he left the trail to go into the thick of the woods. He placed his other hand behind his back and flicked his wrist, gesturing to someone.

Mason tossed him a pocketknife, and how in the hell Carter caught it without looking was beyond me, but they both made everything look so effortless. And Mason, without missing a beat, went back to shielding Lucy the same as Jack was for me.

Carter began directly addressing the traffickers, speaking in another language, presumably Portuguese. He held up his other hand now, keeping both as fists to hide the pocketknife.

"What's he saying?" I tried to look around the tree for a better view of where Carter was heading, but Jack buried his fingertips into my side, practically forcing me to hold still.

"I said not to move, and I meant it," he hissed into my ear, anger still clinging to his words. I had a feeling his clipped tone was partly for me, but also a result of his hyperawareness of the danger.

"How many people? How do you know they're traffickers?" I whispered, my lips almost catching the bark of the tree. "What if they're here for us? For me?" Now that he knew the truth, no sense in trying to paint a different picture than the very ugly one which was my life.

"Three armed tangos in camo. They're protecting territory. Guards," he quickly explained. "I doubt for us. But that doesn't mean they'll just let us go. Not since we found a smuggling route."

It was an awful time to freeze up with fear as memories from my last day in California tried to catapult to mind, but the second I heard the pop of gunfire, my head went there. Right to the past. To the day I took a life. To the day I watched blood spill everywhere inside that bastard's five-car garage.

"Charley." There was a voice in my head. Or was it in my ear? Hands sliding around my body, spinning me around. Palms on my face. Eyes on my eyes.

It was Jack. Not the *him* I feared. But we weren't safe. Not yet. We were in danger.

"We need to run." Jack held my cheeks, searching for confirmation I understood him. "The three men are down. Carter handled one. Gray or maybe Jesse took two kill shots from wherever they're hiding in the woods watching us. But more will most likely come."

*Gray? Jesse? Kill shots?* There'd been more shots while I'd been lost in the past? How long had I been walking down the memory lane of Hell?

"The cameraman took off, so we don't have eyes on us, and my guys will have our six, but we can't stay here. We need to move," Jack continued when I'd yet to get my voice or my feet to work.

He must've realized I was still stuck in my head. Stepping

back, he hoisted me up and tossed me over his shoulder, carrying me away from the chaos. He moved fast, pinning my legs to his chest as my ass bounced on his shoulder, and I flattened my palms on his back.

"Lucy," I cried out when I saw her. She wasn't being carried like me. She was on her own two feet, hand in Mason's while running alongside him.

"Put me down. I'm okay," I told Jack as we came up alongside a dead body. The man was in camo, and his face was painted green. He had a knife in the side of his throat, eyes open.

Carter stabbed him?

As Jack lowered me to the ground, I searched for the other bodies, finding Oliver and Carter taking the dead men's weapons.

"There'll be more," Carter announced as he handed Jack a handgun. "They had radios on them." He turned the knob, killing the staticky noise over the line, cutting off contact with whoever the men had been trying to talk to before their lives had ended. "We need to keep moving until I can get a signal to Gray."

"But didn't your friends shoot these two guys? Where are they?" Lucy asked, doing a three-sixty, as confused as me.

"Close enough for kill shots with a long gun," Oliver told her. "Far enough away they're not already here for an immediate assist."

"Oh." Lucy frowned, then looked at me for what to do, but I was as clueless as she was. And that didn't sit well with me.

"I texted Gray the map we've been using earlier, but we'll need to go off course," Carter said, "which means they'll lose us."

Mason pointed to Gwen's charm bracelet. I wasn't sure

what that meant, but the look that passed between him and the others meant they certainly did. "They'll catch up with us eventually." He reached down and grabbed his pocketknife from the man's throat and my sister turned away when blood spurted from the guy's neck.

"Come on, we need to go," Oliver said, grabbing Mya's arm.

"If the map led us to this trafficking route, does that mean you were right about your concerns? That someone suspects something, and they want us not just cut from the game, but dead?" My question was drowned out by the sounds of an engine—a *motorbike?*—cutting through the air, loud enough for us to hear over the sounds of nature humming all around us.

Jack grabbed my arm, then shot me a dark look. "Move, or I'll pick you up again."

"Fine," I hissed, but I jerked free from his grasp and reached for my sister's hand instead.

"Where you go, I go, right?" Lucy whispered, and I hated the tears I saw well up in her eyes. The full weight of our situation may not have sunk in that morning by the pool, but it sure as hell had now.

"Right," I told her as Jack motioned with his gun for us to move ahead of them.

Just like on the rope bridge, the guys boxed in the women. Carter and Oliver in the front of us, and Jack and Mason behind us. We walked fast, borderline jogging as we navigated through the woods, careful not to trip and injure ourselves.

"Will the cameraman survive to even get help?" Lucy asked a few minutes later as we spotted what appeared to be a clearing up ahead. Were we nearing another river?

"I doubt we'll be getting any help," Mason said just

before Oliver and Carter halted abruptly and I nearly collided with Carter.

As I looked past him, I realized why they'd stopped.

"Illegal deforestation," Oliver rasped, anger cutting through his voice. "They're destroying the rainforest."

"And I bet those narcotraffickers are also using the logging routes to smuggle drugs. And, well, people," Mya tacked on, shielding her eyes from the sun since we currently lacked the presence of the canopy.

"That also means we'll be encountering more armed tangos soon," Jack shared, and I could feel him at my back, his breath on my neck as he brought that reality back to the forefront.

*You think I'm a killer. You think I murdered an FBI agent. You hate me . . . and yet, you're still protecting me.* I did my best to let that last part comfort me. One problem at a time.

"We can't cross this clearing. We'll be out in the open." Mason turned toward us, his back to the desolate land where the campfire smell still lingered. The destruction of those trees had been recent. "But going to the left leads us back to the trail from the map, and we don't know for sure what other bullshit awaits us if we continue on that path."

"You think someone doesn't just want us cut from the show, they want us dead?" I repeated my earlier question they hadn't been able to answer before.

I did my best not to dip into the past again and freeze up as I waited for someone to speak up; I needed to be present and aware of our situation with my sister in harm's way.

"We're in a dangerous part of the Amazon," Gwen said. "If there's a lot of criminal activity here, maybe they sent us this direction on purpose. It's possible they didn't hire anyone to take us down, they're just hoping the jungle does it for them."

"An unfortunate accident. And since we signed waivers before the show, they don't have to assume responsibility. They'd probably even carry on with the show. It'd make for interesting TV, I suppose," Mya added. They were speaking freely, which clearly meant they knew Jack had told me the truth about why they were there.

"I guess that means none of us are wanted by the kidnapper, then," Lucy murmured, still a bit breathless from running.

"I guess not," Mya said. "But I don't get how they found out we were undercover. Our aliases are foolproof."

"Maybe it's not you all they want dead." Lucy's eyes widened in alarm when she realized she'd spoken her thoughts out loud.

"Did you run our faces? Our real ones this time?" I whipped around to peer at Jack. "Is that how you found out the truth about me today?"

Jack's hands settled on his hips as he lifted his chin to the sky, choosing not to make eye contact. And that was my answer, right? They did.

"We may have lost those assholes for now, but we don't have all day to sit here and theorize why they're after us," Mason said, taking the lead in ignoring my quest for answers. "We'll need to take our chances with the open terrain here. If memory serves me correctly, to the right is the Amazon river, and unless anyone wants to become a snack for a caiman or a snake, this is our only option."

"We have weapons now. And knowing them, Gray and Jesse are almost caught up with us," Gwen added, and I turned to see her nodding with the kind of optimism we needed.

"We make a run through the clearing. Zigzag. Got it?" Carter's gruff command left zero room for arguing. *Damn that man is intense.* Before following through on his own plan, he turned toward me and declared, "If you're suggesting it's the Feds after you because our teammate ran your face through our software, it's not them. The FBI has a much different approach in catching their subjects." He scowled at me, then added in an even more clipped tone, "Plus, our program is independent of the government's. The Feds don't even know you're here. At least, not because of us."

That was something, I supposed. But before I could figure out a response to him, the sound of the motorbikes returned.

"Fuck," Oliver seethed. "Time to run."

# CHAPTER TWENTY

## JACK

"You're crushing me. I can't breathe." Charley planted her hands on my chest, pushing me away from her, but until I knew we were one hundred percent in the clear, I'd be keeping my body on top of hers.

We'd successfully made it back to the jungle after crossing the area destroyed by deforestation, but not before I'd had to shoot two people who'd come at me with machetes. Over a decade as a Green Beret, and a fucking dating show gave me my most Rambo day ever.

With the immediate threats expunged, we were forced to get far too cozy in our tight spot—a patch of tamped-down vegetation where an animal, hopefully a small one with no teeth, no doubt lived.

Angry and frustrated with her, but not wanting to suffocate her, I did my best to shift the brunt of my weight to my forearms. A brutal reminder of our intimate moments from the night before.

Carter and Oliver were the only ones exposed, holding sentry at the edge of the jungle with the rifles they'd snatched from the dead bodies, ensuring no one else was on our ass before we began to move again.

To track us using Gwen's bracelet, Gray would need to get word to Gwen's dad. Wyatt could be under enemy fire, but I knew he'd still answer a call about his daughter. Then Gray would be faced with the problem of stopping Papa Bear from up and leaving his current op to come join us, knowing Gwen was being hunted by narcotraffickers.

"It's not what you think," Charley whispered, drawing my attention. Her tone was like a soft caress over my heated, sweat-slicked skin.

Why was she risking her life by talking right now just to try and clear the air? Because screw the air. It was cloudy and confusing, and I highly doubted she'd be clearing shit for me now.

*You killed a Fed.* I still couldn't wrap my head around it. I'd spent the entire morning (before we'd been shot at and Carter had to play slice and dice with Mason's pocketknife) running possible scenarios through my head as to why she'd murdered an FBI agent, attempting to make sense with the limited intel I had.

If the men on her heist team were undercover, maybe it'd been a mistake? She thought they were bad guys. Not that it changed the fact she took a life—a good guy's life.

*And hell, why were you committing crimes in the first place? A getaway driver, seriously? Yeah, you said back in Cape Town you used to be a good driver, but what the fucking fuck?*

I grunted, forgetting she couldn't hear my spiraling thoughts.

Of course I fell for a wanted woman. Wanted for too many speeding tickets was one thing. Murdering a Fed and being the getaway driver for heists? Damn.

I dipped my chin to find her eyes, which wasn't easy to do given our proximity and lack of natural light in our hiding place.

"You keep saving my life. I'm wearing blood from a man you shot ten minutes ago to prove it." Her hand on my chest became a little fist, but she left it resting between us. "Why? Am I worth more brought in alive than dead? Is there a bounty on my head you're now considering going after?"

"You've got to be kidding?" I snarled. She was really pissing me off. "And for someone who's clearly done a good job at avoiding authorities, you'd think you'd be better at keeping quiet, so you don't expose us to the real bad guys."

"I think I hate you," she bit out, and the attack felt false and flimsy at best.

"No, you don't. You *want* to hate me, but you don't." *And same.* I was pretty sure my anger earlier had been more with myself than with her. Mad that I couldn't look at her and feel anything even remotely resembling hate. And considering she killed a Fed . . . I felt all kinds of bad about that.

"How much do you wish you had cuffs on you right now?" she shot back, her raspy tone slipping under my skin.

My dick twitched at the idea of binding her wrists, proof my head was off. The steel rod between my legs didn't understand we were in hiding and not preparing to fuck like animals in the wild.

"I don't know what to think about you." I wanted to make up any excuse possible to absolve her of her sins. I'd become her Michelangelo and paint any ceiling with any number of reasons why killing a Fed and being a getaway driver for a heist crew was "just fine and fucking dandy."

Then my mom's words popped into my head, and I had to mull them over. Chew on them. Take a minute to think about them before I finally spoke to the woman I couldn't stop wanting. *"Forgiveness doesn't mean letting the enemy into your heart, it means letting him out of it,"* had been Mom's favorite saying, and I'd never understood what it meant.

*I still don't.* Because surely, she wasn't saying to forgive Charley for murder, right? "I'm struggling to believe you could—"

"We're safe," Carter cut through my lame attempt to express my chaotic thoughts to Charley. "Time to go."

I rolled to the side, allowing Charley her freedom. Once she was clear from our temporary hiding spot, I stood. Spying my hat on the ground a few feet away, I bent over to snatch it and groaned at the pain in my back. *Yeah, forty is the new thirty my ass. My joints disagree.*

Stretching my back while positioning my hat on face-forward, I spotted Charley rushing over to her sister, hooking a protective arm around her.

*You're not a killer. There's just no way. The report must be wrong. It has to be. Or the Fed was crooked.* I'd take anything. Any scraps that got this woman off the hook since she'd so swiftly hooked my heart. "What's wrong?" I asked, catching the worried look in Mya's eyes. Something was definitely on her mind, and based on how her eyes flicked from me to Charley, it had less to do with the chaos we'd just endured and more to do with my personal hell.

Mya collapsed the space between us to mere inches, reached for my forearm, and gave it a reassuring squeeze. Pressing up on her toes, she leaned in and whispered, "Carter just told us why the Feds are after them."

Mya may have been talking, but it was Charley staring at the two of us that captured my attention.

"I'm so sorry, Jack." Mya's words rung in my ears as she let go of my arm.

Ripping my focus from Charley and back to Mya, I said

after a harsh exhale, "It's just my luck." I did my best to erase whatever pathetic look I was probably wearing and went over to Carter. "So, what's the situation?"

Oliver turned his attention on me. "We just took out two more men that ran through the cleared field en route to us, and Carter overheard a message that another team is being assembled to hunt us down."

"The cartel must have a local place nearby. Given how deep we are in the jungle, it'll hopefully be a small site," Carter said, letting go of the rifle and allowing the sling to catch its weight.

"We stumbled into a beehive, though." Oliver shook his head. "We either take them down, or they keep coming for us." When his brows dipped with worry, I followed his gaze to the blood on my arm.

"Not mine," I casually said, letting him know I didn't need medical attention.

"You're not suggesting you attack first, right?" Charley left her sister's side to join the conversation, and I resisted the impulse to ask her if she was a decent shot or not. Thinking about her murdering someone would reignite my anger and open up all sorts of reactions from my team, and that wouldn't help the situation.

"Whether we go on offense or defense at this point, it doesn't matter." I folded my arms, ignoring the blood sticking to one of them. It must've come from being wedged up against Charley. She'd wound up with blood on her when I'd shot one of the narcotraffickers during our jaunt through the deforested part of the jungle. His blood wasn't on her hands, literally or figuratively, nor was he an innocent man. But it reminded me she did have blood on her hands. It was just eleven years old. And that image was messing with me. "The cartel will keep sending people after us. They must assume we're . . ." I cleared my throat. "Feds."

"It's not what you think," Charley abruptly snapped out her response to my statement like a reflex.

And my sorry ass wanted to cling to her words.

"Would you all stop looking at us like that?" Lucy's demand in the quiet of our standoff was like being doused in ice water. "We're not going anywhere with you if you think we're killers. Let's clear the air. Now." She opened her arms wide as if she could block our movement forward. Stubborn as her sister, so it would seem.

"*You're* not a killer." Charley faced Lucy and snatched her arm. "Just me."

"But you did it to save me. They need to know the truth." Lucy yanked her arm free and wound up whacking Mason in the process. "Shit, sorry."

"It's okay." Mason gave her a little nod. From where I stood, Mason didn't buy whatever Carter had tried to sell about the Lennox sisters being dangerous.

*Shit, neither am I, right?*

Carter was going off intel my best friend told him. But Gray was going by whatever the Feds had about them in their system, and I knew that shit could be easily cooked up. Rewritten and couched in terms to mislead and redirect blame.

Charley slowly faced me, a sad look in her eyes as she asked, "The truth doesn't matter right now, though, does it?"

"It doesn't," Carter spoke before I could, which was good, because my stomach was busy being too nauseous for me to talk. "We need to make it out of this jungle alive, and we still have a mission to complete." He peered at Lucy, then Charley.

"That's assuming even if we make it back to the lodge tomorrow with the 'treasure' they'll let us stay," I pointed out the grim truth. "All I know is that if our kidnapper is somehow responsible for this shit show today, they don't want it happening on camera, which is why the 'accidental' run-in with the narcos."

"Because the show must go on," Oliver muttered sarcastically under his breath. "But does that mean we're going after these bastards now hunting us, or are we setting a trap to pick them off when they come for us?"

Before anyone could answer him, the familiar sound of blades chopped the sky in the distance, drawing our focus.

"Looks like they're not giving us a choice. We're back on the run again," Oliver remarked, grabbing Mya's arm. "And I'm thinking we're going to be taking a swim. How do you feel about waterfalls? I know you hate cenotes."

*Cenotes?* Right, they'd had to swim the jungle in Mexico last year on an op. And from what I'd later learned, Mya hadn't been amused by Oliver's strategy to keep her from screaming while forcing her to jump into a hole in the ground.

"So help me, if you put your grubby hand over my mouth this time, I'll—"

"What happened exactly?" Mason interrupted Mya, then shook his head and waved his hand. "Never mind. I don't want to know."

I hadn't been sure if the forced fight between him and Oliver yesterday had done anything to alleviate the tension between them, but now, I was pretty sure it had. Mason was giving up and moving on, wasn't he? Not that it mattered at the present time, but I felt him slowly surrendering to the idea Mya's heart was elsewhere.

"Let's get to the waterfall, then." I'd much rather take my

chances in the water than get picked off from a rifle in the sky.

Everyone except Charley began following Oliver, and Charley's hands found my chest as she blocked my path to go.

"Not now. The truth won't matter if you die, will it?" I pointed over her shoulder in the direction we needed to run. "I *will* pick you up if I have to," I added, and she released a small sigh before removing her hands from my body.

She frowned and tossed out another weak, "I hate you."

"Yeah, yeah," I grumbled, then grabbed her hand. Our fingers threaded together, and she peered at our clasped palms before meeting my eyes. "You hate me as much as I hate you."

# CHAPTER TWENTY-ONE

## CHARLOTTE

"WE REALLY NEED TO JUMP?" MYA PEEKED OVER THE LEDGE by the waterfall. Her movement dislodged a few rocks, sending them over the edge, lost to the rushing water as she shuffled backward.

It wasn't that far of a drop, and Carter had assured us the water down below should be relatively safe compared to that first night. Honestly, I was fine with jumping. I was still wearing the dead guy's blood, not my favorite accessory, and it beat the alternative of waiting to be sitting ducks out of the water.

"To get to the other side, yeah, we need to go over." Oliver set his hand to her back, and she flinched. "I'm not going to force you *unless* you don't go willingly."

"You got her?" Mason asked, and Oliver looked back at him, his brows dipping as if surprised at the lack of jealous tone there.

Oliver nodded. "Yeah, I've got her."

Was this some type of olive branch from Mason? And why was that even on my radar to care?

I was on the run because of a game show. We were being chased by assailants who either wanted to capture or kill us. And I'd just witnessed my teammates take down several of those pursuers, four of them who'd *"fast-roped from a helo"* —Carter's words—less than five minutes ago. I knew my life was chaos, but damn if this wasn't starting to feel like a bit much.

I focused on Mason who quietly turned his attention to my sister.

"You up for a little refreshing swim?" Mason tipped his head, his question competing with the sound of the waterfall.

It wasn't exactly Niagara, but it also wasn't something you found in my neck of the woods where I'd grown up in Orange County. Of course, both Lucy and I had gone cliff diving into similar waters as these while living around the world, so I knew we could handle it.

"Let's do this." Lucy slipped her hand into Mason's, and they both jumped over the edge.

"We don't have all day," Carter grumbled as he swiftly stepped up behind Mya, grabbed hold of her, and took her over that same edge before she knew what hit her.

"Guess he has her." Oliver laughed. "And he's probably the only guy she won't smack for that." He shrugged, tossed our backpack over, then followed it into the water.

Gwen went next, and I took that as my cue to go. I swiveled to the side, searching for the man I'd watched not only shoot multiple men, but snatch a blade from one bad guy and use it to slice his throat.

When Jack had faced me after killing that man, he'd been breathing hard and looked . . . lethal. He'd glanced at the bloody blade and his lips had parted, and he immediately dropped the knife as if horrified I'd witnessed him take a life in such a brutal manner.

Unsure why I was stalling, fixated on that last round of unknown-enemy whack-a-mole, I asked, "Will the pilot head back and get more people?"

"If there are more people in the area, yes." He removed his hat, then bent it and shoved it into the large side pocket of his cargo shorts. "Let's hope no one is close so we can buy ourselves some time." His voice was flat, no hint of the passion we'd shared the night before. The concern he'd shown me before Carter spilled the "official" version of the truth he'd uncovered was gone.

I wished I could go ahead and spill my own truth so he wouldn't think I was some murderer any longer. Of course, I had to get him to also believe me. And the evidence was stacked up against me.

I held out my hand. My version of an olive branch.

"You don't need me," he said, looking away toward the top of the waterfall.

I swallowed and spoke one very uneasy truth for me, "Yeah, but I want you."

The collapse of his broad shoulders didn't do wonders for my nerves. But when he turned, that heartbreaking look in his eyes told a different story. He'd been hurt before, in a different way than I had, but it was there. Clear as day, and it cracked my walls. Cut through my defenses.

I lowered my outstretched arm. "I did kill someone when I was twenty. It was self-defense and to save my sister. But he wasn't a Fed. I was framed for that."

There wasn't any change from him. No reaction. Just the same curious stare pointed my way. He looked as lost as I felt.

We needed to go over the ledge. Cross the narrow river to place more distance between ourselves and the bad guys. Focus on surviving. But there we both were, frozen in place, having the moment I'd worked so hard not to have for eleven years.

"Believe me or don't, that's the truth." I turned, mentally and physically preparing myself to jump alone, but his arm banded across my midsection, and he drew me flush to his body.

A shuddery breath fell from my lips as he slid his hand up my chest to my collarbone. His fingers splayed across my throat before the pad of his thumb made its way to my mouth, and he brushed down my lower lip.

"I believe you," he whispered into my ear.

My thread of control to "keep calm and plug along"—or whatever the hell that saying was—nearly snapped.

"Why?" I shouldn't have pressed, but it wasn't exactly in my nature not to.

"I have no choice." The gravelly tone of his voice slid down my body and hit me between the legs.

"There's always a choice," I repeated what he'd said to me about going into the jungle just that morning. "Is it because you wouldn't be able to look at yourself in the mirror knowing you had sex with a murderer?"

At the feel of his hand on my chin, urging me to look back to find his eyes, I obeyed his request.

"It's because I don't think anyone or anything can change what I'm feeling for you or stop me from wanting to take you in my arms again." That raspy promise freed a small breath from my lungs.

He abruptly stepped back, hooked his arm around my waist, and set a soft kiss at my temple just before we both jumped.

* * *

GOING DOWN WAS MUCH LESS TRAUMATIC THAN TWO NIGHTS ago, but when I pushed up to the surface in the calm waters, the spray from the waterfall blasted me in the face. I twisted on reflex when I felt something at my back, luckily realizing before I struck out that it was Jack tugging my shirt. He was drawing me away from the base of the waterfall crashing down into what looked like a gorgeous pool.

"Like Carter said, this water should be free of anything that bites, but let's not take our chances." Jack tipped his head to the side, and I looked over to see everyone waiting for us on a narrow strip of grassy land, a bank of trees just beyond them. The forest awaited us again.

Gwen and Mya had removed their shirts and were wringing out the water. Like me, they both had on a bikini top.

As I swam to the ledge, I spotted Lucy peeling off her tank top, revealing two pink triangles that barely hid her breasts. Mason seemed to notice, too. He leaned in and said something to her. My eyes narrowed as I tried to imagine what exactly was going through his head and how hard I'd have to hit him. But his gaze never lowered as he whispered in her ear.

Her eyes widened and she reached up to adjust one of the triangles. Well, damn . . . the jump had shifted the fabric around, and he was politely letting her know her nipple was nearly on the verge of escaping.

*Okay, that's a good-guy thing to do. Point for Mason.*

Jack climbed out only to spin around and offer me a boost up. I hesitantly accepted his palm, and my hand became lost inside his. A perfect and protective fit. And one that nearly brought tears to my eyes.

My dad taught me a few rules about men before his heart

attack stole him from the world. One of which was, *"Never marry a guy who can't hold both your heart and your hand in the palm of his."*

Mom had hated that advice, insisting I didn't need any man to hold anything of mine. But maybe Dad was right? And it seemed Jack could so easily do both.

"You want my shirt?" Jack asked, drawing me to the present.

"You don't need to give me yours."

But Jack ignored me, removing his tee anyway. And my attention was glued to his wet, glistening wall of muscles.

"I don't get how I'm the one wearing blood when you're the one who kill—" *Not going to finish that sentence.*

"We need to find a safe place to set up, so we have the upper hand when they come again." Carter's reality check did nothing for my confidence in our escape as I got rid of my blood-stained tank top.

"What kind of safe place? How is anywhere out here safe?" Lucy asked while I tightened the string at the back of my bikini top, ensuring my breasts were properly covered by the black triangles. One wardrobe malfunction per family was enough.

When I looked up, I didn't miss Jack checking as well. "You're good."

His husky voice had my nipples pebbling as he shoved his soaked shirt my way, his eyes darkening the slightest bit.

I looked around and noticed everyone else, Carter included, had removed their shirts. "I think I'll stay in this for now." A bikini top was more comfortable than the heavy weight of soaked fabric. I was tempted to remove my pants, too, but it might push Jack off another ledge. I decided wet pants and shoes were a mild inconvenience to what we'd already endured.

"Come on, then." Jack slung his wet shirt over his shoulder and started to follow the others into the thick of the jungle.

*Survival 2.0? Or are we at number three by now?* I was losing count of how many times we'd dodged death that day.

"You okay?" Lucy came up alongside me and handed me a granola bar. The wrapper was dry, which meant the backpack had shielded the contents inside from being soaked.

"Are *you* okay?" I asked after taking a bite, a bit famished from all the save-my-life cardio that'd taken place.

Lucy focused on Jack and Carter walking side by side ahead of us. From the sounds of it, they were going over a plan of action for our next steps. "You told him before you jumped, didn't you?" she asked me a few seconds later. "The truth?"

Jack's strong back muscles flexed at her words. He'd overheard her. But he kept walking and talking, giving nothing else away, and Carter either didn't hear or didn't care.

"I told him a little bit," I whispered. "I didn't want to stay out in the open too long, but he needed to know."

"Don't trip." At Jack's order, I faced forward and found him looking back at us.

We weren't on a designated trail, and the ground was littered with obstacles. Good call on the focusing part. I nodded at him, then he returned his attention toward Carter again.

I clocked Oliver and Mason behind us, both armed, keeping a bit of distance between themselves and us.

But now, our greatest threat seemed to be bugs. I couldn't even continue talking to my sister if I didn't want to risk swallowing a mouthful of them. I was fine with silence, though. I could use some time to think.

After about an hour of walking without being attacked by

a person or animal, Jack abruptly stopped and lifted a fist into the air, ordering us to hold positions.

"Is that an abandoned house? Kind of creepy," Lucy spoke up first, and I took in the sight of the three-story structure.

Nature had reclaimed the house, taking possession of the old building. It appeared to be missing half its roof, and I had my doubts as to whether going inside would be any safer than staying out in the open for the bad guys to find us.

"We'll check it out. Clear each room. This could be a good place for us to hide out for now. As long as it won't collapse on us," Oliver said, then he turned to Mason. "You want to stay with them?"

"Sure." Mason nodded, then motioned for us to hang off to the side of the building. Jack shot me a quick look, as if conflicted by the idea of leaving me alone.

"I'm fine," I mouthed, assuming he needed some reassurance that I wouldn't fall, faint, or hell, bolt. "I'll be right here when you get back."

Jack gave me another hesitant look, then snatched a pistol he'd had tucked at the back of his shorts. He checked the clip, mag thingy, or whatever it was called, and frowned at what he found.

"Not enough bullets?" I whispered my thoughts out loud.

"Just two," he answered, his lips still turned down.

"Hopefully, two more than you'll need," Lucy said, and I wasn't sure if that was a joke from her.

Mason handed Jack something, and I assumed it was the thing that held the bullets. For a wanted woman, I sucked at knowing about firearms, even if I did use one to kill a man eleven years ago. Less of a lucky shot and more like impossible to miss with him inches away from the gun.

"You sure you're okay?" Jack asked, focus squarely on

me. Carter and Oliver had already gone inside the house that I'd swear just moaned in protest at them for entering.

I did my best to conceal the shiver that ran up my spine, feeling like I was in an R.L. Stine *Goosebumps* novel. But based on the quirk of Jack's brows drawing together and his lips falling back into that frown he kept sporting, he noticed my fear.

"My sister is a badass," Lucy said, coming up alongside me and hooking her arm with mine, "but she doesn't like scary movies, haunted houses, or creepy carnival rides."

I glanced at her from over my shoulder and rolled my eyes. "Thanks for that."

"I'll go. You stay." Mason opened his palm, and Jack wordlessly handed him the gun.

"I'm not a fan of any of those things either," Mya said, coming my way to stand near Jack as Gwen joined us as well. "But I'd rather be somewhere enclosed while we wait for Gray and Jesse to catch up with us. I'm assuming it'll just be them, and Camila's other teammates will hang back at the lodge with eyes on her."

"We're in good hands, don't worry," Gwen added.

I wasn't used to being the one others had to calm down, but despite them not knowing I was innocent of killing a Fed, they were still being kind to me. It was . . . nice, to say the least.

I peeked over at Jack and watched him drag one of those "good hands" along his jawline while shooting me a pensive look.

"So, about the thing." I swallowed, unsure if it was the best moment to clear the air with Jack's female teammates or not, but I'd prefer they not think I was some cold-hearted killer.

"We're all set," Oliver called out, and that was fast. Too

fast. Because it stole my chance in sharing my thoughts with Gwen and Mya.

Gwen reached for my forearm and gave it a light squeeze. "Maybe catch us up on everything after we're out of the jungle?" She tipped her head, eyes meeting mine like she was trying to determine my guilt or innocence.

"Okay," I whispered, doing my best to force the word out while hiding my fear and disappointment.

"We'll be right in," Jack told them.

Gwen let me go, and I motioned to Lucy to head in, and we shared a quick wordless exchange. A sister thing. Attempting to read each other's thoughts. I narrowed my eyes and gave her a slight nod I'd be okay, and only then did she leave.

Once Jack and I were alone with nature, he came around to face me. He was still shirtless, every rippling muscle on display becoming a slight distraction to my focus.

"Gwen's right," I blurted, feeling oddly nervous now about spilling my guts. I wasn't sure if I could handle his judgment of not only me, but my mom. "Maybe we get out of this mess first before I explain everything? I mean, this doesn't seem to be about me, right? So, I'd rather not make it about me," I rambled.

He was quiet for a moment, but when he spoke, his words rocked me to my core. "There's one thing I do need to know now." He gently cupped my chin, commanding my eyes on his, and I hesitantly peered at him. "After this is over, if I can get you out of whatever mess it is you're in, will you stop running?"

That was an impossibly big "if." And he had no idea just how hard of a task that'd be.

"Do you want to be Charlotte Lennox again?"

I hadn't heard my real name in so long, I was beginning

to forget it was even mine. But God, the way it rolled from his tongue . . . it sounded almost as beautiful as Charlotte London. *Ha, two cities for a full name.* I could handle that. *Wait! What?* "We barely know each other," I frantically said, jumping straight over his immediate question and answering the forever one he hadn't even asked.

"I'd like to get to know you." His tone was so genuine. And the way he was looking at me, I was about to melt into a very cliché puddle. Maybe even ask him to kiss me so I could pop my foot up behind me like I'd seen happen in old-school movies. "But I can't go all in unless I know you're not going to run afterward."

*Geez. The truth. Just like that. Honest and direct. No attempts to mind read or guess. This is another age-difference thing, right? Or is it just a Jack thing?* I'd been ducking the truth for so damn long, did I even know what it was anymore? Hell, I wasn't sure if I even remembered who I was before I became a wanted woman.

"Charley?" He let go of my chin, possibly discouraged by my silence, and I didn't blame him. I was a bit thrown myself. He shook his head and backed up a step, eyes moving overhead to the canopy cloaking us from the sun.

Worried I was about to lose him, I drew myself closer, snaking my arm behind his neck, bringing our bodies flush. He lowered his focus to my face, and I stared up at him, fighting with myself to say the words he needed to hear, but I didn't want them to be a lie. If I said them, I had to know in my heart they were the truth.

*You've got your own walls. Baggage, too. Don't you?* I swallowed. *Who made you afraid to feel something for me without worrying I'd . . .* "Who broke your heart?" I pushed out the question, a tremble flowing along with my words.

His eyes fell closed, and he brought his forehead to mine

as he murmured, "Jill."

# CHAPTER TWENTY-TWO

## JACK

I'D NEVER BEEN SO GRATEFUL FOR MY BEST FRIEND AND HIS "perfect" timing. Before Charley could summon a response to the mention of Jill's name, the soft rustle of vegetation alerted me to new arrivals. I looked up just as Gray came into view, Jesse stopping right beside him, both kitted up and looking like they'd been to hell and back.

"My friends are here," I whispered in her ear, tipping my head in their direction.

She untangled herself from our hold on each other and whipped around.

"You two good?" I stepped alongside Charley. "What happened?" I pulled Gray in for a quick one-arm hug, then turned my attention to Jesse, giving him a friendly nod. We were friends but we weren't hugging-type friends. Not yet, at least.

"Not our blood," Jesse remarked casually, his curious gaze bouncing between Charley and me. "We encountered another team heading your way, and we got to them before they could get to you."

"We good for now, or do we need to relocate?" I asked,

tracking yet another new sound coming from overhead. At least it was only a small monkey gnawing on some food while creeping on us. Having reinforcements arrive was great. Other human intruders, not so much.

"We're fine for now." Gray's answer snagged my attention. Specifically, the *for now* part. "Two guys from Camila's security team are with us, but they're hanging back, covering the perimeter. They'll alert me over my SAT radio if we have company and need to move."

*Good.* We needed all hands on deck if we were dealing with a cartel on their playground. "So, um, as you probably know by now, this is Charlotte." There'd been plenty of awkward back-and-forth looks between the guys and my girl, but no actual intros had been made. *My girl.* Why'd that have to sound so damn perfect even in my head?

"You can call me Charley." She offered her hand; Jesse was the first to take it. A wary expression crossed his face, but I doubted he gave her too firm of a grip.

"Jesse." He let go of her, then deferred to Gray to make the next move.

Gray kept his eyes on her for a few painful seconds, allowing the uncomfortable silence to stretch as he determined whether she was a threat. More likely concerned she was a threat to my heart, not to our team. The man had my back, what could I say? "Grayson."

*No nickname and no handshake? Come on, man. I get it. You're wondering, what the fuck? But she didn't kill a Fed. Give me a little credit.*

Charley lowered her hand, acknowledging he wasn't "there yet" in believing her innocence.

"So." Jesse strapped his pistol to his side holster, buckled it, then looked around. Always the operator. "The cameraman from your team reported what happened, and Camila let us know they're deciding on whether to cancel the show. They've sent a search party to find you all. I don't know if that's to keep up with pretenses, so they don't look complicit in what happened or not, though."

"We should talk in private," Gray cut to it a beat later, still observing me like he was calculating how much therapy I'd need after this op. My best friend had seen me at my worst, then a few levels below that. And sure, I'd been one moody motherfucker in the few weeks since Cape Town, but Charley was back and . . . I didn't even know where to go with the rest of that thought.

"I'd like to hear whatever you have to say," Charley said, a touch of grit to her tone.

"I'm thinking it's *me* who needs to hear what *you* have to say, actually," Gray remarked. Jesse motioned with two fingers he was heading in, likely grateful to escape our awkward situation. "But before we get into your version of what happened eleven years ago," Gray went on once Jesse was inside, "and if that's why these men are hunting you down, we'll—"

"Wait, they're hunting her?" I blinked a few times, trying to absorb Gray's statement. The monkey above us made a little gasp-like sound. *Yeah, you and me both, buddy.*

"Hunting me?" Charley whispered when Gray took a moment to stew in silence as I got my shit together.

Gray rested the heel of his hand on his rifle, which was hanging on the sling across his body. His clothes were painted in more blood than Charley's tank top had been earlier.

Weirdly—but also, thank God—in all the chaos throughout the day, not a single shot had made its way toward Charley or Lucy. I wasn't sure if the bad guys were trying to keep the women alive for a different kind of trafficking (the kind that made me want to puke) or if— "They want her alive," I said at the realization. How had I missed that? Right, my head was off big-time.

Gray dipped his hand into a pocket of his cargo pants, produced a crumpled image and handed it over. "We searched the men after we killed them, and I found this on one guy."

Charley peered at the picture of her standing beside her sister during the kissing icebreaker on night one. The camera had zoomed in on just the two of them.

"I translated the message on the back," Gray added, and I flipped it over to see Portuguese there. "Capture, not kill orders. One-million-dollar bounty."

"A million dollars for us?" Charley murmured, her tone less shocked and more full of fear as she backed up a step.

I looked over at her while handing the photo to Gray, trying to wrap my head around why in the hell someone had placed a million-dollar bounty on their heads. "Too bad you didn't leave anyone alive to question," I said to him, still focused on Charley. If the color didn't return to her face soon, I wanted to be close enough to catch her. "So, the kidnapper isn't changing his MO, right? This is, uh, about something else?" Apparently, today was about her after all. And we'd be needing Charley to clue us in now. No more waiting.

"It's not the kidnapper after me, it's him," Charley whispered, her hand moving to her throat, and she gripped it as if feeling the squeeze of someone else's hand there. "I don't know how he found me here, but it must've been a trap."

"What trap? Who is this 'him'?" Gray asked, shoving the photo into his pocket.

Charley had given me hints about "him" during our conversation in the treehouse, but she'd deflected, successfully stopped me from following the trail of crumbs she'd inadvertently left for me.

"I guess you do need to hear what I have to say," she murmured, swiping her hand up to her cheek in a bit of a daze. "But if he's behind this, we can't stay here. He may not want Lucy and me dead yet, but he won't hesitate to kill you all to get to us."

No argument there. Today was all the proof I needed of that. "Does this mean we have two problems? The kidnapper and the man after her? Or are they somehow one and the same?" Was that even possible? It didn't really add up, but I wasn't sure what to think anymore.

Gray motioned toward the house, signaling for us to join the others. We could all hear her story at once, so we didn't need to play the game of telephone later with our teammates.

"I, um . . . Are the Feds after me, too? Do they know I'm here? Carter said—"

"If they don't know yet, they'll know soon." Gray frowned. "Word will get out that these assholes are on a killing spree searching for two Americans, one wanted for killing a federal agent." His tone was cold and icy, and I reminded myself he still believed she was responsible for that man's death. He didn't know the truth yet.

*Hell, I don't know the truth.* "So, we have three problems. The kidnapper, Feds, and the cartel being hired to come after them."

"I just can't figure out how he found me. Lucy's TikTok account? But no way is he back at the lodge. I would've felt him there, I just know it. And does that mean someone at the show is working with him? Sending images and footage his way?" she quickly asked, making my head spin a bit.

"There could be an insider there, and our kidnapper is elsewhere, and they're being sent videos." Gray lowered his arm, realizing she was too lost to her thoughts to notice his suggestion to go in. "It'd make it a lot easier to answer your questions if we knew the name of the guy after you." He let go of a gruff breath of frustration, then pinned me with a hard look, a request to encourage her to get a move on.

"Fine," she said before I had to nudge her the right way. "But promise we leave after?" She looked at him, wringing her fingers together. "Like you said, more men will be coming."

Gray lifted his chin, not answering her, only silently requesting for her to head inside.

"I'll be right in," I told her, assuming Gray would want a word alone before we all reconvened. Her eyes met mine, softening a bit, and she pushed the loose strands from her bun away from her face, then went inside.

Once the door shut, I turned to find Gray on one knee with his rucksack on the ground. "You seem to be missing a shirt, man." He tossed me a black tee, a smirk on his face.

"We both were, if you didn't notice."

He closed his bag and stood upright. "She had something on. Bathing suit."

I laughed. "If you call those little scraps of fabric barely concealing anything 'something on.'"

Gray lifted his left hand, and my attention landed on his message: his wedding band. "I didn't notice."

"Right, that wedding band come with special superpowers, making other women invisible?"

Gray shrugged. "You'll understand when you're a newlywed."

Then again, maybe I didn't need to be married to get the message. I had eyes for only one woman already, and that woman had my head spinning. "Anyway, what is it you'd rather not share in front of her?"

He turned to the side, putting eyes on the house before squaring his attention back on me, that touch of humor gone.

"Camila told me she set you two up in Cape Town. That it was no accident you met. And it's not an accident you're here."

"Yeah, I gathered as much."

Gray shook his head. "No, you don't understand. This has always been Camila's op, and it started before Cape Town."

My shoulders fell, but at the creaking noise above my head, I shifted my focus to find my new buddy, Curious George, still hanging out and spying on us. "No, this is Gwen's op," I corrected him, because what he'd said made as much sense as Charley murdering an FBI agent. "Camila just knew the cards would fall this way is what you mean."

"No." Gray's quick answer pulled my eyes away from my new pal. "Camila asked Gwen to lie to us. She said if we knew the truth ahead of time, shit would've gone wrong. Not her exact words, but fuck, you know how cryptic she is. But she said she already messed up, and things keep going wrong. And she won't say more for fear things will get even worse."

And by "worse," I had to assume he meant someone would die. "So, what you're saying is Gwen has no friend named Harley? No ex-girlfriend missing."

"There are six missing girls, that part is true. But Camila did ask Gwen to lie and not tell anyone she was involved."

"That explains why Gwen was oddly fidgety and not acting normal at the hangar and on our flight here." The lying was clearly hard on her.

"Camila's barely told me anything, but I have a feeling this all somehow connects to why she brought us to Cape Town last month since she set you and Charlotte up there. And now we're all here."

I barely remembered why we'd even been in Cape Town —to stop the sale of some weapons technology or something. I'd become solely focused (okay, okay, *obsessed*) with thoughts about Charley after that mission. "I take it Camila didn't tell you Charley is innocent, though? Because you sure as hell haven't been looking at her like a framed woman."

"Like I said, Camila gave me the bare minimum. And when I asked her for more, you know what she told me . . ." He shook his head as if shocked at some memory. "That one date I went on with her last year, well, she explained why there was never a date two. She said if there had been one, I'd never have wound up with my dream woman, because Tessa would've died. She saw it happening during dessert. But she said if she shared anything about Tessa coming back into my life and needing my help, then—"

"Shit would've gone sideways," I finished for him, thinking back to the wild string of events leading to my best friend getting married. "I have to believe this is about not only saving those missing women, but also saving Charley."

"Unless Camila wants justice for the murdering of a Fed," Gray tossed out a possibility I didn't want to hear. "And to catch whichever bad guys are after Charlotte, too. Presumably from her old heist crew."

"No, Camila's friends with Charley." I looked over at the house, anxious to go inside and hear the truth. "The fact they know each other is what connects us to everything." Well, that was my assumption. Maybe Camila couldn't share more because she didn't even know everything-everything, which also meant it'd be on us to put the puzzle together.

"But is Camila really friends with Charlotte? That woman works in mysterious ways. So, I have no plans on believing anyone's innocence or guilt until we know more. One of us needs to be objective."

"Fuck, fair enough." Agitated, I expelled a deep breath. "And Carter is seriously clueless that Camila's been pulling our strings?"

"He doesn't know, and Camila was clear on telling me he can't know. Not sure why, but there's a reason, I'm sure."

"Somehow, he'd affect the outcome in a bad way. Got it."

Gray grabbed his rucksack, and we started for the house. "So, does that mean we need to divide and conquer? Find the missing women and solve this case with Charley?"

"I'm thinking so, unless the missing women are connected to Charley somehow. Regardless, I have orders from Wyatt to get Gwen out of this jungle by tomorrow and no later. I'd rather not be on my brother-in-law's bad side. Makes for awkward family dinners."

"Yeah, see, I'm supposed to be the one making ill-timed jokes, not you. I've lost my fucking edge, man."

"You'll get it back once this is over." Gray patted my back. "Now come on, let's go find out if your head is in your ass or you've finally found your 'the one.'"

# CHAPTER TWENTY-THREE

## CHARLOTTE

*JILL* . . . THE NAME KEPT POPPING AROUND IN MY HEAD, driving me a bit nuts. I needed the rest of that story, but I assumed I wouldn't be getting it anytime soon. That shouldn't have been my priority now that I knew who was after us. And yet, I couldn't get the sad sound of his voice out of my head as he'd said her name.

"Okay, I don't know if I can take any more hot men joining us. This guy is on another level, too," Lucy said, drawing my focus her way. "I'd say we stumbled into a rom-com with delicious actors, but there's nothing exactly funny about our situation." Somehow, there was still humor clinging to her tone. Her attention was fixed on Jesse as he spoke with his team, huddled in the corner of our haunted hotel where I sure as hell hoped we didn't plan to stay as guests.

There was still furniture, but it was covered in layers of the earth, and any step we took sent plumes of dust (only a mild exaggeration) shooting into the air, making me gag.

But honestly, it was the way the walls and floorboards howled and cried for mercy when we weren't moving that had me doing some major cringing, burying my fingernails into my sister's side as I held her tight alongside me.

*And wait, rom-com? What was Lucy talking about? This was clearly a romantic suspense. And I was done with it.* I stole my focus back to the door in case we needed to make a quick escape. I had no desire to sit, lean, or lie any-freaking-where. *Get me out of here.*

The only light filtering into the room came from one window Mason had used his still-damp tee to swipe off the dust. Oliver had lit the lantern he'd snatched from the backpack, placing it in the center of the room. That was it. So, when I loosened my hold of my sister to peer at her, I doubted she'd make out my facial expression as I asked, "Are you really talking about how hot everyone is?"

Mason's throat-clear cut across the room, and Casper the *un*friendly ghost (okay, I was imagining that), appeared to be cackling upstairs. *It's in my head. All in my head.* God, I hated scary shit. Even imaginary scary shit. And even more so since there was plenty of real shit to worry about.

"I think Mason heard you." Lucy gently stepped on my toe to demand my attention. "Would you rather me think about the fact we're trying to avoid being killed while ironically standing inside a house where I'm betting people were murdered—and yes, I think those are blood stains on the floor?"

I walked back a step, bumping into the wall, taking Lucy with me.

Mason swiveled around, and I assumed he was looking at us. "You two okay?" Not that I could see that well, because we'd moved, which meant I was seconds away from choking on the ashes of some murder victim.

"We're just dandy," Lucy said as I coughed a few times,

trying to find my breath. She freed herself from my embrace and playfully elbowed me in the side.

*You wouldn't be "dandy" if you knew who was hunting us. But did he set us up, drawing us here? Or is this a horrible accident he stumbled upon us?* Either option sucked, but we were in this situation now regardless of how we got there.

And as soon as I told Lucy who was behind our "jungle excursion" today, she'd forget all about the level of hotness of Jack's teammates.

Casper was already laughing his ass off upstairs at what was to come.

*Screw my life. This can't be real.* We'd gone from a reality dating show to being part of *The Blair Witch Project.*

"They're coming in," Carter announced a beat later, and the door creaked open, sending a little shockwave through the house that could literally be felt beneath my soggy running shoes.

"This place feels like it's going to collapse. Maybe we don't stay here long," Grayson said once Jack closed the door behind him.

I hated that Jack's best friend could barely stand the sight of me. But I had to remind myself he thought I was a killer. Plus, there was that little element of his father basically being the President's right-hand man when it came to all things military. He was bound to be a by-the-books kind of guy, right? And he was going to look out for Jack the way I'd protect Lucy; I couldn't blame him.

"On the same page." Lucy shot her hand in the air.

"Oh, so now you're ready to go, hmm?" I said to her, which earned me another little elbow I doubted anyone could clock in the dimly lit room.

"Here." Jack walked over and offered me a shirt. "This is dry. You want it?"

I looked at it for a moment, unsure what to do. "Everyone else is topless, well, aside from Jesse and Gray*son*, so why shouldn't I be?"

When Jack shoved the shirt in my hand anyway, Lucy took his unspoken hint and left us alone. Still not taking it, he brought his mouth to my ear. "Sweetheart, you're about to tell my team your story, and I'd prefer not to be distracted by your tits that keep trying to play peekaboo around your current attire." That dark edge to his tone slid under my skin and I nearly forgot about the creepy house, especially when his breath blew across my ear.

*Well, I hope that's your breath, and not a ghost.*

"Please," he begged. "Wear it for me."

Once the goose bumps were fully formed for the third time since I'd set foot in that house, I accepted the shirt and wordlessly did as he asked. He tipped his head in a thank-you, and I gulped, knowing what was about to happen—story time. "Are we doing this here? The truth?"

Carter lined himself up alongside Grayson, and said, "I don't think this house can withhold a gunfight when the next team is sent. It'll collapse right on top of us."

"And you think another team will come?" my sister asked him, now the only one not clued into the fact those men were after *us*.

"You didn't tell her?" Jack asked in surprise.

Lucy faced me. "Tell me what?"

Before I could find the courage to share the ugly truth, a voice from Grayson's radio echoed through the room, "You have incoming. Three ATVs carrying eight tangos. Two guys on foot. We'll take out as many as we can and slow them down. But the fact they keep finding you means someone with you is tagged."

"The backpack," Carter snapped out in anger.

"Someone from the show is definitely helping them," Mason noted.

"It'd make sense for the show to track every team's backpack in case of an emergency," Mya tossed out.

"But someone from the show is clearly feeding the cartel our location," Carter said, sounding irritated that he hadn't considered we were being tracked sooner. But from where I stood, given how fast everything had happened, no one needed to be blaming themselves.

"Maybe we don't run," Oliver suggested, his tone calm. "If this place is going to fall, and they think we're hiding in here . . . we let it fall on top of them. Pick off any survivors."

"And save one for questioning." Jesse nodded. "Good thinking."

Jack reached for my hand. "I'm not risking having Charley and the women here in case shit goes wrong."

"Oliver and I will hang back with Jesse and Gray," Carter said. "You and Mason take the women away from here. Once we get answers and take them out, we'll find you." He took the radio from Grayson and tossed it, and despite the shit lighting, Jack caught it with his free hand.

Mason stepped forward. "Oliver's got medic training. If something goes wrong, he should be with the women. You've still got the jungle to deal with out there, not just these pricks. I'll stay back."

"You sure?" Mya asked, her tone soft as she reached for his arm.

Mason looked over at Lucy, then pulled his arm free from Mya's touch. "I'm sure."

Jack brought the radio near his mouth and asked, "What's our timeframe?"

There was static, followed by gunfire in the background, before an answer came back. "Five minutes tops."

"Get out of here," Grayson ordered as Jesse unstrapped a gun from the side of his leg.

Jack let go of my hand and took it from him. "Don't die. Any of you." He set his sights on Grayson. "I made a promise to your family, okay?" After Grayson quietly nodded, Jack grabbed hold of my hand again.

Once the six of us were back outside, I sucked in the fresh air, only to startle at the sounds of gunshots somewhere in the distance.

"You good?" I reached for Lucy's hand with my free one, deciding not to let go of Jack's as we ran.

"Not really," Lucy shot back without facing me, keeping her eyes on the uneven ground. "Who's after us?" she pressed again, the humor now absent from her tone. "The kidnapper?"

Before I could find the courage to tell her the truth, I stubbed my toe and then connected with an exposed tree root on my next step. I dropped her hand, so she didn't go down with me, but Jack didn't loosen his grip, and he kept me from face-planting with the ground.

"You with the falling, you're starting to remind me of Gray's wife. You okay?"

"Yeah, I'm good. Let's go." I hooked my arm with Lucy's and pushed forward as if nothing had happened.

It had to be around seven at night, and while there was still light out, being cocooned by the trees and their sprawling branches made it hard to see the sun in the sky. The sound of engines and gunfire were no longer present, but in its place a chorus of bugs orchestrated a private symphony as we moved. Thank God for the long-lasting bug spray and sunscreen we'd applied before our journey that morning.

"Wait, I think . . ." Oliver stopped and held out his arm. Not paying attention, Mya slammed right into it. He whirled around as she began rubbing her chest in small circles. "You okay?" Why was he mouthing that question? What fresh hell were we about to step into?

Gwen came up alongside Mya, just as Mya whispered, "Yeah, those arms of yours are lethal."

I'd swear I'd spied a sheepish grin from him, even in the shit lighting.

"What's up? You hear or see something?" Jack asked him.

"I think we just stumbled upon one of the cartel's sites." Oliver waved us off, motioning for us to step aside as he approached whatever it was he'd noticed that none of us had.

"Stay here," Jack demanded, his tone soft but decisive. "Give us a second." He retrieved the gun from the back of his cargo shorts and kept his head low, joining Oliver.

I couldn't make out anything there aside from the shake of Jack's head before he turned our way again. He tucked his gun at the back of his pants, which I hoped meant there was no immediate threat.

"What'd you see? Oliver right?" Mya asked him. "Does he have eagle eyes?"

"There's a small site there. Probably an acre of land. Enough light to see everything since there's no trees by the house," Oliver answered, walking back from wherever he had disappeared. "No overwatch towers. A house and a big garage. Only one guard visible sitting on the porch, holding a phone and rifle. Tapping his foot. Anxious. Looks like someone put the fear of God in him."

"And that means?" I asked.

"That he's probably the only one left alive, but he was ordered to hang back," Jack stated, his tone still steady.

"Oh." My shoulders fell, a touch of relief at the news, but I wasn't sure if I was allowed to welcome that feeling into my body yet. We still had to escape the jungle and find a way safely out of Brazil.

"If I shoot him before he knows we're here, and no one comes outside to check on him, that'd answer our question that he's alone," Oliver proposed, looking at Jack as if checking for his thoughts.

"And if people do come out?" Mya asked. "And there's a lot of them? Then what?"

"There won't be," Jack said with confidence I wanted to cling to.

"We could use water and food. Weapons. Medical supplies since ours may have been tampered with, and . . ." Oliver's focus fell to Mya's bikini top for a moment. "Shirts would be nice."

"You're suggesting we go into the enemy's fortress," Lucy whispered.

"I'd hardly call it a fortress. The house looks like it was uprooted from the suburbs and plopped there," Oliver said, his tone light and clearly trying to prevent her from panicking.

"We could look around. See if there's anything that can help us determine who at the lodge is helping them track us," Gwen said, appearing to be on board with the idea. "Maybe they have a laptop I can check, too."

"After I shoot him, and if no one comes out, I'll go in first and clear the property. Make sure it's safe for you all." Oliver folded his arms, squaring back his shoulders as if preparing for an argument with Mya.

"And if the place is rigged? You step on a booby trap

thing and blow yourself up? Then what?" Mya countered, her arms flying over her chest, mimicking him. Oliver's gaze dipped back to her breasts, the limited light filtering through affording him a perfect view of her cleavage.

"Then I guess it's my time, and I'll be meeting my brother on the other side." Oliver's tone was low and rough.

Shit . . . he'd lost his brother? How? When? I pushed down the urge to ask him questions that weren't my business, and Mya's arms collapsed at her sides as she stared at him in silence.

"No one is dying today." Gwen focused on Jack next. "If Carter can't get one of those guys to talk, we can't miss our chance to see if something is inside this place that'll help us determine who's after us."

"I know who's after us," I blurted, then covered my mouth even though it was too late to keep my thought from escaping. Too bad I couldn't reel those words back in. "But, um, not who's helping at the lodge." I assumed Jesse had clued them in during their huddle session back at the haunted house, but then I remembered Grayson and Jesse didn't have a name. Only I had that knowledge.

"And who's after us?" Lucy asked me, the exhaustion in her voice unmistakable.

"Just give me a gun," Mya insisted, not pressing for an answer like my sister, too focused on the fact Oliver was about to be a lone wolf. "If you're going in, I'm going, too. You need support just in case. And we shouldn't leave the others alone out here. Jack needs to stay back."

Oliver chuckled, not loud enough for that one asshole about to meet his maker to hear. "Like hell are you going as my backup."

"It's the only play." Mya stepped in front of him, lifting

her chin. Her petite frame was no match for Oliver's muscular one, and he dipped his head to find her eyes.

"Jack." I grabbed his arm, urging him to look at me instead of the face-off happening between Mya and Oliver. "What's the safest option? Keep running? Or maybe get ahead of these guys by going inside?"

Jack's brows flew together the moment I'd uttered the word "running," like some knee-jerk reaction. "If we can get answers, it'd be helpful to go in. And we could use supplies that aren't tainted by whoever planted that tracker, and God knows what else, in that bag," he finally conceded. "We're just lucky the water and food weren't poisoned."

I let go of him and held my stomach when a rumbling sensation hit me. *Just hunger, not poison.*

"But we wait," Jack said a moment later, then faced Oliver. "Hang back here out of sight until we hear from Gray. They should be done handling those men soon. And Carter will get answers from these fuckers, you know him. Let's have backup before we risk kicking the hornet's nest just in case there's more than one fucking bee."

Oliver turned our way. "Fine." He grumbled something I couldn't hear before telling Mya, "Guess you win, buttercup."

"It's not about winning," she bit back. "It's about you not dying, jackass." Then she spun away from him and started into the jungle, probably more so to place some distance between herself and Oliver than the house.

Gwen trailed after her and Oliver shook his head as Jack ordered, "Stay with them. Just give her a little bit of space so she doesn't kill you herself."

"Roger that." At Oliver's response, I had to assume Jack was higher up in the chain of command for their team.

"Go with him," I told Lucy. "I'll be right behind you."

She gave my arm a little squeeze, then nodded and joined Oliver.

I fidgeted with the hem of my new shirt, wondering if I ought to give it to Lucy instead. "I have to tell you something," I finally shared.

"Yeah, I know." There was almost a touch of humor to his tone, but I could've been imagining that, too. "And I never finished telling you my thing."

*Your thing. Right. Who's Jill? Who do I need to knock out for hurting you?*

"But let's move farther away from that guy while we talk. Well, possibly guys. Plural." He smiled at his last word, and I tilted my head, lost on the joke. "Sorry, was thinking about my mom . . ." He held my wrist and guided me away from the fence.

"Bad guys make you think about your mom?" *That should be my line.*

Once we were about fifty feet away from the perimeter of the house, he replied, "No, my grammar does, but uh, ignore me." He shrugged, and a boyish grin touched his lips. I was happy I could make that one out since his smile eased my nerves a bit. "So . . ."

I wet my lips, my anxiety back front and center. I'd rather talk about his mother than mine. *But here goes.* "Lucy doesn't know all the details about what happened the night the Fed died. She only knows bits and pieces."

He quietly reached for my hand and laced our fingers together, then pulled me closer, bringing our linked palms to his chest, just over his heart. How'd he know I needed those steady beats to get me through this?

"I don't want to hurt her with the truth." I hated the way my voice broke on my whispered words.

"She's an adult now, not a kid like when you took off."

"Yeah, but she also thinks that, um . . ." *Just get it out.* "She thinks our mom died in a car accident." I closed my eyes, thinking back to the night before Mom's accident. How she'd laid everything out for me. The new names and passports. The money. The plan to escape to London after she'd faked her death so we could meet up with her trusted friend. A way to finally escape the bastard who had control over her. But she'd asked me not to tell Lucy anything beforehand.

*"She's too young. She won't understand."* Mom had cupped my cheeks, tears in her eyes. *"When we're all safely in London, I'll figure out what to tell her. But if anything goes wrong . . . you take her to London yourself. You protect her, okay?"*

"What are you saying?" At the feel of Jack's free hand tracing the curve of my cheek, I opened my eyes.

"She was never supposed to die," I told him, my stomach twisting in knots. "Her plan was to fake her death in a car accident so the three of us could run away." He tightened his hold of my hand as I continued, "We were supposed to cross the border into Mexico and fly from there to London together. The car accident worked, and it was even reported on the news. My sister wasn't supposed to see that, though, and before I had a chance to tell her it was okay, that Mom was alive, we were taken from our house."

He grimaced but kept quiet, waiting for more.

"What Mom didn't plan for was her asshole employer sending people for us. He knew I could drive, because she taught me, and he had a heist that'd been months in the works, and since he thought she died . . . well, they needed a getaway driver at the last minute, and they came for me."

"Fuck," he rasped.

"They told me they'd kill Lucy if I didn't do it, and I

knew I had to make it out alive without getting arrested to save her." My body was trembling, but he drew us even closer, so our clasped palms were now all that was wedged between our heartbeats. "After the heist was pulled off, I was taken to his mansion in Malibu."

With his hand still on my cheek, he caught the sole tear that managed to escape.

"We were in his garage. Looked like a small chop shop, but it wasn't one. He's just . . . well, he's rich." I swallowed, trying to take my time to get through this, but also knowing I didn't have all day. "Lucy was in there, and I begged him to let us go. But that asshole had a change of heart. He needed someone to replace Mom on his team. And he decided it should be me. He wouldn't take no as an answer." Chills chased down my spine, and another tear fell, dropping onto his big hand cupping my cheek. "Two of the men there that night were undercover Feds. They broke their covers to try and save us." *This part. Fuck this part.* More tears fell, and Jack let go of my hand to pull me in for a hug, squeezing me against his chest. "Shots were fired. They didn't have a chance to call for backup. I guess they'd been deep under."

"I'm so sorry," he said, his mouth by my ear as he held me.

"One of the Feds managed to get my sister out of there, though. He tucked her away on the property just before he was shot. She doesn't know that. She doesn't know he died to save her life, and I don't want her carrying that burden." My stomach protested the memories. And the tension in my chest was going to crush me with the weight of my emotions as I relived that night.

"And you were framed for that?"

I shook my head. "No, I was framed for killing the other Fed. The one the bastard shot himself."

"Who is he?" He pulled back to find my eyes. "Who do I need to kill to set you free?"

My heart slammed against my chest at his words, at his promise to handle the prick for me. To end my nightmare. "Brant Luther," I hesitantly revealed.

His eyes widened in recognition. Because who didn't know that man?

"The rich *philanthropist?*"

I gave him a little nod, then whispered, "A wolf in sheep's clothing. And he hates me with a passion, because he blames me for killing the woman he loved."

"And who'd he love?" He cocked his head, holding my face with both palms.

I closed my eyes and cried, "My mom."

# CHAPTER TWENTY-FOUR

## JACK

"The guys are fine and already en route to us," Oliver said, interrupting the shock of Charley's last words. "Gray's tracking Gwen's charm bracelet to get to us."

Charley stepped free from my embrace, wiping away her tears to put on a brave face despite the emotions she had to be struggling with.

My heart was still thundering in my chest. I only had pieces of the story, but I had enough to know she was a good person. Not a criminal. And she deserved to be safe, and for justice to be served. And I'd do everything in my power to do that for her.

"Carter get anyone to talk?" I asked Oliver as Mya, Gwen, and Lucy came into view behind him.

"They didn't know much. Charley and Lucy were to be brought in alive and to Peru using one of their smuggling routes," Oliver explained.

I wrapped my arm behind Charley's back to hold her waist, drawing her close to me. I needed that connection and was grateful she didn't reject my touch with eyes on us.

"All I need is five minutes with one of their laptops to see if there's anything of value to help us," Gwen said as we moved back toward the house again.

"Yeah, okay." I motioned for Oliver to hang back with the women while I checked the location. The fence was camouflaged by nature, so I had to peel back some of the branches to get a decent look inside.

The man from the porch was now pacing in the front of the ranch home, a phone to his ear and a rifle slung across his chest. Maybe he'd just been notified the team dispatched to the jungle was KIA.

*You're alone here, aren't you?* The fact he'd stayed behind and never risked his neck to go in the jungle gave me hope he was important enough to keep safe. And that likely meant he'd be valuable for questioning.

Given the few words I could make out—strings of apologies and promises to locate what I loosely translated as "the packages"—I assumed he was talking to his boss.

Carter's fluency would be necessary to grill this guy while Gwen hacked their server to see if there was anything of use on it.

On the verge of turning back to join the others to discuss a plan, I halted when the man swapped his phone for a remote from his pocket. One of the garage doors opened to reveal a Bronco inside. Shit, he was leaving. But on what road?

Returning to the others, I brought them up to speed on what I saw, employing my best sarcastic tone when I shared the best news of the day, "And he's about to leave in a fucking car."

"The smuggling routes," Mya whispered. "There may not be roads for normal use around here, but I bet the cartel have their own roads in and out of Brazil."

"And our best source of intel is about to use one to get away." I snatched my pistol from the back of my shorts. "I'm going in. We can't wait." I gave Charley a little nod, then focused on Oliver. "Stay with them," I ordered and went back to the fence before anyone could protest.

With the man out of sight inside the garage, I used the vines obscuring the fence to hoist myself up. I dropped over and took cover behind one of the trees to wait for him to pull out of the garage.

There was too much distance between us for my 9mm to do any damage with him behind the wheel, which meant I'd need to expose myself. The second he pulled out in the Bronco, I stepped into view. He slammed on his brakes and made eye contact.

One or two beats of quiet enveloped us just before he did exactly what I hoped and floored it.

I walked his way as he gunned it, playing chicken with the SUV while waiting for just the right moment to make my move. He wouldn't be able to shoot me with his rifle while driving, especially at that speed, so the second a handgun appeared outside the driver's side window, I lunged to the right. My back hit the ground, arms extended, as I shot him through the open window at the same time he popped off a shot.

I nailed him in the forehead, and thankfully, he missed me completely.

Moments later, the Bronco smashed into the fence, creating a crater-like hole. No alarms sounded, and there didn't appear to be any sophisticated security on-site. Why would there be? No one came into the thick of the jungle and fucked with the cartel without a death wish.

I took a second to catch my breath, my free hand landing on my chest as I rolled my head to the side to ensure the crash hadn't garnered attention from anyone inside the house just in case my original assessment that the man had been alone was wrong.

"You okay?" Oliver called out a minute later, and I got to my feet as he reached inside the window of the black Bronco.

"He dead?" I asked, wishing I could've left him alive for questioning, but him aiming a vehicle at me and pointing a gun in my face kind of eliminated that choice.

"Yeah," Oliver answered. "Got his phone."

"Let me check the property just in case. Don't let the women come in here until I give you the all clear," I ordered while he leaned in through the window, probably securing the weapons as well.

I hurried inside, checking the rooms for cameras and anyone hiding inside. Once I cleared the last room, which was an office, I grabbed the laptop from the desk there, tucked it under my arm, then started for the garage. Three other vehicles were parked inside. No people.

I made my way back over to Oliver. "We're clear. No cameras inside. And I'm assuming the breach didn't trigger any silent security alarms to another cartel site, but that's only a guess."

"I'm sure their boss already dispatched a new team for the jungle," Oliver said, waving the women inside. "So, we shouldn't stay long."

Gwen and Mya were the first to come inside and Gwen honed in on the laptop, and I gave it to her.

"Here." Oliver handed her the cell phone, too, as Charley and Lucy joined us. "This is password encrypted."

"On it." Gwen went straight for the porch and dropped down onto one of the rocking chairs.

"You good?" Charley asked me, nudging Lucy to the side to block her view of the dead guy in the Bronco. Always so protective, and God, I kind of loved that about her.

I reached for Charley's shoulder and gave it a light squeeze while promising her, "I'm fine."

"For a second I thought you weren't going to move out of the way in time." Charley's whisper of concern traveled from her voice to her eyes.

"You shouldn't have been watching." My hand slid down her arm to reach for her hand. Not giving a damn that we weren't alone, and we had a dead man who'd lost his game of chicken three feet away, I pulled her against me. "And you're not getting rid of me that easy," I added, answering the question I thought—well, hoped—I saw in her eyes.

Her hands went to my back, and her short fingernails bit into my skin. She turned her cheek to rest it against my chest, and I held her there, exchanging a look with Mya. *Yeah, I know. I'm not falling. I already fell. And hard.*

Mya offered me a quick smile, and I knew she was doing her best to hide her emotions before peering Oliver's way. "I'm heading inside to find some supplies."

"I'll come with you," I said as Charley eased back from my arms and brushed away a tear. "Want to join us?"

After a quiet sniffle, she motioned to her sister. "Only if Lucy comes, too."

"You all go. I'll wait here for the others," Oliver suggested, a frown forming on his lips.

It only took me a second to determine why. He was mimicking Mya's look, and her attention was riveted on Oliver's bare chest. "What?" He dropped his eyes to his pecs.

"What?" she repeated, blinking. "I'm just thirsty."

"I bet you are," Oliver murmured, the double meaning not lost on any of us.

Leaving our canteens back at the haunted house was

probably not the best idea. Our dehydration seemed to be playing havoc on our focus.

"Shirt," Mya blurted. "You need one."

"So do you," Oliver bit back, eyes dropping to Mya's bikini top. He shook his head as if realizing he was hazy from the need of water, too, and roughly barked out, "Go. Now." He swallowed. "Please."

I observed the two of them, unsure what to think other than if they didn't screw soon, they might snap. Shaking my head, I stole my attention back to the issue at hand: the need for supplies and for it to be done quickly. "We'll be right back."

With my hand at the small of Charley's back, we walked toward the house. Gwen didn't look up from her screen as we passed her, completely absorbed in her work.

Once inside, Mya took the lead. "Lucy and I can grab water and food."

"Sure, thanks." I let the door shut behind us and faced the main hall. "We can grab weapons and those, uh, shirts we seem to be needing."

Mya whipped away from me, probably wanting to hide her blush, and Lucy went with her down the hall.

I quietly grabbed Charley's hand, leading her in the opposite direction.

"Is your mind racing?" she asked me as we walked the length of the hall. "Because mine is."

"I don't think it's taken a break since the first night I saw you at the players' lodge," I admitted as we turned into a bedroom.

It was eerily quiet, and I struggled with taking the time to encourage her to finish her story. "I know you have a lot more to tell me, but . . ." My attention swiveled to the closet, then back to her, and I let go of her hand.

"Yeah, we should wait until we're somewhere safe," she said, gently placing a hand on my chest. It wasn't a no, just a not here. "Let's see if these guys have good taste, I guess." Her casual tone managed to ease my nerves a bit as she opened the double doors to the closet. Her long fingers flew across the row of shirts hanging there before she settled on one and removed it from the hanger. "Bad guys iron and hang tees? Who would've thought?"

"Not me," I said, returning the small smile she'd sent me while holding out a black tee with U2 emblazoned on the front.

"I'll give this to Lucy." She draped the shirt over her arm, then grabbed a handful of others and dropped them on the bed covered in what looked like a quilt made by someone's grandmother.

I snatched a plain blue tee and pulled it over my head before removing the hangers from the rest. "Weapons room, and we're good to go," I said, feeling damn uneasy about being there any longer than we needed to.

Charley grabbed the shirts, clutching them to her chest like a security blanket, and followed me to the room I'd clocked earlier while clearing the house.

A mess of weapons were all over one table, oddly situated right next to what appeared to have been a game of unfinished beer pong likely interrupted by the call to come find us in the jungle.

Grabbing a black duffel bag from the floor, I knocked the red cups from the beer pong table to the floor, set the bag on top of it and began loading it up. I snatched the only vest I could find and shoved it her way. "Wear this over your shirt. It has a chest plate."

"Bulletproof vest?" She handed it back to me. "If there aren't enough for everyone, I'm not wearing it."

I cursed under my breath in frustration, but there was no sense arguing with her. "I assume there are more vests, but they're currently strapped to dead bodies in the jungle."

"And the vests didn't do much to help them," she shot out with a little shrug.

Okay, she had me there. I grunted and tossed the vest onto the table before zipping up the bag. "Yeah, yeah. Let's get out of here." I tipped my head toward the door, and we made our way to the front porch.

Mya and Lucy were already back outside, but I hadn't expected to see Gray, Carter, and Mason there as well.

"Where's Jesse?" I looked toward the Bronco, not seeing Oliver there. I dropped the bag as Charley began offering shirts to our semi-naked team members. "And Oliver?"

"Camila's other guys are heading back her way, so we don't have anyone on lookout. I sent Jesse and Oliver outside the fence to keep an eye on things." Carter exchanged a grim look with Gray and nearly growled out, "Someone pulled my image from the cameras back at the lodge. All our faces, in fact." The ice in Carter's voice had Gwen flinching.

I supposed Carter still wasn't aware of the Camila–Gwen thing. Of course, I doubted Carter truly blamed Gwen for the fact his face wound up online after he'd warned her "it better not happen." Because, seriously, none of us could've predicted this all going sideways the way it had. *Well, fuck. Except Camila.* "How do you know they identified us?" I finally spat out, then snatched a bottle of water from Mya's bag, realizing my hazy thoughts and lightheadedness were from dehydration.

Before taking a sip for myself, I nudged the bottle into Charley's hand, and she hesitantly accepted it. I focused back on Gray as he pointed to the computer on Gwen's lap, and she spun it around to show the screen with our faces and names there.

*Well, that sucks.*

"Camila just called to let me know the Feds are swarming the lodge. Show is officially canceled," Carter piled on the bad news that'd be a deterrent in potentially completing part of our mission. "And the Feds aren't just looking for Charlotte and Lucy, they're now here for me, too," he seethed, not even trying to hide his disdain for the three-letter agency. "My guess is my plane back in Tabatinga is now under the FBI's control, too."

"Wait, you're wanted, too?" The bottle slipped from Charley's hand, but I snatched it in time and my dry lips craved the water, so I stole a drink myself.

Carter swiveled his attention her way, brushing her off with an icy glare. "It's a long story."

"Aren't they all?" Charley whispered back.

"True." Carter dedicated his focus back to the laptop. "We're going to use their smuggling routes to get to Peru undetected before the Feds catch up with us. I'll have my other pilot fly my second jet there to extract us tomorrow."

"And how exactly are we using their smuggling routes to escape?" Charley asked him.

"Their smuggling routes are navigable by car," Gwen said after switching the screen. "And this map shows us which way to go."

*Well, that's one way to do it.* I squished down the now-empty bottle between my palms. *Do these fuckers recycle?*

"Won't the cartel find us if we're using *their* routes?" Charley's eyes dipped to where I held the crushed bottle before her attention climbed back to my face.

I tossed the bottle back into the bag with our other

supplies, because yeah, maybe I just killed a guy, but fuck littering.

"Not if we get out of here before they have a chance to send in another team," Gray spoke up before I could.

Using their routes wasn't exactly an ideal situation, but our options were limited with how many people were currently hunting us, not to mention the resources they would have at their disposal to track us.

"And even if they do find us, I like our odds," Gray tacked on a moment later.

"And what happens after that?" Charley reached for my free hand, and I swallowed her palm with my own and squeezed. "Don't you still have a kidnapper to catch?"

Or was the kidnapper also Brant Luther? I still needed to reveal that important detail, that I now knew who hired the cartel.

"With the show being cut short, how the hell will we, or Camila, for that matter, figure out who the insider is?" Point to Mya for the million-dollar question.

"Well, there's nothing on the phone or laptop that'll help us answer that," Gwen shared, shaking her head in frustration. "But if there is a connection between the kidnapper and who sent the cartel after us, maybe we should meet up with Camila and her team in Peru and work this case from a new angle?"

"Camila doesn't even know who—" Carter abandoned his words the second the dead man's phone began ringing. "Answer it," he directed, climbing the two steps up to join us on the porch.

Gwen set aside the laptop and promptly answered the call.

"I need a status update," a woman said, skipping a greeting. An American accent from what I could tell. "The tracker hasn't moved in thirty minutes. Do you have the packages?"

Charley stumbled back, taking me with her since I had a tight hold of her hand.

Carter spun his finger in the air, motioning for Gwen to end the call.

"Is that who I think it is?" Gwen asked, eyes wide. "Shannon?"

*Damn, you're right.* "The polygrapher. She's the one working with Brant Luther and the cartel?" At Charley's eyes widening, I realized I'd accidentally revealed the name. *Well, it needed to happen, but shit.*

"Wait, Brant Luther is involved?" Lucy stepped back, and Mason quickly swooped his arm behind her, stopping her from falling off the porch. "No, that can't be." She began frantically shaking her head. "This is all my fault. You were right, Charley. We never should have come here. I'm so sorry."

"You're saying Brant Luther is the one who hired the cartel?" Mason snapped out as Charley pulled her hand from mine to go to her sister. "*The* Brant Luther?"

*Yeah, welcome to my world of what the fuck.*

Carter lifted his phone, a reminder of the time-sensitive situation we were dealing with and that we needed to give Camila a heads-up about Shannon. "I need to call Camila."

"I'll do it while you wrap up the shocking Brant news," Mya offered, stepping forward and opening her palm. "Divide and conquer."

"Fine." Carter handed over his phone, then drove both hands through his black hair. The situation was frustrating, but seeing it get to Carter made it seem just that much more dire. "Let her know to be careful. Shannon might be working with someone else at the lodge, too."

"Roger that," Mya said, and I stepped aside when I realized she planned to make the call from inside the house.

"So, you're saying the man after you is the tech guru and businessman turned philanthropist?" Gwen rose from the rocking chair as the cell phone rang again. Carter waved a hand, an order to ignore the call.

*Tech guru? Right.* I vaguely remembered something about him making his fortune by inventing something techy, and he sold the IP to one of the titans of the industry. *When was that?*

"That's probably why the Feds were undercover back then," Charley spoke up, still hugging her sister. "I think the FBI suspected Brant was stealing intellectual property, among other things, and they were trying to . . ." She paused for a moment, took a steadying inhale, and I spied a nervous swallow. This had to be killing her, and I wanted nothing more than to hold her while she spilled her darkest secrets. But she needed to do this for Lucy. Well, for both of them. And if she'd let me, I'd be here for her when the dust settled. "My mom, she worked for him back then. Brant's the one who killed the FBI agent eleven years ago. He framed me for it. We've been running ever since."

"That's a plot twist I didn't see coming," Gwen murmured. "He became who he is because of that IP deal, and if you're a loose string in terms of exposing how he really became rich, his house of sainthood cards will fall. I can see why he'd want you dead."

"That's one reason, sure," Charley whispered. The rest of my team didn't know about her mom yet. But on the porch of the cartel's home wasn't the best place to get into those details. They now knew Charley was an innocent and in need of our help, though. We'd deal with the rest once this mess was resolved and she and Lucy were safe.

"But is he the one collecting women like they're game

show trophies?" Gwen grimaced as if disgusted by her own comment. "It has to be him, though, right? And somehow, bad luck brought you right into his line of sight."

"The women are blonde. Our age. Badasses somehow. They're all like you. Maybe he—"

"No," Charley cut Lucy off. "He didn't take them hoping they were me." She shook her head, and I agreed with her on that.

"The second he realized and confirmed you two were at the lodge, he changed his MO. Sent people after you, but used the cartel to make it look accidental," I theorized. "If Brant thought any of those other contestants from past shows were Charley, he would've done the same then. Found a way to snatch them straight from the show. No, taking them was about something else. An obsession of some kind?" Whatever his intentions, he was one sick fuck. And far away from being the saint the media had painted him out to be in the last few years.

"Well, if the missing women all look like you," Lucy began, her tone tentative, "that means they also all look like—"

"Mom," Charley mouthed in shock. "He's obsessed with our mother." Her arm banded across her abdomen. "That son of a bitch took those women because they remind him of her."

# CHAPTER TWENTY-FIVE

## JACK

Mʏᴀ ꜰʟᴜɴɢ ᴏᴘᴇɴ ᴛʜᴇ ᴅᴏᴏʀ, ᴀʟʟ ᴇʏᴇs ɪɴsᴛᴀɴᴛʟʏ ꜰᴏᴄᴜsᴇᴅ on her. "Camila's going to have her team grab Shannon the second she tries to leave the lodge. She'll bring her to Peru and meet us there."

"She have any idea on a timeframe?" I asked her.

"The Feds are holding everyone there overnight. Questioning contestants. Going through video footage. And they have agents in the jungle looking for us."

I focused on Gray. "At least you weren't there and on camera. Your father would flip if the FBI found footage of you at a reality show."

"But the Feds are going to see you," Gray reminded me. "It won't take them long to put two and two together. My father will have to intervene either way and do damage control to remove our connection to any of this."

"At least we have that option," Carter said, his tone firm. But I sensed some gratitude there as well, which was confirmed when he offered Gray a nod of thanks.

Gray wasted no time grabbing his radio, issuing orders for

Jesse and Oliver to return so we could leave the area before anyone else showed up looking for us.

"So, does that mean we're sticking to the plan and using the smuggling routes to Peru?" Gwen asked, closing the laptop.

"It's our only option." Carter pointed to the house. "Any security cameras here that need to be erased before we leave? I don't need them having any more proof I'm alive, let alone this team exists."

"No cameras on the property," I let him know.

"Their lack of security out here is a major red flag," Gray said, eyes on me. "Means they more than likely have a bigger compound somewhere else, and this is just an in-between spot for them."

"Like their own personal motel and refuel station on the smuggling route?" Lucy asked, brows shooting up.

"Basically," I answered flatly, that bad feeling in my gut mirroring Gray's. "We need to go." I patted Charley's back, signaling her to start for the garage, then slung the weapons bag over my shoulder.

"I downloaded the map from the laptop and air-dropped it to Gray's and Jesse's phones," Gwen said, walking at my other side. "Three vehicles. Three maps now."

"Thank you," I answered her as we entered the garage with three blacked-out SUVs: a Bronco, Jeep, and Tahoe. "Okay, spread out and see if we can find the keys." A few minutes later, Oliver and Jesse walked through the door.

"Mya, you get to ride with Oliver and Mason," Gray ordered, grabbing keys Mya had found.

"Of course, because that makes perfect sense for us to be together," Mya blurted, a touch of sarcasm in her tone as she tossed keys to Carter.

Gray shrugged off her words and added, "I'll ride with Jack, Charley, and Lucy."

I gave Mya an apologetic look before opening the back door to the Bronco for Charley and Lucy, then tossed the bag of weapons on the seat between them. With my hand on the top of the SUV, I leaned in and peered at Charley. "I'm getting you out of here safely, I promise." I nearly kissed her forehead, those bold green-blue eyes held so much trust and vulnerability, but I resisted and slammed the door shut. "Let's roll out." Sliding behind the wheel, I followed the Jeep and Tahoe to the semi-hidden gate on the property.

A few minutes later, we made it to a narrow dirt road, just wide enough for our SUVs, and Gray opened his phone to the map Gwen had provided in case we fell behind.

"We're about ten klicks from the cross point," Gray shared. "Looks like we'll be heading to the other side of the Amazon so we can cross the border."

"It'll take us thirty minutes at this pace, though," I pointed out as we hit a bump, jostling us around. Pretty soon it felt like we were riding over moguls on a ski slope, but without as much grace.

I shifted the rearview mirror to catch sight of Charley. She was squeezing Lucy's hand on top of the duffle bag. With the truth out of the way, I was sure they appreciated the comfort of being next to each other.

I turned my attention back to the route ahead, and had just issued the warning, "seat belts," when the next hard bump sent me rocking forward, my knee hitting hard into the column of the steering wheel.

How the hell did the cartel manage this path on the regular? And seat belts? When did I become such a dad?

At about twenty-five minutes into the drive, Gray piped

up, "We should be crossing the border into Peru any minute now."

"Oh, thank God," Lucy said, almost as if she'd been holding her breath.

Aside from braking for a few animals, we hadn't been met with any real obstacles so far, which almost had me worried. It was a bit too anticlimactic, and while that was exactly what I wanted, nothing ever went that smoothly in our line of work. So, I kept my head on a swivel, clocking every inch of jungle from left to right, as we drove.

"And it looks like we'll be turning onto an open road and leaving the jungle, too," Gray added, studying the map.

*Fucking finally.* I was more than done with this jungle and ready for paved roads. These situations wouldn't normally bother me, but . . . Charley was there, so.

"Once we're out, will the cartel risk coming after us on open roads?" Lucy asked. "Is the million-dollar bounty Brant offered worth it to them to risk exposure?"

Gray twisted in his seat to peer back at her. "At this point, they'll be more inclined to seek revenge for the fact we killed so many of their men." He shook his head and stole a look at me before facing the women again. "I'm still trying to wrap my head around Brant's involvement in all of this, though. As well as his obsession with your mother. I don't get it."

Looking in the mirror, I noticed Charley's eyes on Lucy. I knew those were details she didn't want to reveal to her quite yet, but they'd need to come out eventually. "I thought you wanted to wait until the group is together to discuss everything," I reminded him, unsure why the sudden inquiry.

"That was before I found out that Brant Luther's involved," Gray said matter-of-factly, a slight edge to his typical no-nonsense voice. I was about to cut through the tension and defend Charley, but then he added, "Nothing pisses me off more than people who parade around as saviors when they're secretly the devil."

*Fuck, okay, good. We're on the same page.*

"The FBI report I read said your mother was part of a heist crew. Did she ever mention what they were stealing?" Gray asked next.

*Like the IP that made Brant uber wealthy?*

"I honestly don't know anything about the heists my mom was involved in, or what I was forced to help him steal by driving the getaway car that night everything went down," Charley murmured, her tone hesitant. "He said if I didn't drive, he'd kill Lucy." Her voice broke at the mention of her sister, and damn, I knew how hard that had to be on her to face her demons and share the past with her sister and in front of us. "I have a feeling the bank heist was to cover up what they were really after, though, because I doubt it was money."

"What makes you say that?" I asked, catching Charley's eyes in the mirror.

"I overheard someone mention one specific vault they needed to hit," she answered as I reset my focus on the road, hitting another major bump.

"Maybe the other heists our mom, um, was involved in were similar?" Lucy sounded so hopeful, but she was probably much more clueless about her mom's secret life than Charley. "Mom never should have gone to Brant Luther for help when Dad died," she added when no one spoke up. "I still don't get how Mom ever got involved with someone like him in the first place."

After another turn and a quick cut to the left so we didn't wind up off road in the jungle, I rasped, "Sometimes people do things they wouldn't normally do to protect those they love." I knew nothing about Charley's mom, but I understood the kind of love a mother could have for her children. My mom may have been a library director, but she morphed into a badass when anyone so much as bothered me.

"Mom had a rough life before she met Dad, you know that. Fell into the wrong crowd. Began boosting cars before she was even sixteen," Charley said, her tone soft but still defensive. "When she met Dad, she gave up that life to start a family. But he didn't want her to work."

"And when she went to get a job after he died, she had nothing to put on her job application other than car thief," Lucy picked up the story, a sigh falling from her lips. "I know. But still. She went from being one of Brant Luther's personal drivers to joining a heist crew. It's crazy."

"That's how she got into bed with him?" Gray shot out, turning in his seat again. "Sorry, I mean, metaphorically."

I checked the mirror again, worried about Charley.

Her shoulders collapsed as she said, "Brant was in love with her, but she didn't love him back. And Brant was a disaster the night of the heist. Bloodshot eyes as if crying. Totally unhinged thinking Mom died in the accident. And then . . ."

"And what?" Lucy reached for her arm and squeezed just before I peered at the road again.

"I was only able to get out of the garage that night because Brant had been distracted by Mom," Charley whispered so low I nearly didn't hear her. "She . . . showed up . . . and jumped in front of a bullet meant for me."

Before Lucy had a chance to react, I spotted something from the corner of my eye. It was dark out, but was that another road? One not on the map. And was the movement I caught just my hypervigilant imagination, or . . .? I lifted my foot from the gas for a second, squinting to try and get a better look. "You see something on your side?"

"Fuck," Gray snapped out, dropping the phone and

shooting both hands to the ceiling a moment later. "Brace for impact. We're about to get hit."

\* \* \*

WHAT THE HELL JUST HAPPENED? WHY'D I FEEL LIKE I WAS in Afghanistan? The day an IED had flipped my Humvee. We'd been ambushed, and that night, death had only been an acceptable option if it was my own, not the men I'd been leading.

Groaning, I tried to fight off the memory of almost losing my team that day and slowly opened my eyes. It took me a minute to take in my surroundings. Smoke, burnt rubber, and the metallic scent of blood filled the air. Was I in an active war zone? No, that didn't seem right. I was—

*Shit. In the jungle.* "Everyone okay?" I rasped in alarm, our current situation coming screaming back at me. The sounds of gunfire weren't from the Taliban, but the cartel outside our Bronco. And we were being rammed again.

I was jammed up in an awkward position with my belt still strapped, digging into me.

"Everyone okay?" I called again just as gunfire echoed all around us, ricocheting off the Bronco.

"We're fine back here," Charley replied.

*Thank God.* But why wasn't Gray talking?

I felt around for the seat belt latch and unbuckled, my body immediately folding into an even worse angle, my neck hollering at me.

Positioning myself with my knees beneath me on the window that was pressed to the ground, I pivoted to the side and felt around for the lights, unable to see a damn thing in there.

Once the inside of the Bronco was basked in the soft glow

of the light, I could finally put eyes on my best friend. He was still strapped in, the belt holding him in place, but his arms and body were limp. Head hanging. Eyes closed. A gash across his brow and blood trickling down the side of his face.

He'd taken the brunt of the impact when we'd been struck, and I had to assume it was a tank or heavy-duty equipment that had flipped us so easily.

"He's not dead, right?" Lucy cried out just before we were abruptly plowed into again, sending me careening into the roof, bashing my head against it.

We kept sliding until we were wedged up against something solid enough to stop us. The jungle howled in protest to our being there as more rounds of gunfire blasted all around us. My team, more than likely, amid battle out there, and I was unable to help.

"Gray?" I shifted around again, trying to get to him. *Please be okay. You have to be okay.* I reached up and checked for a pulse, and my shoulders fell with relief. "His pulse is steady. And nothing appears to be impaling him."

Bullets continued to crack all around us, and the bullet-resistant windows would only hold up so long before the glass eventually did give way. Since the SUVs were used for smuggling routes, it made sense they'd taken precautions and had armored vehicles. *Thank God for their paranoia.*

Although, why were they shooting at us? Did the cartel bastards not get the memo Charley and Lucy were wanted alive not dead? Had something changed? Or did they no longer care?

"The gunfire, is that just from the . . .?" Charley let her sentence hang in the air.

"My teammates are returning fire." That I was sure of, and since we'd yet to be rammed again, I hoped that meant we were on the winning side.

Static popped over Gray's radio seconds later before Jesse's voice filled the vehicle. "Y'all okay in there?"

"Gray's unconscious," I responded. "The rest of us are good."

"Shit, okay. Give us another second. I need to check the tank and ensure they're all dead."

*Tank. Thought so.* "Roger that." I looked back to put eyes on Charley and Lucy again. They were behind my seat, both unbuckled and huddled together in an awkward position. Getting out of the SUV was going to be tricky with the reinforced glass. "We'll need to go out the trunk or climb out from Lucy's side door."

When Gray began coughing, I snapped my focus his way. "Well, that road wasn't on the map," he said before groaning. "You all okay?"

"Better now that you're awake." I reached out, stopping him from unbuckling. "That belt is keeping you from crashing into me."

"Shit, yeah, you're right." He shook his head, blinking as blood hit his lashes. "This must be their own version of border control. Or to ensure no one on their side tries to double-cross them."

"Which is why they left the road off the map," I said just as Jesse came back over the radio.

"We're clear for now. My guess is they'll have people waiting in Peru, though." Jesse paused for a second, then I heard him knock twice at the back. "Try and pop the trunk to crawl out that way. If not, I'll climb to the side to open that door."

I set aside the radio, and thankfully, the trunk opened with a little help from Jesse guiding it as it slid across the dirt road. "Gray's awake now," I yelled back to Jesse and Carter, standing armed behind our vehicle. "But he's hurt. Needs medical attention."

"I'm fine. Relax. Just a concussion," Gray stubbornly protested. "Get the women out, and we'll be right behind them." He looked at me and jerked a thumb. "Exit first. I'll fall on top of you otherwise."

Once the back seat was clear, I pulled myself through the opening to get there, then twisted back around to the front. "Let me help you so you don't hit your head again." Not waiting for him to argue, I leaned in and wrapped my arm around his body, keeping him from falling or fucking up his prosthesis.

"I'm good, I'm good," he grumbled once freed from the front seat. I helped him out, then went back for the bag of weapons before joining everyone.

Charley lunged into my arms, and I dropped the bag to hold her. "I got you," I murmured into her ear, cupping the back of her head, drawing her cheek to my chest.

It was dark out, but there was a flurry of movement around me—my team planning next steps—and there I was, lost to Charley's soft inhalations as she squeezed hold of me.

"I found a first aid kit when I got food and water back at that house," Mya said.

From over Charley's head, I watched Gray wave off Mya's attempt to help him walk around our banged-up Bronco. "I hit my head; I didn't bust up my leg."

Mya lifted her hands and backed up, tossing out, "Oliver can patch you up temporarily until you can get stitches."

"As much as I'd love to hold you . . ." *Forever, in fact.* "We should get going." We were still in cartel-controlled territory, nowhere near safe.

"Right, I'm sorry. I, um." She pulled back, sniffling. "Not sure what came over me. I'm not normally like this."

I brushed the pad of my thumb along the contour of her cheek, taking time we didn't have to ensure she was okay. "Like what?"

"Weak," she said, the word popping harshly from her mouth. Her anger toward herself for feeling vulnerable was obvious, but she had no idea how strong she was.

From over my shoulder, I spied Carter signaling me to "wrap this up." Hell, had I hit my head, too? What was wrong with me? We had to move. We were easy targets out here, but I needed her to know how I saw her. "You're not weak. Not even close. You're one of the strongest women I've ever met." I laced her fingers with mine, not waiting for her to argue with that fact, and we joined the others crowded by our two remaining vehicles.

The headlights of the Jeep and Tahoe were the only light we had to work with in the thick of the jungle.

"What's the plan?" Mya set her back to the Jeep. "Civilization is just around the corner. We'll be out in the open and sitting ducks the second we drive into Peru now that they know we have their vehicles."

I looked over to see Oliver applying a bandage to the gash on Gray's head. Gray's wife, Tessa, was going to grill me about that when we were Stateside, but hell, it could've been a lot worse. The fact we'd survived being hit by a tank and weren't riddled with bullet holes was a step in the right direction. Not that I'd be mentioning that to her.

"So, we don't drive over," Jesse said, sliding his rifle across his body, ready to go round two with the fuckers. Or, well, I'd lost count what round we were at. It'd been a long day. "We walk."

"Then find cars to boost?" Charley piped up, her words garnering everyone's attention. She backed up, bumping into the Tahoe, taking those same panic-like steps she'd taken in the treehouse the other night. "Sorry, but I mean, what choice do we have?" She looked around at us all. "I assume given your training, you all know how to jack a car, but I can help."

"Yeah, we know how to boost a car," I said, trying to rid my voice of any inflection that would make her think I was second-guessing her innocence. And I wasn't. I was just second-guessing her mother's. What mother teaches her daughter to steal cars and drive like she was a Formula 1 Grand Prix racer in the first place?

"Mason and I can walk ahead. Scout out the area. See if there's anyone waiting for us before we leave the jungle," Jesse suggested, already on the move as if Gray or Carter had given him the go-ahead. Forward moving. Forward thinking. I had to remind myself he'd not only been an Army Ranger, he'd been a hitman for the CIA once upon a time ago, and he could handle almost anything thrown his way. Today was proof of that.

"We can't wait here," Gray said. "We'll have your six, but we'll hang back far enough."

"Roger that," Mason confirmed, then secured a rifle and hurried after Jesse who was nearly out of view.

"Did the men in the tank have anything on them that could be useful?" I asked Carter.

"Yeah." Carter dug through the duffel bag of weapons I'd put together back at the house, arming himself as he answered, "A text with orders from their boss not to let any of us make it out of the jungle alive."

"Even Charley and Lucy?" I winced at the news, unsure why I was so surprised considering they'd tried to demolish us in that Bronco not even ten minutes ago.

"Looks like the cartel cares more about retribution than the bounty. Plus, I'd guess they don't have any direct ties with Brant Luther. They probably don't even know the bounty came from him," Gray suggested, holding the side of his head, which worried me.

"I highly doubt the head of the cartel had any clue his men even made the deal to catch Charlotte and Lucy." Carter stood tall, a 9mm in one hand, and a blade half the size of a machete in the other. "He wouldn't give a damn about a million dollars. But his people who make a lot less money than him operating his smuggling routes would."

"So, you're thinking Brant Luther had Shannon reach out to them and offer money on the DL?" Gwen asked. "When the men kept failing and dying, word got back to their boss about what was going on."

"And I'm assuming they had to make up a story as to why some Rambo-like men in the jungle were cutting down his guys," Mya tossed in her two cents. "My guess is they lied to cover the fact they made a backroom deal without his knowledge."

"Well, shit, how many enemies can we possibly rack up in one day?" At Oliver's words, Mya turned and whacked him in the chest.

"One more now that you just jinxed us and said that." Mya shook her head.

"Let's just get the hell out of this jungle. I'm working on arranging a safe house, but we need to put some distance between ourselves and the cartel," Carter said. "Ready to go?"

"I was born ready," Oliver teased, and I knew that was to annoy Mya. Some things, even in the throes of Hell, would never change with them.

"Remind me again why I fought Gray so hard to get you on my team?" Carter with a joke? Or was he serious?

"Hey, that pissing contest over me is why you two joined

forces and created Falcon Falls," Oliver pointed out. "I'd say it worked out."

"Yeah, yeah," Carter grumbled. "Let's just move out."

I knelt alongside the bag of weapons and took two magazines for my 9mm, then Gray killed the lights on the Jeep and Tahoe. "You doing okay?" I asked him once we began walking, following the others.

"With all the shit I've survived in my life," Gray started as we entered the thick of the jungle, "a tank won't be what takes me down. No worries, brother. Plus, you somehow seem to always have my back when I need it."

"Always will." The emotions that hit me as we walked side by side were unexpected to say the least. We were all okay, and we'd make it through this shit storm. That was what we did. Resilient should've been inked on our bodies, because that's what we were on this team. And I needed to remember that in moments like these.

Gray slapped my shoulder, and I suppressed my wince from the pain, forgetting I'd jacked it up in the accident. "But I'm not the one who needs you right now. She does."

I cleared my throat, more emotions pushing to the surface, and I damn near choked on them as I searched up ahead in the dark, only a shadow of movement where Charley walked by her sister. "The thing is," I said with a sigh, my shoulders falling as if weighted down by my realization, "I think I might be the one who needs her."

# CHAPTER TWENTY-SIX

## CHARLOTTE

"So, Mom didn't die in the car accident? Instead, she was there that night, and got shot? I don't understand."

I'd expected Lucy's questions at some point, but I'd hoped she'd hold off until we were on safe ground. After changing course two times to avoid more traps the cartel had set for us, we were finally in the world of streetlights, paved roads, and people. But safe wasn't the word I'd use to describe our situation quite yet.

I stole a look at Lucy, unsure what to say as guilt and pain fought for space in my already hungry gut. It was after nine at night, and I was pretty sure I'd only had a granola bar since breakfast. I remembered Mya had packed snacks back at that house earlier, but we'd never had a chance to eat after we left. *Why couldn't she wait till after we at least ate again to have this conversation?*

"Well?" Lucy prompted, interrupting my hangry thoughts. *Here goes nothing.*

"Mom faked her death. We were going to meet her over the border in Mexico and fly to London together. You were never supposed to see the car accident. She didn't want you to know the plan ahead of time." I rushed through the details as quickly as possible, hoping it'd ease the pain. The streetlamps were just bright enough for me to easily make out her furrowed brows over her shocked eyes. "I didn't get a chance to tell you because Brant's men took us right after. When we never made it to the airport, and Mom saw the heist on the news still took place without her, she must have put two and two together and circled back to come save us."

She stopped walking, forcing me to halt as well. Whipping around, she cried, "Eleven years, Charley. Eleven freaking years. You could've told me."

Unsure whether to pull her into my arms for a hug or give her room to breathe, I found myself simply staring at her. When I tried to scratch together the reason I'd kept the secret for so many years, it sounded weak to even my own mind. "I thought it'd be better for you to think her death was an accident."

Jack turned back, putting eyes on us. He didn't come our way, but he remained in place waiting, still such the protector.

Fixing my eyes back on my sister, I explained, "While you were hiding outside where that Fed stashed you for safety, Mom took a bullet meant for me. And I—"

"So help me God," Lucy rasped, whittling the space between us to inches, stabbing a finger at my chest as tears glistened in her eyes, "if you dare say you feel guilty for her dying, I'll turn around and go back in the jungle and just let it eat me alive." Her wobbly lip screwed with my focus. "She chose the life she chose, and she put us in that position. The only good thing Mom ever did as far as I'm concerned is take a bullet for you."

"We need to go," Carter urged. And as much as I wanted to stay there and hash out everything, to finally shed some of the weight I'd carried for so long, he was right. We had to go, because we weren't on safe ground.

Lucy pulled her hand back. "Wait . . . you didn't tell me because of guilt. No, you didn't tell me so I wouldn't hate her. Blame her even more than I already do." She shook her head and looked toward the others waiting for us just up the road. Carter caught her eye and not-so-patiently waved us over. "She may have wanted us to escape and start over somewhere new, but she was the reason we needed to escape in the first place. She was a criminal." And with that, she obeyed Carter's command to get a move on, leaving me rooted in place, replaying every decision I'd ever made.

"Hey, you okay?" Jack stepped in front of me, a fist beneath my chin, guiding my focus up to meet his eyes.

"Not even a little bit," I admitted, blinking back tears.

Jack's lips parted, his reply cut off when Jesse called out, "There's a shopping center up ahead." We'd reconvened with him and Mason ten minutes ago. "I have Wi-Fi again, and I googled the name of the plaza. They're open for thirty more minutes."

"Then we need to move quickly before the cars are gone from the parking lot," Gray said, stealing a look back our way.

"How long since you've boosted a car?" Jack asked me— a far cry from whatever words of wisdom he'd planned to give me about my sister's reaction to my revelations about Mom. But oddly, it was exactly what I needed him to ask so I could refocus. "I know she taught you to drive, but since you said earlier you can help *procure* one as well . . ."

"It's been a minute." *More like over a decade.* "Technology has changed a lot in cars, but I think I can handle it." I swallowed down the uneasy swell of emotion pushing up into my throat. Was he wondering why she taught me to steal cars? Did he blame her, like Lucy did? Would he think I was as bad as she was if I did this? "If *you* can handle me helping? You're a law-abiding citizen, and I'm offering to use—"

"We need to break the law to save our lives." Dropping his fist from my chin, he brought his hand to link with mine, and we began following the others. "Carter will get names for the stolen cars, and they'll wind up with more than enough cash to compensate after the fact, I promise."

"Is Carter wealthy or . . .?"

"Think Bruce Wayne without the bat suit. A total badass that's loaded with unlimited resources and gadgets." He gave me a small smile, then tugged my hand, a reminder we were in a hurry.

*Batman, got it. Nice ally to have. Scary, but nice.*

"We need three cars if we can manage it," Gwen said once we all neared the parking lot.

From where I stood, there were slim pickings at the late hour on a weekday. In my opinion, our best bets were the two older model Honda Civics and the one two-door Lexus.

"I've got this one." Carter pointed to the Lexus. "Get the Civics."

*Mmm, Batman knows his cars, too.* At least we were on the same page.

Carter wasted no time breaking into the Lexus, never setting off an alarm. And Jesse went for one of the two Civics and got to work.

Without waiting for the go-ahead, I pulled my hand from Jack's and went to the early nineties Honda Civic SI. Mere moments later, the driver's door was open, and I had the car started.

I rummaged through my memory about the car's particular facts. They'd been super popular back in the day, and Mom used to make me memorize different features about cars. *A turbocharged 1.5-liter four-cylinder under the hood that'd give us 192 pound-feet of torque. With the six-speed manual transmission, we'll be in good shape with this one.* It was almost as if that'd been Mom's voice in my head, not my own. "Mind if I drive?" I asked Jack.

His lips tilted into an unexpected smile. "I'd mind if you didn't." He opened his palm and motioned toward the driver's side. "Please." He urged Lucy to hop into the back seat, and she gave me a hesitant look—like she was unsure if she wanted to share the same air with me—but thankfully, she quietly slid into the back seat.

Once behind the wheel, I didn't miss the way Lucy sat behind the passenger seat, knees turned toward the door, arms folded, and eyes out the window. *Yeah, you're pissed. I get it. Hate it. But need you to live, so, I'm ignoring it. For now.*

"Shit," Jack said while getting into the car, then he rolled down his window. "Two police cruisers just pulled into the parking lot. We don't know if they're here for us but head out cautiously."

As if on cue, the police car lights both flicked on, and they began our way. Not a great sign.

"If they pursue, just lose them. We'll find each other after that." Gray handed Jack a phone through the window, then hopped into the passenger seat of the other Civic.

Without hesitating, I took off, and we split into three directions. The two police cruisers chose to follow Carter's Lexus and my Civic. Guess that answered the question if they were there for us. At least Jesse's Civic was without heat.

Not even two seconds onto the road, and they were boldly shooting at us.

"Cartel must've sent them. Not the Feds," Jack hissed, grabbing his gun. But instead of shooting back out his open window, he rested the weapon on his thigh, and I had to remind myself they were still police officers hunting us, even if the cartel paid them off. "You okay?" He looked back at my sister, and when I checked on her in the mirror, I saw her gripping the back of his seat, barely managing to hide the terror in her eyes.

Lucy gave him a tight nod, and then I ordered, "Buckle up."

Thankfully, she did as I asked, and then I strapped in. I needed to completely focus on the vehicle if I was going to turn the Civic into something that could outperform a cop car.

*"It's not the car that makes a race. It's the driver."* Mom's words came back to me, giving me the confidence boost I needed to do this.

I kept my eyes on the road, because where my eyes went, so would the car, and I needed to keep us from crashing.

"There. Turn onto that busier street," Jack directed, pointing up ahead. "They're less likely to shoot at us with other cars around."

Once there, I weaved in and out of traffic, glad—if not a little surprised—Jack was right.

I leaned away from the steering wheel at the perfect arm's length to comfortably drive fast. There was a sharp turn just ahead, and I reduced my speed and applied the brakes at the right time to lose the unwanted speed at the apex, allowing me to maintain control of the car. The second the wheels were straight, I accelerated and flew forward.

Jack and Lucy kept quiet, and all I could hear was my own pulse in my ears.

The Civic SI had a more aerodynamic body with a greater wheelbase than some of the other models, and I did my best to use that to my advantage, but we still couldn't seem to shake the police cruiser.

"How's the gas tank?" Jack leaned over to check while asking. "Half a tank. Good."

"Are you okay?" my sister asked, still clutching hold of Jack's seat.

"I will be when we lose them," I rasped. "Give me a second." After checking my mirrors, clocking their location, I took another turn, then depressed the clutch to disengage the engine from the wheels as I let my foot off the accelerator. I moved the shifter up to the next highest gear, then released the clutch while pressing down on the gas, and I was about to floor it when a better idea hit me. A move Mom had taught me. And that one-second feeling came to mind. "Everyone, hold on." I pulled a quick U-turn, purposefully spinning the car fast before braking hard. "My turn to play chicken."

Facing the police car, along with other vehicles, I gunned it in the same lane as the cruiser, preparing to go head-to-head with them. At the last second, I shifted around them and jumped the median, practically flying over the divider in the road, before landing in the lane, heading back in the natural direction of traffic going the opposite way of the cruiser.

As I accelerated down the road, Jack twisted to look behind us and let out an uncharacteristic whoop. "Nice fucking job."

"Thanks. Did we lose them?"

"You bought us time and distance. Time to get off the main highway and lose them for good," Jack said, pointing to the next exit.

A few minutes later, I pulled over as he prompted and killed the lights. In the dark, parked in an alley, I finally took a deep breath before peering over at Jack.

"When was the last time you drove?" Jack asked, not even trying to hide the shock in his tone. "You, uh, don't exactly seem rusty."

"I practice when I can." I gave him a little shrug. "Just in case . . ."

"Thank God for that. Don't think I could have pulled off what you did in this antique." I couldn't see his mouth, but I could hear the smirk in his voice on that last word.

Our conversation in the pool at the lodge felt like forever ago, and to be sitting there joking even at a time like this somehow felt right. Normal, even. How was that possible?

"Let me call the others." Jack placed the phone on speakerphone, and Gray picked up immediately. "We're good. You?"

"We're good," Gray answered. "And I just got word from Carter, he lost his tail. Camila also texted. She's still stuck at the lodge. FBI won't let anyone leave yet. But that also means Shannon is stuck there, too." He paused for a second. "But there's been a change in plans for our next stop. We decided it'd be better to head to Ecuador. We can't stay in Peru with heat on us now. Carter's going to arrange a safe house."

*Drive to Ecuador? How far was that?* "We'll need to boost new vehicles since we've been marked in these," Gray continued.

"How are we getting across the border if we're all wanted now?" Lucy asked, an edge of timidness in her tone.

"Money goes a long way. It's the universal language," Gray answered.

"Right," I said. "Bruce Wayne without the suit."

Gray chuckled. "So, she knows."

"She knows," Jack replied with a quiet chuckle.

I leaned back in my seat, totally spent, then lazily rolled my head to the side to check on my sister. She hadn't released her death grip on the sides of Jack's seat. I forgot she'd never been in the car on any of my joy rides over the years. This was all new for her. Not to mention the fact she'd only just learned Mom didn't die in the accident that night, but Brant Luther shot and killed her. She was overwhelmed. Still angry with me for lying.

"What do you say?" Jack's question pulled my focus back his way. "You up for round two of stunt driving and illegal border crossing?"

A shocking smile met my lips. "There are two things I can do all night long."

"I know one of them," Jack returned, his voice deep, suggestive, hinting at our night together. "Tell me driving like you're in a *Fast and Furious* flick is the other one."

# CHAPTER TWENTY-SEVEN

## CHARLOTTE

"Hey, you." Jack's sexy voice rousted me from the foggy haze of that place of in-between-sleep.

I blinked a few times, trying to get my bearings. I was leaning across the console, my head on Jack's shoulder, while clutching his hand like a lifeline as it rested on his leg. "How long did I sleep?" I rasped, my voice still heavy with sleep. Releasing his hand, I sat up and rotated my neck, unsure if the pain there was from the weird position I'd slept in or from the military-type tank knocking our SUV over like it was weightless.

"You've been out since we got breakfast three hours ago." Jack quickly flexed and wiggled his fingers before lightly grasping the steering wheel. Guess my grip on his hand was tighter than I'd realized.

I checked the time, then peeked over my shoulder at my sister, still working at the knots in my neck. "Same for her?"

Lucy was on her side, hands beneath her face, and her knees bent up to fit in the back seat of the Jeep Cherokee we'd jacked shortly after I'd morphed into the stunt driver my mother would have loved, using skills she taught me I'd only ever used that one night eleven years ago. And yet it felt like it was only yesterday.

"A little bit after you. And she, uh, asked me questions I couldn't answer, assuming you'd told me the whole story, I guess."

"Shit, I'm sorry." My messy bun was long gone, and my hair was tangled around my face. I checked my wrist for a hairband, but I must've lost it at some point. "Are we, um, getting close?"

"Almost there. We crossed into Ecuador while y'all were asleep. Clearly, without hiccups. We passed through a more, I guess you could say, *discreet* border crossing. I followed Carter through. Never even had to roll down my window."

"Guess money really is the universal language, especially considering those cartel thugs were willing to go after a bounty without their boss knowing." I looked out the window at the stretch of mountains that were so close it was as if I could reach out and touch them. "You must be exhausted by now. You should've slept while I drove earlier," I chided, focusing back on him as he tilted his head my way. I caught sight of his tired eyes for a moment, but there was a hint of a smile on his lips as he turned back to the road.

"After last night's epic display of road skills, I trust your driving more than my own. What I don't trust are assholes who could come out of the woodwork, and I'd prefer to be awake until we're at our final destination." He grimaced, and I wasn't sure why until I looked ahead and saw a truck loaded with trees. "Yeah, speaking of that . . . I'll be forever traumatized by trucks hauling wood because of that movie."

"I never saw *Final Destination*, but I've seen the TikToks about the scars it's left on your generation."

"Ouch." He laughed, then checked the rearview mirror as if worried he woke my sister. "My vintage-antique self, hmm?" Angling a quick look my way, he eased off the gas pedal a touch, placing more distance between us and the truck up ahead.

"Oh yes, so, so old." I winked, shocked that I was even in a remotely playful mood after everything we'd endured in the past twenty-four hours. It was seven in the morning, and I hoped the new day wouldn't bring new problems.

"I got a text from Carter twenty minutes ago." His tone was much deeper than moments earlier, a reminder we weren't out of the woods just yet.

I adjusted my seat belt, so it wasn't digging into my ribs while peering at him. "News?"

"The FBI rounded up the rest of the contestants from the jungle, and after questioning them and everyone at the lodge, they finally allowed them to leave. Camila's team nabbed Shannon on her way to the airport."

My shoulders collapsed at the good news. It was still hard for me to wrap my head around the fact both Jack and I had a connection to Mila. That she was the reason we'd been brought together.

"Camila's currently flying with her security team and Shannon to meet us at our new safe house as we speak," he added. "And I promise, once we're together, we'll get to the bottom of everything going on."

I knew he had a lot of questions he wanted to ask me—including if Brant Luther would really kidnap women because of his obsession with my mom—but I was pretty sure he was biting his tongue, knowing I'd prefer to wait and share.

After that, silence filled the Jeep for a bit, time inching by at a sloth-like pace. I was eager to get off the road somewhere safe and also clean up. At least we hadn't had any assholes come out of the metaphorical, or literal, woods after we'd boosted the Jeep Cherokee.

My stomach groaned, and I slapped a hand to my abdomen in embarrassment since we'd eaten a few hours ago. The guys had stopped at a place in Peru that was open 24/7, and Oliver had gone inside and pretty much bought everything off the menu, claiming Peruvian food was some of the best on the planet. After devouring every morsel while Jack drove, I was definitely in agreement with Oliver, even if I had been starving.

"We'll get you something when we get to the house," Jack tossed out. "I'm hungry again, too. We burned a lot of calories yesterday."

"I'd rather burn calories a different way," I said suggestively.

At the feel of his hand on my thigh, I looked down and set mine on top of his before our eyes met. "Me, too." And based on the dark look in his eyes when he peered at me, I was pretty sure he wasn't thinking about a stair climber.

*Makes two of us.* "Eyes on the road, mister," I teased.

He flipped his palm over on my thigh, and I obeyed his silent request to link our fingers together, loving how easy things were between us. We just seemed to fit together like two matching puzzle pieces. I knew he had a past, though. One that had broken him.

With a little more time to kill, and no desire to talk about myself, I found myself saying, "Tell me about Jill."

The Jeep slowed a touch at my words, but then he resumed speed and checked the mirrors. Carter's Land Rover was now between us and the *Final Destination* truck, and Jesse was at the wheel of the minivan traveling behind us. When we'd boosted our current vehicles from a neighborhood—yeah, we'd all felt guilty about that—Mya had joked that since Jesse was now a dad, the minivan suited him best. Jesse had tossed her a comical look while hiking his pants up, a total dad thing to do, in my opinion.

"If you don't want to talk about it, it's okay," I finally said when he didn't respond after a few uncomfortable seconds had gone by. "I'm the last one to press about personal stuff." *But do I need to run Jill over with my car?* A chill flew down my spine at the morbid thought, but I already hated this woman for hurting him, so I'd at least let the mental image of smoking her in a car race simmer in my mind.

"It's not that, it's just . . . do you really want to know?" He peeked at me from over his shoulder, and I nodded. After a sigh, he shared, "Jill's my ex-wife."

I wasn't sure why my stomach protested that fact, but it'd done a hard flip. Was this . . . jealousy? Because at thirty-one, I'd never been in love. I'd never given a man my heart. This was a completely foreign feeling for me, and I wasn't sure how to handle it right now. *Is this what Lucy goes through?*

How could Jill not have seen how lucky she'd been? Sleeping in bed next to Jack. Hearing his "I love yous." Having his hands trail over every square inch of her body the way he'd done to me the other night. Clearly, they weren't—

"She wasn't the love of my life," Jack continued in a low voice, basically finishing my trainwreck of thoughts, and he squeezed my hand.

"But you married her." I wet my dry lips, trying to digest the fact some woman named Jill had badly fumbled the ball by losing a man like Jack. My normal instinct would be to blame the guy. But I just . . . refused to believe Jack had botched things.

"I did." He switched lanes and took the exit off the highway at the sign that said we were in Cuenca. I hoped that meant we were nearing our destination. I was so tired of being on the road, being out in the open. But at the same time, I craved the extra moments with Jack. To hear his story. To know more of who he really was.

"I was young and in the Army. Still a Ranger at the time."

*Right. You became a Green Beret.* And he'd brilliantly displayed his skills keeping us alive in the jungle.

"We met at a local bar in Fayetteville, North Carolina, where she was from. A lot of guys I served with, well, they either avoided marriage because they were worried it'd distract them while deployed, or they wanted to be married to give them an extra reason to make it through the war." His tone dropped lower, gravellier as he continued, "I was obviously in the second camp. I wanted love. Someone to talk to on the hard days. There, uh, weren't many good ones during the war. But having someone to come home to, well . . ." He kept his eyes on the road, and I heard the strain of guilt in his voice as he added, "When I say it out loud, it sounds like I used her, but I swear that's not the case. I thought I loved her, and maybe I did. But I was young and didn't know what I know now."

"I can't imagine a man like you using a woman," I said, feeling the need to reassure him I didn't think less of him. God, I was the last person to judge someone. "What, um, happened?"

"She wanted me to leave the Army. I eventually gave in and did what she asked. Tried real estate, and I hated every fucking second of it." He lightly chuckled, pausing before adding, "I think a lot of those who serve struggle with civilian life, though. It's just so different. I don't know how to explain it."

"I get it." I nodded, though he wasn't looking at me, eyes still focused on the road as he followed Carter around multiple turns.

"Jill wound up leaving me because I couldn't hack it in the civilian world. During the divorce process, I found out she'd been cheating on me throughout our marriage. But yeah . . . she wasn't the person I thought she was."

"I'm so sorry." Tears formed in my eyes, hating that a man like him had ever been hurt. I remembered him telling me in Cape Town about wanting the kind of love his parents had, and he'd never found it.

"In some ways, I get it. I mean, we're asking our wives to hold down the fort while we're gone for months or more at a time, and it's a lot of fucking work. They get lonely. And just because I was loyal . . ." He shook his head. "So, uh, after the Army I wound up with the CIA," he said, shifting gears. "If you saw the movie *13 Hours*, basically that's what I did. Protected CIA officers or ambassadors. Things like that. Gray's sister, she, um . . . well, I watched over her."

"And how'd you end up in this line of work?" I asked, deciding not to continue the Jill conversation since he'd made the abrupt subject change back to work. If he wanted to leave her in the past, I'd leave her there, too.

"Gray created a security company, and he finally got me to join. Then we wound up partnering with Carter later on. So yeah, here I am. Operating is still my life." He swallowed and shot me a look, as if there was a question he wanted to ask me: *Can I handle him operating? Would I ask him to quit like she had?* The question didn't come, though, and he quickly returned his attention to the road ahead.

Carter had stopped outside a gate just off the roadway. We parked behind him as he reached out his window and punched in a security code. No house in view yet, but I assumed it was farther back on the property. From my estimations, we were right by the Andes Mountains in the southern region of the country.

I looked back at my sister, wondering if she was fake sleeping, allowing us a "private" moment to talk. No way was she that deep of a sleeper. No, that was me.

"So, what do you want to do with your life once your name is cleared and this nightmare is over?"

I whipped back around to face him just as the gates were opening, allowing us entry. "I've never even . . . I don't know. I never thought I'd have a life outside of running. I never allowed myself to daydream the possibilities."

He let go of my hand and cupped my cheek, the car remaining stopped despite Carter pulling through the gates. "It's time you start thinking about that, because it will happen. Pretty soon you'll get the chance to do what you want with your life."

"You really think you can help clear my name?" My tears were going to fall, and I'd be unable to stop them. This beautiful, wonderful, strong man was giving me hope, and I'd never let myself feel that way before.

"Of course." His thumb smoothed along my cheek.

"And what about Brant?" I closed my eyes, remembering the moment Brant Luther had cupped my cheek, swiping his thumb over my dimple as he slid the blade of a knife along my rib cage, cutting me.

"You'll never need to worry about Brant Luther after this, I promise." I flicked my eyes open at the darkness in his tone, just in time for him to look deep into my eyes as he said, "Because I'll be personally killing that son of a bitch."

# CHAPTER TWENTY-EIGHT

## CHARLOTTE

"Forget Bruce Wayne," Lucy began, "I think Carter is more on the Iron Man level in terms of his money and access to stuff."

Standing alongside her, we took in the view of the "safe house." Its Mediterranean style transported me back to Spain, or when I lived in Sicily for a few months three years ago.

"When it comes to this man," Mya said, nudging Carter in the side where they stood by their Land Rover parked on the U-shaped driveway, "you don't even know the half of it." She lightly chuckled. "Then again, neither do I. He's a mystery to us all, and we work with him."

"Real funny," Carter said glibly, removing his unscathed sunglasses. All this beauty and mystery surrounding us, and what I really wanted to know was how in the world his Ray-Bans survived our episode of *Survival?*

*Really, Charley, that's what you're focusing on?* "So, we're staying here for how long?" I asked, forcing myself to get with the program.

Jack swiveled my way, pulling himself from the quiet conversation he'd been engaged in with Gray and Jesse near the minivan. "We stay until we locate Brant Luther, and then we figure out next steps."

"Wait. We don't know where he is?" I questioned as I left my sister's side to get closer to Jack.

"Camila touched base just before we pulled in," Gray began, settling into operator mode again. "Her jet should land in about forty minutes, but after we gave her Brant's name, she did some research while en route. Seems he's been off-grid ever since—"

"The first season of that game show two years ago," I blurted, putting it together. "He really does have those women."

"There have been rumors he's had some health issues," Gray continued. "We can't be sure of the specifics, and his corporate PR team has done their best to make sure of that."

*Corporate PR my ass.* I'd done my research over the years to keep tabs on Brant, and it'd made my stomach turn to see how he'd gone from raising eyebrows that warranted undercover Feds at his office to being some charitable do-gooder who "gave away" twenty percent of company earnings every year to charities. My guess over the years was that he used the charities to launder his dirty money.

"I'm trying to make sense of all this," Lucy said, joining my side again. "You think while he was getting treatment, he suddenly snapped and decided to abduct women because they looked like our mom?"

"Maybe he thinks they're Mom?" I replied to her, and Lucy peered at me, skepticism in her wide eyes. "But in my opinion, Brant's a sociopath. He definitely was one eleven years ago when Mom started to fear him." *Well, so she told me.*

"Either something triggered him to begin abducting women who look like your mother these past two years,"

Gray said, "or he's been doing it for a long time and flew under everyone's radar."

"True, this could just be a new way he's going about it." The idea was unsettling and made me want to vomit. "Did Shannon talk? Confirm Brant's behind this?" Why hadn't I asked that yet? That was an important detail.

"Camila's working on it. Using her own form of a lie detector test on her," Gray shared with a smirk.

"Polygraph the polygrapher," Gwen murmured, catching Carter's eyes for a moment. "If Camila doesn't get her to talk, I'm sure our resident Iron Man will." She winked, then angled her head toward the house.

Carter muttered something too low for me to hear as I asked, "If Camila knows things somehow, can't she put her hand on Shannon's arm or something and just see the future? I have no clue how that works, but . . ." That worked in movies, and we were practically in one, so why not?

"She can't get a read on Shannon. And Camila doesn't, um, see into the past," Carter explained, his shoulders relaxing; although, I had a feeling no part of that man was ever truly relaxed.

"And that means?" Lucy asked before I could.

"Camila not being able to get a read on Shannon's future probably means Shannon doesn't have one," Gwen said, interpreting Carter's cryptic words.

"Does that mean you all plan to kill Shannon?" I folded my arms, unsure how I felt about that. Yeah, she helped the cartel track us down, and she was more than likely involved in the women going missing as well, but . . .?

"I'm not planning to kill her, no," Carter said flatly, then he motioned toward the house. "Let's get inside. Once Camila's team is here, they'll secure the perimeter for us. In the meantime, we have cameras and alarms if anyone gets within five hundred feet of the house."

"And how'd you happen to come across this place? Even Iron Man has limits," Lucy quipped, her tone playful.

"It belongs to a friend of a friend who owes me a favor," Carter answered from the side door of the home near the detached garage. He typed in an access code and the light on the panel turned green. "I arranged to have clothes and toiletries brought here for us. All the closets and bathrooms have everything you need," he said while opening the door. "And the kitchen has been fully stocked with food."

Carter walked through the door, and everyone immediately followed. With Jack in tow, we entered the house, making our way down a long hall that emptied into the grand foyer. The outside had been breathtaking, but the inside was next level with a fountain gurgling near the marble staircase.

*Oh, so this is how the other half lives?* Glancing over at Lucy, she shot me a quick look and I could tell despite how she seemed these past few minutes with everyone, she was upset with me. Upset that I had kept secrets from her this entire time. *Oh, Luce, I only did it to protect you.* I subtly shook my head to clear the emotion rising in my throat and focused back on Carter. "So, can you trust this friend of a friend not to tell the FBI or cartel we're here?" I had to assume the answer was yes, but I needed him to spell it out for me before I'd allow my body to relax and exit the fight-or-flight mode I'd been in since yesterday morning.

Carter's brows stitched together, clearly disturbed by my lack of trust in his judgment. "Yeah, the man who owns this property hates both the cartel and the Feds."

"And he's probably more scared of you than both of those groups," Gwen tossed out, patting Carter's shoulder. "Well, I don't know about everyone else, but I need a shower." She pointed to the stairs. "Let me know when Camila's here."

"Second bedroom should work for you. It'll have what you need," Carter told her, speaking through barely parted lips for some reason.

Gwen whirled back, her gaze skating up and down Carter's body. His clothes looked as rough as all of ours after the day in the jungle yesterday. "And what is it that I *need* exactly?" Despite the playful smile from Gwen, I'd swear there was a hint of allure in her tone that I had to chalk up to fatigue. Because she couldn't be flirting with him, right?

Gray stepped around Carter, blocking Gwen's line of sight of the man, but bringing him close enough for me to catch the strong grit of his jawline. "Gwen," he rasped.

I remembered Jack telling me Gray's brother-in-law was her father; so, he was Gwen's uncle. Of course he wouldn't want his twentysomething-year-old niece making eyes at his co-team leader. Heads would probably roll back home if her dad was anything like these guys.

"I was teasing. Relax." Gwen yawned and then resumed her trek up the stairs, disappearing a moment later.

"Why do I feel like Gwen's flir—"

"Don't say it," Carter cut Oliver off, and he couldn't mask the agitated look on his face. Well, maybe it was less distress and more . . .

. . . Frustration. *Ohhh, you need to get laid. Yup.* I recognized that look. He just didn't want it to be with Gwen. *Good call, big man.*

Gray faced Carter, that tight line of his jaw still there. "Something happen back at the lodge I should know about?"

And Gray just read the room.

"You had eyes on us while we were there." Carter angled his head, the challenge clear in his eyes. His Ray-Bans may have survived the jungle, but they were about to get crushed by his palm. "You tell me."

"Okay, boys." Mya stepped between them and stretched out her arms. "Neither of you slept on the way here. You're way grumpier than normal. Just go clean up. Our attitudes are not the only things that stink around here right now."

"Yeah, you definitely need a shower," Oliver said to her, obviously trying to break the tension that was still heavy in the air between their team leaders.

"Same here. I'm offending myself," I piped up, trying to join Oliver's attempts to stop a possible face-off by two tired operators. Plus, I really did need to wash up. My hair was wild over my shoulders, and I'd also lost my "nipple coverage" when I'd removed the bikini top to get comfortable during my nap on the way there. And based on Jack's clenched jaw, eyes on my chest, we both realized I was braless in front of a bunch of men at the same time.

My arms flew across my breasts, but of course Jack seemed to be the only one who noticed since all other eyes were on the Carter-Gray standoff.

Well, and then there was Oliver, who was busy eye-fucking Mya who appeared to have lost her bikini top at some point as well. Catching his eyes, Mya immediately dropped her arms as barriers between Gray and Carter at the realization and mimicked my move.

*Oh, you're playing with fire, Mya. That man looks like he wants to rip you apart, buuuut in a good way.*

I twirled around, searching for the other point of that triangle of theirs, and discovered Mason hanging back near the double doors, arms folded over his chest, remaining quiet. His eyes weren't on Mya but on the tiled floor.

"Clean up. Meet me in the library. Third door down this hall," Carter grunted, stealing my attention. My head was already spinning with everything we'd dealt with; I didn't need whiplash from the group dynamics as well.

"I take it you've been here before?" Lucy peered at Carter, and he nodded before taking the stairs two at a time.

"I'll walk you two to one of the rooms," Jack offered, nudging his chin toward the stairs.

"I'd rather have a room to myself for now," Lucy said, clearly not ready to let go of her anger, and walked around me to get to the stairs.

"Lucy, wait." I reached for her, hating the friction between us. "Let's talk."

She gently pulled free from my touch, and my knees buckled at her rejection. "You had eleven years to process everything," she whispered, her back to me. "Just give me time, okay?"

"I'll make sure she finds her way to a bedroom and not some sex chamber," Mya joked, coming to my rescue. Well, I assumed it was a joke. "And Jack can still show you to yours," she suggested, eyes on him.

It wouldn't eliminate the hurt, but maybe being alone with him wasn't such a bad idea. A tight hug from Jack was something I could use right about now. *Maybe I don't deserve his comfort.*

Before I could allow that thought to marinate, Jack linked our hands together and addressed Jesse, "Let me know when Camila's here."

"Roger," was all Jesse said, as we bypassed my sister and Mya and went up the stairs ahead of them.

Once on the second floor, Jack let go of my hand and, after peeking into a few of the rooms, settled on the bedroom at the end of the hall.

I peered at the bed, which had a black leather headboard and bold red comforter with red and black leather pillows.

I angled my head and stepped closer, trying to make out what was peeking out at the edge of the bed. Mya's earlier joke came back front and center when I picked up what appeared to be a metal rod attached to—

"Is that what I think it is?" Jack interrupted my examination of an object I'd only ever seen in a movie. A movie that I had totally watched for the plot. And by the plot, I meant the hot actor who starred in said movie.

"It's like Mya's the psychic one."

"Nothing surprises me when it comes to Carter's associates. And I use that term loosely." Jack reached for the steel bar, which had ankle cuffs on each end. And not the fuzzy ones. No, it looked like something belonging to a torture room from the 17th century.

Still kind of hot, though, if I was being honest with myself. "So, this is to restrain your legs, and—"

"If you squirm or try to move, the bar extends, forcing your legs even wider."

"Great, the jaws of life for my legs. Guess that's one way to find out how flexible I really am," I teased.

He set down the sex-torture object, turned away from me, and tore a hand through his hair. He was adorable, trying to hide the fact the idea of having my legs spread wide open turned him on.

*I mean . . . I was hella turned on, though. So . . .*

"The shower is, uh, open to the room, huh?" His nervous laugh as he pointed out the obvious was a nice redirection. An interesting way to distract his thoughts. Maybe mine, too.

"That's one sexy shower. Theme of the room. Sex." Now my cheeks were hot. It wasn't like this man hadn't already devoured my body with his mouth. Why was I getting shy now?

Jack coughed into a closed fist, and even with his back to me, I could tell he was adjusting himself. Erection. Check.

I stepped next to him to take in his view of the shower, which also provided a view of the scenery just beyond the house. On the other side of the clear partition was a huge picture window open to the mountains. "At least we can pee in private," I joked, pointing to a room off to his left I assumed had the sink and toilet.

He looked over his shoulder at me and smiled. "I should let you wash up."

"Or you could stay?" *What am I doing?* We'd just survived a quick bout in Hell, and I had no desire to take a joyride back to that hot inferno anytime soon, but was I horny? *Why yes, yes, I am.*

"What about what you said in the treehouse the other night?" He left my side like he needed to place some distance between us. Maybe so he could think with his head and not his *other* head. What I didn't expect was for him to go all the way to the open doorway. Arms rigged across his chest. He leaned his right shoulder against the interior frame, and despite the lazy posture, the man still gave off "I'm hard as a rock" and "fuck me" vibes. Nothing soft or sweet about him right now.

Replaying his question, I had to remember what I'd said in the treehouse, because that felt lightyears behind us. But I was also slightly distracted by how he was staring at me. In a room with a sexy shower. And a bed with ankle cuffs meant to provide him perfect access to have his way with me. And God what a way that'd be . . .

"You know the truth now, though. Well, most of it." *There we go, voice. You still work.* "Things have changed."

He pushed away from the door, barely hiding what appeared to be a wince. I was more than a little concerned he'd hurt himself in that accident last night. But then he closed the door and turned the lock. "Is that right?" He slowly faced me, a hard look washing across his features.

"Yeah, they have," I confirmed with more confidence that time. And then, without hesitation, I removed my shirt and tossed it to the tiled floors.

His eyes dipped to my breasts. A slow, slow journey as he took his time to look at me. And I took my time checking the bulge in his cargo shorts that even the heavy bulk of material couldn't hide.

"Shower with me." I swallowed, eyes back on his face, and his gaze flew up to meet mine. "Well, maybe a hug first. Because I'm a fucking mess over getting shot at multiple times, watching people die, my sister hating me and—"

Before I could finish my words, he pulled me against his chest, caging me in his muscular arms. And the way he protectively held me allowed the floodgates to open as tears streamed down my cheeks.

"Should I hate my mom for what she did?" I asked, my voice thick with emotion. "She worked for Brant for years. Yeah, she said he was unhinged, but wasn't he always a bad guy? Why'd she stay so long if she knew it put us in danger?" Why'd she finally decide to leave? "She taught me everything she knew. Almost as if she planned for me to follow in her footsteps, you know? But then she said no whenever I, um . . ." How could I tell him the next part? What if he hated me? Judged me?

"What is it?" he asked, pulling back to find my eyes.

I chewed on my bottom lip while also chewing on my thoughts, determined to get through this. I didn't want any more secrets. "I was at community college, bouncing around from major to major, confused about what I wanted to do with my life. And then I dropped out a few weeks before she died. I asked her to get me a job with her crew. It was alluring. Driving fast cars. Weaving down streets." God, my stomach hurt at admitting this. I couldn't even get the words out because I hated them so much. I'd spent eleven years busting my ass, working harder than I'd ever thought possible to provide a life for my sister, and I hated knowing Mom could've done the same. But she chose to be a criminal instead. And, once upon a time, I was more than ready to follow in her footsteps.

"You were twenty, Charlotte." He cupped my face. Hearing him pull out my first name felt like he was about to drop something serious on me. "That's still young. And you saw your mom as this kickass woman who could race like she was a professional driver, and you looked up to her . . . You wanted to be like her. And you can't blame yourself for that." He angled his head, drawing his face closer to mine. "I bet you asking to join her crew is why she quit and wanted to run away. She may have taught you skills in case you ever needed them to survive, but she clearly didn't want that life for you."

Was he right? Was it never about leaving Brant, but about protecting me from becoming like her? And did that mean I was—

"No. Not your fault. Don't go there. And when this is all over, you have to find a way to let go of the past. It's what we do now that matters."

I wanted to believe him. To buy into that idea. Maybe one day. One moment at a time. "Then live in the now with me," I said decisively.

His brows slanted as he studied me. "What do you want me to do?"

I gulped, turning my eyes to the shower. "I think you know exactly what I want you to do."

# CHAPTER TWENTY-NINE

## JACK

My PALM WENT TO THE WINDOW AS THE DOUBLE showerheads rained down over us. "What if someone's watching us?"

"Who's going to see us? Someone hiding on the mountainside?" She distracted me from my worries by wrapping her arms around me, drawing her naked body flush to mine. Her tits smashed into the hard wall of my back, and I hooked my arm around to catch hold of her hip.

"If they did, I'd need to burn their retinas with my—"

"Heat vision?" she teased, her breath fanning across my shoulder blade. "Don't tell me, you're Superman in our Avengers-Justice League crossover event. From a reality show to a superhero movie, it makes perfect sense."

"The fact you know the difference between an Avenger and someone in the Justice League just makes me l—" I cut myself off before I dropped the L word on her.

Swapping places with her, I set her back to the window, her ass cheeks pressed against the steamy glass, likely leaving a ghost of an imprint there. She bit on her lip, and it took all my resolve to play off my near admission, relying on

307

misdirection to save my ass. And possibly my heart. "You just fit in so well with my team, I mean. Your humor. Bad jokes and all." I winked, trying to play it cool, even though I was fucked when it came to this woman and how she so quickly owned my heart.

"Bad jokes, huh?" She chuckled.

From her laugh to the way she fit so perfectly in my arms, I was completely taken with her, and I was damn near tempted to go ahead and fuck her against this window for any random person or animal to see. Okay, maybe more than tempted. I was a bull charging the flag, ready to go and forget objectivity. Subjectivity. Hell, all the "tivities." *What is wrong with me?*

"Yes, horrible jokes," I said with a smile I hoped was more charming than devilish. Because heaven help me, my dick was as hard as that rod attached to the bed with her naked in my arms. And it had been ever since she'd held that ankle cuff in her hand while visions of licking her cunt, not sugarplums, danced in my motherfucking head.

*Still* biting her lip, clearly to torture me, she lifted her chin, eyes boring into me, a challenge to keep up with whatever I was planning to do next. *Oh, I'm going to get you clean before getting you really, really fucking dirty, sweetheart.*

Carter had clothes stocked for our room. But what about condoms?

Reaching down, I slid my finger along her seam as the water continued to rain down over us. She arched into me, and I reveled in how wet she was. It wasn't from our shared shower time. I did that to her. And fuck if that wasn't a good feeling. "Tell me you want this," I groaned. Damn, I needed this woman.

Her hand skimmed between our bodies. Long fingers flew

over my abdomen to the ink at my side. She paused there for a moment before sliding her hand down to cover mine. Eyes never leaving mine, she murmured, "Make me forget the last twenty-four hours, Jack." Then her long lashes swept down, hiding my view of her eyes as she added, "Make me forget the last eleven years, too."

My forehead dropped to hers, and I stilled my hand between her legs. "I don't think it's possible to fuck away our problems, sweetheart," I admitted, my tone rougher than I'd intended. Desire was coursing red-hot through my veins, drowning out my concerns for Peeping Toms on the mountainside or possible bad guys en route.

"Are you sure?" Her voice cracked.

*Damnit.* I wanted to scoop her in my arms and steal her away to some place safe from the chaos of our situation. But that'd be running, and she said things had changed. We just needed to clear her name so she could live again.

"Charley . . ." I pulled back as her eyes fluttered open and gorgeous blue-green irises stared back at me.

She rested her hand on my cheek and licked her lips. "Then make love to me and promise me everything will be better soon."

"Make love," I echoed back. Damn Cupid and his fucking arrow. There was absolutely nothing I wouldn't do for this woman.

Trade my life for hers? Without a second thought.

Kill for her? Done. Planned to do it again.

Fuck her senseless against the window and forget the outside world existed? You bet your ass.

"Yes, make love," she repeated, tears joining the water droplets from the shower on her cheeks. "I have an IUD. I'm safe."

"Same." My lips tipped into a slight smile and her giggle

tripped my brain back to reality. "Not the, uh, IUD part. The other thing. Safe."

She copied my smile, her one dimple on full display. "I don't know how much time we have, so . . ." She walked her hand back up between our bodies and set it over my heart while she continued to palm my cheek with her other, staring into my eyes.

I knew deep down in my gut she was my "when you know, you know" girl. I finally understood how the guys on the team felt when they described their feelings about their wives. It was still a lot to take in given the short amount of time we'd spent together. Though, we'd packed a lot into that one night in South Africa, as well as a lot in the last few days. I didn't want to scare her away by being too intense.

We both flinched at a hard knock at the door, followed by Jesse yelling, "There's been a change in plans. Meet us downstairs in five minutes!"

I closed my eyes and snapped out, "Roger." My team were a bunch of unapologetic cock blockers. Couldn't the "change in plans" news wait until after I gave my woman what she needed?

Charley gripped my biceps and rasped, "How fast can you come?"

My eyes flew open, and my heart raced as she reached between us and fisted my cock. "How does zero to sixty sound?" I teased, thinking back to her *Gone in 60 Seconds* driving skills from the night before. "See, bad jokes. Can't help myself."

Her tongue poked between her lips, a slight taunt. "Not so bad. Kind of adorable, in fact. How about you make love to me later and fuck me *fast* and *furiously* now."

*I see where this is going.* Her play on words drew a laugh from me. And I'd happily give her the owner's manual to not only my jokes but to my heart, mind, and body. "Roger that," I said hoarsely, then set my mouth over hers, stealing a kiss I wanted to last a lifetime. But the countdown was on. The hourglass had been flipped, and I wanted her to get off before anyone else came knocking.

Letting go of my cock, she buried her fingernails into my biceps, drawing her body flush to mine. Rotating her hips, my throbbing dick rubbed against her core and the feel of her slick heat was heavenly.

I slid my hand down her thigh and hiked up one of her legs to wrap around my waist, opening her up as I buried my fingers between the folds of her pussy. Wrapping my other hand back around to her ass, I squeezed tight before finding and circling her bud with my finger. Fervently strumming her clit, I applied a little pressure to her tight hole, and I swore the moan that unleashed from her lips could be heard in the fucking mountains beyond the window she was pressed against.

I captured her lips, swallowing that moan, and I knew exactly what I needed to do in order to pull that coveted orgasm from my woman. "I'm going to devour your pussy first," I told her, my lips nearly catching hers as I spoke. Her blown pupils confirmed exactly what I'd thought. Dirty talk was perfect foreplay. "Then I'm going to fuck you against this window while you come. You'll ride my cock through your orgasm. That work for you?"

She blinked a few times, then confirmed her answer with a nod, eyes wide with anticipation.

My attention was drawn to the drops of water rolling down her chest between her full tits. Unable to stop myself, I cupped her breasts and gently squeezed. Lowering my head, I licked the water from her breasts, swirling my tongue around each nipple before dropping my gaze lower.

God, her body was incredible. Her stomach was perfectly soft. Full hips to grab hold of, and her ass was on another level of fuck-me amazing.

But those eyes. That smile. And the way she laughed and hit me back with jokes was what sent me over the edge.

"We're probably down to four minutes, mister." She playfully bit her lip again, the little tease.

I captured her sassy mouth with mine, tongues meeting, dueling, forging an even deeper connection between us.

Reminding myself our time was limited, I lowered her leg and dropped to one knee, taking in the sight of her puckered and ready for me.

The second I ran my tongue along her seam, she held the sides of my head in place. "Fuck my face, sweetheart, like you're riding my cock," I demanded, wanting to see her wild and free.

She whimpered when I pushed two fingers inside her, then took control, shifting up and down, rubbing against my mouth, hitting her sweet spot just how she liked it. How she needed it. I urged her along with my tongue, coaxing her close to that breaking point. I shifted one palm to her ass cheek, keeping that sexy cunt tight to my mouth so the friction as she moved was more intense for her.

"Jack," she cried. "Oh my God. Yes, yes."

I waited a moment for her to climax, for her taste to flood my mouth before adding, "Be a good girl and come for me, Charley."

Seconds later, she let go of my head and gripped my shoulders, urging me up. Her needy voice was music to my ears. "Now. Fill me now. Please. While I'm still coming." So. Fucking. Perfect.

I pushed off the floor, bending my knees to get her into position, nudging the head of my cock to her soaked center.

She hooked her leg over my hip again, and I slammed into her without hesitation, pinning her to the window.

*Holy—* Sex bare with her was going to officially do me in. It was too damn good. Eyes-in-the-back-of-the-head, kill-me-now good.

One hand slammed to the window over her shoulder as my other gripped her side to keep her in place while her pussy muscles tightened deliciously around my cock.

With her tits smashed to my chest, water spraying over us, I thrusted in, over and over, never pulling all the way out, not wanting to break our connection. Breathing hard, I did my best to keep my eyes on her, not allowing them to squeeze tight in resistance to not coming too fast. I wanted to stay with her for as long as possible. The team could wait.

*Fuuuuckkkk.* I cursed again. Maybe out loud, or maybe in my head? Hell if I knew. My ass muscles were squeezed as tight as my teeth were clenched, still refusing to be a one-minute man. *Ninetyyyy secondsss, at least.* My brain was mush, even my inner thoughts were breathless and spent.

"Holy shi—Jack, you feel so good," she said while tightening her walls around my dick again. "Oh God, I didn't know it could feel this good. I've never . . . without . . ."

Knowing I was her first bare sent me over the edge. I exploded inside her, my body almost convulsed from coming so hard.

When she finally set her leg down, I slowly stepped back, pushing away from the window as I slid from her warmth. Watching my cum drip down her inner thigh, mixing with the shower water, had me wanting more. *I wish we could have a round two right now.*

"That was intense," she panted, leaning against the window for support.

"I'd say so." I angled my head, trying to process what just

happened. "Um, now that you're good and dirty, I suppose I should clean you up before we get out?"

I had to force myself to rip my eyes away from the masterpiece before me to find the soap. There were what I assumed to be new loofahs hanging on a little hook by the shower handle. Reaching for one, and a bottle of body wash, I squirted the purple liquid onto it.

I wanted to take my time washing her, time I knew we didn't have. More things to save for later.

She watched me with a sated, but provocative look in her eyes as I knelt before her again. The bandage from her leg was gone, the wound closed. It looked good, but I'd make sure to have Oliver check it later just in case.

Intensely focused on the task at hand, I ran the loofah up the inside of her thigh, cleaning my remaining cum from her skin. When I swiped the loofah across her pussy, she bucked at my touch.

"I'm thinking we're going to need to go again later," she murmured, and I looked up at her, probably sporting a goofy, love-drunk smile.

*Hell to the motherfucking yes.*

"But much slower next time," I promised, gently massaging her clit to clean her up, never losing her eyes in the process.

She angled her head toward something in the bedroom, and my dick managed to go from lazy to awake damn fast. "Oh really? You want that?" I assumed she was referring to the bedside "jaws of life," which was going to make me laugh every time I replayed her words. Well, also horny.

"I'm thinking it could be . . . fun?"

I smirked. "Spreading your legs open so I can fuck you with my mouth would most certainly be pleasurable for me," I rasped the truth, then slowly stood.

I soaped up her breasts next, taking my time on her nipples. We were beyond five minutes. But no one had come knocking yet, and I'd take an extra minute or two if my teammates were going to give it to us.

At the sight of the scar beneath her ribs, I backed up, unable to stop myself from asking, "How'd that happen?" I had scars all over my body. All by-products of the job. No mystery there. But this one bothered me. There was a story behind it, and I had a feeling it'd tamp down my ever-growing erection.

She brought her fingers to the two-inch faded mark. "It happened that night. Brant Luther had smoothed his hand over my dimple, a reminder of my mom. Then he slid the knife over my shirt, cutting me."

I remembered her flinching when I'd touched her dimple, and now I hated myself for producing that memory for her. My hand went still as I waited for her to continue.

"Brant was going to take his time killing me. He blamed me for Mom's accident even though it made no sense. But one of the guys from his crew stopped him. He was a friend from my mom's old crew. The one who got her the job with Brant. They started arguing about what to do with me."

Listening to her recount it all, her voice almost aloof, I could tell she was trying to distance herself from the memory just to get the words out. I wanted to wrap her in my arms and tell her it would all be okay, but I knew she had to finish sharing first.

"Mom's friend distracted him but not long enough. Brant went over to his bench and swapped his knife for a gun." She frowned and covered her scar with her palm as if trying to stop the bleeding from eleven years ago. "That's when Mom burst through the side door near where I was standing, and Brant fired. I think it was in reaction to being startled, but

Mom was in front of me, blocking me. The bullet hit her right in the chest." She paused for a breath, and I couldn't wait any longer and pulled her in my arms.

I'd already wanted to kill Brant, but the more I learned, the more I knew there'd be no mercy.

An "are you coming" knock at the door made her flinch. I tightened my hold on her and hollered, "We'll be right there," before anyone could ask what was taking us so long.

"Both Brant and her friend looked shocked to see her alive," she continued in a daze, ignoring the interruption, "and Brant let go of the gun and ran to Mom. He was holding her in his arms, and she looked at me, then at him and whispered something I couldn't hear just before she . . ." She shook her head, her lower lip trembling as she recalled the painful memories. "I knew she was dead, and I hated leaving her, but I had to get to Lucy. I, um, had the gun, the one he shot both her and the Fed with, and I didn't hesitate to shoot one of his men trying to stop me from leaving to get to Lucy."

"What about the other guy? The man you said was your mom's friend?"

She pulled back to find my eyes. "I had the door open, prepared to leave, and he yelled for me not to move. I turned around to see him aiming at me, but I saw the look in his eyes. He couldn't do it. So, I ran."

Thank God she'd read him right and he never pulled the trigger.

She sniffled, swiping at her cheeks as if trying to hide the tears that blended in with the shower spray. "I found Lucy, and we rushed back to our house. I had to take the chance to go back for the passports and money Mom had left for us. Brant sent men after us, but we got away."

"I'm so sorry," I said, squeezing her tight again, forgetting time was sensitive and my team was waiting. All that mattered was holding this woman in my arms.

Camila may have brought us together for a reason, but I'd be damned if I didn't believe it was fate.

And now I had to survive the rest of the mission to find out if Charley truly felt the same way about me.

# CHAPTER THIRTY

## JACK

"I know, I know. You don't need to say anything," I muttered the second I was within earshot of Gray in the library. Carter, Mya, and Gwen were crowded around the stately desk at the center of the room, working with the limited resources we had: one stolen laptop from the cartel's home and Gray's iPad.

Charley went over to sit with Lucy on the couch in front of the bay window that overlooked the mountains. At least Lucy wasn't shunning her. Eye contact made between the two of them. Good start.

"I *could* say something about what I *think* you were doing up there, in the middle of an op, with a person of interest, but that would make me a colossal hypocrite, wouldn't it?" Gray's smirk came and went fast, a quick switch of gears from best friend mode to team leader. "Camila's plane is rerouting to Bogotá. She'll be here later this evening."

"Wait, what?" Charley's head whipped our way, her hands gripping her thighs to steady herself. "Why? What happened?"

"She got Shannon to talk at the last minute," Carter said,

318

facing us, leaning against the desk. "Apparently, Shannon's not just the polygrapher. The show was her brainchild. Stephen is the public name and face for it."

Gwen was seated behind the desk with the computer, busy typing as if Carter's words weren't news to her. Considering how long I'd taken to get down there, they probably weren't.

*Worth it.*

Mya quietly looked up from the iPad, meeting my eyes for a moment before they flicked to Charley and back to me. I took it as a sign she was happy for me and whatever was happening with Charley's and my relationship. Damn, I hoped it wasn't too early to use that word.

I had to assume Jesse, Oliver, and Mason were now securing our perimeter since they were MIA and Camila's team was going to Colombia.

I folded my arms and leaned against the side of the bookshelf to my right. *Mom would have loved this library.* But it wasn't the time or place to miss my parents, so I focused back on Carter. "And what's in Bogotá that'd have Camila rerouting there?"

Carter gripped the bridge of his nose as if not keen on the idea of Camila heading to Colombia without him. Camila could hold her own, though. She ran a security team and was a former intelligence officer. I'd witnessed her kick some ass just last month in Cape Town when we'd helped her stop the sale of the high-tech prototype of a new weapon created by our government that'd been stolen.

When Carter continued to remain tight-lipped about the details, Gray filled in some blanks for us. "Shannon didn't recognize Brant's name or photo when Camila showed it to her. She said he's not who forced her to work with him."

"She could be lying," Charley said before I could. "Especially about the forced part. But Brant has to be

319

involved. It's the only thing that makes sense. Is Shannon working with anyone else? Stephen?"

"According to her, no. And Camila pressed her pretty hard," Gray said.

"Didn't they use a lie detector test on her, too?" Lucy asked, her tone soft.

"People know how to beat them." Charley eyed me while quirking her brow, letting me know I'd shown my hand during that icebreaker round.

"I'm sure Brant is involved," Gray declared before I could speak up. "My guess is he sent someone he trusted to do his dirty work, though."

"Right, of course." Charley nodded in agreement, and Lucy gave Charley's forearm a reassuring squeeze.

"So, what's in Colombia?" I asked again, diverting my focus to Carter.

"The blackmail video Shannon secretly took during her first meeting with who hired her," Carter shared. "We need his face so we can run it through our system. If he works for Brant Luther, we might get a hit through CCTV footage for his last whereabouts. And wherever he is, I'm betting Brant will be, too."

"And hopefully the missing women," Gwen said without looking up as she continued to type on the keyboard. She was probably still diligently trying to track down Brant while waiting for the video from Camila.

"So, did Shannon tell Camila what he looks like? Or maybe how this all happened?" Lucy asked, still holding her sister's arm.

My eyes were drawn back to Charley. Although she didn't get that great of sleep last night in the Jeep, the shower and sex seemed to have revived her a bit. She looked more alert and fresher now than when we'd arrived. Her hair was hanging wet over her black long-sleeved shirt, and I was just glad Carter had thought to have whoever shopped for us buy bras.

"Shannon said there were two men, but the second guy stood there like security while the one guy did the talking. According to her, the man in charge was about fifty but appears to take good care of his health, so he looks more like forty," Mya answered, jerking my focus back to her. "Light brown hair. Green eyes. Beard. American accent." Mya set aside the iPad and pushed away from the desk. "Shannon claims she had no clue any contestants went missing. She said the guy showed up before the start of the second season and offered her money to allow him input on who made it to the final three."

"And did he have a say in how the women were selected?" I couldn't help but ask.

"No. He gave her some preferences, but he never had a hand in choosing who was on the show," Mya answered. "She said he never even asked for the contestants' names ahead of filming."

"You'd think he'd want more involvement." *Shannon has to be lying, and she managed to beat the polygraph test.* "So, what happened when he made her the offer?"

"Shannon said she turned him down. He left her alone for a few weeks, only to reach out online with an interesting, and very illegal, incentive to change her mind," Mya explained. At least that part sounded somewhat legit.

"Bribery and blackmail, the pillars of criminal activity," Gwen tossed out with a shake of the head.

"At that point," Carter picked up, "Shannon was all in. He also required her to email him all recorded footage at the end of each night to a specific address on the dark web," he added, rubbing his hand along the back of his neck. The man looked exhausted, and fatigue wasn't a look I was used to seeing him sport.

"He probably gives the footage to Brant to watch," Charley murmured, eyes trained on the burgundy carpet beneath her bare feet.

"I'm struggling to believe Shannon was ignorant to the fact women were going missing after taping each season," I said, thinking back to his requests for "specifics" when it came to who he'd prefer selected.

"And we heard her voice on the call. Shannon was working with the cartel's men. Gave them our locations from the tracker in our bag," Gray pointed out.

"Yeah, but even then . . ." Gwen's words trailed off. I looked her way, waiting for her to finish that sentence, but her attention was fixed on Carter. Guess that part wasn't her story to tell.

Carter's spine went stiff, and he rotated his neck. "Apparently, this guy ran our faces to get IDs and used some of our backgrounds to motivate her. I'm wanted by the government for . . . things. Charley for murder. Mya's a former journalist."

"Oh." Charley raked her fingers through her wet hair, drawing in a deep breath.

"Our unknown suspect convinced her we were dangerous. Told her Mya would expose the truth in a story about her show," Carter went on. "He cut a deal with some of the cartel's men, and Shannon was their point of contact. He ordered the impromptu jungle adventure, so it'd look like an accident when we were captured. Just one of those things that could happen if you ventured into the cartel's territory."

"Regardless of how much Shannon did or didn't know, she's guilty in my book," Gray said, securing his arms across his chest.

"Agreed. As soon as Camila goes to Shannon's bank in Colombia and retrieves the video, she'll send it our way. Then we can work on getting a hit on his identity, as well as his silent friend." Carter turned his attention to Gwen. "In the meantime, Mya and Gwen are hunting for clues as to Brant's whereabouts."

"Can you trace the videos Shannon sent electronically to our mystery guy?" I asked Gwen.

"I need her laptop and a bit more to go on. I'm swimming in the dark using this piece of shit. I'd have more luck with a Nokia phone from the nineties," Gwen remarked while flicking the screen of the cartel's computer.

"Hopefully, we'll get photos and names, and we won't need her to do that," Carter said.

I finally pushed away from the bookshelf and shoved my hands into my jean pockets, unsure what to do with myself. I felt freaking useless, and I hated it. But then an unexpected idea sailed through my mind seemingly out of nowhere, and I lifted my eyes to the ceiling, processing it. "Camila wanted us on this op, and it's somehow connected to Cape Town, which means Brant must be connected to our job in South Africa. My guess is Camila didn't know his name then. What if that stolen tech we stopped from being sold was stolen by Brant's crew, and that's—"

"What do you mean 'Camila wanted us on this op'?" Carter cocked his head, staring me down. Damnit, I'd forgotten Camila explicitly told Gray that Carter couldn't know this op wasn't Gwen's.

Time to start backpedaling. "I mean . . . it was fate I met Charley in Cape Town, and they're friends, so—"

"I'm the liar," Gwen blurted. "I don't want you lying for me, Jack." She stood and circled the desk to face Carter. "Camila needed us undercover at that show, but she said she couldn't be the one to ask us to go. I had to make up a story. This has always been her op."

"Gwen," Gray bit out, stepping forward. He looked genuinely worried, as if her sharing that information was going to have some strange *Final Destination* butterfly effect and fuck with the future. Just like Camila had worried might happen.

But maybe we'd already altered what was going to happen anyway? Maybe it was safe for us to lay the cards out on the table now that we'd made it past the show and the danger it presented?

Carter looked up at the ceiling, a deep breath inflating his chest as he worked out how to react.

I stole a look at Charley, ensuring she was still okay. She gave me a small nod, but I also knew she had to be uneasy about what would inevitably come next: her turn to tell the full story to my team. To explain why we were up against Brant Luther in the first place. At this point, I pretty much had all the pieces, but it'd still be helpful to hear them all at once to better grasp the full picture.

"Go back to what you were saying," Gray said when Carter had remained oddly quiet.

When nobody else said anything, I looked at Gray and realized he'd been speaking to me.

"Camila only asked us to help her stop the stolen prototype from being sold last month. That her team would handle who those men worked for," I shared. "At the end of that op, I bumped into Charley at the bar the night before we flew out. Camila was supposed to be there and bailed on us— the *both* of us." *A fact I'd only recently learned.*

"If Mila, um, *Camila,* knew I was in danger there, then why the theatrics? Why not just tell me I needed to go?" Charley asked, eyes on me.

"That butterfly effect thing?" Gwen offered, more like a question than a statement.

"Because it was Brant's men that we stopped. They were selling the stolen tech," I said, finally piecing it together. "Someone from Brant's team more than likely planned to head to South Africa to figure out how and why things went south. And my guess is that someone would've stumbled upon Charley there."

"And that man is probably who we're looking for now," Charley whispered, shock laced into her agreement. "But because you and I met, and I saw your weapon in your hotel room that morning, I panicked and moved that day. Stealing the chance for him to bump into me there."

"Right." I dove my hands into my pockets, feeling so damn uneasy about all of this.

"But then I was upset we moved just when I was starting to fall for that guy there," Lucy joined the conversation, "and I received the invite to the show." She turned toward her sister on the couch. "And I made you feel like shit for moving, so I convinced you to let us go on the show when you otherwise would've said no."

"Fucking butterfly effect," I hissed in agreement with Gwen's analysis. "Camila said she kept messing things up. By taking the job in Cape Town, we inadvertently sent the man after Charley and her sister there. And then because I met Charley and scared her off . . ." I cleared my throat.

"I wound up in Brant's path anyway." Charley banded her arm across her abdomen. "What if him finding me is meant to be? What if I can't escape this fate?"

"You're forgetting an important piece, though. We wouldn't know women were missing if not for this new course of direction," Gwen said, her tone soft. "Camila couldn't run facial recognition from an image in her mind

325

when she realized someone was after Charley, but she could connect enough dots to lead her to the reality show. And to the fact something was going to happen to Charley there. And that was when she put it together that women had disappeared after the show."

"You're a really good actress," Carter interjected in an antagonistic voice, shaking his head. "Acting shocked back at the lodge about Camila's—"

"Don't blame her," Gray snapped out. "Gwen doesn't work for her or for us. She can do whatever the hell she believes is right."

Gwen lowered her focus to the tiled floor, and I hated the look of shame Carter's clenched jaw and disappointing stare seemed to inspire. "I'm sorry."

Carter focused on Gwen, and his shoulders dropped as whatever pent-up frustration he was dealing with seemed to dissipate a touch. "I'm . . ." he said around a swallow, "sorry. I was out of line." He waited for her to meet his eyes before continuing. "Camila's a stubborn pain in my ass when it comes to her safety, and I should be mad at her, not you."

"Let's just focus on the fact we know what in the hell is going on now. Brant Luther's still a thief, and now he's abducting women, too," Mya spoke up, cutting through the tension with a gentle hand. "And he wants Charley and Lucy bad enough he was willing to pay the cartel a million dollars and raise a shit storm with the Feds as a result, to get to them."

"And no, it's not fate something bad will happen to you," I said, eyes on Charley. I couldn't shake her words that were drowned out in the noise of the blame game among my team. I cut across the room, not giving a shit we had eyes on us, and hauled her into my arms. "I'm not letting anything happen to you."

"I, um, I can try and use this piece-of-shit laptop to hack the CCTV cams near where we worked in Cape Town. See if I get a hit on anyone connected to Brant Luther's legitimate organizations," Gwen offered. "Their photos and names will be on his company's website. And maybe Charley will recognize someone from the footage." Her voice was tentative, as if getting on Carter's bad side had rattled her normal control. It was weird, and a little disconcerting. Gwen didn't usually have a problem pissing off anyone.

"There's too much footage to look through. Just focus on finding Brant right now while we wait to get an ID on the man doing Brant's bidding," Gray suggested, hands planted on his hips as if realizing he needed to take charge given Carter seemed a bit off. "But I think it's time we hear the whole story. Why does this man so desperately want you?"

Charley peeled herself free from my arms and faced my best friend, but before she could answer him, Carter's cell rang.

"It's Camila. Hold on." Carter answered the phone, and listened quietly for a moment before hissing, "Just be careful. She could be leading you into a trap." Another pause. "And I know this is your op. And I'm pissed you kept it from me." One more beat of silence before he walked over to Charley and offered her the phone. "If you're up for it, Camila wants a word."

# CHAPTER THIRTY-ONE

## CHARLOTTE

No, I wasn't up for a conversation with Mila. *Ca-Mila.* Not yet. I needed a second to breathe. To process. To not be mad at her for lying to me. Even though I really had no right to be angry since I'd lied to her about my background, too. I didn't want to be a hypocrite, but . . .

"I don't want to talk right now." I pushed away the phone. "I'm sorry."

Carter quietly brought the phone to his ear and left the library to have what I assumed would be a private conversation-lecture with her.

"It's okay," Jack said to me, rubbing his thumb along my forearm. "When you're ready, you'll know."

I nodded at him, loving how much this man accepted even the irrational parts of me, then distracted myself by heading over to one of the fully stocked, floor-to-ceiling bookshelves. Racing my fingers along the spines of what appeared to be mostly classics, I asked, "Should I go ahead and explain the story? Or wait for everyone to be here?" I paused at the sight of one book on the shelf above me, then reached for it. Jack London's *Call of the Wild.*

"You can go ahead," Gray said, and I turned toward the room, clutching the book protectively to my chest. Jack's eyes traveled from my face to the book, but I doubted he could read the title from how I had it glued to my body beneath my forearm.

Jack stood alongside Gray, who had yet to change from the looks of it; Gray was still wearing the same military-looking clothes, bloodstains and all.

I took in the sight of the man I'd shared a romance novel-worthy scene with not too long ago and couldn't ignore the fact I'd kind of loved how he'd lost himself in the moment.

Jack pushed his hands through his messy locks, still wet from said swoon-worthy scene. He'd opted for jeans that clung in all the right spots, and a navy-blue long-sleeve shirt, sleeves pushed to the elbows, exposing his corded forearms.

Giving me time to find the words, Jack turned toward the window that overlooked the mountains, inadvertently distracting me with the fit of his jeans. Shaking my head, I closed my mouth, hoping I hadn't drooled while ogling the man I'd so quickly fallen for. It was time to recount my life and how we wound up in this predicament. Not my favorite subject matter.

"Maybe if you sit, that'll help?" Mya offered, and I looked over at my sister on the couch. In her hot-pink top and jeans with holes in them, she looked like a beautiful young woman in a room full of her peers, and it suited her.

If I told my story, would it get us one step closer to her having a normal life?

"I'll stand." Clutching the book like a lifeline, I went over and stood by the couch alongside Lucy, not wanting to have my back to anyone while I delivered what felt oddly like a eulogy.

Jack faced me again, but stayed put, hanging back by Gray.

At least Lucy now knew all the dark parts I'd kept from her, so I didn't have to burden her with any more unexpected news.

"Could you start from the beginning?" Mya asked, her tone soft as she perched a hip on the desk. "I know some of us know bits and pieces, but it'd help to hear everything from start to finish."

I brought the hand not clinging to the *Call of the Wild* to my throat and drummed my fingers there, trying to remember the art of speech. A few deep breaths later, I told them about my mom and the hard life she'd had growing up. How she'd joined a heist crew before the age of sixteen. Met my dad, then gave up that life when she gave birth to me at nineteen. And wow, she'd just be turning fifty now. *Mom's closer in age to Jack than I am.*

"Claudia stopped boosting cars when she was pregnant with you, but then when your dad died of a heart attack, your mom struggled with finding work," Mya recapped my rambling. "So, she returned to the only work she'd known."

It sounded so simple coming from Mya. If only . . . "Someone from my mom's old heist crew reached out and offered her what was supposed to be a legitimate job with Brant Luther. That's when she became one of Brant's chauffeurs. I met that friend a few times, but he never gave me a name. And when I asked my mom for it, she told me the less I knew, the better. I realized the job was more than likely not legitimate after that, and I pressed her for the truth." I swallowed at what I had to say next, then ripped off the Band-Aid.

I revealed everything that went down. Mom telling me the truth about her real line of work. How she taught me to drive, and even how to steal a car, not that I'd ever done that. *Well, until last night in Peru.* Then I detailed Mom's sudden decision when I was twenty to leave the country. Her escape plan. The fake car accident. The plane tickets to London from Mexico.

I told them all of it. How Brant's men took us from our home before I could even explain to Lucy that Mom never died in that accident. How they forced me to drive the getaway car for their planned heist that night since Mom was "dead." And then when Brant decided he wanted me as part of his team for good, and hadn't liked my answer of no, he'd tried to kill me.

"And that's when the federal agents blew their own cover. To try and save us," Lucy whispered. It sounded as much a reminder to herself as everyone else that we were innocent of their deaths.

"They gave their lives for us, and I wound up pinned for murdering one of those agents. I couldn't even reach out to his family to offer my condolences and share how grateful I was for . . ." *Saving Lucy.* I swiped away a few errant tears and pushed on. "Brant started fighting with Mom's old friend as he tried to convince Brant not to kill me. He wouldn't listen. I was already bleeding at that point." I covered my scar with the book even though nobody could see it. "Mom showed up, startling Brant, and he fired his gun. It was obvious he didn't mean to kill her. The anguish in his voice, and the pain in his eyes . . . he was screaming, and even crying, while he held her in his arms." I paused, beginning to get choked up. "It should have been me, holding her in her last moments, but . . ."

Jack started for me, sensing I was struggling, but I shook my head. I needed to get through this on my own. I had to be strong. He gave me a hesitant nod, then backed up a step, realigning himself alongside Gray.

"I reached for the gun Brant dropped—the one he'd used to kill the Fed—and shot the man who tried to stop me from escaping. Mom's friend aimed at me, demanding I stop . . . but he couldn't pull the trigger and kill me. So, that's how we got away." I blinked back a few tears.

"And Brant blames you for Claudia's death," Mya said softly.

The emotions I was trying to keep at bay pushed forward and the book slipped free from my grasp. "I need a minute. I'm sorry." I abruptly rushed from the room before anyone could get out a word, slamming into Carter in the hallway on his way back to us. "Shit, sorry."

He clutched my arms, halting me in place. "Are you . . ." A hard swallow from him as he met my eyes. "Okay?" He'd practically choked on that question, as if it'd been hard for him to show signs of emotion or offer comfort to someone else.

"I just need a second."

His eyes left mine, moving beyond me, I assumed to Jack or my sister, who had likely followed me from the room. "Third door down on the right will take you to the sunroom. Take as many seconds as you need."

I nodded my thanks, and as soon as he let go of me, I made a beeline in the direction he'd told me to flee.

Once inside the sunroom, I fell to my knees, unable to stop the weight of guilt from taking me down.

The hardest part of reliving the past, something I'd never shared with anyone else, was knowing I left Mom behind. I couldn't bury her. Mourn her properly. And I hated knowing I had to leave her with that bastard.

Seconds later, Lucy's soft arms wrapped around me from

behind. "Shhh, it's okay," she murmured into my ear. "I got you," she promised.

* * *

"How are you?"

I looked up from my untouched lunch where I sat at the breakfast island in the kitchen to see Jack there in the doorway. "Better, all things considered."

It'd been a few hours since my hasty bolt from the library. Since then, Lucy had cooked everyone lunch, but she'd also kept everyone, including Jack, away from me. I'd needed space. Of course, I hadn't meant from Jack, but I'd been too exhausted to even voice those words to her.

"You should eat." He leaned his hip against the counter and folded his muscular arms over his chest. His hat was on. Maybe a new one? Backward facing, so I could clearly make out his concerned eyes.

"I don't have an appetite." I pushed away the plate, frowning. "I'm sorry I ran earlier."

His shoulders dropped a touch at my words, but he didn't unlock his arms. Those beautiful eyes of his softened as he studied me. And the harsh lines of worry on his forehead became a touch less intense. "You didn't run. You were speed walking like the elderly at the mall. Very different."

I had to feel my lips to believe there was really a smile there. But yup, he'd cracked me. Wide-freaking-open since the moment we'd met, if I was being totally honest. And it was time for honesty after eleven years of hiding.

"Well, um, if you're not going to eat, then maybe you can join us back in the library? Camila just emailed us the video footage. Two men were on camera. No audio and not a great angle of their conversation, but she said both men were from

333

her . . . uh, visions." He cleared his throat, giving me a moment to take in the news. "We sent their images to our teammate, Sydney, back in D.C. to run through our facial recognition program, but we were thinking—"

"I may recognize them?" I stood, nodding eagerly. Ready to help find this asshole and, hopefully, save those missing women. *And please, please still be alive so we can save you all.* "Is Camila and her team on their way back here? No problems accessing Shannon's vault to get the blackmail footage she had hiding there?"

Jack held my hand, his touch comforting as we walked together. "No hiccups."

"That's good news. So, why'd you sound so nervous when you delivered it?" I stopped in the hall, waiting for an explanation.

His lips flattened into a hard line, and he cupped the back of his neck with his free hand. More distress. Not a good sign. "Camila just sounds off. I don't like it. Plus, in my experience, when something seems to be going flawlessly, well . . ."

"Is that code for a storm is brewing, so we better prepare?" He nodded quietly, and I wasn't sure how to respond other than to return his nod and carry on.

"Hey, you doing okay?" Mya was the first to greet me once we both entered the library.

"Hanging in there." *Trying, at least.*

Gwen was talking to Lucy near the desk, showing her the laptop. And when my sister's eyes went wide, I stiffened. I knew that look.

"You recognize either of them?" Gwen prompted, and I withdrew my hand from Jack's to go see the screen for myself. "He appears to be the one in charge since he's sitting, and the other guy is hanging back behind him."

"I think I recognize them both," Lucy whispered as Gwen offered me a view of the laptop, and I faltered a step. "That's Mom's friend. The man who got her the job in the first place. He's the one after us and helping abduct women for Brant?"

Shock cut through me for two reasons: the man talking to Shannon was, in fact, Mom's "friend" who'd once let me live. And the other guy was— "That's the guy I shot and killed," I finished my thoughts out loud. "Well, shot. Apparently not killed."

Feeling a hand on my shoulder, I heard the concern in Jack's voice as he softly asked, "You okay?"

"I'm not a murderer," I whispered after a throat clear, trying to get my head on straight after that truth bomb.

"You were never a killer," he reassured me.

"We'll get names for them soon," Gwen said with confidence, pulling my focus from Jack and setting it back on the screen.

I narrowed in on the man who was seated. He looked, well, uncomfortable to be there. But . . . "Can you rewind that clip? I'm pretty good at reading lips."

"Yeah, I was trying to do that before you came in." Gwen paused the footage, then went back a few seconds so the camera was focused on Mom's so-called friend. A "friend" who was now having me hunted by the cartel.

I followed along with the man talking, making the same shapes with my mouth as he did, trying to process what he was saying.

"We don't need to wait to hear from Sydney," Mya said, eyes riveted to her iPad. "His face is on the company's website. He's not only the CFO for Brant Luther Enterprises Charitable Foundation, he's also Brant's younger—"

"Brother," I finished for her, reading that word form on the man's lips just as Mya said it.

"Right," Mya said. "That man is Erik Luther. The man standing behind him is part of Brant's security team."

I stumbled back, and Jack's arm hooked around me for support in an instant.

"If Erik was part of Mom's old heist crew, does that mean so was Brant? Did Mom know them both before she met our dad?" My mind was spinning with possibilities.

"According to a quick web search, Erik is fifty. Never married. No children. Resides in Pasadena, California," Mya shared as she appeared to be searching in real time. At least the shitty tablet was sufficient for a quick web search.

"Erik's Mom's age. Isn't Brant a lot older than him?" I asked her.

"He's sixty-five," Mya answered, looking up from her screen.

"You think Brant was the crew runner back in the day, and your mom and Erik were part of the team?" Gwen tossed out the idea as I continued to wrap my head around everything, including the fact the man I thought was dead was very much alive, and apparently out for revenge.

"It's possible, I guess," I murmured in a foggy daze, growing nauseous.

"I'll have Sydney try and find where Erik and this security guy are now. Once Camila arrives with a better laptop," Gwen began, "I can help out." She flicked her finger at the cartel's laptop. "This one doesn't have the power I need to hack into anything. Not even enough juice to create a fake impersonator account of a celebrity on Instagram."

"I, um, can't make out anything else Erik said," I shared after trying one more time, doing my best to focus.

"That's okay." Jack smoothed his hand up and down my back in comforting motions, and then I turned to see Carter entering the library, phone in hand but not at his ear. Mya quickly updated him, including the fact we now had a name, and how Erik was the one to "let me go" by not shooting me that night eleven years ago. *Only to come for me now.*

Instead of responding to the news, Carter simply said, "Camila's insisting she talk to you." He held out the phone, and I took a deep breath before crossing the room.

I sighed. "I need to take this alone."

Jack shoved his hands into his pockets and gave me a tight nod.

I shot Lucy an apologetic look, feeling responsible for this mess, even though I knew it wasn't my fault. And then I waited to get to the sunroom before I brought the phone to my ear.

"Charlotte?"

"Camila," I whispered back. "It's me."

An apology I'd half expected didn't come. Instead, she cut right to the point. "I have to tell you something very important, and I want to tell you now, so you have time to process." Her bone-chilling tone made my legs weak, so I sat on the bucket swing, eyes pinned to the mountains as I waited for her to continue. "Something changed. I don't know why or how, but it did. And I . . . I can only see the outcomes. Two possible outcomes. In one scenario, I can see you alive after this is over. In the other, I can't see anything."

I leaned back in the swing and closed my eyes, terrified of the direction this was going. No future meant I'd die. "How do we make the scenario happen where I live?" I murmured, my heart beating wildly.

"There's only one way I can see that happening, but I know you won't allow it." Camila's accent cut through a bit more that time as emotion caught in her tone. "I'm so sorry I failed you."

"Just tell me," I rasped, opening my eyes, blinking back tears.

"If you live, Lucy dies. And possibly the five missing women, too," she rushed out.

*Five? I thought there were six. But wait, what . . .?* "You're saying it's either me or Lucy and those missing women?" I peered toward the door, ensuring no one was there as I processed the news.

"I'm either going to your funeral or hers. But if I didn't tell you this, it'd be hers for sure. If I tell the team this, though, you both wind up dying. And maybe the missing women, too. I don't know more than that," she said, a tremor shooting through her voice.

"Don't tell them," I blurted. "Please." I sniffled, coming to terms with the reality of the news.

"I wish I could help or do more, but I'm afraid if I try to intervene again—"

"No." I abruptly stood. "We can't risk something going wrong and Lucy or those women dying." I shook my head, refusing to allow that possibility. "This was how it was always supposed to happen I think."

"But you deserve your life, too. And I don't know how to give that to you." Her hoarse voice had me choking up even more.

"It's not up to you to change fate. It's meant to be," I forced out. "But, um, I need you to tell Lucy and Jack something for me after this is over." I didn't need Lucy feeling guilty that she lived when I didn't. I couldn't handle that. I wanted her to fall in love and marry the man of her dreams. To have the dog barking in the yard with her kids swinging on the playset out back on warm summer days. "I can't have either of them feeling guilty." Tears streaked my cheeks, but I refused to ugly cry. I had to keep my shit together. For just a little longer. "I need you to convince them to move on with their lives." Pictures of my time with Jack flashed to mind, and I held on to them as I whispered, "Tell Jack to never give up on finding the woman of his dreams since I can't be her."

# CHAPTER THIRTY-TWO

## JACK

"What'd you say to her?" I paced the library, tearing my hands through my hair. "Camila, damnit, tell me. Charley's pale. Hiding something from me. So, tell me." I slammed my palm to the wall by the bookshelf, trying to get a grip. But no one was in there to see me spinning out of control.

"I just told her I'm sorry for . . . well, for everything." Camila's voice broke as if she was barely hanging on herself. That wasn't like her, and it was incredibly sobering. "I'm sorry. I have to go. I'll see you when my team arrives. We'll be at the house in two hours."

The call died, and I nearly chucked the phone across the library.

Charley had refused to talk when I had pushed for answers after she'd returned from the sunroom to give Carter back the phone. After she'd left the room, I'd pretty much snatched the phone from Carter's hand to call Camila myself. The team had quietly left for the kitchen to continue their work there. But with our limited resources, we were all feeling fairly fucking useless and on edge.

I took a second to regroup, then a few more just because I was failing, and as I started to leave the library, I spotted the book Charley had been holding earlier.

Picking it up, I eyed the cover of what appeared to be a collector's edition of *Call of the Wild*. I took the book with me, holding it tight in my hand like a roadmap I'd be lost without.

Lucy was near the stairs, and she lifted her chin as I approached. "Charley's taking a nap upstairs. She asked to be alone."

"Even from me?" I frowned, my shoulders dropping to match how defeated I felt.

Lucy nodded, then started upstairs without another word. She had to be sensing something was wrong. Well, beyond what was already wrong.

I joined Mya in the kitchen a few seconds later, handing her the phone. "Where's everyone else?"

"Gray's making a call in his room upstairs. Probably finally changing, too. Not sure where Carter and Gwen disappeared." Mya looked up from the laptop. "And Jesse, Oliver, and Mason are still outside ensuring we don't get any uninvited guests." Her eyes fell to the book, and she added, "Go to her. Trust me, she doesn't need space. She needs you."

"Mind reader, too? I think we have enough of those on our team right now." I'd meant that as a joke, but my words sounded more asshole than snarky comic. "Sorry." My shoulders dropped a little more, like I was Atlas struggling to hold up the world. "I don't want to bother her." *But I really do.*

"Charley looked like she saw a ghost after that call." She flicked her wrist, dismissing me. "So, go."

Without saying more, I set down the book and left the

room. Mya was right. Fuck space. I had to make sure she was okay.

I took the stairs two at a time, rushing to get to Charley, only to halt just outside the second bedroom when I overheard Carter grating out, "Regardless of what Camila ordered, you shouldn't have kept secrets."

I was prepared to bust into the room and defend her, confused why he was lecturing her right now, but Gwen's clipped response stopped me. "But I'm good at keeping secrets. I've kept what happened between us last month to myself."

*What. The. Fuck?* My hand hovered over the doorknob, unsure what to do. Listen first and then storm in, or storm in and ask for forgiveness?

"That should never have happened," Carter snapped out. "I should have kicked you out the second you walked in on me. Not let you stand there frozen in shock, watching—"

"Watching *some woman* deepthroat you while you sat naked on your office couch casually sipping whiskey," Gwen tossed back. "You just stared into my eyes while she . . . And I . . . can't get it out of my head."

My blood was damn near boiling, but I was apparently as frozen in shock as Gwen had been when she'd walked in on Carter getting serviced by a woman last month.

"You *need* to stop with all this," Carter said after a curse. "And no more teasing. It's going to give the guys on the team the wrong impression about us. And let me be clear when I say nothing will ever happen. Not with you, and not with . . ."

As his words trailed off, Gwen asked, "Since when do you care what people think? I know you're not truly scared of my father, let alone anyone else on the team."

"It's not about fear, it's about respect." After a tense moment (for all of us), he went on, "But I lost the last bit I had for myself when I let you stand in my office for sixty seconds too long."

I bowed my head to the door and closed my eyes, trying to get a handle on my breathing and heart rate. I wanted to go in. Tell Gwen to back the fuck off. That Carter wasn't good for her. But from the sounds of it, Carter was doing a decent job himself. As much as I hated eavesdropping, I had to be certain he didn't falter and change his mind, falling into the temptation of a beautiful woman staring at him during a stressful-as-fuck operation.

*God, I might puke.*

"You know, for a man who tries to come across as heartless, you're far from it," Gwen said, her tone softer this time. Less fight there than before.

"Please don't mistake the fact that I won't fuck you because I don't want to ruin my relationships with my teammates and your father for me having a heart." Carter's words were crisp but cutting. "Now, let's put this shit behind us so things are no longer awkward." When Gwen didn't speak up, he added, "You have your whole life ahead of you, Gwen. You're still figuring out who you are. Trust me when I say I don't belong in your life as anything other than a—"

"A friend?" I barely heard her whisper.

"I can't be your friend. Colleague, yes. But I don't have friends. Particularly not female friends."

"Camila's your friend," Gwen shot back. Like a bullet to the brain, hearing Camila's name reminded me about her mystery conversation with Charley. The conversation that'd sent Charley over the edge and in need of alone time.

"Camila's . . . different," Carter said, almost dragging out the words.

I pushed away from the door, wishing I had a time machine to go back and unhear that entire conversation. Or brain bleach. Carter naked on a couch, watching Gwen from across the room while a woman swallowed his cock. That was something I did NOT want in my head.

"Camila's Camila," Carter replied to a question I must have missed while trying to remove the unwanted images from my mind. "Now go. Please."

They were both quiet for a moment before Gwen answered, "Fine, I'll respect your wishes. I wouldn't want to come between you and anyone just to have you fulfill some fantasy. I, uh, know you and I'd never actually work out."

At Carter's reluctant sounding, "Thank you," I bowed my head in relief and took off back down the hall to get to Charley's room.

It took me a second to shake off the chills and lose the nausea brought on by that unexpected conversation. But maybe it was good I heard it? I trusted Carter a bit more for gently (his version, at least) letting her down. And then there was the fact he apparently did give a damn about our opinions and feelings (not that he wanted us knowing that).

I quietly opened the bedroom door, finding Charley asleep on top of the covers. Well, she appeared to be sleeping, but she could've been faking it.

"Charley?" I prompted, closing the door before tossing my hat onto the nearby leather chair.

When she stirred but didn't open her eyes or speak, I joined her on the bed.

I wanted answers about the real conversation she'd had with Camila, but I also wanted the color to return to her face first before I pressed.

I hooked my arm over her side, her ass nestled against my cock, and the back of her head rested near my chin. Closing my eyes, I decided maybe, just maybe, I'd give myself a few minutes of rest, too. It'd been a long time since I'd actually slept.

I wasn't sure how long I was out, but Gray came into the room without knocking and announced, "We found Brant and Erik's location. Time to make our move."

\* \* \*

"WHERE ARE THEY?" I BOLTED UPRIGHT, BLINKING AWAY THE last bit of sleep still holding on as Charley did the same.

Gray's eyes fell to the end of the bed, and shit, he had to see the "jaws of life" there. "Um." He focused back on us, blinking now as well. "Cayman Islands. Sydney pulled up aerial surveillance of where we believe the Luthers are staying."

I reached for Charley's hand and squeezed. "How bad is the site we'll need to breach?"

"Not too bad. Gated entrance. Two overwatch towers on the north and south sides of the estate with men more than likely positioned there. The mansion is right on the ocean, which means we could quietly infil that way. Lots of hammerheads and tiger sharks in those waters, though."

"When's the last time stamp for Erik being seen there? Could he already be gone if he's realized Shannon is MIA?" I asked him.

"CCTV footage Sydney pulled had him landing at the airport there two hours ago. My sister took over from there and used her network to continue to ping his location through traffic cams, which led us to the address where we assume Brant is as well." He folded his arms, an uneasy look crossing his face that didn't do wonders for my stomach considering we had a location and a timeframe we could work with. "If Brant's there, he's been holed up there for a long time.

Sydney can't get a match for him on the island on any recent cams."

*There it is. The reason for the stress.* No definitive proof our main asshole was onsite, but we'd have to take our chances. Worst case, we'd get Erik, and he'd lead us to Brant.

"We can take Camila's jet. She just landed, and she's waiting there for our decision on what to do next." Gray checked his Apple watch. "If we leave now, we can hit the estate a little after midnight."

"I'm going, right? Or am I staying here?" Charley asked, and I peered over at her, concerned to see that despite the nap, the color hadn't returned to her cheeks.

*What are you keeping from me?*

"We have two options, which is why Camila's still at the airport waiting for our decision on this," Gray said, and I pivoted back his way, my heart racing. "First option, the women stay here, and Camila and her team guard them. She doesn't believe they were tracked or followed, but let's not operate under the premise of hope."

*Yeah, fuck "hope it's okay."* I needed guarantees when it came to Charley's safety.

"Second option, the women fly with us, but they wait at the airport in the Caymans while we complete our mission," Gray suggested. "But we can't all fit on Camila's jet. And Carter's backup jet is still en route here. So, Camila's team would have to wait for his jet and fly separately, which will push our mission later. I don't want to be chasing daylight, so it'll be tight, but it's still doable."

"And you think Lucy and I will be safe at the airport?" Charley asked him, squeezing my hand harder.

"Camila doesn't think her team was followed to and from Colombia, but if she's wrong, I don't like the idea of my team being so far away if this house gets hit. And as much as I'd like to trust Camila's men, I don't know them well. I'd rather you be near us, so I do think the airport is the safer option. Security there. Less chance Brant, a so-called reputable businessman, will openly target it, possibly drawing attention to himself and his company."

"Do you agree?" Charley asked me, and I looked at her as she blew out a shaky breath.

"I think so. But it'd help if you tell us what Camila told you on the phone." I hated being so blunt, but her safety was on the line.

"Camila told us everything will work out how it's supposed to," Gray said in a steady tone.

I wanted to believe him, but . . .

"Airport," Charley said. It was a solid declaration, but I didn't miss her drawing her free hand to her throat and pinching the skin there. "Let's do that."

I turned my attention back to Gray. "We'll be down in five, ready to roll out."

Gray nodded, then left and closed the door behind him.

"Tell me what Camila told you." I let go of her hand, only to reach for her arm so I could guide her onto my lap. She straddled me, wrapping her legs around my body, and I cupped her cheeks while staring into her eyes. "Please."

Her eyes became glossy as she shared, "She told me everything will work out, but, um . . ."

Fuck, my heart couldn't take this. "What is it?"

She dropped her focus to my chest, guarding her eyes from mine. "She said you and I won't end up together. I'm not your 'the one,' Jack. And I—I need you to be okay with that. Promise me you'll be okay with that."

My stomach protested her words. My heart. Mind. Every damn part of me seized up and rejected that idea. "Why in the hell would she tell you that? I don't understand." I shook my head, then set my fist beneath her chin, demanding her eyes, but she wouldn't give them to me. "Charlotte," I said around a swallow, "there's only two ways we don't end up together. You don't want me, or I die tonight. So, which is it? Because like hell is anything happening to you, so that option is off the table," I bit out, my tone gravelly.

"I already said too much," she cried. "I shouldn't have told you anything." A soft curse floated from her barely parted lips before she pushed away from my chest, trying to escape. I drew her back, pinning her tight against my body and she whispered, "What if I changed something? What if I messed up and now someone dies because I told you that?"

"No one is going to die, damnit." I was on the verge of losing my ever-loving mind if she didn't come clean with me. And I needed her to, desperately. Because I knew I'd never get shit from Camila if I tried. She was a steel fucking trap.

"I'm sorry. I'm . . . just don't do anything different. I'm begging you." Tears streamed down her cheeks now. "Please." She swallowed and caught a tear on her lip with her tongue. "You need to forget this entire conversation."

My shoulders collapsed yet again, this time with almost violent force as I put it together. "Camila can't see your future. She doesn't know what's going to happen to you because . . ." The last time I'd experienced this kind of pain in my chest, this kind of all-consuming panic, was when I found out my mom died. And I . . . "No," I said, my vision blurring from my own tears. "If taking you to the airport gets you killed, then no. New fucking plan."

"No." Her eyes widened in fear. "You're not allowed to know this or else—"

"Or else what?" I held her biceps, scrapping any plan of ever letting her out of my sight. I'd be sitting the mission out and watching over her until Camila found a way to see her future again.

"If you change the plan or tell Gray and the others about this, then *both* Lucy and I die. And possibly the missing women, too." She sucked in a ragged breath, her chest hitching with the effort to speak past her tears. "I—I messed up. I wasn't supposed to let you know. And now if Lucy and anyone else dies, it's my fault." She began sobbing hard while she clenched my shirt. "I'm dead no matter what. Please don't change anything and let me be the reason my sister dies."

# CHAPTER THIRTY-THREE

## JACK

CAMILA, LIKE CARTER, HAD CONNECTIONS. THAT MEANT WE had a private hangar reserved for us at the Mariscal Lamar International Airport, about twenty klicks from the safe house. She was talking to Charley near her jet, and . . . what was I doing? Well, I was allowing Oliver to wrap my knuckles after he relentlessly insisted, noticing my hand was a bit busted. I may have lost my mind and put a few holes through the walls in the bedroom after Charley had told me it was her fate to die, and I couldn't stop it from happening.

I kept my eyes on Camila while Oliver finished up, waiting for my turn to talk to her. I needed her to tell me she was wrong about her visions and that Charley would be okay.

"So." Oliver spoke for the first time after doctoring me, forcing my attention back his way.

"So," I repeated, unsure where he planned to go with that line of thought as he zipped up the medic bag he'd borrowed from Camila's plane—a much better kit than the one he'd used to patch up Gray's forehead.

Oliver did a not-so-subtle throat clear and shot a quick

look toward Charley and Camila. "I take it Camila gave you bad news?"

*Not me. Charley.* And what in the hell was I supposed to do with the news? I held my hand, the stinging pain there matching the achy throb in my shoulder.

Stealing a moment to think, my gaze drifted over to Shannon sitting on the ground, back to the wall near some boxes. Hands and feet bound. Mouth gagged. She must've been a pain in Camila's ass on the flight. Fuck, she deserved that treatment just for working with the Luther brothers.

Before I could pluck together some form of answer for Oliver, I noticed Camila leaving Charley's side, appearing to head in my direction. "I have to talk to her, excuse me."

Oliver picked up the medic bag and left me alone near the hangar door to wait for what I hoped would be a change in Camila's story. One that ended with a happily ever after.

"She told you," Camila said, her tone less angry and more apologetic. "And no, she didn't tell me she told you. I can see it on your face. You have the eyes of a grieving man."

"I'm not grieving, because she's not dying," I hissed, stabbing my finger toward the ground while keeping my voice low so my teammates didn't hear me. "Did anything change?"

"Did you tell your teammates? Are you still planning to board my jet and fly to the Caymans?" She wouldn't meet my eyes, and I hated that. It meant nothing changed for the better if she couldn't even look at me.

"No, I didn't. And yes, we are," I said roughly as I let go of my wrapped hand. An injury that no one had asked questions about.

I hadn't punched the walls in front of Charley. I'd lost control in private. Then I'd dropped to the floor and broke down and cried.

After I'd let myself grieve about a future that hadn't happened yet, I remembered who the fuck I was and pulled myself together. Because I WOULDN'T let her die. Not on my watch. I'd find a way. Or I'd . . .

"I'm sorry." Camila reached for my forearm. "You can't save Charley without sacrificing others."

I stared at her hand for a moment before jerking my focus up to glare at her. "And if I tell the team, somehow more people die?" I forced out the horrible words.

Camila nodded, and I peered over at Charley talking to Lucy and Gwen.

I caught Charley's eyes for a moment, and she shook her head. A silent apology for breaking my heart because of her "destiny."

"Fuck your visions." There went the control I'd worked so hard to get ahold of again after leaving the safe house.

"If Charley lives, and her sister dies, she won't be able to handle that. Just like you couldn't survive Gray dying because you lived."

Camila wouldn't hammer home any rational points with me on that. I wasn't exactly capable of thinking clearly to see the logic in her words. I was stuck in the land of tunnel vision. And **SAVE CHARLEY** was the bold mantra cutting through my head on repeat. *No matter what,* tagged onto that thought as well.

"Don't do this to me." My voice broke and I dropped my chin as her hand slid up my arm to grip my shoulder. On reflex, I backed away from her, feeling the need to blame her even if it wasn't fair to do so.

"I'm so sorry," she murmured before leaving my side to head toward Carter.

I swallowed, trying to pull myself together again, then went over to where Gray stood talking to Jesse. "Two of

Camila's men will go in my place when we arrive. I'm staying with the women at the airport in the Caymans."

Gray opened his mouth as if to protest. He'd want me on the op, and I hated not having my best friend's back, but I knew he'd be okay. Charley, well . . .

"Okay," Gray said without rebuttal.

I nodded my thanks, then went over to Charley, reached for her hand, and she wordlessly walked with me outside the hangar.

"Five minutes, and we fly out," Carter called to us, but I didn't look back to acknowledge his words.

"We'll hold course," I told her, gently gripping her forearms as she peered into my eyes. "But I'm going to do everything in my power to not let *anyone* die." After a few tears slid down her cheeks, one hitting her wobbly lip, I rasped, "I'll fight with my last breath to keep you alive." I held as steadfast and calm as I could when I shared, "My dad couldn't survive without my mom, and I don't need years of knowing you to understand how he felt. I won't survive without you." The confession was too soon, too early, but we were already on what felt like borrowed time, so she had to know how I felt. "*If* for some reason I can't save you, I'll be sure to take out as many motherfuckers as I can on my way out the door with you." I reached for her wrist, smoothed my thumb over the words inked there and declared, "Where you go, I go."

# CHAPTER THIRTY-FOUR

JACK

GRAND CAYMAN, CAYMAN ISLANDS

*"FOCUS ON THE THINGS YOU CAN CONTROL."* MOM USED TO remind me of that whenever it felt like the world might swallow me whole. When life kept throwing things my way to see if I could catch it, juggle it, or if I'd just give up and drop it. And of all the times I'd fumbled the metaphorical ball of life, this was one damn time I refused to let a mistake happen.

No, I had to find a way to control what felt like an uncontrollable situation.

As we prepared to land, I looked down at my hand. Charley was clutching it like a lifeline. I knew she wasn't terrified of flying, so I could only assume it was about what was to come. She had barely spoken on the flight, blotting away any tears that'd managed to break free before her sister could see them. The few times I'd caught her mid-sniffle, she'd give me a little tip of her lips in apology as if feeling bad for expressing her emotions. And each time I'd witnessed it, I'd felt like I'd been run over.

At the feel and sound of the pilot putting down our landing gear, I sat taller and looked around inside the cabin at everyone on board. Camila was sitting with Carter near the front of the twelve-passenger jet. Two of her men had joined our flight, and they were facing Jesse and Oliver, engaged in conversation.

Lucy was in the aisle opposite of us. She'd fallen asleep at some point, and her head was resting on Mason's shoulder. From the look of it, Mason didn't seem to mind. Charley followed my line of sight but didn't loosen her grip on my hand as she checked on her sister who was now stirring as if realizing our descent had started.

"I've got you," I whispered, redirecting her focus. Her stunning eyes met mine, and we stared at each other, lost in our own thoughts and our own little world, as our descent continued.

Well, until Oliver barked out, "We've got a problem."

My stomach twisted and I swung my eyes to the window to locate the problem. A swarm of flashing red and blue lights lit up the runway like a Christmas village.

A rush of adrenaline burned through my veins, and I looked around at my surprised teammates, landing lastly on Jesse. He had to be having flashbacks from our operation in France. He'd been taken down hard in his attempts to stop the love of his life from being taken from him on the tarmac that day. I remembered the anguished look on his face and how it'd affected his wife, Ella, and I couldn't let that happen to Charley. I didn't give a shit if it was crazy or not, this woman was the love of my life, and I'd find a way to—

"They're here for me," Charley murmured, her tone more resigned than shocked.

"Oh God," Lucy cried, fully awake, the alarm evident in

her eyes. She hooked her arm with Mason's, most likely hoping he'd anchor her in place and keep her protected.

Mason met my eyes, a solemn look there I recognized all too well. I shook my head, letting him know we were beyond fucked. We had to be real about what might happen. Prepare ourselves to deal with it. Pretending it might not happen wouldn't help anyone.

*"Focus on the things you can control."*

I blinked and turned my focus to Gray. "Call your dad. Wake him up."

Gray was already standing, phone in hand. More than likely on the same page before I'd issued the directive as if the one in charge.

"Right, the Secretary of Defense," Charley whispered, twisting back to look inside the cabin toward the others. "But, um, if the Feds are here with the local police, and they take Lucy and—" She cut herself off, peering hopefully at Camila for an answer to her unasked "does this change anything?" question, but Camila shook her head in apology.

"Make sure your dad lets the President know Gwen's on board as well," Carter noted to Gray.

"Why would that matter?" Lucy asked, her tone as fragile as glass.

"My dad's one of the President's go-to men. As in, he goes to him for shit no one else can do." Gwen's roundabout way of explaining her father's top-secret job offered a little hope without giving too much away. "He also works with the President's son." She winked.

And then there was that.

"We can use all the extra encouragement from the White House we can get to pull off the Feds and the local PD," Gray shared before heading in the direction of the cockpit to make the call.

"I still don't see how the Feds knew we were flying here," Oliver remarked, standing in the aisle, eyes still trained out the window.

I followed his gaze to see six men in the familiar blue FBI raid jackets. Most of the local PD were hanging back in their cruisers, likely only there for support "just in case" we started something. I had to assume air traffic control was barking out orders to our pilot that we couldn't hear with the cockpit door closed.

"Shannon set us up, didn't she?" Mason spoke up, and I turned to see him peering at Camila. "The vault in Colombia was a trap."

Shannon was on board Carter's second jet with eight of Camila's other teammates, but they were about three hours behind us, still in the air. And *had* she set us up? Did Shannon manage to play Camila and her team? With Camila seeing glimpses of the future, how'd she pull that off?

Camila was on her feet now; her body slumped a bit in defeat as she pushed her dark hair away from her shoulders. "She must've spoken with Erik Luther before my team grabbed her this morning and came up with a backup plan."

"You think Erik planted the bait—the video of himself—in the vault for us to find?" Carter asked her, going through the motions of strapping on a chest plate beneath a vest as if preparing for war.

It was fucking madness. We couldn't shoot at the FBI or the police. Well, we could, but again—madness. Of course, Carter did have a lot at stake there, too.

"My guess is Shannon always had the evidence there. I would've detected her lie otherwise." Looking slightly confused, Camila's voice lacked the confidence I was used to hearing. Maybe with all the other noise, she misread this. And if she was wrong about this, maybe that meant Charley's future wasn't set in stone?

Somehow, this fucked-up situation just gave me hope.

"But maybe Shannon confessed and told him about it. Erik and Brant decided to turn that to their advantage instead of killing her for it," Mya suggested. "Regardless, I'm sure we would've been screwed whether we stayed at the safe house in Ecuador or came here. They would've had a team follow Camila back there if we didn't take the bait and come here when Erik showed his face on camera for us to find him."

"This is my fault." Camila's words were little more than a whisper, but it was enough for Carter to do something slightly shocking. He hooked his arm around her back and pulled her close, holding her tight to his side. He kept her there, his thumb moving up and down her arm in silent support. "If I'd never gone to Colombia, they'd never have found us."

Carter dipped his chin as Camila peered up at him, locking his eyes on hers. "This is *not* your fault. Not even you can know everything." And with the grit and growl I was used to hearing, he added, "Now quit blaming yourself before you really piss me off."

"So, you're saying," Lucy began, still clutching hold of Mason, "Erik Luther had eyes on the bank in case Shannon showed up. And that served as a signal to him to change plans?" When Mya nodded, Lucy followed up with, "But why would Erik tip off the Feds? Why go that route?"

"He can't openly storm the airport," Mason told her, "but he can have the Feds take you two and then . . . well, take you from them once you're Stateside."

"I haven't been to the U.S. in so long, I . . ." When Lucy leaned back in her seat, seemingly resigned to whatever was about to happen, Charley reached across the aisle and held her hand. She'd become almost stoic, somehow channeling a sense of calm when I knew she had to be anything but.

"So, what do we do?" Gwen asked just as Gray exited the cockpit to rejoin us.

"My father's waking up the President, and he'll get ahold of the FBI director and see what's going on. Hopefully buy us some time." Gray's announcement was tempered by orders to exit the plane. The command, delivered by an agent outside over a speaker, was jarring and abrupt, ratcheting up the tension once again in the cabin. "We'll have to do our best to talk our way out of this until the director can call the special agent in charge here." Gray removed his 9mm from his side holster and set it on the front-row seat. "Let me handle this." He nodded at me as if to say, "don't worry"—*too late for that*—before he disappeared from my line of sight. A moment later, I spotted him outside the window on the tarmac, confronting the man I assumed was in charge.

"Give me a second." I let go of Charley, stood, and made my way toward the cockpit to get closer to the door to hear what was going on outside.

"Your father won't be too happy you were harboring a fugitive," the agent said, and there was no way he'd spoken to Admiral Chandler already. He must've recognized Gray. If the cartel had our photos from the game show cameras, of course the Feds did, too. "We're just here for the fugitive and her sister. Give us Charlotte and Lucy Lennox. We're not here for you. Not even your buddy, Carter Dominick. Kind of wild, you of all people are working with him."

I rested my sweaty palms on the door of the cockpit as I tried to rally and find my breath. Figure out next steps.

"I hate splitting up from them," Jesse said from behind, sounding resigned to our fate, and I turned to look at him, my body tensing, "but if the Feds aren't coming for the rest of us, we can follow them. Intervene when Erik and Brant's men try to ambush the Feds."

*No, because Charley still dies. How in the hell do I change this? Fuck these visions, damnit.*

"The FBI may not be taking us, but like hell are they letting us leave this airport anytime soon," Carter added, breaking away from Camila to confront me.

"I don't know what to do," I admitted, hating I felt as unsure as I had my first day outside the wire in an active war zone. "I'm not thinking clearly, but I do know we can't go up against those uniforms out there. It'd be a bloodbath, and that's not—"

"Of course we won't," Jesse cut me off, then deferred to Carter for an alternative. Glad I wasn't the only one who wasn't even sure of what that was.

"We track them. If the admiral can't stop them from leaving in time, the second Admiral Chandler orders the FBI to stand down and let us fly out, we find them. Then we come back for the missing women." Carter's tone was confident, but he didn't know about Camila's visions about Charley's fate.

I looked over to see Gwen clasping her charm bracelet to Charley's wrist. "Just in case," she said, and Charley stared at the bracelet before looking my way, distracting me from Gray now arguing with the agent outside.

Spotting Gray's 9mm on the seat, I moved around Jesse to pick it up, then tucked it at my back beneath my shirt and went outside before anyone could stop me.

"What the fuck do you mean you're staying on the island tonight before flying them back to the States?" Gray hissed, fearlessly going head-to-head with the agent.

"Orders are orders," the agent snapped back.

"And who gave you those orders?" I shot out, both sets of

eyes cutting to where I now stood on the tarmac. "Who tipped you off? Brant and Erik Luther? The same men who accused Charlotte of killing the undercover Fed eleven years ago?" I stepped closer to the man, presumably the special agent in charge, and three of his men came up behind him as if worried I'd go for the jugular. Hell, maybe I would. "Charlotte didn't kill that agent. The man who gave you the tip we're here did."

The clench of his jaw and the shifty way he looked toward the jet and back at me struck me in the gut. "Money. The universal language. The Luthers paid you off." I tilted my head, studying him as rage violently ripped through my body. "How long have you been working for them?"

"*That's* why the Feds closed the case and never looked into the Luthers again despite two of their agents being killed that night," Gray added, picking up on my line of thought. "They had help on the inside then, just like they do now."

"Don't listen to them," the special agent remarked, addressing the other men. His voice wavered the slightest bit as if worried they might switch sides and join us.

*Please God, let them do that.*

"Board the jet. Get Charlotte and Lucy Lennox," the special agent commanded, then signaled to two agents to head inside. "Don't think about trying to stop us from leaving here." He tipped his head toward the six local PD cruisers, his threat clear.

Remaining in control, not lost to my rage at the moment, only lost to my sole focus of needing to stay at Charley's side, I grabbed the pistol from the back of my pants and went for the traitor, punching his smug face before pointing the 9mm his way.

The asshole held his jaw while another agent pulled his Glock on me. "You're under arrest for assaulting a federal agent, and you're coming, too," the man directed before the agent in charge could protest.

*Game on.*

"Jack," Gray hissed—knowing exactly what I'd done—while I surrendered my weapon without a fight.

I quietly lowered to my knees. If this bastard traitor planned to take Charley and her sister from there, they'd be taking me, too.

I looked to my left to see Charley and Lucy joining us. The agent escorting Lucy appeared to be treating her with civility and not like a criminal. The other guy, though, shoved Charley to the ground like he believed her to be a murderer.

I attempted to lurch his way, snarling in disgust at his treatment of her, but hesitantly backed off when he pulled out a taser. I couldn't help her if they hit me with that damn thing.

I bit back a few dozen curses as they cuffed Charley's hands behind her back, pushing her to her knees next to me. She appeared to be in a bit of a daze, and it killed me that I could only comfort her with my words and presence.

"They're innocent." Gray approached the lead agent again, stabbing a finger at the air. "Do *not* take them from the airport before you speak with my father. I guarantee you'll regret it."

The special agent in charge waved his hand in the air, ignoring Gray's attempts to stop him. "The women are coming in my Tahoe," he said, motioning to one agent to get a move on. "This animal can ride with you two."

"Hell no," I shot out, trying to stand and go after him, but two agents grabbed hold of my arms, pulling me back. "Don't you see he's crooked," I hissed, hoping that unlike their prick boss who'd been bought and paid for by the Luthers, they were on the right damn side in this.

"The police have orders not to let you follow us," the

agent tossed out, eyes on Gray. "Let's see how long your father takes to make the call." He checked his watch. "My guess is we'll have a pretty good head start."

"You fucking traitor." Gray charged him and the agent who'd been rough with Charley deployed his taser. My stomach wrenched at the sight of my best friend being taken down like an animal in the wild.

"Stopppp," I yelled, my voice breaking.

"Back. The. Fuck. Off." Carter crouched alongside the agent and Gray on the tarmac. "Or you'll find out why your boss is too afraid to take me in tonight, too." No weapon in hand, Carter just stared down the agent that held Gray with the taser to his back. "Your boss is going to die," Carter seethed as the agent finally relented. "And let's be clear, if I find out you're corrupt, too, I'll be coming for you as well."

The agent straightened to his full height, stared into Carter's eyes as if debating whether to challenge him, then he flicked his index finger, motioning to the others to head to the SUVs.

"We'll be right behind you," Carter gritted out with a tight nod my way before he reached for Gray's unmoving body, rolling him over.

"Jack," Charley cried out, commanding my attention. "I—"

The crooked Fed shoved her into the back of the SUV, robbing her of the chance to finish what she was trying to say to me.

"Everything will be okay. We'll come for you all," Mya called out, quickly making her way to Gray and Carter.

But Mya was wrong. Because if Camila's visions were right, nothing would ever be okay again.

* * *

"YOU KNOW WHO I AM, RIGHT?" I BARKED OUT, HOPING TO get the two Feds to speak to me after several unsuccessful attempts within the last ten minutes. We were in a well-lit tunnel, allowing me to see everything, including the fact there was no other traffic. And I had a horrible feeling once we exited the tunnel, we'd find out why we were alone in there.

"Jack London. Green Beret. CIA Ground Branch. Now private security," the driver finally spoke up, catching my eyes in the rearview mirror. Maybe he had a bad feeling, too?

"Then uncuff me and arm me before it's too late, and—" I let my words drop at the familiar sound just outside the tunnel. A sound that lodged that dread even deeper in my gut. Because it couldn't be my guys. Not yet, at least. Carter was good, but no way had he managed to get free from the airport and secured a helo, too. "They're here."

"*Who* is here?" The driver paused as if detecting what I'd just heard. "Is that a helo?"

The agent in the passenger seat turned back to look at me. Maybe searching for answers I'd been trying to give. Answers and intel they'd ignored.

"The men who killed those Feds eleven years ago and framed Charlotte Lennox. The men who hired the cartel to take us out in the jungle yesterday. *That's who's here.*" The powerlessness I was feeling, being away from Charley and Lucy, unable to help them, burned and fueled my hatred for the entire situation. "And since you know who I am, un-fucking-cuff me and let me help you before we all die."

Static cut through their radio, followed by the unmistakable sound of a gunshot, and the SUV in front of us —the one carrying Charley and Lucy—abruptly stopped.

"What the hell just happened?" the driver asked, slamming on the brakes so we didn't rear-end them. But the

SUV with the two other agents behind us bumped us, sending us forward into Charley's SUV.

"My guess is your special agent in charge just shot the agent in the Tahoe with him, and men are about to fast-rope down from a helo to come kill us while they take the Lennox sisters away." I kept my voice as steady as possible despite my pulse pounding in my ears in anticipation of what was to come: Camila's "prophetic" visions playing out. "Give me a fucking gun," I demanded, then maneuvered my hands around to find the release on the seat belt, trying to free myself of one obstacle. "I'm going to die if you leave me here. My guess, so will you."

"What do we do?" the newbie-looking agent in the passenger seat asked the driver.

I twisted back to see the two agents in the vehicle behind us getting out, but then they dropped behind their doors at the sounds of more gunfire.

"Shit, he's right. Three armed men just entered the tunnel," the driver said, going for his sidearm. "Uncuff him. Give him a weapon," he said decisively, rolling down the window and opening fire on the intruders in the tunnel heading for the SUV in front of us.

"Hurry." I gave him my back so he could uncuff me.

"They've got the women," the driver shared between shots.

I whipped around the second I was free, took the Glock being offered to me, and didn't hesitate to open the door. Shielding myself behind it, I immediately returned fire.

One asshole went down fast when I double-tapped him in the chest as the agent behind the wheel of our SUV took down the second tango with a headshot.

The crooked agent grabbed Charley, using her as his shield as he walked backward to escape, a gun to her head.

The third assailant that'd dropped in from the helo was doing the same with Lucy.

"Shoot and they die," the special agent in charge yelled.

"Jack!" Charley screamed. I thought she was going to beg me to save her—or let her go—but when something struck my shoulder just before she vanished from my sight, I realized she was trying to warn me.

I spun around, suspecting the agent in the third SUV shot me in the shoulder because he thought I was trying to escape. Instead, I was greeted by the sight of the man who'd tased Gray shooting the other agent alongside him. Another fucking traitor.

Regaining my bearings, I raised my good arm in one fast movement and fired. Kill shot. Two more just in case—to ensure he was put down for good—and then I turned back toward the tunnel exit, grateful the agents that'd been with me had my back, keeping me from getting shot in it.

Ignoring the searing pain in my shoulder, I ran by our SUV, hauling ass to get to Charley before— "I'm too late."

# CHAPTER THIRTY-FIVE

## CHARLOTTE

*He's okay. Jack has to be okay. He can't . . . I mean, Camila would've told me if Jack was going to . . .* Damnit, I needed to pull it together. I took a deep breath, trying to calm my racing thoughts. I couldn't afford to lose it now. I didn't want to inadvertently screw up Lucy's fate by not being able to maintain my focus.

We'd only been in the air for ten minutes, but it felt like a lifetime. And right now, I wanted nothing more than to hug my sister. Provide her some sense of comfort. But I couldn't. My hands were still cuffed behind my back and Lucy's were now zip-tied on her lap. It was too hard to talk over the helo blades chopping the air, so I waited for her attention to turn my way and mouthed, "It'll be okay." A false promise in the dimly lit space, but hopefully a little light of hope for her.

A heartbeat later, my shoulder collided with hers when the pilot stopped suddenly and began hovering in the same spot. The traitor Fed sat across from us talking into the attached microphone on his headset, and the passenger by the pilot— the monster who'd used my sister as a shield—twisted back to look at us. He gave him a thumbs-up, and I assumed that meant we were clear to land.

I highly doubted we were at the spot the team had pulled up aerial surveillance for back in Ecuador. No, that had only been a trap to get us here.

The second we landed, and the pilot killed the engine, Lucy shocked me by using the chance to yell, "You're a disgrace. A murderer. A traitor and—"

"Shut up," the agent snapped back, sounding more annoyed than angry. He leaned forward to unstrap us in preparation for moving us out of the helo, but my sister went for surprise two.

She lunged toward the bastard. With her clasped hands, she brought her fists up beneath his chin like it was a volleyball. *Holy shit*. She got him good, but all she did was piss him off.

I didn't need Camila's gift to see what was coming next. I bolted up, bumping my head against the ceiling to block his swing and took the punch to my jaw instead. My head snapped left as pain radiated throughout my entire skull at the impact.

"Stupid bitch. Always taking the hits for your sister." He shoved me on the seat as Lucy murmured an apology to me.

A moment later, the door slid open, and I blinked at the bright lights behind two men standing there. My stomach dropped the second they stepped closer. Erik Luther and the man I'd thought I'd killed stared at me.

*You let me go eleven years ago, why kill me now?*

"The other agent didn't make it," the crooked Fed said, joining the two men on the ground. "And we left some men alive back in the tunnel. I hadn't planned on going back to my old life, but now—"

"What happened in there?" Erik's hands were at his sides, and his eyes remained locked on to mine. "Did you hit them?" The ice in his tone was a curveball of hope, and I latched on to it eagerly.

"What? They got feisty when we landed." The agent swiped his palms alongside his pants, wiping away blood that wasn't there.

Erik turned slowly, his hand reaching behind his back, and he became the killer he hadn't appeared to be right before my eyes. He shot the Fed in the face without hesitation. And on instinct, I shifted in front of Lucy to shield her from the sight of the man dying, like she was fourteen, and I could protect her from all the bad things in the world.

Erik casually tucked the gun at the back of his jeans, grabbed something from his pocket and swiped at the blood that'd splattered onto his face and neck. "Out," he said to us while tucking the material back into his pocket.

The security guard—who, based on the harsh look in his eyes, clearly wanted me dead—flicked his wrist, motioning for us to move.

When neither of us budged, because why would we walk into a shark's mouth on purpose, Erik turned our way and reached up. "Easy way or hard way?" He tipped his head to the side, eyes meeting mine, then offered his hand.

I swallowed, unsure of what to do. Where would I even go? Ask the pilot for an Uber lift out of there?

"Charlotte." The way Erik said my name didn't sound as much like a demand to hurry as him asking me to trust him.

*I think the fuck not.*

"Hard way it is." The security guard sidestepped him, coming for us, and Erik faced him.

"I've got this. Take the Fed away from here. Make sure

you pin the hit in the tunnel on the cartel. Connect everything to them. Dump the Fed's body in Peru, near the border where our team handled those other men," Erik ordered as the other man from the front seat exited the helicopter.

The security asshole looked at me, then back at Erik, and something in his eyes made me even more uneasy. And that was saying a lot given our situation. "Brant gave me orders to never leave her side." He held firm in his stance. "Chuck can handle the Fed and the coverup." He twirled his finger and the other man—Chuck, apparently—hooked his arms under the Fed's armpits and wordlessly did as instructed, starting to drag away the traitor. "I answer to Brant, not you," he tacked on as if Erik might object.

What was going on? And could we somehow make a run for it while these two were distracted in some sort of pissing contest?

"Wait," the security guy called out to Chuck, who halted instantly. "Did you check them for trackers?"

*Shit, shit.*

"No." Chuck dropped the Fed's body and started back for the helicopter. That had me moving and I jumped out, then turned, waiting for Lucy to do the same.

Erik went over to the Fed, searched his pockets, then came over to me. "Turn around."

"What are you doing?" Security Asshole asked.

"Brant won't want to see her cuffed," Erik said in a biting tone.

Once he freed me, I kept my hands behind my back long enough to unclasp the bracelet, allowing it to fall, hoping the grass would hide it from sight. "You were my mother's friend," I said to distract them from what I'd done, stepping away from the bracelet in preparation for Chuck to check me for trackers. "Why are you doing this? I've never opened my mouth about what happened. It's been eleven years. You didn't need to come for us."

"You shouldn't have been on that show," Erik said, and I thought I detected a tinge of regret in his eyes. Why did it feel like he truly didn't want to find me? What was really going on?

"Pretty sure it was lucky for us they were." Security Asshole motioned to Chuck with another twirl of his finger, instructing him to check us.

"You're not going to get what you want," Erik said as Chuck waved some baton thing down my body. I was too distracted by Face-Off 2.0 to be thankful the nearby bracelet didn't set off the alarm.

Security Asshole looked my way and hissed, "You're wrong about that. When he's done thinking she's Claudia, I won't be bringing her here with the others. I'll finally get my revenge for this bitch shooting me."

"Brant's going to think I'm my mom?" Shit, and also . . . oh God, that made sense. Sort of. *But wait, what?*

After Chuck cleared my sister, he chucked the baton-thing back into the helicopter and went about his business of casually dragging away the dead body.

"He will." Erik sounded as if the idea stressed him out as much as it did me.

But Erik put us in this situation, so why was he so upset about it? It didn't add up.

"Bring Lucy with the others. We'll board the helo and wait," Erik said a few seconds later.

Security Asshole peered my way as if unsure he'd be following that order. And it was just long enough for me to realize what his words also implied.

"We're being separated?" I clutched my chest, forgetting the pain in my jaw. *This is why I . . . don't make it. But*

*Lucy does. The tracker is here, and I'm pretty sure I'm leaving.*

"No," Lucy cried, then lunged for me, hooking her arm with mine with fierce intensity.

I didn't want to cry, but this was our goodbye, and my fate was already predetermined. I wasn't sure who'd be the one to kill me, but it was inevitable. "I love you, sis." I untangled her arm from mine so I could pull her in for a hug, and she broke into a violent sob against my chest.

"You knew this, didn't you?" she whispered through her cries. "Camila told you."

"I love you," I repeated, doing my best to stay strong for her. "It'll be okay."

"He'll come for you. He won't let this happen," Lucy bellowed as the asshole began pulling her away from me.

I knew the "he" of the story was Jack. But I also knew he wouldn't be able to save us both, and he knew what I wanted. My sister to live.

"I love you, Charley." She tried to get to me, but the asshole hauled her into his arms, pinning her to his muscular chest, and I fell to my knees as I watched her being taken away from me.

Once she was gone from my sight, taken into the mansion in the distance, Erik crouched alongside me. "I never wanted to find you two. This wasn't supposed to happen."

I braced my hands on the ground as I struggled to find my breath. "You sent the cartel after us. You made this happen. Baited us here. You're lying." I lifted my chin to look at him, feeling strangely unthreatened by a man who'd done those things.

"I didn't have a choice. My brother's head of security, who he trusts even more than me, recognized you on camera at the show. He wanted to take you straight from the lodge, and his idea would've been an outright massacre. Getting you into the jungle with your . . . friends . . . and hiring the cartel to try and take you was the only way I could give you a chance."

"What?" I pushed away from the ground only to fall back onto my heels.

"When I realized your teammates weren't who they said they were, I hoped they'd . . ." He shook his head and stood, and with trembling legs and a shocked mind, I did the same. "Those cartel thugs were never supposed to hurt you. And the men who tried to at the border, well, I dispatched a team there to take out any survivors. They're all dead."

I continued to stare at this man in shock, unable to process everything. Was he lying? Was the security guy always the threat to me, both in Cape Town and on the show? "I don't understand," I cried.

"I let you get away that night eleven years ago because you're Claudia's daughter. I bought you as much time as possible so you could escape. You really think I did that just for you to wind up in my brother's grasp again? And now with his sickness, he'll think you're her. Fuck." He cursed again, cupping his jaw. "I'm not a good man, Charlotte, not even close." His arm fell to his side. "But my brother's a monster. We're not the same."

"I don't understand any of this." Tears I'd managed to hold back began to slip down my cheeks.

"I won't let him touch you." Erik's attention shifted to the house, and I followed his gaze to see Security Asshole coming out. "And I won't let Jordan hurt you either."

*Jordan?* So, the asshole had a name. I liked Asshole better.

"I'm sorry, Charlotte," he added, then motioned for the

helicopter before taking hold of my arm, his touch surprisingly gentle.

I forced myself to move with him. "Why should I believe you?"

Erik paused outside the helicopter door and leaned in and whispered, "Because you're my daughter. That's why."

# CHAPTER THIRTY-SIX

## JACK

"THE BULLET WENT CLEAN THROUGH. I'M FINE," I HISSED AS Oliver stabbed the needle into my arm against my protests. "I don't have time for this."

"You're not fine," Mya snapped out, joining us outside the tunnel. "Let him help you. You'll be useless on the op otherwise."

I grunted, then bit down on my teeth as Oliver did something to my shoulder that was less than pleasant. I focused on Gwen, sitting on the ground near the entrance of the tunnel. Using the SUV's headlights to see, she monitored Lucy and Charley's location through the charm bracelet on her laptop. *God bless Wyatt's obsession with his daughter's whereabouts.*

In an interesting turn of events, Gray's father managed to not only pull the police off our team's plane at the airport, but he requested they also help us out on behalf of the President. Starting with the team being Uber'd to the tunnel via police cruisers. And once the Feds—who'd miraculously survived the ambush in the tunnel—let their FBI headquarters in on the betrayal, the Bureau was willing to play ball without a nudge. It was now a joint mission of sorts.

Thankfully, a couple of the Feds' SUVs had only suffered fender benders, so we had adequate transportation for the op. I honestly didn't care about their condition as long as we all made it to Charley and Lucy in time.

"Never thought I'd see the day Carter worked with the Feds," Oliver said as he finished whatever patch job he was doing on my shoulder.

"I'll work with anyone as long as it means getting to them in time." I did my best not to say too much—to keep my mouth shut about what else I knew. I was still worried about Camila's warning.

"We'll get to them." Mya was working hard to sound confident, which I appreciated.

"Okay, you're all set for now." Oliver patted my good shoulder. "But since you won't take morphine, you're going to need to use your anger as a pain reliever for now."

"Yeah, that won't be a problem."

As my team finished prepping for the mission, I went over to Gwen and squatted alongside her to view the screen. "They haven't moved in a few minutes," she announced. "I think they're at their final destination."

I winced at her choice of words. *Final destination. Please, don't say that.*

"Where?" Carter came over, kitted up for war. I needed to prep too, but seeing their location on the screen made me feel like we were closer to getting them back. And honestly, I wasn't ready to give up that reassurance just yet.

"I've got an address. They're at an estate that was rented out two years ago to a British investment banker. My guess is that's their cover story for being here," Gwen explained while

Oliver helped me stand. I gestured to Jesse, acknowledging I was ready to gear up.

"How far away?" Gray asked, strapping on his Kevlar vest. Like me, he insisted he was fine to operate, brushing off being fried by a taser as a mere flesh wound. I wanted to protest him going in less than one hundred percent, but knowing he would be at my side also brought a level of security and comfort I needed.

"Ten kilometers, give or take," Gwen said, shooting to her feet while balancing the laptop on her palm.

"Here." Jesse helped me into the Kevlar vest since my shoulder made it difficult to lift my arm. I strapped a Glock 19 to my side and confirmed he'd already packed the vest with 30-round magazines. "And this bad boy is courtesy of Camila's lead sniper." Jesse offered me the M4A1 Carbine rifle. It was more ergonomic and had a better trigger response than the regular M4.

I nodded. "This will work."

Next, Mya handed over the wireless comm, and I shoved it into my ear. "You're Alpha Four tonight," she said, unable to mask the worry in her voice with fake confidence.

*Yeah, I'm worried, too.* "Roger that," I answered as she gently hugged my good side.

"Be safe." Mya's trembling tone was going to fuck with my head. "Go get your girl back, Jack."

"Yeah." I cleared my throat. "I plan on it."

"The place has a regular six-foot fence. So you won't need a breaching charge. You can scale it. In fact, the security seems fairly light," Gwen shared. "We don't have time for an aerial view or to put up a drone for heat signatures, but something just feels . . . I don't know."

*Feels what? What don't you know?*

"Like they weren't planning on company? They gave us the other location, so they're probably assuming we'll mount a campaign there instead," Gray said, trying to reassure Gwen's concerns. Concerns I now found myself sharing. "And if I had to guess, when the police check the address we gave them for the other property, it'll be empty or rigged to blow."

"You did give them the heads-up, right?" Gwen asked him, and Gray shot her his "of course" knitted-brow look.

But I was still hung up on the op being an easy infil. Anything that looked easy usually had us bottoming out and falling into the depths of Hell, where we'd have to claw our way back from the dead.

* * *

"ALPHA TWO, COME IN. DO YOU COPY?" I WAITED FOR Gray's response from his position on overwatch. My team had infiltrated the property far too easily. We'd only had to jump a fence. Hell, not even any barbed wire to stop us. Talk about a red flag.

"This is Two," Gray said over comms. "You have an armed tango about to round the corner by the front porch. He's all that stands in your way of entering the home."

*One guy? One fucking guy? That's it? Red flag number two.*

From my crouched position behind a boulder at the front of the property, I took a knee for extra support—fucking shoulder injury—lifted the rifle, steadied my aim, and took the shot the second he came into view. "Tango down," I confirmed, then stifled a groan as I pushed back up to my feet, my shoulder on fire. But the pain radiating there had nothing on my heart.

"This is One," Carter cut over the line. "I have my sights on a helipad in the back of the home, but no helo."

*Please don't tell me they left and the tracker stayed behind because someone* . . . "Roger that," I said, my voice shakier than I was comfortable with.

"Charlie mike, Alpha Four," Carter said despite the news, telling me to continue mission, and I did. I kept pushing forward.

Gray popped into my ear to let me know of another tango on approach, and I took him down before he could so much as raise his AK.

"This is Alpha Three. I have . . . people in my sights. I think the missing women are among them. This is, *welllll*, weird." Jesse's words had me hanging back on the porch.

"What do you mean?" I rasped, my heart thundering in my ears.

"They're having a pool party. Pretty sure some of those women we identified as missing are drinking and living it up by the pool with a couple sporty jock-looking guys." Jesse sounded tentative. Well, more like shocked.

"I'm sorry, what?" Gray shot out. "Say that again."

And Jesse did. Word for fucking word.

"Do you see our targets?" Carter was referencing both Charley and her sister, as well as the Luther brothers. "Any of them?"

"Negative," Jesse answered. "What do you want me to do?"

"This is One. Let me clear the house first. Everyone, hold your positions."

Hanging back outside while Carter searched the house for Charley and Lucy wasn't what I wanted to do, but I'd be damned if I compromised the mission and became the reason something happened to Charley due to my irrational state.

*But what IF following orders is why—*

My thoughts were muted by the sounds of gunfire inside the house, which also prompted screaming from the back, and the poolside music stopped.

"This is One. The house is secure. Tangos down," Carter shared once the gunfire ended.

"This is Five," Oliver said. "You're all clear from my vantage point."

"This is Six," Mason spoke up. "Clear from the north side as well."

At that, I rounded the porch and entered through a side door. "Do we have eyes on the package? Anyone, come in. Does anyone have the package?"

"Just one," Carter said.

"They took Charley," I heard Lucy say over Carter's comm. "She's gone."

I stopped in the hall, my body going numb. "No," I seethed, my knees buckling.

At the sight of Carter at the end of the hall, escorting Lucy, I did my best to get a grip. The mission wasn't over yet.

"Jack," Lucy cried, breaking away from Carter to rush my way. "She's gone."

I let the sling catch the rifle to hold her.

"The Fed was dead before we got here," Carter informed me, meeting my eyes. "I'm going to talk to the team. We'll find where Charley was taken."

I nodded at him over Lucy's head and held her for a few more seconds, knowing Charley would want me to comfort her sister.

Mason appeared at the side door. "Are you okay, Lucy?"

"No." She peered around me, and Mason flicked his wrist, quietly motioning for her to come to him.

I let her go, and she walked into his waiting embrace.

*Damnit, I need to find my girl.* I sidestepped the two of them and went outside. Camila was there now, talking to the police and Feds, as well as the "partygoers," who apparently included the missing women. "What'd they say? Do they know anything?" I asked her as Gray made his approach.

Camila turned to me as the police and Feds focused on talking to the bikini-clad women and the guys in swim trunks out by the pool. "The women are here because they chose to be here. But there are only five of the six. I showed them the picture of the woman from season one, and according to them, she was never here."

I clutched my aching shoulder as I studied her, wishing she'd hurry up and tell me the future changed and that everything would be okay. "What do you mean they 'chose' to be here?"

"Erik Luther offered them a lot of money to play house with his brother and pretend to be Claudia Lennox," Camila explained. "They each have a two-year contract and had to sign an NDA. Once Brant was done with his delusions in believing the woman to be Claudia, which lasted anywhere from two to four months, Erik brought them to this house to finish out the duration of their contract. The girl from the second season said her time is up next month, and she's supposed to receive her million-dollar payday."

"You mean the one who looks pissed we're here?" Gray's eyes fixed on a blonde throwing her hands in the air, ranting about being robbed of a million dollars.

"The women really chose this?" I asked in disbelief. "They weren't taken against their will?" That was good, but it didn't change the fact Charley was still in the hands of dangerous men.

"According to them, no. I guess I got that wrong."

Camila's eyes narrowed on me. Was she suggesting she got "something else" wrong, too? Like Charley's fate?

"The women identified both Erik and Brant's head of security for us," one of the Feds said, joining our "debrief." He looked at me and added, "Erik offered them a sweet deal they said they couldn't refuse." He shrugged. "Money, the universal language," he tacked on, throwing back what we'd said at the airport about the crooked Feds.

I blinked a few times, trying to pull my thoughts together. "I need to find Charley. She can't be far away." *Think, damnit.*

"Every way off this island is now being monitored," the Fed shared. "They have to be here somewhere."

"And our men just checked the other address you gave us," one of the local officers said as he joined our group. "The house the Luthers used to bait you is empty. Not even rigged as a trap. But the women confirmed that was where they lived with Brant before coming here."

"Did we leave anyone alive here so we can question where they might be now?" I spit out, ready to claw at my hair, but I needed to keep calm to get through this.

"Alive, yes. Conscious? No. Carter's working on waking one now, but we doubt he'll know anything. The Luthers wouldn't risk that," Camila noted, her focus on me.

"Get Gwen on the phone." I keyed in on Gray next. "Have her search nearby properties that have a helipad. And then narrow the search down to ones rented or purchased this week. They'd need a new place fast to pull this off."

Camila nodded. "Gwen's already on it."

"And we're working to get a hit on any recent air traffic for helicopters to get us a search perimeter," the Fed said.

"Thank you." I waited for the agent and officer to leave and, even though Gray was still there, turned to Camila. "Tell me there's hope, that something changed. Tell me Charley doesn't die. Tell me you misinterpreted that vision, too."

Camila bowed her head and whispered, "I'm sorry, Jack. I, um, can't tell you that."

I backed up from her, bumping into Gray, and nearly fell into the pool. He caught my good arm, keeping me from going down. Frustrated and furious at how fucking useless I was, I turned, preparing to walk away when Camila threw her hand out, nearly knocking me into the pool anyway.

"Wait." Her eyes widened as she seemingly stared off in a daze and yelled, "Something did change. There might be hope. But she doesn't have much time." Still focused on the pool, she murmured, "She's going to drown."

# CHAPTER THIRTY-SEVEN

## CHARLOTTE

INSIDE THE LAVISH SECOND-FLOOR SUITE AT THE MANSION I was taken to, Erik checked his watch, then removed what appeared to be a hearing aid from his ear, but maybe it was a communication device. He shoved it into his pocket, and we were finally alone for the first time since we'd flown to the new location.

"Why aren't we just leaving? Why even bring me here if you don't want me near Brant?" Standing by the king-sized bed, I clutched the white dress Jordan had shoved at me to put on before he'd left the room to let Brant know we were waiting for him.

"Jordan and his men wouldn't have let me run away with you and Lucy. I had no choice but to come here. And you saw how heavily guarded this place is. Almost all of Brant's men are here, which will make the task of your friends saving your sister much easier." Erik kept his voice low as he went over and drew the floor-to-ceiling curtains open, exposing two French doors. He unlocked and opened them, allowing a gentle breeze into the room, the smell of the Caribbean Sea wafting in with it.

*But wait, what?* "What do you mean?" I tossed the dress to the side, thankful it was a simple and plain silk sheath rather than wedding-white and frilly.

Erik pushed his hands into his pockets and faced me. Was he really my father? Was it possible? "You had a bracelet on when you exited the helo. Not one when we got back on. You were being tracked," he remarked in a steady tone. "But when Jordan reaches out to his men to check on them, and no one answers, he'll tell Brant to evacuate here as a precaution."

*Oh.* I was starting to feel strangely numb. Less breathy and panicky as I'd been before, but I wasn't sure why given the fact a man obsessed with me would be in the room in a few minutes. Maybe because some part of me believed Erik was my father, and despite not knowing me, he appeared to give a shit about me.

"Tell me you have a plan to get me away from him, then." Okay, hello, panic, again. Because the blank look on Erik's face had my stomach turning.

"I can't kill everyone here. I'm only one person. And my brother's men are loyal. Money won't do the trick in getting them to turn. Not everyone can be bought." He squeezed his eyes closed. "I'm hoping your men manage to track us here before it's too late."

"You're hoping my . . ." I blinked, shaking my head in shock. "Did you leave some clues, at least?"

"This is the only property that's been rented in the last two days with a helipad. If they're smart, they'll connect the dots." He opened his eyes, angling his head. "Are they smart, Charlotte?"

"They're smart." *But if they'll be able to find me so easily, why do I die? What happens between now and then? Crossfire? No, Jack would be careful. That can't be it. And I refuse to believe Jack died in that tunnel, so he'll be coming.*

*So then, what? Shit, why am I thinking about how I'll die instead of focusing on how NOT to die?* "Tell me everything, though. Please. I want to understand why this is all happening."

He came closer to the bed, and when I flinched at his proximity, he walked back a step. I had to remind myself he still worked with Brant, a psychopath. And he himself was a criminal. He'd killed that Fed without remorse, so he was dangerous, too.

"I've known your mom since we were both sixteen. We boosted cars together. One night when we were eighteen, well, the adrenaline got to us, and . . ." He cleared his throat, letting me fill in the "we had sex" blanks. "She told me a few weeks after that she met someone and wanted to straighten out her life. When I found out she was pregnant, she promised me you weren't mine." He was talking fast, no doubt because we were short on time, but I could detect the slip of emotion edging into his tone. My brain was trying to play catch-up and truly comprehend what he was trying to tell me. Everything I'd ever thought I knew was a lie. "Claudia cut me out of her life, and it wasn't until your—well, the man who raised you—died that I made the biggest mistake of my life . . . If I had just left her alone and not pushed her into working with me again, she'd be alive. And you'd be living a very different life."

This was too much to process. My head was spinning. I started to sit, but then a framed photo on the dresser caught my eye. I went over to it and lifted it with trembling fingers. Mom standing by her Mustang, stunning in silk, her hair curled, framing her high cheekbones.

"I took that photo of her." Erik came up alongside me. "The day she bought that car. She'd been so excited to have one she hadn't stolen."

"But the money was dirty. Same thing." Now I sounded like Lucy.

Erik took the photo from me and set it facedown on the dresser. "For the first few years your mother worked with us, things were fine. She did what she had to do to earn enough to support you and Lucy. Nothing more."

I faced him, realizing he was defending her, just like I had over the years whenever Lucy and I talked about her.

"But then the jobs got riskier. And the higher the risk, the higher the reward. My brother built his business off the backs of others' success."

"Stolen success." A dejected feeling cut through me, and it was hard to digest the fact I'd once envied my mom's "job" and had considered it a suitable career path.

Erik looked up at the ceiling as if unable to meet my eyes as he told me the rest. "About a year before she died, my brother started developing an unhealthy obsession with her. She didn't return his affections, and that only triggered him more. I tried to protect her as much as I could, but when you started pushing to follow in her footsteps, well, I'm assuming that's why she tried to fake her death and run away. If she'd told me her plan, I could've helped her."

*You loved her, didn't you?*

"I tried to stop Jordan from forcing you to drive in your mother's place for the heist, but I was overruled. And then when . . . well, everything went down . . . Your mother's last words to my brother were a plea not to kill you because you were his niece."

Oh, God. *That's* what she said? I remembered her whispering something while clutching hold of Brant as he'd held her, crying.

"I told him she lied to try and save you, but he wanted proof. He took the blood from the knife he cut you with and

387

threatened to . . . well, destroy both of us if the woman he loved had a child with me."

"What'd you do?" This was all so wild, but so many things were adding up.

"Money can thankfully buy some people off, and I paid the guy at the lab to give me the real results and offer my brother an alternative. The test confirmed you were my daughter. And now I know why she did her best to limit my time around you. She knew I'd quickly see the truth in your eyes. Given my family, I don't blame her for not wanting me to know."

He was right. The truth was right there in front of me. And I would've figured it out back then. *We share blood, and that means I'm related to Brant, too.*

"Brant gave up searching for you once the bloodwork came back and he was satisfied with the results, but clearly, Jordan didn't. He wanted revenge since you shot him." Erik went back to the open French doors and reached for his back, going for the gun there. Oddly, the sight didn't worry me.

"Why the dating show, though? Why is he fixating on women who look like my mom?"

He faced me, resting the weapon against his outer thigh. "Brant started having delusions a few years back. One day he was watching that reality show, and he swore one of the contestants was Claudia. He became obsessed with finding her. I tried to get him help. Brought him down here." A deep breath later, he added, "He had Jordan kidnap the woman, and by the time I got to them both, Brant had already killed her. She'd refused to give in to his delusions that she was your mother."

I cupped my mouth, fighting the urge to be sick. Now I knew why Camila had alluded to only five women being saved.

"I should've killed Brant then, but he's always heavily protected. Even from me. I'm not . . . like him. I may be a criminal, but I'd never hurt a woman." He tore his free hand through his hair, eyes shifting to the door as if he could hear steps that I couldn't. "Brant tried to go after another woman in broad daylight a few weeks after that incident, mistaking her for Claudia. I realized I had to do something or more women would get hurt."

"You came up with the idea to use the show?"

Erik nodded. "I needed to control the situation. Control Jordan without him realizing I was. I pitched the idea to him, explaining it'd be the best way to prevent Brant from destroying his business by publicly attacking someone again. So, whenever there was a contestant he favored, I offered them money in exchange for pretending to be Claudia."

It was hard for me to believe anyone would agree to that, but I supposed if the price was right, some people would struggle to turn down the offer.

"The last thing I expected was for you and your sister to wind up on the show. Jordan was Shannon's point of contact, and I never got involved in the process until my brother made his choice. I couldn't stomach it. But if I had, I would've recognized you and gotten you away before Jordan ever ID'd you two."

I considered his words, my body shaking at the heavy weight of them. "I want to believe you. But it's just—"

"I know," he said as the doorknob turned. "I wouldn't believe me either, I suppose." He turned to the side, hiding the gun clutched in his hand behind his back.

Jordan, along with Brant and one other armed man, filed into the bedroom.

"Claudia?" Brant questioned, stopping in his tracks.

Seeing him again in the flesh had me choking up. Even

after eleven years, I could still see him holding my mother's lifeless body on that garage floor . . . But I didn't want to follow in her footsteps. I couldn't just sit here and wait to die. She'd want me to live, and more than ever, I wanted to live. I wanted . . . *I want Jack.* Damnit, I had to figure out how to change my fate.

"She's not Claudia," Erik spoke up, not wasting time, and Brant twisted to look at him, dark brows lifting in shock. "You know that. The doctors told you that you're dying, and reliving the past is not going to save you from death."

*Dying?* No sympathy from me, but Erik had left that part out of his story.

"You can't keep tricking your brain into believing these women are Claudia. And Claudia never loved you. You need to stop this madness," Erik pressed, remaining firm near the open balcony doors.

"Stop," Jordan demanded, drawing his weapon from a side holster as if sensing there was about to be a showdown between the brothers.

*Perhaps pistols at dawn?* My life was already wild enough the past few days, at this point, I'd expect nothing less.

"She looks just like Claudia." Brant walked my way and snatched the white dress from the floor. "You're her. Don't lie to me."

Chills wrapped around my limbs, but I did my best to remain tough. To believe my fate was written in the stars, and not in the sand. "We do look alike. Because we share blood," I spoke up. "I'm her daughter. So, I suggest you walk back a few steps and don't try and touch me." I elongated my neck, trying to gain another inch of confidence in facing off with this psycho who killed my mother. "I'm also your niece."

"You faked the test, didn't you?" It was Jordan that time, peering at Erik.

From the corner of my eye, Erik lined himself up with me, and I caught a quick nod. "There are some lines even you won't cross, Jordan. And letting Brant near his niece is one of them."

Jordan looked at me, then at Brant who continued to stare at me, squinting as if trying to solve a Rubik's Cube.

"Too bad I never liked you, Erik, or maybe I'd give a fuck if she lived or died," Jordan snapped out before turning his attention on my other problem: Brant, who was still looking at me like . . . *shit,* like he thought I was my mom.

Brant's dark hair was wet and tousled as if he'd recently showered, and with his free hand, he shoved his thick fingers through his locks and lifted his Travolta-like dimpled chin like a directive before pushing the dress my way. "Claudia."

Erik maneuvered around me, blocking me from his brother, and I took the chance to place a little more distance between us, practically stumbling out onto the small balcony. "She's not Claudia," he grated out.

"What are we going to do?" Brant's other guard, still hanging back by the door, asked.

Jordan tapped his ear as if someone was talking to him, and then I startled at the sound of gunfire. "We're under attack." He lifted his weapon, aiming it my way as he barked out, "Kill them and get the boss out of here."

Before I had a chance to react, Erik raised his arm and fired just as Jordan shot back. A flashback to my mother jumping in front of me to take the bullet popped into my head as Erik flung himself before me, taking a bullet to the arm. *You saved me.*

Brant charged Erik, and everything was a blur of movement. With my back to the balcony railing, I had nowhere to go . . . and then time stopped. I wasn't sure where the bullet came from that struck me, but everything was going dark as the momentum propelled me over the railing. And that's when I saw—

. . . *Jack.*

# CHAPTER THIRTY-EIGHT

## JACK

THE SIGHT OF CHARLEY FALLING FROM THE BALCONY, HER eyes closing right before she went over, had my heart stopping. Running on pure adrenaline, I pushed through the room as fast as possible. Two men were lifeless on the ground, and I double-tapped the guy at my nine o'clock in the chest, leaving Brant as the only obstacle to get to Charley.

He was in the process of going for a weapon, blood staining the side of his white dress shirt. As much as I wanted to make Brant's death painful, I didn't have the luxury. I needed to get to Charley. Without an ounce of remorse, I shot the fucker right between the eyes before quickly maneuvering around him to get to the balcony.

*Please don't be dead. Please, God.* I looked over the railing and Charley was in a pool . . . floating facedown.

The memory of Camila's words launched me into action. Getting up onto the railing, I chucked my rifle, then made the dive into the deep end. I swam over to her as the gunfire filled the air like fireworks as my team continued to take down tangos. I grabbed hold of her with my bad arm, ignoring the shooting pain, and swam us over to the side of the pool.

Using all my strength, I hauled her out of the water and gently set her on her back. Her head rolled to the side, and she wasn't breathing. But the pool hadn't been colored in blood, which meant . . .

After pulling myself from the pool, I ripped open her shirt, prepared to do CPR. *Oh thank fuck.* I breathed a sigh of relief at the sight before me. She was still wearing the chest plate I'd asked her to put on beneath her shirt while on the flight from Ecuador. I'd completely forgotten about it. The plate had taken the hit, but the impact of the shot had still knocked her out. She'd be bruised and in pain when she came to, but . . .

Tossing the plate to the side, praying my teammates kept cover over us, I tilted her head back and sealed my mouth over hers, giving her five rescue breaths. Then I pressed down hard, a third of the depth of her chest. After thirty compressions, I gave her two more rescue breaths. I kept repeating the cycle, my body starting to shake, tears joining the pool water coating my face.

"Come on, Charley, breathe for me, sweetheart. Please," I begged as I pushed down on her chest, trying not to hurt her, the bluish coloring on her face the last thing I wanted to see. "Please," I choked out. "I'll do anything. Fuuuuck, I promise. I'll do anything." Was I begging God to save her? I wasn't sure, but I . . . "Just come back to me, Charley. Please," I yelled in desperation, panic taking over.

"Jack," someone yelled from behind me. Was that Oliver? "Jack, let me help."

A montage of every moment Charley and I had spent together flooded my mind, nearly making me hysterical. "No, no. She's going to be okay. HAS to be okay." *No, you're not dying.*

Just as Oliver knelt alongside me, Charley jolted and moved, and she began coughing. I quickly urged her head to the side, so she didn't choke on the water she was spitting out. She gasped for air, her oxygen-starved lungs acting on instinct, and I broke down and sobbed at the sight of her breathing, eyelids fluttering open.

"Can I take over now?" Oliver asked, a hand on my arm. "I have to make sure—"

"Yeah," I whispered, shifting to the side to give him room to help her while remaining on my knees near the two of them. It was eerily quiet, and I finally realized the gunfire had ceased.

"She okay?" I heard someone else call out. Or maybe they were in my ear on comms? I was too fucked up to know.

"Jack." Charley clutched her throat, attempting to sit.

I couldn't stop the sobs still destroying my chest as I moved over and hooked my good arm behind her back, drawing her against me.

"I think I died," she whispered into my ear as we held each other. "You brought me back to life."

I pulled away to see her eyes, which were still a bit red, but her color was returning to her face.

"And, Jack, maybe this is crazy, but I'm pretty sure I met your mom. Mine was there, too." Tears flew down her face. "Your mom told me to hang in there, that you were waiting for me."

I broke down at her words and tugged her against me. Whether it was true or not, I just, well . . . "Fuck, Charley," I choked out, clutching her tightly, somehow believing that yeah, my mom just met the love of my life.

\* \* \*

"THANK YOU FOR HAVING MY BACK OUT HERE, SO I COULD . . ." *Get my girl.*

"Always, man." Gray looked at Charley before pulling me in for a hug, careful of my shoulder.

I did my best to push aside my emotions as Mason joined us by the ambulance where Charley was being seen by a medic and shared, "Erik's gone."

Gray coughed into his fist for a second, discarding his emotions as well before he snapped out, "What do you mean he's gone?"

"He was on the floor in that bedroom when I killed Brant and the other guy," I said, unable to make sense of it. "Jordan was dead, too."

"Erik must not have been dead, and in all the chaos he slipped away." Mason had kept his voice low, and his expression read, *Don't shoot the messenger.*

We were about a hundred or so feet away from the pool where Charley had fallen into, and to be honest, I could go a lifetime without going near rivers or pools.

Jesse and Oliver came over a few seconds later, and we didn't waste time in exchanging ideas about next steps to go after Erik.

"Erik's not a danger," Charley said softly, breaking through our discourse, and she motioned away the medic while sitting upright on the stretcher. "He saved my life. Took a bullet meant for me."

"That, um, seems strange." Mason blinked, turning a questioning glance my way, and I sure as hell didn't have an answer for him.

"Not so strange since he claims to be my biological

father." Charley's words stole my attention, and I went back to her side and reached for her hand. "And I think I believe him, too."

"Say what?" Mason almost choked on the words, but for some reason, I wasn't quite as shocked as him.

When Charley began detailing everything that had happened after the tunnel ambush, including what Erik had told her, it all somehow made sense in a strange way.

"Will you go after him?" Charley asked, looking at me. I could feel the Fed at my six on approach, and I shifted to the side to catch his eyes.

Since the agent had never offered a name, I opted not to press for it. But I'd be forever grateful to him for his help.

"We'll try, but I get the feeling he won't make it easy on us to find him," the Fed said, sliding his hands into his pockets. "We found a hard drive with what looks like enough evidence to not only take down the entire Luther operation but give a few lives back. Well, at least return the patents they stole to their original owners. This is a big win for the Bureau." His brown eyes shifted over my shoulder, and I spied an SUV rolling in, most likely bringing Lucy, Camila, and the others now that it was safe to join us.

The property was clear but swarming with uniforms, and I was anxious to get out of there. Carter had made a quick exit once all tangos had been confirmed down and Charley was safe, worried the FBI might have a change of heart and decide to *try* and take him in.

Charley squeezed my hand as she asked the agent, "Am *I* still on your wanted list, or am I free now?"

"The names of the corrupt Feds working with the Luthers over the years were also on that hard drive, so they'll be the ones we're going after, not you. You're clear, Miss Lennox."

I felt the tension leave Charley's body and I allowed myself to relax a little at his words. "You and your sister can have your lives back. You're no longer wanted by us. And from what we also learned, Erik Luther cleaned house with the cartel who attacked you all the other day in South America. They won't be coming for you either."

I still didn't like Erik, but at least he saved me from having to take out the trash to help protect Charley. We appeared to both be devoted to keeping her safe.

Charley bowed her head but kept hold of my hand, and I could tell she was fighting the urge to cry. Hopefully, tears of relief. Her nightmare of being on the run for eleven years had come to an end.

"Charley!" At Lucy's voice, she whipped her head back up to see Lucy.

"Lucy." Charley let go of my hand and hopped off the stretcher, running to meet her sister.

Gwen and Mya sidestepped the two as they embraced, but Camila hung back near the sisters as if wanting a moment with Charley. And fucking A, I was crying again at the emotional intensity of their reunion.

"Well, if you all would like to get out of here before even more uniforms show up," the Fed said, tilting his head toward the gated exit, "I wouldn't blame you." He cleared his throat, eyes going to Gray. "Tell your buddy, Carter Dominick, the FBI released his jet in Brazil. He can have it back. And your father has issued leave-him-be orders. So, he can stop looking over his shoulder. From us, at least." He winked.

Gray stepped forward and offered his hand. "He'll appreciate the news."

The agent smiled, then shook my hand next. "I'm sure. Though, from what I've heard, the U.S. government is the least of Dominick's problems."

*True.* "And hey, thanks for having my six back in the tunnel, and believing my innocence."

"Don't mention it. You know, it's not every day I get to fight alongside someone with your background. I'd say it was a pleasure, but getting shot at never is." The agent tipped his head goodbye, then left me alone with my team.

"Not a bad day's work," Gwen chirped with a small smile and a clap of her hands. Her bracelet was back on her wrist, and I was glad she'd found it back at the other house before rolling out. "Or, well, a night's work."

"Glad to see you're all okay," Mya commented, her gaze swiveling back and forth between Oliver and Mason.

Mason gave her a little nod, then he quietly walked toward Lucy, who was heading our way as Camila and Charley talked.

"Since we're dating show teammates and all," Oliver began, "maybe I can get a congratulatory hug from you for killing four assholes tonight? No, wait, make that five." He pointed at the house. "On my way to the pool, some guy with a bad case of FOMO wanted to meet his maker, too. So, I decided to oblige him."

"A hug for killing five baddies, huh?" Mya smirked. With the bright lights illuminating the whole backside of the property, it was impossible to miss the blush spreading across her cheeks at the fact Oliver, joking or not, had asked for a hug in front of us all. "I guess I can manage that."

"You two need a room?" Gwen nudged Mya in the side when she'd yet to actually give Oliver the hug he'd more than likely been joking about.

"We should get the hell out of here," Gray said, motioning for us to get a move on.

We walked away from Mya and Oliver, heading toward the gates where our SUVs were parked outside. Were they really getting along? That was weird. But nothing about the last several days had been exactly normal, so . . .

"You sure Charley and Lucy will be good to go back Stateside?" I asked, walking alongside Gray and Jesse.

"Yeah, my dad messaged me that they're good," Gray confirmed, and my good shoulder dropped another inch in relief. My bad one was still out of commission from any movement.

When we closed in on where Camila and Charley were hugging, we stopped and hung back, giving them space.

As the adrenaline left my body, my injured shoulder began reminding me of exactly how pissed off it was. I set my hand over the temporary wrap, realizing I probably ought to get it looked at before we flew home.

"You think she'll want to go back to California?" Jesse's question caught me off guard. "Or maybe live near your place in Virginia?"

I was only renting a place in Virginia because Gray and his wife were in that area. And as much as I wanted to find something there long term, well . . . was it too soon for me to tell Charley I'd go wherever she went? *If* she still wanted me in her life after this. Just because she saw a vision of my mother didn't mean . . .

Fuck, now my heart was aching more than my shoulder. We hadn't even had a real date yet. I was putting the cart before the horse, or whatever it was my dad used to say.

"I don't know," I whispered, unsure what to think as Camila and Charley approached us.

Charley set her sights on her sister who was still talking to Mason, then she focused back on me.

"I'm so sorry about everything," Camila said when they reached us. "But I think it all worked out how it was supposed to."

"And Erik? Do you know what will happen to him?" Charley asked her.

"He won't be a problem for you, that much I know," Camila said with a firm nod, then she peered around the sprawling estate still buzzing with activity. "I take it Carter took off?"

"That he did," Gray said with a smile.

"I'll find him. He can't be too far." Camila patted Gray on the shoulder. "I'll be seeing you all soon."

"Oh yeah? Another op? Can't we have a little break?" Gray asked in a semi-teasing tone, and Camila lifted her brows and winked before walking toward the direction of some of her teammates, still talking to the uniformed officers.

"Sooo." Jesse slapped his palms together and held them in a prayer position. "I'd like to get home to my wife now."

"What do you say?" I turned to Charley, deciding Jesse was right and my shoulder could wait. "Ready to go?"

She stepped closer and set her hand on my chest, covering my heart. "There's somewhere I'd like to go when we're Stateside. Somewhere I need to be."

I nodded in understanding. "Visit your mother?" I couldn't imagine never having the chance to properly mourn my parents, and she'd been robbed of that.

"Yes, that's what I'd like to do first," she said, her tone hoarse, likely from nearly drowning, but also from the emotions catching up with her. "Can we have a second, please?" She looked at the others, motioning between me and her, and they quietly left us alone. Well, as alone as we could be with thirty uniforms in the backyard near the pool that had nearly stolen her from me.

"Something you want to say?" I cupped her cheek and smoothed my thumb over her dimple. Instead of flinching, she leaned into my touch.

"There is." Her eyes fell closed.

*Fuck.* She was going to run. Tell me she wanted to visit her mother's gravesite alone, and that she needed time away. And could I give her that time?

"I don't own much, but what little I have is in Spain. I need to pack up my things. I don't know where to go after that, or what I'll even do. I never let myself plan a life that didn't involve constantly being on the go," she rambled, her voice trembling.

"Well, the beauty of it is, you now have your whole life ahead of you to figure it out," I murmured, reaching for her wrist. I smoothed my thumb over the ink that said **Never Let Go** written there. "If you need time, I, um, understand." *I just hate it, and I want to take back those words, because screw time. I want you now and forever.*

Her eyelids parted, and her glossy eyes met mine. "I do need time." She wet her lips, and my heart was on the verge of shattering into multiple pieces that'd cut me apart from the inside out. "But I was wondering if you'd spend that time with me?" She swallowed. "Ever been to Spain?"

Chills racked my body, and every fiber in my being may have snapped from relief. Pretty sure she might have to catch me this time, because I was going to fall. "I have." My turn to gulp.

She stepped back and opened her palm. "Feel like going again? I'll totally be putting those muscles of yours to work packing and carrying boxes, but . . ."

I accepted her palm and gently tugged her against me. "I'll follow you anywhere," I rasped. "And you can use me all you want."

She chewed on her lip and playfully lifted her brows. "Promise?"

I reached around her back, not giving a damn if we had eyes on us and squeezed her ass over her wet jeans. "Fuck yes, sweetheart," I said before slanting my mouth over hers, not waiting for her to meet me halfway this time. Because now I knew she was as all in as I was.

# CHAPTER THIRTY-NINE

## CHARLOTTE

### VIRGINIA - THREE WEEKS LATER

"I'm serious. Really. No more social media or dating for a long time," Lucy said around a bite of celebratory cake.

"Sure, sure, I bet you're serious." Instead of cake in my hand, I was holding and petting Gray and Tessa's cute little dog, Lucky. "I've heard this before. You're taking a social media and dating break," I went on. "Mmmhmm."

"I'm detoxing."

Then why was Lucy staring at the handsome Marine with the backward cap and shades on, talking to Oliver across the crowded backyard of Gray and his wife's home?

"We have a new start at life, and I want to put my old ways behind me," she continued. "Maybe I'll even go to school. Honestly, no clue what I'll do, but I'm starting to dig the East Coast vibes."

I set Lucky down, and he darted over to Carter's dog, Dallas, to play with him. He got around extremely well on the prosthesis Gray had created for him, and my heart swelled at the sight of the furry little tripawd cuddling against Carter's big dog. "You're digging someone who happens to live on the East Coast is more like it."

"Mason lives in New York, not here. And I think we should just be friends," Lucy said while finishing the last bite of her cake.

"Mason and Mya were once upon a time ago just friends." Jack had filled me in on their full backstory over the last three glorious weeks we'd spent together.

It'd been difficult visiting Mom's grave in California, but he'd been there for me. Holding my hand while I'd introduced him to my mother. Then he gave me a moment alone where I silently told her how I knew he was the one.

We'd then spent several days in Spain packing up what was left of my life there. Of course we may have stayed a bit longer than needed to enjoy Palma together . . . without many clothes on.

Once back in the U.S. again, and in between meeting several of Jack's friends, along with apartment hunting with Lucy, Jack and I spent every moment together. We were a little addicted to each other. And every warning I'd ever given my sister about not falling too hard, or too fast, for someone, had gone out the window with Jack.

Yep, I was head over heels for the man. And even though we'd yet to say the L word, it was on the tip of my tongue, dying to break free from my mouth.

"Yeah, well, that didn't end so hot for Mya and Mason, did it?" Lucy pointed out, drawing my focus back to her and the party.

I looked over at Mya holding Jesse's adorable son, Remi. She was trying to encourage Carter to take him, but the man shook his head and . . . did he just panic walk backward into Mason to escape?

When Camila came over and took Remi from Mya

instead, Carter removed his sunglasses and just gaped at her. And, well, that was interesting.

"Well," I began, remembering again what we'd been talking about, "I think things ended for Mya and Mason the way they were supposed to."

"Now you sound like Camila," Lucy said, her tone soft and playful. "But I still think Mason's hung up on Mya. And who wouldn't be? She's smart, funny, and gorgeous."

"Those are also descriptors for you, by the way." I rolled my eyes at her, forgetting I had on sunglasses, so she missed it.

"Well, like I said, I'm turning a new leaf. Doing things differently."

I was about to open my mouth and offer some more words of wisdom, but then remembered I needed to stop momming her. It was time she lived her own life. And I had to let go. Well, not let go-let go. She'd always be my family, and I'd always worry about her, but I could still do that and let her find her own way.

Lucy tossed her plate in a nearby trash bin, then came back alongside me where I'd chosen to hang back and people-watch. I was still a bit nervous to be there with so many people who knew the real me. It was a lot to take in.

Jack had told me Camila said she'd be seeing us again soon, but neither of us had expected it'd be this soon. At least it was for something celebratory. Jack had been incredibly over-the-moon happy when he'd learned his best friend and his wife were expecting. Being there to celebrate with Gray and Tessa seemed the perfect reason to reunite with everyone.

Time and time again, Camila really did prove she somehow knew things. Heck, she'd kind of been right about my future. I did die. I just came back, thank God.

And she'd even been on point about Shannon from the

reality show not having a long life. She didn't survive her first week in jail, getting caught up in a fight there. I hadn't wanted her to die, but she did work with the cartel who tried to kill us, so I didn't shed any tears at the news.

My head was still spinning from everything that went down, though. Sadly, the body of the woman Brant had killed after season one had yet to be found. And Erik was still MIA. I had a feeling we'd never hear from Erik again, and I supposed I was okay with that.

Lucy nudged me in the side, her way of telling me to put myself out there and mingle again. But I needed a few more seconds of "introvert time" after having done meet and greets with the over forty people at the party. Despite the backyard bustling with strangers, they'd all done their best to make me feel like anything but that. More like family.

I'd lost track of names quickly. Not only were Jack's teammates there, except Griffin and his wife since their baby was just born early (and thankfully, healthy), but there were also a bunch of Navy SEALs at the party along with their spouses and kids. Including the President's son Gwen had mentioned on the plane last month.

But that wasn't the only wild meeting at the party. The funny Southerner from Alabama who took over as DJ for the party, flooding the speakers with country music, was married to a woman who had once been an FBI agent. It should have made things super awkward given my past, but as it turned out, we had a lot in common. Ana's parents were criminals, and she'd once been wanted by the Feds, too.

"I need a cheat sheet for the next party with everyone's names and photos," Lucy said, reading my thoughts.

"Ditto."

Another elbow from her as she asked, "Soooo, do you

think you'll move out of our new apartment to live with Jack since you've been sleeping there every night?"

I set my sights on Jack as he twirled Wyatt's younger daughter, Emory, around. I frowned as I spotted him wince when he tried to dip her. Stubborn—yet, oh so amazing. And his shoulder was probably bothering him again. "Um, we haven't talked about moving in together," I finally answered as Wyatt took Emory from Jack. Apparently, I wasn't the only one who saw the wince.

I was pretty sure Wyatt was almost as intimidating as Carter. Not that he'd been rude or unkind to me, but the daggers he'd shot Carter earlier while lecturing him about what he'd heard "happened" at the reality show . . . I'd even felt the heat, and he hadn't been looking at me.

Carter had remained quiet but seemingly unfazed as Wyatt did the fatherly thing dads loved to do, embarrassing the hell out of Gwen.

*"It was innocent,"* Gwen had said, looking a little flustered. *"And just work."* Something in Gwen's eyes had told me another story, but she'd arrived with a date—a professional racecar driver, who also seemed to give Wyatt chest pain. So, I assumed she left whatever feelings she may have harbored for Carter back in South America.

"Well, I'm sure Jack will ask you to move in soon," Lucy spoke up a few seconds later, and I followed the direction her attention was focused. On my guy. "The man can barely handle being away from you even now. But he's giving you space."

She was right. Jack recognized I needed to take a breather, and he was letting me rejoin the folds of the party when ready. God, I loved that man.

"Well, I'm going to go do the extrovert thing and join the

crowd of hotness out here. I feel like I'm at a book boyfriend convention."

I chuckled, then waved her off and went in search of something to drink to cool down.

"I know everyone has been making you job offers, but I have one for you as well."

Mid-reach for a White Claw, at Camila's comment, I pulled my hand back and closed the cooler to face her, finding Remi still nestled in her arms.

I'd been hit up by several of the wives at the party with invites to come work with them. The offer I was most seriously considering was working for Jesse's sister, Rory, with canines that helped veterans transitioning to civilian life.

"I'm moving to the area," Camila went on before I could answer. "It's time for a change myself."

"So, your new headquarters will be in the D.C. area?" I asked her, and she returned her focus to me while simultaneously tickling Remi.

I'd never thought I could have kids because of my lifestyle, but being with Jack, and seeing this cute little boy with dark hair and blue eyes in Camila's arms, had me hopeful for children in my future.

There were so many things I wanted to do now. *Maybe I ought to make a list?*

"Meh. I don't really need a headquarters, but if you want to work with me, I can find a position for you on my team."

"I appreciate that, really. But your job requires a lot of traveling, and I think I'd like to stick to one place for a bit. Plant some roots, you know?" *No more running.*

"Well, if you change your mind, the offer stands."

"Can I ask you something?" I whispered, unsure why I was doing this, but the question was about to come out anyway. "Can you see my future?"

Camila's smile reached her eyes as she replied, "I do. And it's bright."

* * *

"I'M NOT GOING TO LIE, I WAS SCARED OF THIS BEAST AT first, but I think I'm getting used to it." Parked on Jack's driveway later that evening, I straddled him on the seat of his new Harley. "Thanks for the lift home." I smiled. "Well, to your home."

With both our helmets and protective eyewear removed, I could make out his stunning eyes. And as we sat there in silence, the powerful motorcycle between my legs, I was eager to trade out the Harley for Jack between my legs instead.

We'd had quite a few hot moments in the last three weeks, all ending with orgasms. Including the time I'd surprised him with a "jaws of life" just like the one back in Ecuador. Well, a softer-for-my-ankles version.

Jack hadn't wasted any time, using the device to spread my legs open and torture me with his tongue, before fucking me senseless while I rode the crest of my high. How was that only three days ago?

"It can be your home, too," he commented in a deep, almost hesitant voice. The sun had set, but we were still living in that in-between-day-and-night time of the evening, which meant I could make out the soft look of worry in his eyes that matched the tone of his voice. "Too soon?"

I brought my forehead to his and sighed. "Not too soon. Nothing will ever be 'too soon' with you. With us." I slid my hands to his shoulders, careful with the one I needed to remember to make him ice later. "I'm not going anywhere.

No more running," I promised him in case he was still nervous about that.

"I know. That's not why I'm . . . acting weird. Well, stranger than normal today."

I peeled my hands free from him as I sat upright, searching his eyes, waiting for him to explain.

"I found a package on my doorstep while you were in the shower this morning. It was unaddressed, and I should have given it to you right away, but it was from Erik. And I thought maybe you should open it after the party in case it upset you."

I blinked in surprise. "What?"

"Shit. I'm sorry, I shouldn't have waited. It wasn't my call to make." He shifted me back from where I sat and hopped off the motorcycle, then helped me do the same.

"No, you were right to wait. My mood would've been messed up, and I was already nervous to meet all your friends. It was more like meeting your family." Hell, even the Secretary of Defense had been there. He was Gray's dad, after all, and the party had been a baby announcement. That didn't make it any less nerve-racking. "So, um, what was inside the package?"

He grabbed the helmets and eyewear from where I'd set them on the ground, and we headed for the front door of his home. "A letter with your name on it, so I didn't read it. But there was also two hundred and fifty grand in there."

I stopped at his words, shock coursing through me. "I don't want his money."

"I didn't think you would." He frowned. "Come on." Once inside, he set aside our stuff, and I hung back in the bright foyer, still in a bit of a daze. Jack retrieved the package and handed me a folded-up sheet of paper, and I slowly opened it.

Dear Charlotte,

I'm sorry I took off last month, but once I knew you were okay, I figured it'd be best for me to just go. A small part of me wishes things were different. That I wouldn't have to forever be looking over my shoulder, but this is the life I chose. It's my turn to be on the run now, I guess.

Your mom was right back then, not wanting me in your life. I would have made a shitty father and wouldn't have deserved you then. Not that I'm doing so hot now either. I really am your father though, well, by blood at least. The man who raised you was your dad. And from what I can tell, he did a stand-up job.

I have a feeling you won't accept this money since I didn't make it legally but think of it as I'm trying to do something right by you.

You'll also get another letter this week that contains the lab work proving I'm your biological father (in case you wanted proof). But you won't hear from me again after that, I promise. Well, not unless you need me. I'll keep an eye out, but something tells me with *that boyfriend of yours around, you won't ever need me.*

*I'm sorry things happened the way they did, but I hope you have some peace now. I hope you get everything you've ever wanted. Sorry for my part in it taking so long.*

*Take care,*
*Erik*

*P.S. - Below is the location for where Jordan buried the woman Brant killed from the first show. She deserves to rest in peace.*

I MINDLESSLY HANDED JACK THE LETTER WHILE REACHING into the envelope to peer at the wads of cash, still in shock. And honestly, I didn't need the lab work to know Erik was my biological father. I felt that in my bones. Just as surely as I knew he was right to stay out of my life. This was for the best. My past needed to stay there. I needed to live in the now.

"Did the two FBI agents who died that night eleven years ago have family?" I whispered, blinking back tears.

"I think so, yes. Pretty sure they were married with kids," Jack said while folding the letter.

I held the envelope of money out to him. "Can you divide this between their families?" I sniffled, fighting back more tears. "Make it anonymous?"

Jack looked at the package, then back at me. "You're one

of a kind. You know that, right?" He put down the money and letter, drawing me into his arms. "God, I love you so much."

Tears spilled down my cheeks at his admission, finally saying the words I'd longed to hear from him. I shifted back to find his face and cried out my own truth, "I love you, too, Jack London. I love you so much. You're my home now. You're my forever."

# CHAPTER FORTY

## CHARLOTTE

### ONE WEEK LATER

Jack shot me a lopsided smile from where he stood in front of me on his driveway. "So, don't be mad at me," wasn't exactly the best way for him to start a conversation after we'd spent the day apart.

On instinct, I whipped my arms across my chest, nervous for him to go on, but curious as to why he looked so nervous. Plus, there was the whole "don't be mad at me" thing, too.

"There may have been a reason Lucy kept you busy and away from me all day," he said as he began unfolding a piece of paper I realized was mine.

*Lucy managed to keep a secret from me? I'm impressed.*

"I found your to-do list the other day."

I reached out, ready to snatch it in embarrassment, but he held it up over his head, damn him. "Not a to-do list. A wish list." *And oh jeez, there are some things on it about us.* My face was more than likely as red-hot as my body felt. It was the first time I'd made a list since I was in high school. I craved the "normal" things I'd been missing for so long. Even

415

the walks to the mailbox, knowing I now had an address and mail could be delivered to the real me, not an alias, felt amazing.

"Wish list. To-do list. Same thing." He shot me a cocky, devilish smile—the kind that usually resulted in us falling into bed together—because he knew what that handsome look of his did to me. Especially when he gave it to me while shirtless.

"Not really. There are things on there I'll probably never be able to do or have. So, *wishes*." I backed up a step, feeling a touch nervous about his thoughts on a few of those "wishes" I had on the list.

"Mmm. Never say never." With the paper fully opened, he reached into his pocket, and a moment later, the garage door opened. "I know this house is temporary, but since we may stay here a bit longer than planned, I bought all the supplies needed to build the fence you have on your list."

*Am I lame for wishing for a fence?* Another normal thing I wanted. But that fence had a purpose. Better protection for a future dog. Or maybe kiddos while playing out back. "You're going to build us a fence?" The reality of it all hit me hard— he was serious about trying to cross some items off my list.

"I am. I plan to put some of my friends to work this weekend. Beer and bourbon as their payment."

I laughed. "Not a bad trade for their manual labor."

"I thought so." He reached for my hand. "Next up on the list, well, you have 'find out what you want to do with your life for work.'"

"Not so much a wish, I suppose, as a to-do. You're right about that one."

He quietly walked us into the garage, maneuvering us around his Harley and the supplies for the fence, ensuring I didn't trip and fall over anything. "I know you haven't figured out what you want to do for work yet, but you've been busting your ass for over a decade working multiple jobs." He stopped and faced me, still holding my hand. "I'll support whatever you want to do. I know your dad didn't want your mom to work, and if you don't want to work, I'll support that, too. I'll take care of you. If you want a break for a month or a lifetime, I've got you." His voice was rough with emotion, and as what he said sank in, my eyes became glossy with recognition and appreciation.

*Damn.* I wasn't sure what I wanted, or if I could really allow him to take care of me like that. But then I remembered I'd never really had anyone take care of me since Mom, so . . . maybe. For a little bit, at least, until I made my decision. I really did have a ton of offers to choose from thanks to Jack's friends' wives who were all so helpful and friendly in that department as well.

"Shit, you okay?" He let go of my hand and set his fist beneath my chin, guiding my eyes to his.

All I could do was nod, my emotions pushing from my chest and into my throat.

"Well, next on the list, and I'm a bit confused by this one, but you said you wanted to go camping."

"That's confusing?" I asked around a laugh that came out a bit strangled because of my choked-up state.

He removed his hand from my chin and opened the door leading to the house. "After our jungle adventure, I'd thought you might want a break from the outdoors." We started down the hallway, heading toward the living room, and I was curious what he had in store for me next.

"Camping feels like one of those normal family things I missed out on," I explained. "Is it a silly wish?" At the entrance to the living room, I halted at the sight before me. "Oh my God."

Jack turned off the lights, then hit another switch, and the ceiling was lit up by stars. The furniture had all been pushed to the side, and he had a huge tent set up in the center of the room. The front flaps were tacked open, and the floor around the tent was covered in pillows and blankets. Lanterns shone on each side of the tent, and a cheese board was set out in front. Because, well, cheese. Why wouldn't we want that?

"Until we're ready for the great outdoors and I can stomach the sight of a river or pool again, I thought . . . domesticated camping. Is that a thing?" He laughed. "Indoor camping? Whatever it is, I thought we could sleep here beneath these stars. No call of the wild tonight. Well, I mean, I have plans to make you call out a few swear words while you come, but—"

"I love you. I love this." I faced him and slid my forearms over his shoulders, drawing my body closer.

"Good, because I love you, too. And I'm not done yet. More wishes to go."

"You've already done so much. You don't have to fit it all in one night." I pressed up and kissed him, and he slid his tongue between my lips to meet mine. And what a toe-curling kiss it was. God, this man was something else.

Everything really did work out how it was supposed to. I was sure of it. Just as sure as I was that I'd truly met his mom the night I died. Because when Jack showed me a photo of his parents, I'd recognized her.

"Two more wishes tonight. Maybe a third if *I'm* lucky," he whispered against my lips a moment later.

"Well, I certainly won't stop you from fulfilling my dreams, mister." I kissed him again, then he took my hand and held up the list between us.

There were quite a few more wishes there, so I had no clue which would be coming next. Naked in an overwater bungalow with him, only the sounds of the ocean surrounding us didn't seem quite possible tonight. But the naked part? Hell yes, that'd be happening.

Jack motioned for me to sit on the pillows near the tent, but he remained standing, and although the room was only lit by stars, I caught the nervous look crossing his face. "Back at that reality show," he began, his tone trembling a touch, "I was asked what I wanted more than anything, and . . ."

"To be a husband and father," I blurted at the memory, falling back onto my heels as my heart raced. Wife and mother were on my wish list. *Are you . . .?*

Jack let go of the paper and it sailed to the floor as he reached into his pocket and took a knee in front of me. He produced a small box, and a gasp escaped my lips as tears began sliding down my cheeks when he opened it. "My dad gave me Mom's ring when she passed, but I never gave it to . . ." He closed his eyes and took a deep breath. "Will you be the mother of my children, Charlotte?" His lids parted. "I mean, marry me first. Marriage and then children. In that order. Well, probably that order." He cursed under his breath. "I'm messing this up."

I reached for his wrist and pushed up on my knees, cupping his face with my other hand. "This is perfect." I nodded, tears slipping down both our cheeks now. "Yes, I'd love for you to be the one to make those wishes of mine come true. I'd love to be your wife. To be the mother of your children," I choked out.

"You will?" His glossy eyes held mine, and I leaned in and kissed him.

"Yes," I said, a bit breathlessly. He removed the ring from the box and slid the solitaire diamond on my finger. "Charlotte London. Sounds incredible to me."

"Your name will be kind of a book title now. *A Tale of*

*Two Cities*. My mom would love that," he said with a grin, then let go of the box and pulled me against him for a hug. "Damn, I love you so much."

"I love you, too." I couldn't help but remember Camila's words to me at the party last weekend. She was right again. My future did look pretty bright. I hadn't expected it to happen so soon, but it was . . . exactly how it was meant to be. "So, mister, what is this third and final wish you spoke of tonight?"

"Mmm." He let go of me. "I'd rather show than tell you." He grabbed his shirt from the back of his head and removed it. "What do you say?"

I teased my brows up and down, and thought back to my list, realizing he was about to grant me the *make love beneath the stars* one. "I do love a good game of show-and-tell," I said before he flipped me, and I released a little squeal of excitement as he settled his forearms on each side of me.

He murmured in my ear, "Tell me what you want me to do to you, sweetheart."

I swallowed and held the back of his neck and arched into my future husband and whispered, "Ohhh, I think I'd rather show you."

# EPILOGUE

## JACK

### UNDISCLOSED LOCATION - A MONTH LATER

"You guys weren't kidding about him being Batman. You really have a lair," Charley commented as we left the tunnel to enter my team's "bunker" hidden by waterfalls in the mountains of Pennsylvania. She'd had "work a mission with Jack" on her to-do list, and who was I not to oblige my fiancée's wishes?

"Batman?" Carter scoffed, then whistled for his dog, Dallas, to hurry along since he'd become distracted by a . . . well, bat, on the way there.

Carter knelt before Dallas and scratched him behind his ears. The man showed more emotion to Dallas than any of us on the team. But then I remembered that conversation I'd eavesdropped on between him and Gwen back in Ecuador. The man did, in fact, have emotions. Apparently, he just didn't know how to express them.

"We'll find the cleaner, don't worry," Gwen piped up, plopping down behind Carter's desk to work, not wasting any time. "At least we got close enough back at the hotel to hack his computer."

Jesse walked up behind her, watching her flick on all the screens to work.

Charley sat on the couch near the desk and drew one knee to her chest, eyes still moving around the place, taking it all in.

I dropped down next to her and hooked my arm behind her back, still in shock she was with us, that I'd given in and let her join a mission—with Carter and Gray's permission—now that I'd been cleared to operate again post-shoulder injury.

"So, this cleaner guy you're chasing cleans up crimes? That's why he's called that?" Charley asked.

Charley didn't know every detail surrounding our op, mostly because I didn't want her too embedded in the mission. I still needed to keep her safe.

"Yeah, and we're honestly more focused on going after his clients who hired him, but still, we'd like to take him in as well," Gray spoke up before I could. "And now that we have his list, well, once Gwen decrypts it, we'll be able to move forward."

When a silent alarm in the cleaner's room at the hotel had been tripped, our mark had escaped, and we'd failed to finish part two of our mission in taking him in. It'd been our bad luck the hotel had been jam-packed with people attending conventions, which made it harder to track him. But we'd also picked up a tail in the way of security, and Charley, acting as our getaway driver, was the reason Jesse and I had made a clean escape.

Damn, that woman knew how to drive. Like really, really fucking well. She'd executed a perfect extraction, driving like a bat out of hell (okay, kind of funny given we were in

Batman's lair right now) to get away undetected. I was proud, just unsure if I wanted her on another mission after this one.

"So, are you officially working with Falcon full-time?" Charley asked, turning her attention on Gwen.

Mya, Sydney, and Oliver had been unable to join us on this op. Griffin was wrapping up his paternity leave, going a bit stir crazy not operating, so he'd soon be joining us again. But we really had needed the extra help from Gwen and my fiancée.

And God, I loved that word, almost as much as wife (and with any luck, I'd be upgrading to husband from fiancé sooner rather than later).

"Consider me a freelance do-gooder. I'll go whichever way the wind blows," Gwen said with a smile. "And right now, it's blowing in Pennsylvania, because I need some space between myself and my clingy ex."

"Oh no, I liked that guy," Gray deadpanned, his attempt to joke failing, but it was still kind of funny to see him try. "Things didn't last long with him."

"Like I said, he was clingy. Still is, even though I ended things." She showed her phone's screen, and it was lit up with notifications, presumably from the racecar driver. "I'm not trying to play hard to get. I just am hard to get."

"Need me to handle him?" Carter's question didn't sound like a joke. Probably wasn't.

"Nah, I'm good." Gwen set her phone down and reset her focus on the screens. "So, how's Lucy?" she deflected, clearly not wanting to talk about Mr. Clingy. "I heard she's traveling."

"Yeah," Charley said on a sigh. "Her detox from social media was short-lived, and she's doing an adventure documentary thing in Thailand right now." She dug her nails into her jeaned thighs. "I'm trying to be okay with it."

"Not a dating show, right?" Gray asked, shooting her a nervous look.

"God, no. I think she's done with that stuff," Charley returned with a light laugh.

Carter stood and Dallas trotted over and jumped up on the couch, curling up next to Charley. A perfect distraction to keep her from worrying about her sister.

"She'll be okay," I promised, knowing my team (or even the Marines, considering the crush I was sure Mason was harboring for Lucy), would always be there for her sister.

Dallas rolled to his back, giving Charley his stomach to scratch.

"She's like you. Strong," I added in case she was still having doubts about not stopping Lucy from taking off. Lucy had been the one who wanted to stop running back in Brazil, and now ironically, she was the one doing it on purpose.

She smiled at me, then set her focus on Gray. "I never did ask, what happened to those five women who'd been living, um . . . well, you know." Charley circled her free wrist in the air, as if unsure how to spit out the question in its totality. I couldn't blame her. Brant had been "playing house" with women who looked like her and her mom, and it was sick.

"Pretty sure the Feds felt a little sorry for robbing them of the money promised for 'services rendered,' so they doled out a couple bucks to them from the Luthers' account. Not a million, but it was something," Gray let her know. The fact Erik had set it up so the women were willing participants and not forced to be there was some sort of consolation, I supposed. And based on the information Erik had provided, the woman from the first season was finally resting in peace where she was born in Milwaukee.

I let go of a deep breath, not wanting to think about that or Charley's biological dad anymore. I wasn't sure if we'd truly seen the last of him, but I hoped so. "Wellll, if you don't think you'll be needing us for tonight, we may head back to the hotel and wait for your call for next steps." I pulled my arm away from her back and reached for her free hand and squeezed it.

"Wait, stop there," Jesse rasped a second later, and I looked over at him leaning in toward one of the screens. "Enzo Costa's twin sister. Shit, she . . . the cleaner must've . . ."

I didn't recognize the name, but at the distressed look on his face, I released Charley's hand to stand and go over to him.

"I have to tell Enzo about this. He needs to know the truth." Jesse reached into his pocket for his phone, and he was a little pale, shaking his head as if he'd seen a ghost.

"The cleaner covered up a crime connected to your friend?" Gwen asked, looking as confused as I was.

"Don't call the Costas," Carter quickly ordered, then looked to Gray as if requesting to back him up on that. "They'll want to interfere with our op. You can tell Enzo when our mission is complete."

Jesse lowered his phone to his side. "It's about his sister. I can't not tell him right away."

"And they can't save her. It's thirteen years too late," Carter said in a deep voice. "The intel sharing can wait until we've completed our mission."

"What if we work with the Costas on this? Combine forces and resources," Jesse proposed, and I'd be looking up who in the hell the Costas were later.

Carter shook his head. "I can't work with Enzo's brother, Constantine. It wouldn't . . . end well." His gruff tone suggested the conversation that never really started was over.

Instead of pressing, Jesse cursed under his breath, then

peered at Gwen, a silent request for *something*, before he started for the exit. "I need a minute," he tossed out before leaving. I had a strong suspicion he'd be breaking orders and taking that minute wherever the hell Enzo Costa lived, regardless of Carter's directive.

I looked over to see Charley approaching me, and she reached for my hand.

"What the hell was that all about?" Gray asked, deciding to do the opposite of Jesse and probe for details.

Carter shoved his hands in his pockets and focused on Gray. "Constantine Costa dated my wife before we were married, and he broke her heart." His voice dropped lower when he added, "You put us in a room together, and one of us won't be making it out alive." With that, he whistled again, and Dallas came to his side. "Let me know when you have more information," he said to Gwen. "I'll be needing a minute, too."

"Jesse's going to tell Enzo," Gray said just before Carter neared the tunnel to exit.

"Yeah," Carter grumbled back, "I know."

"Well, damn," Gwen said once Carter was gone, and it was just the four of us. "That was tense and unexpected. Sometimes I forget he was married."

"What happened to his wife?" Charley asked, her tone gentle.

"She was murdered," Gray answered flatly. "Her killer has been brought to justice since then, but Carter doesn't like to talk about his past."

"Wow, that's . . ." Charley let her words trail off, more than likely putting together some of the mystery of why Carter was the way he was.

"You two head back to the hotel and get some rest," Gray said with a nod our way. "I'll hang back with Gwen. We'll let you know when we have something we can use to move forward."

"You sure?" I mean, I'd just asked to do that, but after the tense exchange, I felt bad leaving.

"Nothing for you all to do here," Gwen said without looking away from the screens.

"Go, that's an order," Gray said as he pulled Charley in for a hug. "You did good, by the way. Not sure if Jack can handle you, uh, doing that ever again . . . but thank you." And it felt good that my best friend got along so well with the love of my life, and Charley also adored Gray's wife, Tessa. We were all, well, family now.

"I think I'll leave the operations to you all from now on." Charley smirked. "Take Jesse's sister up on her offer to work with her instead."

I didn't even try to hide my smile. Charley would be great working with service dogs, as well as veterans. I was sure of it, and proud of her. Also, damn relieved she didn't want to join any more missions.

"Besides, I'd rather make Jack's heart race in a different way." Her cheeks became pink. "I'm going now," she added with a light laugh.

I exchanged a quick look with my best friend, and he gave me a little nod, letting me know he was happy for me.

"See you two later." Holding Charley's hand, we started for the tunnel exit. I was anxious to get her alone at our hotel.

"Everything will be okay between Jesse and Carter, right?" she asked as we navigated the elaborate tunnel system.

"They'll be fine. I'll call Jesse later and see what the deal is with this Enzo Costa person he knows." I stopped walking and faced her. "But nothing for you to stress about. The mission will end how it should."

"A happy ending?" She fisted my shirt, and I backed her up against the wall, setting my hand over her shoulder.

"Always." I smiled, leaning in closer.

"Wellll then, maybe we should go work on our own mission?" She teased her lip between her teeth, the little temptress.

"Mm. Thought you were done with missions?"

"There's one or two I need to be involved in."

"Oh yeah." I wiggled my brows. "Like baby-making practice?"

She tightened her hold on my shirt. "Absolutely. And it's an honorable mission. One that has a risk, though."

"Risky, hmm?" I lifted my brows, my eyes falling to her luscious lips. They were taunting me, reminding me of the way she'd damn near swallowed my whole cock that morning as a wake-up surprise. What a fucking way to wake up, too.

"Yeah, well, you see, I had the IUD removed three days ago. So . . . there is a risk of a very much *wanted* pregnancy."

Now my heart really was racing. Maybe my mom wasn't there to meet the woman of my dreams—who was very much now real—but I knew she was looking down on me, seeing me whole and complete. And heck, maybe she really had met Charley on the other side. Thank God she'd nudged Charley to run back over to me, though.

I brought my lips to hers. "I guess we need to move forward with Operation Get Married sooner than I thought. Because from where I'm standing, practice makes perfect. And we've done quite a lot of baby-making practice."

"You're such a dork," she said with a soft chuckle, her eyes bright and full of love. "But you're my dork."

"Damn right." I winked, and she arched into me, feeling the heavy weight of my cock there. "And you wouldn't have it any other way."

She kissed me before whispering, "You're exactly the man I've always wanted, Jack." With emotion in both her voice and her eyes, she added in a tender tone, "And I plan to give you the life you've always wanted, too."

THE FALCON FALLS TEAM CROSSES OVER INTO ENZO COSTA'S book, *Let Me Love You.*

READY FOR CARTER DOMINICK'S STORY? *THE FALLEN ONE* releases April 2024. Mya & Oliver's book - title pending.

# MUSIC PLAYLIST

**Spotify**

*Life Goes On* (feat. Luke Combs) - Ed Sheeran, Luke Combs

*Chasin' You* - Morgan Wallen

*No Wahala (Remix)* - Kizz Daniel, 1da Banton & Tiwa Savage

*Call on Me* - Bebe Rexha

*Mi Gente* - J Balvin

*Only Want You* (feat. 6LACK) - Rita Ora

*Slow Low* - Jason Derulo

*Faith* (with Dolly Parton) - feat. Mr. Probz - Galantis, Dolly Parton, Mr. Probz

*Stand by Me* (feat. Morgan Wallen) - Lil Durk, Morgan Wallen

*Forever* (feat. Elley Duhe) - Gryffin, Elley Duhe

*Fast Car* - Tracy Chapman

*You Found Yours* - Luke Combs

# CROSSOVERS

## Previous Falcon Falls books

Griffin & Savanna - *The Hunted One*

Jesse & Ella - *The Broken One / The Lost Letters*

Sydney & Beckett - *The Guarded One*

Grayson & Tessa - *The Taken One*

\* \* \*

## Aside from the Falcon Falls books - where else have you seen some of these characters?

**Gray Chandler** was first introduced in *Chasing the Knight*, and he's also in the epilogue of *Chasing the Storm* (Stealth Ops Series: Echo Team books)

**Jack London** was also in *Chasing the Knight*.

**Gwen Montgomery** - Wyatt's daughter - introduced in Wyatt's book, *Chasing the Knight.* She joins the Falcon cast in *The Taken One.*

**Mya Vanzetti** is a journalist in the contemporary romance, *My Every Breath.* And she is Julia Maddox's friend in *Chasing the Storm* (where she helps save Oliver's life). She joins Falcon Falls Security in Sydney's book - *The Guarded One.*

**Carter Dominick** was also in *Chasing Fortune* and *Chasing the Storm.* He guest appears in *Let Me Love You.*

**Camila Hart** was first introduced in *The Guarded One.*

**Jesse & Ella** - are first introduced in *Chasing Daylight.*

# FAMILY TREE

**Falcon Falls Team members:**

Team leader: **Carter Dominick - Army Delta Force/CIA**

- A widower (lost his wife)
- Dog: Dallas

Team leader: **Gray Chandler - Army SF (Green Beret)**

- Now married to Tessa (now pregnant)
- Dog: Lucky

Other family members:

- Admiral Chandler & Mrs. Chandler
- Natasha (sister)
- Wyatt (brother-in-law)
- Nieces: Emory Pierson & Gwen Montgomery

**Jesse - Army Ranger / CIA (hitman)**

Family / Friends:

- Wife: Ella Mae (son: Remington "Remi" Tucker McAdams)
- Sister: Rory
- Parents: Donna and Sean
- Friends: AJ, Beckett, Caleb, and Shep Hawkins
- Beckett's daughter: McKenna (adopted son: Miles)
- AJ & Ana's son: Marcus (Mac)

## Griffin Andrews - Delta Force

- Married to Savanna (baby now born)

## Jack London - Army SF (Green Beret) / CIA (Ground Branch Division)

- Divorced (Jill London)
- Now engaged to Charlotte Lennox (her sister is Lucy Lennox)

## Oliver Lucas - Army Airborne

- Tucker Lucas - brother (deceased)
- Tucker was engaged to Julia Maddox before he passed away.

## Sydney Archer - Army

- Married to Beckett / Son: Levi
- McKenna and Miles Hawkins (stepchildren)

\* \* \*

**Stealth Ops Team Members** *(Falcon is a spin-off from the Echo Team books)*

**Team leaders:** Luke & Jessica Scott / Intelligence team member: Harper Brooks; Bear (canine)

**Bravo Team:**
  Bravo One - Luke (married to Eva)
  Bravo Two - Owen (married to Samantha)
  Bravo Three - Asher (married to Jessica)
  Bravo Four - Liam (married to Emily)
  Bravo Five - Knox (married to Adriana)

**Echo Team:**
  Echo One - Wyatt (married to Gray's sister, Natasha)
  Echo Two - A.J. (married to Ana)
  Echo Three - Chris (married to Jesse's sister, Rory)
  Echo Four - Roman (married to Harper)
  Echo Five - Finn (married to Julia)

# ALSO BY BRITTNEY SAHIN

Find the latest news from my newsletter/website and/or Facebook
group: Brittney's Book Babes

**Other resources:**

Bonus Scenes

Publication order for all books

Books by Series

Pinterest Muse/Inspiration Boards

Tiktoks

\* \* \*

**Standalone Military Romance**

*Until You Can't*

*Let Me Love You*

**Falcon Falls Security**

*The Hunted One* - book 1 - Griffin & Savanna

*The Broken One* - book 2 - Jesse & Ella

*The Guarded One* - book 3 - Sydney & Beckett

*The Taken One* - book 4 - Gray & Tessa

*The Lost Letters* - *Novella* - Jesse & Ella

*The Wanted One* - book 5 - Jack & Charlotte

*The Fallen One* - Carter's book

**Stealth Ops Series: Bravo Team**

*Finding His Mark* - Book 1 - Luke & Eva

*Finding Justice* - Book 2 - Owen & Samantha

*Finding the Fight* - Book 3 - Asher & Jessica

*Finding Her Chance* - Book 4 - Liam & Emily

*Finding the Way Back* - Book 5 -Knox & Adriana

**Stealth Ops Series: Echo Team**

*Chasing the Knight* - Book 6 -Wyatt & Natasha

*Chasing Daylight* - Book 7 - A.J. & Ana

*Chasing Fortune* - Book 8 - Chris & Rory

*Chasing Shadows* - Book 9 -Harper & Roman

*Chasing the Storm* - Book 10 - Finn & Julia

**Becoming Us:** *connection to the Stealth Ops Series (books take place between the prologue and chapter 1 of Finding His Mark)*

*Someone Like You* - A former Navy SEAL. A father. And off-limits. (Noah Dalton)

*My Every Breath* - A sizzling and suspenseful romance. Businessman Cade King has fallen for the wrong woman. She's the daughter of a hitman - and he's the target.

**Dublin Nights**

*On the Edge* - Adam & Anna

*On the Line* - follow-up wedding novella (Adam & Anna)

*The Real Deal* - Sebastian & Holly

*The Inside Man* - Cole & Alessia

*The Final Hour* - Sean and Emilia

**Sports Romance** (with a connection to *On the Edge*):

*The Story of Us*– Sports columnist Maggie Lane has 1 rule: never fall for a player. One mistaken kiss with Italian soccer star Marco Valenti changes everything…

### Hidden Truths

*The Safe Bet* – Begin the series with the Man-of-Steel lookalike Michael Maddox.

*Beyond the Chase* - Fall for the sexy Irishman, Aiden O'Connor, in this romantic suspense.

*The Hard Truth* – Read Connor Matthews' story in this second-chance romantic suspense novel.

*Surviving the Fall* – Jake Summers loses the last 12 years of his life in this action-packed romantic thriller.

*The Final Goodbye* - Friends-to-lovers romantic mystery

# WHERE ELSE CAN YOU FIND ME?

I love, love, love interacting with readers in my Facebook groups as well as on my Instagram page. Join me over there as we talk characters, books, and more! ;)

<u>FB Reader Groups:</u>
Brittney's Book Babes
Stealth Ops Spoiler Room

Facebook
Instagram
TikTok

www.brittneysahin.com
brittneysahin@emkomedia.net

Made in United States
Cleveland, OH
04 June 2025

17482452R00267